NILE Cat

by

Angela Cecil Reid

Shortlisted for the RUBERY BOOK AWARD 2021

A B.R.A.G. Medallion Honoree. (Book Readers Appreciation Group)

"A terrific young adult thriller... Set in Victorian and ancient Egypt"

Pat Remler, Egyptologist, author of *EGYPTIAN MYTHOLOGY A - Z*

'*Nile Cat* is a grand middle-grade adventure that sweeps readers back in time, first to Victorian-era Egypt and then to the reign of King Ramesses II. The twins grow in self-confidence as they learn to speak up for themselves and show courage amid dangerous situations... I truly enjoyed the wondrous sight-seeing chapters of the Giza pyramids and Saqqara. This is a great introduction for young readers to learn about ancient Egypt as they unravel the mystery of Rose's dreams and Mr Baxter's strange behaviour. *Nile Cat* is a marvellous, hard-to-put-down read. I wonder if a sequel is in store? Highly recommended.'

Historical Novel Society (An Editors' Choice review - August 2021)

'Set in Egypt, this is a compelling adventure story for young adults. Highly recommended.
... Now to the important bit. Can I recommend this book? The answer is yes, very much so. Who to? I suspect most teenagers will find this book enjoyable and possibly without even knowing it – the best way – educational too. The author has worked so hard to offer the reader a fascinating setting, a complex thriller, and a set of characters you'll be sad to say goodbye to. I just hope there's going to be a sequel.'

A Wishing Shelf Book Review

Book Design: Petya Tsankova
Cat Motif: Bokica/Shutterstock.com
Photo: David Carillet/Shutterstock.com

ISBN paperback: 978-1-8381147-0-1
ISBN ebook: 978-1-8381147-1-8

This paperback can be ordered through all bookstores and Amazon. The e-book is also obtainable from e-platforms such as Amazon and iBook, among others.

SandChatBooks.com

To my family

'Ankh wedja seneb'

'Life, prosperity, health'

An ancient Egyptian blessing

CHAPTER 1

December 1871, Port Said, Egypt

It was just after dawn when I leaned over the ship's rail and watched the man who wanted to kill me, ride away on a donkey. His legs were so long that his feet almost touched the ground. He was urging the donkey forward. It wouldn't move.

'Look Rose, it's Mr Baxter,' said my sister Lily.

'I can see that.' I would recognise that spindly figure with his mop of grey hair and thick, round spectacles anywhere.

The donkey boy pulled the lead rope but the animal's hooves were planted squarely in the dirt and its ears were back. Mr Baxter raised his hand, and I realised he was holding his silver-topped walking cane. The cane came down hard on the donkey's back, once, twice, three times. The donkey brayed and flicked its back hooves high into the air. Then it set off at a gallop with its rider hanging on tight to the saddle, his elbows and legs flapping like a pull-along toy. The donkey and its rider disappeared in a cloud of dust, the donkey boy in hot pursuit. I would have laughed if I'd been less afraid.

'Why did he have to hit it?' said Lily. 'He could have waited for the boy to get it moving.'

I nodded. But I knew Mr Baxter would not care about hurting a donkey. 'I hope he never, ever comes back.'

'You hope who isn't coming back?' Papa's voice behind us made us jump.

He was looking very smart in his lightweight tweed suit and waistcoat. His moustache and sideburns were freshly trimmed, and his hair combed smooth and neatly parted.

'Mr Baxter,' said Lily, 'has vanished on the back of a donkey.'

'Really?' said Papa. 'He wouldn't have had his luggage with him then. Not much room for luggage on a donkey.'

'No luggage,' I agreed.

'Then he'll be back before the ship leaves.'

'He hit the donkey with his cane. Three times.'

Papa raised an eyebrow. 'Donkeys can be very stubborn. Sometimes that's the only way to get them moving.'

I glared at him.

He shook his head 'Sorry, Rose. Not everyone is as concerned about animals as you are. For many people here in Egypt, life is hard. It's not a surprise that their animals have a hard life too.'

I supposed he was right. Life was hard in London as well. I'd seen horses like skeletons, struggling to pull their heavy loads through the streets. I hated it.

'But Mr Baxter isn't poor,' I protested. 'He is travelling First Class. And I hate him not just because of hitting the donkey but also because he follows us, Lily and me. Wherever we are on the ship, there he is. Watching us. He scares me.'

Papa frowned. 'Why on earth would he be the slightest bit interested in either of you?'

I shrugged. 'I don't know. But he is.'

Papa shook his head. 'Your imagination will get you into real trouble one day, young lady.' He pulled out his pocket watch and studied it. 'Now I must go or I will be late for my meeting ashore. Coaling will begin soon and it is a terribly dusty, dirty business. So your mother wants you back in our cabin before it starts.'

'But Papa,' I protested, 'do we have to go right now?'

'Perhaps,' he said with just the hint of a smile, 'you can stay for a few more minutes. But the moment the dust starts flying, you must both go to your mama, particularly you, Lily. We haven't brought you all the way from England to escape the London pea soupers for you to breathe coal dust here.'

When the fog swirled up the River Thames from the sea, it mixed with the coal dust in the smoke from all the factories and the fires in everyone's houses. Sometimes it was so thick it was hard to see a foot in front of you. Or even breathe. Then we called it a 'pea souper'. It often lasted for days and could kill people with weak lungs like Lily. She had pneumonia when she was just a baby and nearly died. Her lungs never fully recovered and when the air was bad she struggled to breathe.

The early morning sun warmed our backs as we leaned over the rail and watched Papa cross the gangplank and walk purposefully away. Behind us lay the clear blue waters of the Mediterranean, in front of us was the bustling city of Port Said. It was a whole new world of low flat-roofed houses and palm trees.

Since Mr Baxter and the donkey had vanished at a gallop, I didn't know what to feel. I'd longed to come to Egypt ever since I'd been really little and Papa, who was an Egyptologist, had started telling us stories about the Egyptian gods and kings. Now that I was actually there, all I wanted to do was return to the cabin, lock the door and wait for the ship to take me home.

'What's wrong, Rose?' asked Lily staring anxiously at me. 'Are you really still worrying about Mr Baxter?'

It was my job to look after Lily, not to fill her head with worries. 'I am sure you and Papa are right,' I lied. 'Maybe I'm just not thinking clearly because I slept so badly.'

She didn't look convinced.

'I had such peculiar dreams,' I added quickly, hoping to distract her.

Lily frowned. 'Not your old nightmare?'

'No, it was different.'

'Tell me.'

I gazed at Lily for a moment, deciding what I should say. It was like looking into a mirror. Copper-red hair, green-flecked eyes and pale, pale skin. Except in Lily's case her hair was twisted into neat, shiny ringlets, while my hair hung straight to my shoulders. She was my older sister, but only by twenty minutes. We were fourteen years old and twins, but even though we looked the same on the outside, inside we were very different.

'You know when your hair is washed, you get water in your ears and you can't hear properly? It was like that. I could hear voices but they made no sense, the words were like gurgles. I couldn't see properly either. It was like looking through Papa's magnifying glass. When you hold it too close to something, it goes all blurred.' I shivered, remembering how scared I had felt as I struggled to make sense of it all. And how I had failed.

'I see,' said Lily with a frown.

But it was clear she didn't see at all. I closed my eyes for a moment. I needed to think, about Mr Baxter, about my dream, about the secret I mustn't tell...

I could feel Lily's eyes on me. 'There's something wrong, isn't there?'

One of the most special things about being twins was that we often had the same thoughts at the same time. Lily always said it was just coincidence, but I was sure it was more than that. It was like our minds were linked somehow. And trying to keep secrets from her felt wrong, like wearing boots that didn't fit. I needed to distract her.

'I was just thinking,' I said brightly, 'that two weeks ago we were in freezing, cold London and now we are here in Egypt. Isn't it wonderful?'

She didn't reply at once. Instead she adjusted her hat so that its brim shaded her face, patted her ringlets into place, smoothed out an invisible wrinkle in her skirt and gave a deep sigh. 'I think being in Egypt will be all right. But I wish Mama and Papa would not fuss about me so much.'

'At least they care about you.'

Slipping her arm through mine, Lily said, 'They care about you too, silly. It's just my lungs. If they worked properly, then they would treat us just the same.'

I doubted it. Apart from breathing and maybe drawing, Lily did everything better than I did. But she needed looking after. Autumn in London had been unusually damp and cold, so Lily's cough had been particularly bad. Papa had thought the warm, dry air of Egypt would be good for her. I hated to think how ill she might have been if Papa hadn't decided at the very last minute that we must all come with him on the *SS Australia*. He works for the British Museum and usually spends the winter up the Nile excavating tombs in the Valley of the Kings. This was the first time we'd been allowed to come too. So far, Papa's plan had worked. I hadn't heard her coughing for days. The fresh sea air had already done her lungs good.

'But it's not just about your lungs, is it?' I complained. 'It's other things too. Like Mama saying how you always look as neat a new pin. She never says that about me.'

Lily giggled. 'I can't think why. Have you seen yourself today?'

'No.' My head had been too full of my peculiar dream – and Mr Baxter – to worry about mirrors. As usual Lily's calf-length linen skirt and her cotton blouse looked as if they had just arrived fresh from the laundry, and her bootlaces were neatly tied in double bows. I glanced down at my crumpled skirt and my knotted laces, and sighed.

Lily was leaning over the railing, peering down at the scene below us. 'I expect you are longing to draw all that.'

Usually I'd love to sketch the disembarking ladies who looked like a flight of rainbow-coloured butterflies, and the little grey donkeys in their brightly coloured harnesses standing patiently beside the donkey boys in their ankle length robes, or *galabeyas,* as Papa had told us they were called. There was even a heavily laden camel. All of this should have been irresistible. But not today. Even though I had my little tin of charcoal and drawing chalks in my pocket as usual, my sketchbook was in the cabin, and it could stay there.

Just then a seagull swooped low over the deck then soared up to the very top of the mizzen mast, where it perched to preen its feathers. When Lily and I'd first seen the ship and realised it had a funnel as well as sails, we'd been impressed. It was so very modern.

'When does the ship sail and when does it steam?' I'd asked Papa.

He'd explained that when the wind blew in the right direction for the *SS Australia* to sail on her course, then the sails would be unfurled, otherwise the engines would be stoked up and we would steam our way through the waves. To make enough steam, she needed coal. Lots of it. Port Said was where her coal bunkers were to be filled for the voyage through the Suez Canal and onwards to India and finally to Australia.

I climbed up onto the bottom rail and leaned right out over the side so I could see further along the street. To my enormous relief, there was still no sign of Mr Baxter. Before Lily could ask me what I was doing, I said, 'I was just wondering if Aunt Dora had received Papa's telegram saying we were all on our way to stay with her in Cairo?'

'I suppose she will still be in mourning for Uncle Arthur.' Lily paused, then smiled. 'Perhaps she won't want us and we'll go to stay in a grand hotel. I'd like that.'

'But maybe she will like some company anyway? She must be lonely since Uncle Arthur died.' Our uncle had also been an Egyptologist. He and Aunt Dora had lived in Cairo for years, and Papa often stayed with them when he was in Egypt. Uncle Arthur had died in the spring. Papa told us his heart had failed suddenly and there had been nothing anyone could do to help him.

Lily nodded. 'But I hope Aunt Dora won't take us on endless expeditions to tombs and temples and up pyramids. I know you loved all those stories about the ancient Egyptians Papa used to tell us, but I thought they were dreadfully boring.'

I had to laugh. 'Honestly Lily, if Aunt Dora doesn't take us round all those places, Papa will.' Another thought made me smile. We were going to see Max. And he might show us round, and even Lily would like that.

I glanced at her. She was staring into the far distance beyond the wharf. 'What are you thinking about?' I asked.

'Max,' she said.

Of course. I'd thought of Max, and so she had too.

Max was our elder brother, and he was the best brother in the whole, wide world. He was kind, funny and really clever. He was eighteen now and had left school last summer. He was training to be an Egyptologist on an excavation near Alexandria. We missed him terribly. But he probably didn't miss us much given that his nickname for us was still "the Holy Terrors," even though we hadn't played tricks on him for years.

'Of course he will come and visit us in Cairo,' I said, 'and maybe later on we can go and see the tomb where he has been digging.'

At that moment, a soft voice came from behind us.

'Excuse me, ladies.'

We swung round. Hakim, our cabin steward, was standing a few feet away. 'I am most sorry, Miss Lily, your mother insists you return to her now.'

Lily sighed. 'I'm just coming.' She looked at me. 'Don't be long, Rose,' and then she and Hakim were gone. As I watched them disappear inside and I was left alone, all my fears came flooding back.

CHAPTER 2

It had been Hakim who had welcomed us on board that very first day in Southampton. A dark-skinned, dark-eyed steward in a spotless white jacket with shiny, silver buttons had introduced himself.

'My name is Hakim,' he'd said with a small bow and a huge smile. 'I am to be your cabin steward. Anything at all that you want, I can find for you. If you have questions, I will attempt most hard to answer them. Now please to follow me.'

So we followed him. Everywhere I looked there was dark varnished wood and gleaming brass. We passed the saloon, furnished with long, narrow tables and benches.

'This is where you will eat your meals during the voyage,' explained Hakim.

There were also clusters of green leather armchairs and small tables at each end of the saloon where several passengers were already sitting reading newspapers or playing cards.

'Will this be your first visit to Egypt?' Hakim asked me as we walked.

I nodded.

'You will have a most wonderful time. Are you visiting the great pyramids?'

'Oh yes,' I said. 'I've wanted to see them since forever.'

Hakim smiled. 'They are indeed most magnificent.' He turned to Lily. 'And you, Miss, are you looking forward to seeing the sights of Egypt?'

'I'm sure they will be very nice,' she said carefully, 'unless

I die from sea sickness before we get there.'

Hakim's brow furrowed. 'I am most certain that will not be the case. I have a most efficacious tonic made from ginger and a touch of liquorice, which I will bring for you if you feel unwell.'

I didn't dare look at Lily as I knew how much she hated both ginger and liquorice.

'That's quite enough chatter, girls,' said Papa from behind us. 'I am sure Hakim doesn't want to know all our business.'

Hakim shook his head. 'No, it is good. I am always most interested in my passengers.'

'Where is your home, Hakim?' I asked.

He studied me for a moment. 'Not many passengers ask me about my home,' and he nodded approvingly. 'I was born in Bombay, a most busy and most beautiful city in India.'

The next moment we reached our cabins. Mama and Papa were shown into one. Ours was just next door. The first thing that hit me was the smell, which was a strange soup of furniture polish like Daisy, our parlour maid, used at home, all mixed up with burnt oil and seaweed.

'It smells strange,' said Lily, wrinkling her nose.

'It will be better once you have let it air for a while,' said Papa from the doorway. 'In any case, you'll soon get used to it.'

The cabin was smaller than I'd expected, and darker. The only light filtered in through a porthole no bigger than the globe in the schoolroom at home. A brass oil lamp hung from a hook in the ceiling. Fixed to one wall was a wash stand, while built into the opposite wall were two snug births, one above the other, each hidden behind its own little curtain. A wooden ladder ran from the top bunk to the floor. Against the far wall, below the porthole, was a small leather sofa.

Lily was frowning at the ladder. She was terrified of heights of any sort.

'Shall I take the top bunk?'

She threw me a relieved smile. 'Please do.' She peered round the cabin. 'But wherever are we going to put all our luggage?'

'We will have our cabin trunks in with us,' explained Mama as she joined us. 'The other trunks will go in the hold and not be seen again until Suez.' She gave a short laugh. 'I'm glad crinolines are no longer the fashion. I believe I would have hardly fitted inside the cabins wearing mine.'

I glanced at her dark blue, travelling dress with its neat bustle, and thought she was right, imagining her in the huge birdcage of wire and tape that she used to wear under her dresses. Papa had been relieved when the fashion for crinolines had ended as he said many women had died when their skirt had caught fire, or become trapped in the wheels of a passing carriage.

I was, however, more interested in the porthole. I climbed on the sofa and peered out. Lily joined me. We found we were looking onto the deck, still crowded with passengers waiting to be shown to their cabins.

Later Lily and I stood on that deck and watched as the English coast faded into a blue mist. There was a brisk wind behind us so all the sails were set and the ship creaked and shuddered as waves fizzed past the hull.

A gust tugged at my skirt and blew my hair across my face. 'In just two weeks we will be in Egypt,' I said. 'It doesn't feel real. I keep thinking that any moment I will wake up in my bed at home.'

Lily squeezed my arm. 'Of course, it's real. And although I really didn't want to come, I'm glad we did.' She peered down at the froth of dark, green water. 'As long as it gets no rougher than this.'

Seagulls swooped around the ship filling the air with their wild, sad cries. A shiver of excitement tingled through me. I felt we were setting out on the most amazing and wonderful adventure. I didn't know about Mr Baxter then. He would change everything.

CHAPTER 3

Lily and Hakim had only just gone below deck to escape the coal dust when I heard a great commotion coming from the opposite side of the ship. I crossed over to have a look. A large barge heavily laden with black mountains of coal had drawn up alongside the *Australia* and hundreds of men dressed in brown *galabayas* were lining up beside the barge waiting to fill the baskets on their backs with coal. They then set about scaling the series of ladders now running up the ship's side to the coal bunkers. I saw the first men reach the top, and clouds of coal dust rose into the air. I was just thinking that I'd better join Lily and Mama in the cabin when Mrs Hodges arrived on deck.

'My dear Rose,' she said coming to stand beside me, 'are you enjoying your first sight of Egypt?

'Oh yes, Mrs Hodges,' I said, although her sudden appearance had made me think of something I would rather forget.

She beamed. 'You remind me of how much my dearest Lottie also enjoyed her first sight of this wonderful country.' Then her face grew serious. 'You have remembered your promise, haven't you, Rose? No one must know our little secret.'

'I've remembered,' I whispered unhappily.

'Good girl,' said Mrs Hodges. 'Now I must go. I have a meeting with an old friend ashore. I'll doubtless see you later.'

Shortly afterwards I watched her cross the gangplank and hurry away along the street in the direction taken a short while earlier by Mr Baxter and his donkey.

I remembered first meeting Mrs Hodges on the deck as we watched England disappear over the horizon. She was round and fluffy, like a well-fed rabbit. She had just accompanied her eight-year-old daughter, Lottie back to England and left her at a boarding school. Her sister would look after Lottie in the holidays.

'We've lived in Egypt for several years,' Mrs Hodges explained, 'but now Major Hodges has been posted to Bombay and I must join him.' She dabbed at her eyes with a handkerchief. 'But the Indian climate isn't good for children. Cholera, typhoid and so many other diseases. And then there are the snakes and spiders, all so dreadfully poisonous. I had to take Lottie back to England. She couldn't come with us...' her voice trailed away. 'All that marvellously cool, clean air in England, she will like that.'

'The air's not very clean in London,' said Lily. 'But it is in the countryside. We have cousins in Norfolk and we go to stay with them in the summer. We do all sorts of things outside, like go for walks and have picnics, because the fresh country air is good for my lungs.'

'And I climb trees with our cousins,' I added. 'But Lily doesn't. She likes to keep her feet firmly on the ground.'

Lily shrugged. 'I don't go on the camping trips either.' She shuddered. 'Far too many spiders. I really don't like them. Too many legs.' She glanced at me. 'But at least I'm not scared of the dark.'

I grimaced. I hated the dark. I knew it was stupid. I knew there weren't monsters hiding in the shadows, but that never stopped me looking and listening for them.

'Oh, it all sounds most exciting,' gushed Mrs Hodges. 'Lottie would love to do all that.'

'Will you see her again soon?' asked Lily.

'Perhaps not for years.' Mrs Hodges shook her head sadly. 'India is such a terribly long way away and travel is so expensive. The Major says we might visit her for her twelfth birthday, but he's not certain even of that.'

We felt sorry for Mrs Hodges. We couldn't imagine being away from Mama and Papa for four whole years. But as the days passed, she seemed more resigned to the situation. She frequently sat with us, knitting some unidentifiable object, and dabbing lavender water on her wrists and neck at frequent intervals, which she insisted was most refreshing. If she wasn't knitting or dabbing, then Mrs Hodges was popping peppermints into her mouth from a tin, which proclaimed they were "The Original Curiously Strong Peppermints". She once offered them to us and they were indeed Curiously Strong but also Absolutely Horrid.

From the first moment she seemed interested in us, wanting to know all about our lives, our school, our home, but we soon realised it was really just an excuse to talk about Lottie. One time, when she saw me sketching the battle-scarred tabby cat kept on board to keep the ship's rat population under control, she said, 'You do draw well, Rose,' then added wistfully, 'Lottie loves cats,' and gazed longingly at the picture.

'Please do have it.' I tore the sketch out of the book and handed it to her.

'Thank you so much, I shall send it to her,' she said, rolling it up and tucking it into to her knitting bag.

One day Mrs Hodges asked us where we were going to be staying in Egypt. I told her about Aunt Dora and that Uncle Arthur had been an Egyptologist.

'Oh, goodness,' she said looking startled. 'I hadn't realised. Was your uncle, Arthur Sinclair?'

'Yes.'

'Then I know your aunt and uncle. I once took Lottie to visit your uncle's excavations. It was shortly before he died. He was most kind to Lottie when he showed us round the temple he was working on. He and your aunt were generous enough to ask us to dine with them.' Her face clouded over. 'Indeed, I wonder if...'

She hesitated, apparently changing her mind about what

she wanted to ask, adding only that, 'Lottie says she would like to be an Egyptologist when she grows up.'

'Does she really? I would very much like to meet Lottie. I think we would be friends.'

Mrs Hodges' mouth twisted into a wistful smile. 'I am sure you would, dear Rose,' and reached for her handkerchief again.

A few days after that, we reached Naples and several new passengers came on board. I wasn't interested in them. We would be in Egypt in two days' time, nothing else mattered. I didn't see Mr Baxter coming on board. I didn't realise my life was about to change.

As the *SS Australia* sailed out of the harbour, I returned to the cabin to fetch my sketch book. As I passed Mrs Hodges' cabin the door was open, and I saw her peering into her trunk. She must have heard me because she looked up, smiled and beckoned me inside.

'Ah Rose, my dear,' she said, 'I have been looking for an opportunity for a private word with you. I have a great favour to ask.'

'Oh... really?' I said, as Mrs Hodges firmly shut the cabin door behind me.

She hesitated, then continued in a husky whisper, 'But you must promise me that you will tell no one about this conversation.'

I shook my head. 'I'm not sure I can do that, Mrs Hodges. I don't have secrets from Lily.'

'Please, Rose. If you tell Lily, you might be overheard discussing the matter. The walls on the boat are thin and sound travels. It's terribly important that no one knows about this.'

Even though I knew I shouldn't make such a promise, I was by then so curious that I heard myself agreeing that I would keep her secret, whatever it might be.

'Well,' she said, 'perhaps you remember that I told you that Lottie and I'd visited your uncle's excavations?'

I nodded.

'Well, I'm afraid Lottie is dreadfully naughty sometimes.'

'I think all children are naughty sometimes.'

She gave a watery smile. 'Dear Rose, I knew you'd understand.' She rummaged in a nearby box for a few seconds. She pulled out her hand, the fist clenched. 'Your dear uncle was so kind showing us things. You remember I told you that after we'd visited the excavation, he and your aunt invited us to dinner. Well, when we'd finished eating, he took us to the library to see his Collection of Curiosities.' She must have seen the question in my face. 'Things your uncle had collected that looked intriguingly ancient, but were really just clever copies.'

'I see.'

'Your uncle kept part of this collection in a small wooden box. He allowed Lottie to look through it while we talked.' She took a breath and gulped rather like a fish. 'A few days later, we heard your poor uncle had died. So sad.'

'Yes, indeed,' I said, wondering what was coming next.

'Well, it was only when Lottie and I reached England and I helped unpack her trunk at my sister's house that I came across this.'

She took hold of my hand and pressed something into it. I peered down to see a small statue of a cat lying in the curve of my palm.

The cat was only as tall as my little finger. It was cut from some sort of dark-grey stone and gleamed like polished glass. Every detail from its delicate, pointed ears to the tip of its neatly curled-around tail had been so very carefully carved. It sat on a small oval base and stared up at me through half-closed eyes. It was the most perfect thing I'd ever seen.

Mrs Hodges was staring at it too. 'Maybe it is just a copy of an ancient amulet, but it is lovely.'

I nodded, speechless.

She said softly, but I could hear the fear in her voice. 'Dear Rose, if you can help, I would be so grateful'

'What do you want me to do?'

'Will you return the cat to your aunt?'

'Of course.'

'It's imperative that no one must know Lottie is a thief. I'm sure you are aware the penalties for stealing are harsh, even for children. If your aunt chose to report her to the authorities, even if the cat isn't valuable, Lottie could be sent to prison and then reformatory school. Her life would be ruined.' Mrs Hodges dabbed frantically at her tear-filled eyes. 'Do you think you could possibly slip it back into that box without anyone knowing?'

I couldn't take my eyes off the little statue. 'I'll do my very best,' I whispered, knowing that keeping the secret from Lily meant I shouldn't even think about it.

Mrs Hodges gave me another watery smile. 'Thank you, dear Rose. I knew I could rely on you. This is our secret.'

It felt wrong to agree. But the little cat in my hand felt like a secret worth having. I nodded. 'I won't say a word to anyone.'

That night I lay in my bunk with the little cat tucked safely under my pillow, and tossed and turned for hours unable to sleep. It was too stuffy to draw the bunk curtains so moonlight poured in through the porthole, bringing with it an uncomfortable feeling that someone was out there watching me. Twice I crept down the ladder and peered out onto the deck. Each time there was no one there.

To distract myself, I slid the little stone cat out from under my pillow. The moonlight turned it to silver in my hand. It lay there, all the carefully carved details highlighted by the cold, white light. It seemed even more beautiful than before. As I gazed at it, I noticed that whenever I moved, its eyes followed me. Just a trick of the moonlight, I told myself as I hastily slipped it deep under my pillow.

My thoughts returned to the promise I'd made to Mrs Hodges to keep the cat secret from everyone. I hated keeping it from Lily. But what was really worrying me was how I was going to keep my promise and return it to the Collection of Curiosities. My mind was still spinning with unanswered questions when I eventually fell asleep. Perhaps that was why I'd dreamed about words that I couldn't hear and things I couldn't see. And when I woke up, the shadows of my strange, blurry dream haunted me and wouldn't let me go.

CHAPTER 4

The next morning Lily and I ate breakfast alone. Mama and Papa were still in their cabin. They gave us strict instructions that when we had finished eating we were to take our books onto the upper deck and read quietly. But the wind strengthened and kept flicking the pages of our books. After losing my place three times, I gave up.

'Come on, Lily. Let's play Hide and Seek.'

Lily yawned. 'Honestly, Rose. I think we're a bit too grown up for that sort of thing.'

That was it. She was wearing a green silk bow in her hair. It was too tempting. I grabbed the end of it, the bow untied and the ribbon was in my hand.

She stood up and held out her hand. 'Give it back.'

'No, I'll hide it and you'd better seek it or it may blow away.' I held it high so it fluttered in the wind. Lily glared at me. I laughed and set off at speed along the deck. It was the only time for running games as most of the other passengers were still in their cabins or having breakfast in the saloon.

'Give it back at once, Rose Evering!' shrieked Lily, as she set off after me.

I could hear her pounding along behind me.

'You'll have to catch me first,' I raced towards the lifeboats. I could hide the ribbon there quite easily. I'd spun round the first lifeboat when I realised there was a man standing directly in front of me. I just had time to see he was tall and thin, like a gangly-legged spider with a mop of grey hair, before I cannoned into him. I slid onto the deck, landing in a crumpled heap at his feet.

A hand on my shoulder pulled me sharply upright.

'What on earth are you playing at, young lady?' said a deep, gravelly voice.

At that moment, Lily shot around the corner. She only just managed to stop from bumping into us both.

'Goodness me,' he said peering at us through a pair of thick, round spectacles. 'This is like seeing double. You really are identical.' His face twisted and changed into something else, some other expression. 'And your hair,' he added softly, 'is on fire, like the sun as it sinks into the desert. Quite wonderful.' He let go of my shoulder but kept looking at us, his eyes flicking to and fro between us, as if not believing what he was seeing.

People often looked a bit surprised when they first saw us together. But not like this. A memory stirred. When we were small, Mama took us to visit the Reptile House at London Zoo. Lily was horrified by the snakes but I was amazed by them. Their skins glowed with brilliant colours and intricate patterns, which I longed to draw. But their cold, black eyes followed our every move, flicking between us. It felt like the snakes were sizing us up as possible prey. I felt the same now.

'I am sorry, sir, about my sister,' Lily was saying. 'Did she hurt you?'

'No, no, not at all,' replied the man, shaking his head as if to clear it. 'I was standing in her way. It is a great pleasure to meet you both.' He bowed. 'Mr John Baxter at your service, ladies.'

Lily bobbed a curtsey and nudged me to do the same.

'If you should ever...' He paused as if trying to order his thoughts, then muttered under his breath so I could only just make out the words, 'No, no, of course you will not...' His voice trailed away, he bowed again, swung round on his heel and hurried away along the deck, still muttering to himself.

Lily stared after him. 'How odd. Did you bump into him very hard?'

I shook my head. 'Not really.'

Just then, Papa appeared, looking anxious. 'I've been searching for you two. Mrs Hodges told me she had seen you both racing along the deck.' He touched Lily's forehead. 'You feel a little warm. Please don't rush around so. It's not good for you.'

'I'm fine, Papa, honestly.'

Papa ruffled her hair. 'I saw you talking to someone,' he said as we made our way back to where we had left our books. 'I hope you weren't bothering him?'

'No, Papa,' I said firmly, giving Lily a quelling look.

Papa frowned. 'He looked familiar. Did he give you his name?'

'Mr John Baxter,' said Lily, glaring at me.

'Is he indeed,' said Papa thoughtfully. 'I understood he was still in America.'

'Do you know him, Papa?' asked Lily.

'We've never met, but he is an Egyptologist. Your uncle sent me a photograph of some excavations at Sakkara. Mr Baxter was in the photograph. Those glasses are really quite distinctive, and that hair. Indeed, I have just read a most interesting book he has recently published, *Death and Magic in Ancient Egypt*.'

Just then Mama appeared and swept us off to our cabin for a French lesson. The deck was busy now with passengers taking their daily exercise, which involved walking up and down the deck making polite conversation as they went. It happened every morning before the sun grew too warm. I forgot about Mr Baxter until much later when I saw Papa talking to him in the dining saloon.

Papa eventually came and sat down at our table. He gave me a stern look. 'I hope that will be the last time I have to apologise for your unladylike behaviour, Rose.'

I could feel the heat in my cheeks. 'I'm sorry, Papa. Was he very angry?'

Papa shook his head. 'Once he discovered who I was, he insisted we must dine with him in Cairo. He was a great admirer of your Uncle Arthur.'

I glanced across to where Mr Baxter was seated not far from us, and realised he was watching us intently. He was wearing that hungry-snake look again. He looked away the moment he realised I was watching him. I felt ice cold in spite of the heat. I hoped he would soon forget about inviting us to anything.

I tried to put him firmly out of my mind until I realised that wherever we went on the ship that day, two minutes later, there he was too. It could have been coincidence, and indeed he paid us little obvious attention. Sometimes he would be writing in what looked like some sort of journal, at other times he would be reading a book or smoking his pipe while he gazed into the distance apparently lost in thought.

Mama sent us up on deck after tea, our sketch pads under our arms. We were instructed as usual to work quietly and not to cause any commotion. There was no wind and the sails were tightly furled. Clouds of steam and black sooty smuts were rolling out of the funnel towards the stern of the boat, so we made our way to the bow. We found a couple of chairs and moved them into the shade of a lifeboat.

Lily giggled. 'I think I'll draw them,' and pointed at some nearby passengers dozing in their deckchairs.

'It's that seagull for me,' I said looking up at a huge seagull perched on the nearby cabin roof. 'It looks like he's posing.' The seagull would be just perfect for a charcoal sketch. It was a magnificent mixture of greys, white and black.

Out of the corner of my eye, I noticed Mr Baxter arriving on deck and making himself comfortable in a deck chair about ten feet away from us. He pulled a small book out of his pocket and was apparently soon engrossed in its pages.

I returned to my seagull. It took a few minutes before a strange feeling crept up on me. It was a sort of prickling in the back of my neck. I glanced at the cabin porthole below the seagull's perch, and noticed Mr Baxter's reflection in the glass. It was amazingly clear. Now, when he thought we couldn't see him, it was clear that behind his glasses, his eyes were fixed on us. He wasn't a snake, but a wolf. A wolf staring at Red Riding Hood just before he swallowed her whole.

Afterwards, I tried to catch him out by swinging round suddenly, pretending I was looking for someone else. And there he'd be, staring at Lily or me. He'd instantly look away, and I'd pretend I hadn't seen him. I also noticed that when he was apparently reading, he seldom turned a page.

CHAPTER 5

Coal dust was swirling in the air all around me. It was time to go below. I crossed the deck to take one last look at the wharf, which was by now almost deserted. There was still no sign of Mr Baxter or his donkey. Hope began to rise. Maybe he really wasn't coming back.

On my way I passed Mr Baxter's cabin, just around the corner from ours. When I reached it, the door was open so I paused and peered inside.

Hakim was straightening the sheets. There was a coat hanging on the back of a chair and papers spread all over the sofa. There was even a pipe propped up on a pipe-stand on the little table. My stomach lurched. Papa was right of course. Mr Baxter certainly intended on returning before the ship sailed. Hakim turned and saw me watching him.

'Can I assist you with anything, Miss?'

'I was just wondering what time we will leave Port Said?'

'Coaling will take most of the day. We will not begin through the canal at night. We will depart tomorrow morning.'

'I see,' I said, hope running away like water down a drain. There was plenty of time for Mr Baxter to return. Suddenly having to spend the day in the cabin where there was no chance of being watched, didn't seem like such a bad thing after all.

Coaling did take forever. We had time to finish our books, get half way through another one and stitch our samplers as well. Lily's stitches were always perfect, but mine looked like they had been done by a frog with hiccups. After coaling had at last finished and the crew were busy washing the coal dust off the decks, we went for a walk with Papa through Port Said. Mama stayed on board to rest.

The streets were very narrow and lined by little open-fronted shops and small houses with flat roofs and green shutters. Everywhere we went, we had to push through crowds of beggars, street sellers and shoppers, along with countless chickens, goats, camels and donkeys. The smell of people and animals was overwhelming, and I forgot all about Mr Baxter.

After a while, I realised that Lily was looking paler than ever. Worried she might faint, I took her arm.

She gave me a small grin. 'I'm fine, honestly.'

I didn't believe her, so we walked on arm-in-arm behind Papa. The sun was sinking and the temperature dropped. We passed a whole row of food sellers standing behind their large bubbling pots. The spices tickled our noses. I began to feel hungry and wondered how long it might be until supper.

After a while however, I began to feel something was wrong. There was that tingling at the back of my neck. I swung round, staring into the crowds. There was no sign of Mr Baxter, or indeed of anyone else, watching me. I was just thinking I must have imagined it when the crowds parted briefly to let a camel and its rider pass. In the gap immediately behind the camel, I caught a glimpse of a mop of grey hair. Before I could be certain it was Mr Baxter, the camel passed by and the gap closed. I swallowed, my heart galloping uncontrollably.

'For goodness sake, child, what is wrong with you? You look as white as a sheet,' said Papa impatiently.

I shook my head. 'I'm quite well, Papa.' But I couldn't help thinking that he never spoke like that to Lily.

Had I seen Mr Baxter? If I had, he would soon be back on board. My stomach twisted at the thought.

Papa took Lily's hand and I trailed behind as we walked on.

Soon we found ourselves in the middle of a furious argument between two street sellers, and Papa decided we had seen enough. He marched us back to the ship in time to change for dinner. Mama was already dressed in a grey silk evening dress. She looked wonderful with her red-gold hair swept high on her head and her favourite string of pearls round her neck.

'I thought I would celebrate our arrival in Egypt,' she said softly, her eyes on Papa.

He smiled at her. 'My dear, you look beautiful.'

Lily and I splashed water on our faces and changed our blouses, then we all made our way to the dining saloon.

Since arriving on board, we had been allowed to stay up for dinner. Every night we sat in the same places, at the same table, and when Mr Baxter joined the ship, he was given a seat at the table next to ours. By the time we went in to dinner, I'd convinced myself he would be sitting there as usual. To my great relief, his place was empty.

'He's not here,' I hissed at Lily.

Papa frowned at us. 'Stop whispering, girls, it is extremely rude. In any case, I heard what you were saying. Mr Baxter has no doubt chosen to dine with friends. He may even stay the night with them. As an Egyptologist, he will have many contacts here in Egypt. I am sure he will be back before we sail. I do not want to hear another word against the poor man. If he was a friend of your uncle's, he's our friend too.'

Just then a steward arrived with our food. I realised I wasn't at all hungry. I stared at my plate. Some sort of spicy chicken and rice stared back at me. I forced down a few mouthfuls.

Lily yawned loudly. I guessed to distract Papa.

He looked anxiously at Lily. 'You must be tired. You may be excused. It is time you went to bed.' He glanced at my half-eaten meal, adding sharply, 'Your sister will follow shortly. I will not tolerate a wasteful child, so eat up, Rose.'

Lily threw me a sympathetic look as she left the dining saloon. I knew better than to argue and eventually managed the last mouthful of rice. 'Please may I get down, Papa?' I asked at last.

'You may,' he said, 'and I will not hear another word about Mr Baxter. Do you understand?'

I bobbed a curtsey. 'Yes, Papa,' I said, then hurried after Lily.

That night I lay wide awake, my mind running endlessly over all that had happened that day. Papa's rhythmic snoring, which I could hear clearly through the cabin wall, and Lily's steady breathing in the bunk below should have soothed me. Yet I just felt more awake. I slid my hand under my pillow and wrapped my fingers tightly round the cool silkiness of the little stone cat. A feeling of calm washed through me. I closed my eyes and slept.

CHAPTER 6

'THE BOOK OF MIUT'

I

Miut opened her eyes and knew at once things were not as they should be. The stars glittered in the night sky and the moon-disc was still high above the temple walls, yet the gates must already be open. Soft voices filled the walkways and footsteps whispered across the stone-slabbed courtyard below.

She peered over the ledge and examined the darkness between the columns. There was no sign of the boy they called Hori. Hunger growled in the empty cavern of her stomach. Maybe he would be here soon. But she had been absent from the temple for many passes of the sun-disc. Would he have forgotten her?

Miut began to groom herself. Her rough tongue washed and smoothed her fur from the sand-coloured fluff of her chest, past the dusky stripes on her back and the night-black spots on her legs, right down to the tawny-gold tip of her snake-ringed tail.

By the time she had finished, grey tinged the blackness above. Soon whiskers of gold would stretch out from behind the hills and Ra would sail his sun-boat across the sky. Far above her on the roof of the nearest tower, a priest stood motionless, staring skywards. He called out, his voice echoing round the temple. It was the signal. The day must now begin and everyone should be at work. Footsteps hurried away, voices quietened and soon the courtyard lay silent again.

Just one thought now filled Miut's mind. She must fill her belly. If Hori did not come, should she visit the kitchens alone? But the girl with kind eyes was more generous when the boy was there.

Perhaps she would have to try her skills in the grain store. There she would find enough mice to feed a hundred cats. If only she could catch them. Miut extended eight tiny, curved daggers and scratched them slowly across the stone. Sharp claws alone would not be enough – she needed speed and cunning too. Now that her belly was swollen and heavy with kittens, speed had deserted her.

As if they had heard her thoughts, the kittens moved deep within her, their legs fluttering against her sides like the wings of birds. The movements grew stronger each day. Grey-blue light now filled the courtyard. Surely Hori must come soon.

Just then a whistle pierced the silence. Miut pricked her ears and peered down into the courtyard. Hori was standing in its centre. He was as tall and slender as a young palm, and as strong. His hair was dark and wild about his head. The white of his kilt was stained with patches of black and his knees were covered in dust. He must have felt her gaze on him as he raised his eyes and looked directly up at her. His eyes were the colour of the Great River in flood and as they met hers, relief and fear mixed in his face.

'Miut, where have you been? I have been looking for you for many rises of the sun. Now there you are, perched up high like a bird. Come down at once.' He slapped his thigh encouragingly.

Six springs took her to the ground. She landed heavily and half-stumbled. Picking herself up, she stalked over to the boy, her tail raised straight and high behind her.

'Goodness, little goddess,' he said with a smile, 'you are not so little now. Either you have been gorging on granary rats, or else...' he laid his hand on the swell of her belly, and the kittens moved beneath his fingers, '... you will soon be a mother. Your first time. I will have to look after you, I think.' Hori stroked her head, then her neck. His fingers found the small leather pouch, which hung there.

'What is this?' he asked, trying to prize open its mouth. 'The cord is too strong. I will need a blade. Later maybe. First, we must fill your belly with food.'

He straightened and gazed across the courtyard at the two great, golden doors opposite. They stood open and deserted. 'Even the guards have other duties today,' he murmured.

Hori gently touched Miut's head. 'Come, Not-So-Little-One, we will take the shortest path,' and he set off with Miut following closely at his heels. As they reached the far side of the courtyard, he paused to stare up at the painted scene, which covered the wall above the great doors.

'King Rameses went into battle when he was not much older than I.' The boy's voice was soft, his eyes fixed on an immense figure of a young man standing in a chariot. Two galloping horses pulled him through the field of battle as hundreds of smaller figures fled from the flying hooves.

Hori's eyes glittered. 'One day I too will have great adventures… I will not just record the adventures of others. I…'

Distant voices drifted in on the breeze and someone laughed. Miut's fur rose. She knew the laugh and the man. He was built like a river bull and had the eyes of a long dead fish.

'Miaow,' she warned.

Hori glanced round. 'The guards ... we must hurry.' He scooped Miut into his arms and slipped through the doorway.

They were in a place Miut had never visited before. It was a vast hall of shadows and rows of towering columns. Rays of light seeped in through the gratings in the ceiling far above her head and the painted figures decorating the columns glowed red, green and blue at their touch.

Miut's nose twitched. There was something in the air… she sniffed. Not mice… it was different. There was dust in it, sour oil and something she had never smelt before. It was bitter and full of power. Her claws spiked Hori's arm.

'Ouch,' he said, unhooking her claws from his skin. 'You can walk.' He placed her firmly on the ground.

She padded close behind the boy as he wound his way silently between the columns. They reached a narrow side door. He eased it open and they passed out into a large courtyard. The door clicked shut behind them. Miut blinked as light flooded her eyes.

They had just started across the courtyard when Miut's ears pricked. The distant sound of chanting voices had broken the silence.

'Awake in peace, great god, Osiris,
The doors will open and we will bring you offerings.
We will feed you and clothe you.
We will fill your cup with wine.'

The voices were close enough now for the boy to hear, for he stopped abruptly and looked wildly round.

But the voices were almost on them. 'There is nowhere to hide,' Hori whispered. He bowed his head and waited.

'We have cleansed ourselves in the sacred waters of your temple.
We will honour you, Lord of the great River, and all that grows in the fields,
And Lord of the Afterlife to come.'

A small group of priests rounded the corner and fell silent. Their shaven heads gleamed and their white robes were spotless. The priest who led them had his left leg bandaged, and he leaned heavily on a stick. The rest held platters piled high with food. Miut's whiskers quivered as the sweet smell of freshly baked bread and warm bird flesh filled her nostrils.

She sat beside the boy, her tail wrapped carefully around her. She purred as the leading priest limped forward.

The eyes of the Lame-Priest widened as they rested on her for a single heartbeat before flicking to the boy. 'Hori! Why are you here?'

The boy raised his head. His eyes widened. 'Father! I thought you were still at home, and you could not leave your bed. Your leg…?'

The Lame-Priest cut him off. 'Is it healed? No. It still causes me pain.' He frowned. 'But why are you here? How dare you walk unwashed in the Temple of Osiris?'

'I woke late,' Hori's feet shuffled the sand, 'and Miut had to be fed so I…' his voice dropped away.

'Took the shortest way,' finished the priest.

The boy's mouth twisted. 'Yes, Father. I am sorry.'

'If I had one pigeon for each time you have told me you are sorry, I would have the tallest pigeon tower in the Two-Kingdoms.' The priest's lips tightened. 'Do not take this path again. The temple is dangerous for those who do not understand the ways of the priesthood.' He turned to the group of watching priests.

'Wait for me inside,' he ordered. 'I will join you shortly.'

The tallest priest stepped forward. 'But Khay, we must not delay. Osiris awaits us.'

'I will not be long, Paser.'

Miut's tail twitched impatiently as hunger grumbled in her belly.

The Tall-Priest did not move. His eyes rested on Miut. His dislike was as a breath of night-cold wind.

'Osiris is the god of our temple,' reproved the Lame-Priest, drawing himself to his full height with the aid of his stick. 'I am his High Priest. He will understand I need to speak to my disobedient son. Now go, Paser.' His voice was sharp and firm.

Silently the group of priests turned towards the door to the Great Hall. When the door had closed behind them, the Lame-Priest's expression softened. He put his hand under Hori's chin and raised it, so that the boy was looking directly at him.

'My son, I have missed you,' he said, his voice as warm as a summer breeze. 'Has Dedi kept you busy?'

The boy nodded. 'I have done little but write endless lists of all that must be taken to the High Priest Heteb's tomb before he is carried there. It has been dull work.'

'So now you crave adventure?'

Hori's eyes flamed. 'Oh yes, Father. More than anything.'

Miut watched the Lame-Priest intently. He was staring at the boy's face as if he was searching for something.

'I do have a task for someone with a wise and brave heart,' the priest said at last, 'who I can trust with a secret.'

Hori drew in his breath. 'Please, Father, give me the task. I will speak to no one… and I hope I will be brave… and, with the help of the great god Thoth, I shall be wise.'

The priest frowned. 'I am not sure you are ready for such

responsibility. Yet Heteb believed you have promise and he was a man who knew about people.'

'I shall miss him.'

The priest gently touched the boy's shoulder. 'Many of us will...' he paused and then continued grimly, 'but not all. Come to me in the House of Life when you have eaten.' He hesitated, and after a quick glance around, added, 'Bring Miut with you.'

'But Dedi will be expecting me.'

'I will deal with Dedi. Now feed this daughter of Bastet before she grows impatient and casts her spells against us.' He turned to follow the path of the other priests, leaving Hori staring after him.

Miut needed food and she needed it now. 'Miaow,' she pleaded.

The boy sighed. 'Come on then, little mother. We will find Anath. Then perhaps you will give me some peace.' He swung on his heel and Miut followed him as he walked briskly towards the gate leading to the kitchens.

Their way took them through the temple gardens. They passed bushes of sweet-scented roses. They were as red as the setting sun-disc and armed with spikes as sharp as cats' teeth. Palm trees cast pools of shade onto the path. Ahead of them mud-brick houses clustered against the temple's outer wall, like cells in a honeycomb. Miut raised her nose and sniffed. The air was heavy with the smell of baking bread.

The kitchens were busier than Miut had ever seen them. There were tables laden with platters of newly plucked birds, baskets filled with shining mounds of river-wet fish, loaves of bread and cheeses wrapped in cloth. Other baskets held pomegranates, figs, melons and dates.

Miut saw the girl at once. She was as tall and as slim as the boy. Her black hair was tied into a plait at the side of her head. She was filling a basket with bunches of purple grapes, her white robe was spattered with juice. As soon as each basket was full, it was carried away in the directions of the docks.

Miut broke into a trot, weaving her way between a moving mass of legs. She could hear the boy close behind her. She reached the girl and nudged at her robe with her nose, purring loudly. The girl leaned down and stroked the top of the cat's head.

'I see the little goddess has returned at last.' She studied Miut thoughtfully. 'Though you are not so little anymore.' The girl turned her eyes to the boy, her mouth tightening. 'I have not seen you for many days, Hori. Have you too been away?'

The boy grimaced. 'I am sorry, Anath, but I could not come. Dedi has kept me too busy. Food was brought to us in the House of Life. Will you feed Miut?'

The girl studied him, her head inclined like a sharp-eyed dove. 'Heteb was a most powerful magician and priest, and as the sun-disc sinks into the desert, the great feast beside his tomb will honour him. I think he will not mind sharing a little with his favourite daughter of Bastet, the greatest of all the cat goddesses.'

The boy smiled. 'Thank you,' he said, his eyes fixed on her as if nothing else existed.

Then she was gone, only to return almost at once with a bowl of fish and crumbled bread in one hand, and a plate of meat and fruit in the other. She laid the bowl on the ground in front of Miut, who pounced on it as if she had not eaten for many days.

'You poor, starving creature,' laughed the girl, 'eat well. Let the kittens within you grow strong.'

She handed the plate to Hori who was sitting on the ground beside Miut. He too fell on the food, picking apart the meat with his fingers. The girl knelt at his side and said quietly, 'Hori, you must look after her.'

'What do you mean?' said Hori through a mouthful of meat.

The girl glanced over her shoulder before continuing, 'I have heard things. You do in the kitchens. Everyone comes here. And while they eat, they talk.'

'What have you heard?' asked the boy, wiping his plate clean with a piece of bread.

'Just whispers. Some people do not like it that your father will be the next High Priest. They do not like you and they do not like her.' The girl glanced down at Miut. 'They call her the "Favoured

One" and there is only hate in their voices.'

'So who are these people?' asked Hori, licking the meat juices off his fingers before swatting away the cloud of flies gathering around his plate.

The girl frowned. 'You could guess their names.'

The boy gave a small laugh. 'In that case, do not fear for us. They have no power… they are all talk and their words are full of hot desert air.'

The girl shook her head. 'That is not true. They do have power. I do not want you to be…' her voice trailed away.

'What don't you want me to be?' Miut felt the stillness in Hori as he waited for the answer.

The girl answered sharply. 'I fear for Miut, not you. Should anything happen to her, I will never speak to you again.' She leaned closer to the boy. 'I have also heard the rooms of High Priest Heteb were ransacked soon after his death. Who would do such a thing?'

Hori shrugged. 'Maybe there are thieves even in the Temple of Osiris. I will ask my father.'

'He is recovered? He has returned?' The girl's voice was eager.

'I saw him just now. He is better, but not recovered. His leg still pains him.'

The girl looked grave. 'Many bad things have happened in the temple recently. I fear the gods have turned from us. We must believe when the High Priest joins them in the afterlife, he will make them smile on us once more.' Her eyes touched the boy briefly before resting on Miut.

Miut had finished her meal and was lying down. Her belly was full and she was content. She began licking clean her fish-oiled paws.

Hori's eyes never left the girl. 'If something did happen to me, Anath, would you care?

The girl leaned forward to pick up the empty bowl and plate. For a long moment, she paused to study Hori's face. A smile flickered briefly, then without another word, she jumped to her feet and vanished into the crowd.

Hori stared after her. 'Is there hope for me there, little goddess?' His voice was just a breath in her ear.

Miut purred and nudged her head lovingly against him. Far above them, the priest on the tower called the hour. Miut looked up and saw the sun-disc had risen above the temple wall.

Hori got to his feet. 'Come on, Miut, we must go. My father will be waiting.'

Miut did not move. Her belly was full and now she longed only for somewhere cool and dark to rest. But the boy caught hold of her and swung her onto his shoulder. Too full and too lazy to scratch her disapproval, Miut laid her head against the smooth warmth of his shoulder. The movement of his walking lulled her. She closed her eyes and slept.

CHAPTER 7

A hand was shaking me awake.

'Wake up, Rose, please,' Lily was saying.

I forced my eyes open. Lily was already dressed. She threw me an apologetic look. 'You'd better hurry, or you will miss breakfast.' The door closed behind her. I was alone.

I lay for a moment. My head was whirling... temples... priests... magicians... cats... It was the strangest feeling. It was as if I'd actually been there. I'd smelt the scent of the flowers in the temple garden and the bread baking.

I clambered out of my berth and down the ladder. After splashing some water on my face, I felt a little better. I pulled on my clothes and made for the saloon.

'What's wrong?' hissed Lily when I joined them. 'You look terrible.'

'I'm alright, truly,' I hissed back and forced a smile, guessing Mama and Papa wouldn't notice how I looked. I was right. They were deep in conversation with Mrs Hodges.

To my enormous relief, there was still no sign of Mr Baxter.

'He's still not here,' I hissed at Lily.

She rolled her eyes. 'He may be having his breakfast in his cabin.'

I realised she was probably right and all my fears came racing back.

'Now,' said Mama as she finished eating, 'we'll soon be on our way. I think you'll enjoy this, girls. Did you know that the canal is considered to be a modern miracle?'

Lily shook her head.

I took a deep breath and said in a rush, 'It's a hundred miles long and took ten years to build. Thousands of Egyptians dug miles of it with shovels and it's only one ship wide, with wider passing places. Ships join a convoy of other ships to go through it, and they have to pull into a passing place to let convoys coming the other way go past.'

'Goodness, Rose, however do you know all that?' asked Mama.

'I asked Hakim.'

Papa pursed his lips. 'Please ask me if you have questions and stop bothering the crew. You will keep them from their work and get them into trouble.'

Just then, there were raised voices and a great clattering and banging coming from the deck outside the saloon.

I felt a sudden burst of excitement. We were leaving Port Said, and maybe Mr Baxter too. 'Please, Papa,' I said 'may we go and see what is happening?'

He sighed. 'If you really must, Rose. What about you, Lily? Perhaps you should return to the cabin and rest?'

Lily shook her head. 'Thank you but no, Papa. I slept well. I'd like to see us leave.'

As we left the saloon, Mr Baxter's place remained empty. A few minutes later we were watching from the upper deck as the *SS Australia* dropped her mooring lines and moved slowly out into the harbour to join the southbound convoy.

The wharf was now almost deserted. There was no donkey and no Mr Baxter to be seen. Either he was in his cabin or he really had vanished.

As we steamed into the canal, we were in the middle of the convoy. Some ships were laden with cargo, others were passenger ships like ours. The canal was far too narrow for ships to sail through it, so they had to steam. The long line of masts swept high into the pale blue sky, sails tightly furled, while steam clouds rose from all funnels.

To begin with, the banks of the canal were low and we were

high enough on the deck of our ship to be able to see over them. It was odd though. Beyond the canal banks on either side of us was a vast lake which stretched away into the distance, its glassy surface only broken occasionally by small, low islands and forests of reeds.

'This is Lake Menzalah,' explained Papa. 'it is very shallow. The channel for the canal had to be dredged, and the dredgings were heaped up to form the banks of the canal.'

I was watching a strange patch of red in the water ahead. As we steamed closer I saw it was actually a huge flock of scarlet flamingos parading around the shallows with their long, stick legs and snake necks. They rose into the air with clattering cries as we drew level with them.

At last we reached the far shore of the lake and the canal went into a deep cutting. All we could see were the steep, golden banks of the canal rising high above us, so close that at times it felt we could just reach out and touch them. Occasionally, we saw long processions of men carrying baskets of wet sand up the banks to empty on to the desert above.

'Keeping the canal clear of sand is a never-ending job,' explained Papa.

Eventually, Mama said it was time for our French lesson and led the way back to our cabin. I trailed along behind. When we came to Mr Baxter's door, it was shut. Was he inside or was he still at Port Said?

I hesitated. I needed to know. The others were well ahead of me. I raised my hand but, before I could knock, Mama's voice stopped me.

'Rose. Whatever do you think you are doing?' she said sharply. 'Come here at once.'

I swung round to find her frowning at me from the far end of the passage.

As I caught up with everyone, I told myself firmly not to be so ridiculous. It didn't matter if Mr Baxter was on board. Soon we would be at the other end of the canal in Suez and from there we would catch the train to Cairo. We would never have to see him again.

Just as I was about to shut the cabin door I heard a soft *'Meeoow',* from somewhere close by. I looked round expecting to see the ship's cat I'd sketched the day before, but there was no cat in sight. I remembered Miut. Usually dreams fade, but this one was so clear in my head. It felt as real as the little stone cat in my pocket.

Mama's voice cut through my thoughts. *'Dépêche-toi, s'il te plait,* Rose.'

I hurried up, and turned my mind to the challenge of French conversation. Lily was so good at French and I was so very bad.

CHAPTER 8

After lunch, we all went back on deck and sat in our favourite place in the shade of a lifeboat. Lily read and I sketched, while Mama and Papa talked to each other. I soon found myself listening.

'I mean,' said Mama, 'Dora and Arthur adored each other, whatever will she do without him?'

Papa ran his fingers through his hair and frowned. 'Money may be a problem. If so, we must persuade her to come back to London with us.'

'That would be the most sensible thing for her to do,' sighed Mama. 'It would be nice to have her close by.'

Papa patted her hand and added reassuringly, 'Indeed it would. Now I fear I must leave you as I have some papers to read through.' He set off for their cabin and peace returned.

The canal cut straight through the desert like a deep, open wound. Occasionally, there would be clusters of flat-roofed houses or some sort of stone monument. Mostly, there was nothing to see except the bleached gold of sand against the hot, blue sky, which, after a while, made my eyes ache.

There weren't any convenient seagulls to draw; I would have to sketch a person. I reluctantly started on Mama. I knew I would never be able to get her right, and anyway my head was full of priests in white robes and the smell of baking bread. Hori, as slender as a palm, was walking beside me...

'Rose, Rose.'

It took a few moments for me to realise Mama was talking to me.

'Goodness,' she said, 'you are concentrating hard. May I see what you are working on?'

I glanced down and Hori's face stared back at me. He was standing in a temple garden surrounded by rose bushes. I couldn't show her that. She would ask questions I couldn't answer without her worrying that I'd gone mad. I flipped my book shut. 'Please Mama, I would like to finish it before you see it.'

She sighed. 'Very well. Anyway, we will be arriving in Ismailia very shortly. We stop there for a few hours to collect or drop off, some passengers. Maybe we should go ashore and have a look round.'

My stomach somersaulted into my boots as I realised that if Mr Baxter had been left behind in Port Said, this was where he could re-join the ship.

After passing through a particularly deep cutting, the view opened out and, off to our right, I could see the flat roofs of a small town, and the first trees we had seen for hours. I guessed it must be Ismailia. It was an oasis of green against the bleak gold of the surrounding desert.

Papa returned, and we all went to stand at the bow, as the ship steamed out into a huge lake of shimmering, blue water. Ismailia stood right on its edge.

'It is quite remarkable,' said Papa, 'ten years ago there was nothing here but bare desert, and now Ismailia is one of the most attractive towns in Egypt.'

There was a landing stage in front of the town, but it was too small for our ship to come alongside. Instead we headed to the centre of the lake to pick up a mooring. Several ships from our convoy were already moored nearby. As I watched, a small crowd of people began gathering on the landing stage. I scrunched up my eyes and strained to see if there was a tall, spindly man with a mop of grey hair and round glasses amongst them. It was only when I was sure he wasn't there that I realised

I must have forgotten to breathe, as I suddenly felt quite dizzy.

'He's not there,' whispered Lily, 'not that I care.'

'Nor me.' But I did care. There must have been a reason for him watching us.

Soon several small boats started from the shore ferrying the waiting passengers out to join various ships, and to take anyone ashore who wanted to go. As each boat came alongside, I anxiously checked whether Mr Baxter was on board.

The last boat had just unloaded when I noticed Hakim hurrying towards us along the deck.

'Excuse me, sir,' he said with a small bow to Papa. 'I have been requested to bring this to you.' He handed Papa a small brown envelope.

Papa frowned. 'Who would be sending me a telegram?' He tore open the envelope and unfolded the paper inside. I watched his face tighten as he read. He looked at Mama. 'It isn't good news, Florence.'

Mama's face was even paler than usual as she whispered. 'Is it Max?'

Papa handed her the telegram, then looked at us. 'It seems he had some sort of accident yesterday. Now he has a fever. Mr Raphael asks us to come as soon as we can arrange it.'

Max was hurt? I stared at Papa, holding my breath. Mr Raphael was a colleague of Papa's, and he was running the excavation near Alexandria where Max was working. Lily took hold of my hand. Even in all that heat, her fingers were ice cold.

'Of course, we must go to him,' said Mama, starting to her feet, 'at once.'

Papa put his hand on her arm. 'Please don't look so alarmed, my dear. I'm certain if he was in any real danger, Mr Raphael would have told us so.'

Mama forced a smile and said brightly. 'Maybe he would, but we will go now in any case.' She turned to Hakim. 'Is there a train to Alexandria from here?'

Hakim nodded. 'Indeed. You may go to Zigazag and change

to another train, but it will be a long and most uncomfortable journey. Or you go to Cairo and take the morning train from there. That will be the most comfortable way.'

'I do not care about comfort,' said Mama sharply. 'I would like to go to Max now, wherever he is.'

Papa looked at her. 'I know you do. But what about the girls? Wouldn't it be better for us to take them to Cairo and leave them with Dora? We have no idea what this fever is. We need to be able to concentrate on Max, not worry about the girls.'

It was only then I realised they were planning to leave us behind. 'Please, Papa,' I begged. 'We must come with you. We could help nurse Max.'

At this he snorted, which I thought was most unkind. 'Really Rose,' he said, 'the thought of you or Lily nursing anyone is most unlikely. Lily would faint at the sight of blood, and you would be off drawing something, having completely forgotten the time, and we would have to send out endless search parties for you. No, you must stay with your aunt.'

I scowled down at the deck, but there was no point arguing once Papa's mind was made up.

'Shall I send a reply, sir?' said Hakim.

'Indeed, you must,' said Papa. 'Please telegraph that we are on our way to Cairo now and will be in Alexandria tomorrow.' He pulled out a small notebook from his pocket, tore out a page and handed it to Hakim. 'And send a second telegram to Mrs Sinclair at this address, informing her we shall be arriving this evening.'

He rested a reassuring hand on Mama's arm. 'We can all spend the night with Dora, then you and I shall take the first train to Alexandria tomorrow.' He turned to Hakim. 'Do you know when the Cairo train leaves?'

'I believe in one hour. Shall I inform the captain you will be leaving the ship?'

Papa nodded. 'Please do.'

CHAPTER 9

As soon as we reached our cabins Mama began folding our clothes into our cabin trunks. 'Our hold luggage will just have to follow on,' she said.

It wasn't long before our things were packed. As we made our way to the launch, we passed Mr Baxter's cabin for the last time. Mama, Papa and Lily were ahead of me. This time the door was open.

I hesitated in the doorway. There was the now-familiar ship smell of polish, burnt oil and seaweed, but there was something else, which was strangely familiar. I wrinkled my nose trying to identify it, but failed. A trunk stood open on the floor and Hakim was kneeling on the floor, hastily packing Mr Baxter's belongings into it. He glanced up and seeing it was me, stood up. 'It is most unfortunate you are leaving the ship like this, Miss.'

'I am sorry too.' I gestured at the trunk. 'Isn't Mr Baxter coming back?'

Hakim shook his head. 'Indeed not.'

'You have heard from him?'

Hakim frowned. 'There was a telegram. It instructs for his cabin trunk to be packed and all his luggage sent to his address in Cairo. I must despatch it now, from Ismailia.' He gave me a worried look. 'It is all most strange, Miss.'

'Do passengers often get off the ship and disappear?'

'Not at all, Miss. Indeed, the gentleman was most unusual.'

I certainly agreed with that. But at least he had gone out of our lives. Cairo was a large city, so I would probably never see him again. I could see Lily waiting impatiently for me at the end of the passage.

I was just about to say goodbye when Hakim said, 'He was most keen on knowing more about your brother.'

I stared at Hakim. 'What do you mean?'

'He asked questions.'

'Such as?'

'Where he was making his excavations? How long he would be there? Who he was working with?'

'What did you tell him?'

A fly was settling on Hakim's cheek. He brushed it away with his hand. 'I did not know many of the answers. I said only he was digging somewhere near Alexandria.' He was gazing anxiously at me. 'I am sorry, Miss, was that wrong of me?'

'No. Not wrong at all,' I said although my thoughts were spinning like a waterwheel after a rainstorm. Why had Mr Baxter been asking about Max?

Hakim put his hands together and gave a small bow. 'May your brother recover very soon, and may all your dreams come true.'

I returned his bow. 'Goodbye, Hakim, and thank you for everything.' I managed a smile and then fled to a very impatient Lily, my head swirling at the thought of my dreams coming true. There were bad dreams, nightmares. I knew too much about them. There were good ones too, ones that you didn't want to wake up from. Which sort were Miut and Hori?

'What were you doing?' Lily asked anxiously. 'Mama and Papa will be waiting.'

'I'll tell you later.'

She pulled a face, and then we were flying along the deck to the ship's steps. Mama and Papa were already in the launch, looking anxious. As we clambered down to join them, I realised I couldn't say anything more about the strange curiosity of Mr Baxter. Max was all that was important now.

The crew were just about to cast off when Mrs Hodges

appeared looking red faced and flustered, a large handbag in one hand and a parasol in the other. Two sailors followed her carrying a large blue, and much battered, cabin trunk.

'Oh dear, oh dear,' she twittered as a steward helped her onto the launch, followed by her luggage. 'I am dreadfully sorry to have kept you waiting. Hakim told me your son has had an accident. Will you go to him at once?'

Papa stood up to make room for her to pass him. 'As soon as we can. We will leave the girls with their aunt in Cairo and head for Alexandria in the morning.' Papa sat down beside her. 'But I do hope that nothing so worrying has forced you to leave the ship too.'

Mrs Hodges shook her head, and some of her hair escaped from under her sun hat.

I realised she looked unusually dishevelled.

'Not so terrible, but like you, I had a telegram. There is a problem with the boarding school which my dearest Lottie is attending. She is most dreadfully unhappy and my sister is at her wits' end. She isn't strong, you know, my sister that is, not Lottie. I may have to return to England. I will travel to Cairo and stay with a friend, while I decide what must be done.'

As the little boat headed for the shore and the hot desert breeze ruffled the water, I thought what a busy place the Ismailian Telegraph Office had been that morning.

I realised that Mrs Hodges was talking about us.

'But can you not all travel to Alexandria directly?' she was asking.

'We could,' said Mama and went on to explain why we were being left in Cairo.

'But Mrs Evering,' Mrs Hodges was looking intently at Mama, 'please let me take the girls to Cairo. I will deliver them safely to their aunt.'

Mama threw a desperate glance at Papa.

'But Papa,' I started before his most quelling look silenced me.

'If you're sure they would be no trouble,' said Papa, 'that would be most extraordinarily kind.'

Before we had even reached the shore, it was arranged that Mama and Papa would set off for Alexandria directly, and we would go with Mrs Hodges to Cairo and Aunt Dora.

I stared wide eyed into the distant horizon to stop the tears that threatened to overflow. I refused to cry. I wouldn't upset Mama and Papa. They had too much to worry about already. But going to an unknown city, to an unknown aunt, with neither Mama nor Papa, felt wrong. It was like I was standing on the edge of a cliff – about to fall off.

CHAPTER 10

The train was waiting for us only because Hakim had sent a boy on to tell the stationmaster that we were on our way. The door to the compartment was open.

'You will have a wonderful time,' said Papa. 'Look after each other. Be good. And no quarrelling. Remember your aunt has had a very difficult time recently. You are not to add to her troubles.'

Mama wrapped her arms round me and hugged me tightly. I nuzzled my head into her shoulder, breathing in the warm, sweet smell of her. I never wanted her to let me go.

'You and Lily will be fine,' she whispered, 'just do as Papa says.' She then added, 'Keep Lily safe. I trust you, Rose.'

'I will, I promise.'

She gave me an extra tight squeeze, kissed my cheek and let me go.

Before I could say a word, we were clambering up into the compartment. The door slammed shut behind us. There was a piercing whistle and the train shuddered and hissed into life. Clouds of steam swirled around the platform as I pulled down the window. Lily and I leaned out and waved at Mama and Papa who waved back. We kept on waving until they were just tiny black dots in the distance.

Mrs Hodges settled herself into the window seat opposite us, opened her bag and pulled out a small leather-bound book with '*Magic in Ancient Egypt: The Mysterious Truth*' embossed in gold on the front cover. I wondered if the ancient Egyptians had magic wands and pulled rabbits out of hats.

'Now girls,' she said, 'I wish to finish my book. I am sure you can amuse yourselves for a while.'

So we did. To stop myself worrying about where we were going, or about Max, or my dream the night before, I opened my sketchbook and gazed out of the window at endless miles of desert broken up by the occasional camel train, or an oasis of green palms and clusters of flat-roofed houses. I decided I would draw a village scene. It was difficult to keep my pencil steady as the train was rattling around so much. In the end, I gave up and read instead. Later Lily and I slept. The sun began to sink, turning the rock-strewn sand to a rich golden pink. Ahead a forest of minarets, towers and domes spiked the sky. Cairo.

Lily whispered in my ear. 'What if we hate Aunt Dora? What if she hates us?'

'She'll be really nice. She's our aunt after all!' I whispered back, hoping desperately I was right. As I tried to push my sketch book back into my bag, there was an extra big jolt and it fell onto the floor at Lily's feet.

She picked it up. 'Can I see what you were drawing?' She flicked it open. 'Oh, that's lovely, Rose. Really not too wobbly. And I love the way you've drawn that little cat. It's beautiful.'

My stomach twisted as I studied my picture. There, by the corner of a small mud brick house, almost in its shadow, lay a cat. A cat I didn't remember drawing at all.

CHAPTER 11

Cairo station was filled with people of every shape, size and race. Men in suits and ladies in long sweeping dresses mixed with Arabs in their colourful robes and dark-eyed Egyptians in their desert-coloured *galabayas*. Porters were piling luggage from the train onto hand carts, and everyone seemed to be shouting at each other.

I realised Lily was staring round with huge, shimmering eyes like a rain cloud waiting to happen. I took hold of her hand and hissed, 'It'll be fine, Lily, for goodness sake, buck up.' Not that I felt particularly bucked up. My head ached and my legs felt like I was wearing boots filled with lead. Lily glared at me, but at least her eyes stayed dry.

It was almost dark by the time a porter had loaded our luggage onto his handcart and we followed him outside the station to where ranks of horses and open carriages were waiting in the fading light. Mrs Hodges spoke to the driver of the nearest carriage, which had a sad, rather dusty-looking chestnut mare between the shafts. I stroked the mare's nose. It was as soft and smooth as the silk of Mama's best dress. I wished I had a sugar lump for her. I patted my pockets. No sugar, just some short ends of my colouring crayons and a pencil. At home I often had both in my pockets, which meant that the London horses often got rainbow-coloured sugar lumps, but they never seemed to mind.

'Come on, Rose,' Mrs Hodges' voice cut through my thoughts, 'get in the carriage, we have not got all night.' I glanced at her, surprised by the unfamiliar sharpness of her tone. But she had turned way and was instructing the driver. I caught Lily's eye and she shrugged. Maybe Mrs Hodges was as tired as we were.

A few moments later, we were all in the carriage, our cabin trunks strapped high on the back. The station clock was striking six o'clock as the driver flicked his whip and the mare leaned into her harness. As soon as the carriage began to roll, she broke into a trot.

The narrow streets were busy at first, then gradually emptied. Lanterns flickered above doorways, voices called out of dark alleys, a distant donkey brayed. Eventually the only sounds were the brisk thudding of the mare's hooves and the rumble of the carriage wheels. Where the streets widened into small open squares, moonlight fell in silver lakes darkening the surrounding shadows.

Lily fell asleep leaning against my shoulder. But I couldn't close my eyes. I just watched this strange and mysterious city go past and wished more than I'd ever wished for anything before, that Mama, Papa and Max were with us in the carriage, not hundreds of miles away. The thought of Max sent my heart racing. What if he was really ill? What if... I clenched my fists. I wouldn't think of anything worse. I remembered Mama's words. I had to be strong, for me and for Lily.

At last the streets broadened out and were lit by gas lamps, like we had in London. The light pooled at the base of the lampposts, but between the pools, the darkness was thicker than ever. Suddenly the carriage swung to the left and the driver pulled on the reins and the horse slowed to a walk. Large shadow houses lined the street we were in, each set back behind shadow gardens.

'Finally,' said Mrs Hodges straightening her hat, 'we have arrived.'

The horse jolted to a halt in front of a high wall and a pair of iron gates. They were closed. Lily and I climbed out of the carriage and peered through the bars. It took a few moments to make out that behind the gates was a jungle of straggling bushes and trailing ribbons of creeper, and beyond the jungle, the house towered above us, silhouetted against the night sky. A dome like the top of a giant pepper pot sprouted from the roof. Not a glimmer of light showed through the shuttered windows.

Lily breathed into my ear. 'Does this look like the sort of place Aunt Dora would live?'

I glanced back at the carriage. Mrs Hodges was instructing the driver as to which bags to unload.

'It must be right,' I said firmly. 'Mrs Hodges has been here before.' But my thoughts were racing. Maybe Aunt Dora hadn't received Papa's telegram? Maybe she was away? What would we do if she was? Before my fear could turn from a trickle to a torrent, the driver picked up our bags and Mrs Hodges pulled at the gates. The hinges opened with a protesting screech and we followed her up the cracked and crumbling steps to the front door. She grasped the bell pull. We heard a jangling somewhere deep inside the house. And then we waited...

CHAPTER 12

Mrs Hodges again raised her hand to the bell pull. The sound of a bolt scraping back stopped her. The door swung open to reveal an elderly man dressed in a long black robe. On his head he wore a neatly tied blue turban. He was holding an oil lamp which spluttered in the night breeze. He was no taller than us, his face was as dark and wrinkled as last year's walnuts and his eyes as black as night.

He raised the lamp so he could properly examine our faces. His eyes widened. He seemed startled. As I'd feared, it seemed we weren't expected. My thoughts spun. What if Aunt Dora was away? Where would we go?

Then I realised that the startled look on the man's face had vanished and instead he now seemed almost excited. I breathed again. So he must have been expecting us, only maybe he hadn't been warned we were identical twins.

He said softly. 'Two girls and one face, with skin as pale as the moon... and such hair... even in the darkness it glows. It is true indeed that it is as red as the sun as it sinks into the desert.' His voice trailed to silence.

His words niggled at me. There was something oddly familiar about them. But what? I wished I was more awake, my brain felt like tangled wool.

'Goodness gracious,' said Mrs Hodges brusquely, 'do let us in, my man. We are expected, I assume.'

The man bowed his head and stepped back to allow us to pass. 'Apologies, Madame. I am Ezra. I keep the house for Mrs

Sinclair,' he said. '*Ahlan wa sahlan*. You are most welcome here in *Bayt el Dil*.'

'*Bayt el Dil*,' I repeated letting the unfamiliar words roll in my mouth, tasting them.

Ezra stared intently at me. 'The House of Shadows,' he said softly.

We were standing in a room lit only by the lamp in Ezra's hand. It seemed more like a huge, gloomy cave, than a hallway.

He turned to Mrs Hodges with an apologetic expression. 'Mrs Sinclair has had to go out. She hands you her apologies. She asks if you would like to call on her and the young ladies in the next day or so, when you will be made most welcome.'

Mrs Hodges nodded quickly and seemed relieved not to have to wait. 'Of course. It is getting late. My friends will be wondering where I am. Please give my regards to Mrs Sinclair.' She gave us both a brief hug. The smell of lavender and peppermint enveloped me as she murmured in my ear, 'Remember, Rose, remember our secret.' Releasing me she said brightly, 'Now be good for your aunt, girls. I will see you very soon.' Then she was gone and Ezra shut the door firmly behind her.

I stared after her, my thoughts spinning. That strange half-recognised smell in Mr Baxter's cabin had been Mrs Hodges' lavender and peppermint. What had she been doing there?

A few seconds later there was the squeak of the gate, followed shortly by the steady clip clopping of the horse as it set off down the street. It was like the last chain binding us to the world we knew, had shattered. Even with Lily beside me, I felt terribly alone. Glancing at her I saw she was staring at the door and knew she wished Mama and Papa were here as much as I did

I told myself firmly not to be ridiculous. Aunt Dora was our aunt. She would look after us. I turned my attention to the room we were standing in. Through the gloom I could just make out the curve of a dome far above our heads. A great glass chandelier hung from the centre of the dome, but there were no candles in the holders. And no fittings for gas lights. I remembered the gas lamp in the street outside. It seemed that gas was yet to make it inside. Worse than no light, however, were the monster cobwebs, which hung like sailors' hammocks between the branches of the chandelier. I wondered how big the spiders were which had spun those webs.

'Just how big are the spiders in Egypt?' whispered Lily, her hand grasping mine, her eyes fixed on the monstrous webs.

Ezra must have heard her as he looked up at the chandelier. 'The maid was unwell and returned to England. She has not yet been replaced.'

I realised two things. One was he had not answered the question about the size of spiders. The second was that the maid must have left a long time ago.

'Come,' said Ezra turning away, raising the lamp so its flame pushed back the shadows a little further. 'I will show you to your room.'

We followed him across the hall, his sandalled feet padding silently over the marble-slabbed floor and along a corridor that appeared to cut the house in half. At the far end, moonlight was filtering in through a glass-panelled door, filling the corridor with silver light. Delicate watercolours of ruined temples and views of the Nile hung on the walls. A small one of three pyramids at night caught my eye. I stopped for a proper look.

'That's so boring. Pictures of buildings always are,' said Lily peering over my shoulder.

'It's not. It's beautiful. Look at all the detail.'

Beside the glass-panelled door stood a tired-looking grandfather clock. It chimed seven times as we reached it. I felt a flash of surprise that it wasn't later; the day seemed to have gone on forever. Ezra was waiting for us beside an open door.

Our bedroom was a large, square room with a high ceiling. The shutters were closed and the air was hot and stale. Ezra pulled a taper from a holder on the dressing table and used it to light the small oil lamp which stood on a large chest of drawers. The only other furniture in the room were two beds, a substantial wardrobe, a washstand and a water jug.

'I will fetch your luggage,' said Ezra, and vanished.

Lily threw herself on to the bed nearest the window. 'Oh, Rose, how I wish Mama and Papa were here.'

'And Max,' I said, wondering how he was, and if Mama and Papa were with him.

There was a knock on the door and Ezra reappeared dragging our cabin trunks.

'Mrs Sinclair has returned,' he said, 'but she has some urgent matters to deal with. I will fetch you to her when she is ready to receive you.'

'Can we look round the house while we are waiting?' I asked and was surprised when Ezra's eyes flashed an angry look at me.

'Indeed, you may not. There are many precious things which must not be disturbed. Please stay in your room until I return.'

I was about to ask him if there was anyone to help us unpack, but then remembered he had already told us the maid had left. Anyway, before I could ask anything he had left the room. The door clicked shut behind him.

'Come on, Lily, we should put our things away.' I dragged my trunk over to the chest of drawers.

Lily didn't move. Her eyes were shut.

'Do get up,' I snapped, because I was tired and unsettled by Ezra's anger. 'I'm not your maid.' I went over to give her a shake, then, with a shock, realised how drawn her face was, and that under her eyes were shadows like bruises. Mama had told me to look after Lily, but what if I failed and she became really ill?

Lily opened her eyes and gave me a small smile. 'It is just one of my headaches.'

I knew what Mama would do. I poured some water from the jug into the basin, and taking a towel, I wet it, then squeezed it dry. I laid it on Lily's forehead.

She sighed. 'That feels lovely and cool.'

I set about unpacking for both of us, while Lily lay pale and still on the bed. I tried to put everything away neatly and quietly. There seemed to be a good deal, even though most of our luggage was still in the *SS Australia*'s hold.

Lily liked things being just in the right place, so I put the cotton stockings, bloomers and wool vests together in one drawer, while our flannel petticoats went into another. I folded away the cotton blouses and pinafores as carefully as I could, and hung our linen skirts and dresses in the wardrobe.

Once I'd finished I lay down on the other bed. I tried not to go to sleep. Surely Aunt Dora would be ready to see us soon. My stomach gurgled and I realised I was starving. Our last proper meal had been breakfast and that seemed like years ago, as did my conversation with Hakim. Why had Mr Baxter been so interested in Max? Not that it really mattered because Mr Baxter had gone, vanished into the dust on the back of a donkey.

CHAPTER 13

After a while Lily felt better and got off the bed. She sat down in front of the dressing table mirror and began brushing her hair. I watched her mirrored self for a few moments. She still looked so pale.

'Let me,' I said.

She handed me the brush. I continued pulling it through the ringlets, softening them to loose curls with long sweeping strokes. The rhythm calmed me and I forgot about the strangeness of the House of Shadows. It must have been some minutes later I felt a draught. I looked into the mirror and saw that the door behind us was now open and Ezra was standing in the doorway behind us. He was perfectly still, his eyes fixed on us, his face expressionless.

He started when he saw I was watching him.

'Mrs Dora is waiting for you,' he said abruptly. 'Please come with me.'

I picked up our lamp and we followed him.

Lily gave me a nervous glance as we left the bedroom. 'I hope she likes us.'

'I am sure she will,' I said as reassuringly as I could manage.

The passage clock was striking eight as Ezra led us down a dark staircase into a narrow hallway. The door in front of us was closed. Ezra knocked sharply three times, then turned to us with a small bow. 'Please go inside directly,' he instructed, and without another word he disappeared up the stairs.

I stared after him.

'What's wrong?' asked Lily.

'Didn't you see?'

'What?'

'When we were in the bedroom, I saw Ezra in the mirror. He was standing in the doorway watching me brush your hair.'

'Maybe he had never seen red hair before. Or twins.'

'Maybe,' I agreed, as I pushed open the door and led the way into the room beyond.

We found ourselves in a dimly lit library. The air smelled of dust, leather, burning oil and old paper. Bookshelves lined the walls and the floor was dotted with open boxes, some empty and some half full of books and papers. There were two large windows with closed wooden shutters, and window seats with cushions. Between them stood a handsomely carved grandfather clock, its steady ticking filled the room.

The only other sign of life was a spluttering oil lamp, which stood on a large desk opposite us, between mountains of books and papers. There seemed to be no other furniture except for a wood and glass cabinet standing at the far end of the room, and a pair of leather-backed arm chairs.

'She's not here,' Lily whispered, 'let's go back upstairs.'

'We can't,' I hissed. 'I am sure she'll be here in a minute.'

I was peering round wondering if this might be where Uncle Arthur kept his Collection of Curiosities when a woman's voice interrupted my thoughts.

'Oh dear,' she said, 'I am sorry. I didn't hear you come in. You must be Lily and Rose?'

I spun round to see someone, who must be Aunt Dora, peering out at us from behind the paper mountains.

Lily and I curtsied.

'Yes, Aunt Dora,' I said, 'Ezra did knock.'

'I'm afraid I was miles away reading some letters,' said Aunt Dora, pushing back her chair and standing up. She gestured towards the nearest boxes. 'Do please excuse the muddle. I have so much to sort out. If only your dear Papa were here to help me as he promised he would be. Of course, I understand he has to be with your brother, but...' her voice trailed away as she examined us.

She was tall and thin, still dressed in full mourning for Uncle Arthur. On her head was a small cap of black lace and her dress, which swept the floor, was plain black silk. She wore no jewellery at all. Her skin was as pale as Lily's and mine, and her hair was silver grey. A pair of spectacles hung from a string round her neck. She put them on and studied us.

'Goodness me,' she said at last, 'it's like seeing double. I know one of you must be Rose and the other must be Lily, but who is who? I have no idea.' She gave an apologetic smile.

'I'm Rose,' I said. 'I have straighter hair because I don't spend hours tying my hair in rags each night to make it curl.'

'And I'm Lily,' said Lily frowning at me, 'and I just like my hair to look nice.'

I was about to tell her just what I thought about her curls, when I noticed that the corners of Aunt Dora's mouth were twitching as she continued, 'Your father warned me you two could argue the hind legs off a donkey.'

I realised she was trying not to laugh, and suddenly I felt a great deal better. Though the mention of a donkey had brought with it a vivid picture of Mr Baxter disappearing on his donkey. But before my mind could wander any further along that road, Aunt Dora picked up the lamp.

'I was sorry to hear about Max. I hope your parents will find him recovering well when they get to Alexandria. Now in Egypt, we like to give our guests gifts to make them feel welcome. I have something for you both. Come with me.'

She led the way between the many boxes to the cabinet. Through the dusty glass I could make out that its shelves were dotted with small, carved figures. Some carried baskets, others held hoes or knives, one even had a bow in his hand and a quiver full of arrows on his back. They were beautiful.

'These are lovely,' breathed Lily.

'Indeed they are,' agreed Aunt Dora. 'They are *shabti* and they are magical figures that the Ancient Egyptians placed in a rich person's tomb.'

'I know...' I couldn't stop myself interrupting, 'Papa told us about them. The ancient Egyptians believed that if a dead person had been good when he was alive, he would come to life again after death. So they placed things in his tomb that they thought he would need in the afterlife, like spears for hunting, a boat, a bed, chairs, as well as food and drink. He would need servants to look after him so he would say a spell and the *shabti* would come to life and bake bread, catch fish or even farm his fields.'

Aunt Dora looked approvingly at me. 'You are quite right of course.' She added questioningly, 'Rose?'

I nodded.

'Good, I will try remember who is who. It'll be easy, just as long as you don't start curling your hair, Rose,' Aunt Dora smiled. 'I think your father has taught you a great deal about Egypt.' She looked at Lily. 'Are you interested too?'

'Not really,' admitted Lily. 'I always thought Egypt was rather dull.' She paused then added, 'But not now I'm actually here, of course.'

Aunt Dora nodded. 'I'm glad to hear that,' she said gravely, but her mouth quivered. She turned back to the cabinet. 'These are some of the objects your uncle found while he was excavating.'

I'd noticed some of the figures had animal heads. I knew they were Egyptian gods and goddesses. I recognised some of them from a book Papa had given us. One was particularly striking with a man's body carved out of grey stone, and a black head with pointed ears, and a long snout. It was Anubis, the jackal-headed god of the Underworld.

Dora pulled a key out of her pocket and unlocked a drawer in the base of the cabinet. She lifted out a small wooden box. I guessed this must be the box Mrs Hodges had told me about. My heart was suddenly beating so loudly I was sure Aunt Dora and Lily must hear it. I wrapped my fingers tightly around the little cat in my pocket. I'd promised to put it back, but how could I let it go?

'Now this is something quite different,' said Aunt Dora, placing the box on top of the cabinet. 'This is your uncle's Collection of Curiosities. These might look ancient, but they are particularly clever forgeries and have little real value, but some of them are still very beautiful.' Her mouth lifted into a small, sad smile. 'In Egypt, remembering someone's name helps them live again in the afterlife. I would like each of you choose something from this little box. Whenever you look at it, remember your uncle's name.'

My heart leapt. This was my chance to do exactly what I'd wanted to do ever since I'd first held the little stone cat.

Aunt Dora opened the lid to reveal a tangle of bracelets, brooches and necklaces. Some might have been silver, but they were so dull and tarnished it was hard to tell. There were also strings of coloured beads and a jumble of small, carved animal and human figures.

'Now who wants to go first?'

'Lily should,' I said, 'as she's the eldest.'

Lily threw me a surprised look before peering into the box. She plunged her hand in and rummaged about for a few moments before pulling out a dull-looking bracelet shaped like a snake. She gazed at it doubtfully.

Aunt Dora handed her a cloth. 'Give it a good polish.'

Lily rubbed at the blackened metal. Soon the whole bracelet was gleaming.

She slipped it over her hand. It twisted elegantly round her wrist. 'It's beautiful. Are you sure I can have it? It looks like it's made of silver.'

Aunt Dora nodded. 'It is. It looks wonderful on you.'

Lily threw me a quick look. 'It's lovely, isn't it?'

'Yes.' All eyes had been on Lily polishing her bracelet. No one had noticed me slipping the cat into the box and tucking it down out of sight. I felt strangely empty without the cat in my pocket.

'I believe it represents one of the snake gods,' Aunt Dora was saying, 'but I'm not an expert so I don't know which. Arthur bought that off a street seller in Aswan. Now Rose, what would you like?'

It was my turn to plunge in my hand and rummage. For a terrible moment I thought my cat had vanished. At last, at the very bottom of the box, I found it. My fingers closed tightly round its cool silkiness. I pulled out my hand and opened it. The cat stared unblinkingly up at me.

Aunt Dora gently took the little stone cat from me and examined it carefully. I watched her, holding my breath. She had to let me keep it. She just had to.

'Well, Rose,' she said at last, 'it is rather beautiful. I think the amulet has been carved from a stone called haematite. I have no idea where Arthur found it. On a market stall I expect.'

'But may I have it?' I whispered, suddenly terrified Aunt Dora would say there had been a dreadful mistake and it should not be in the Collection of Curiosities at all.

Dora nodded. 'Of course,' and she handed it back to me. 'The ancient Egyptians used to believe amulets had magical powers and would bring them luck. In ancient times, people carried these cat amulets to gain the protection of the cat goddess, Bastet.'

But he will not mind that he shares it with his favourite daughter of Bastet.

Had Papa ever told us stories about Bastet? I didn't remember any. So how had I dreamed about a daughter of Bastet?

'What sort of protection?' asked Lily.

'The strengths of the cat.'

'Such as?' I whispered.

She looked thoughtful. 'I imagine you could be as brave as a cat defending her kittens from danger. Or you could be as fast and as silent a hunter. Perhaps you would be able to see better in the dark. I believe cats see well even when there's very little light, though I think their whiskers help them find their way when it is completely dark.'

'Cat magic,' I said slipping the cat safely back into my pocket.

Aunt Dora nodded. 'That's a nice way of putting it.'

Just then there was a whirring from the direction of the grandfather clock, followed by a series of loud chimes.

'Goodness me,' said our aunt, turning towards the door, 'half past eight already. It is dreadfully late. You must both be exhausted. We will sit in the garden and Ezra will bring us something to drink. You can tell me all about your parents and poor Max's accident.'

CHAPTER 14

Ezra was waiting at the top of the stairs. He seemed out of breath. I did wonder if he might have been listening at the library door and hurried up the stairs when he heard we were coming out. But why would he be that interested in our conversation? I pushed the thought away.

Aunt Dora led the way out through the glass door onto a small terrace. High above us the moon hung huge and white in the starry sky. Below us, the small, square garden was lit by moonlight and by lanterns, which flickered in the evening breeze. Urns overflowed with flowers turned to silver by the moonlight, and a central fountain sent water sparkling into the air. We followed our aunt down a flight of stone steps and over to a small wooden table and chairs, where three glasses and a large jug waited for us.

We sat down, and Ezra filled the glasses with a pale, cloudy liquid.

'This is a most popular drink in Egypt,' he said, handing us each a glass, 'it is *assir limoon*. It is made from lemon juice, water and sugar.'

He waited while we sipped it. It was cool and delicious. It was when I put down my empty glass that I realised that Ezra had not taken his eyes off Lily since we had been in the garden. I looked at Lily to see if she had noticed, but she was chatting to Aunt Dora.

When we had finished our drinks, Aunt Dora smiled gently. 'You must be exhausted, and I have work to do this evening sorting through more of your uncle's papers.' She glanced at Ezra.

'Tonight, the girls will eat in their room. Please could you make up a tray for them.'

Ezra bowed, collected our glasses and made his way back inside the house.

Aunt Dora waited until he was gone before saying, 'He really is marvellous, you know. An excellent cook. He insists on doing everything, since we lost Tilly.'

Tilly must be the maid Ezra had mentioned. 'Has he been here long?' I asked.

Aunt Dora shook her head. 'He came to us shortly before your poor uncle died. He was highly recommended by a kind friend of your uncle's. We needed someone trustworthy as we had been burgled a few weeks before. They were interrupted as nothing was taken. It was worrying all the same.'

'It must have been horrid,' said Lily.

Aunt Dora nodded. 'When poor Tilly fell ill so soon after Arthur died, I had to send her back to England. Training a new maid seemed too difficult. Ezra even does my accounts. The Copts are excellent mathematicians, you see. I leave it all to him.'

I was curious. 'What's a Copt?'

'It means he is Christian, not Muslim,' explained Aunt Dora. 'The Coptic Christians were here already when the Muslim army invaded Egypt about twelve hundred years ago. Indeed, many believe the Copts are the true descendants of the ancient Egyptians who built the pyramids. You can usually recognise the men as they often wear black gowns, and blue or black turbans.'

She stood up. 'Now girls, it is time for supper and bed. I hope you won't mind dining in your bedroom tonight. I will have some soup in the library while I am working through your uncle's papers.'

She paused, frowned and continued. 'That reminds me, that friend, the one who recommended Ezra, is going to help me with your uncle's affairs, now your Papa has had to go to Alexandria.

He's starting first thing tomorrow, so you'll meet him at breakfast.'

'May I stay for a few moments longer,' I pleaded. 'It's so pretty. I would love to bring my sketchbook out here another night perhaps?'

'Aah yes, Rose. I remember your dear Mama telling me how you loved to draw. Stay, but just for a few minutes. Lily, you had better come in now before the temperature drops. We cannot have you getting a chill.'

The garden was very quiet after Aunt Dora and Lily had gone inside. I sat there taking in all the details of light and shade. After a few minutes I noticed something move in the shadow of a palm. I held my breath. Perhaps it was a rat? Papa had told us that there were millions in Egypt. Or was it a snake? I knew there were plenty of those too.

I wasn't afraid, just curious. Suddenly a breeze stirred the palm fronds and rays of moonlight stabbed the darkness. There was something lying there. I realised it was a cat. It was so still that for a moment I wondered if it was dead. But then an ear twitched.

Maybe it felt me watching it as its eyes flicked open. It blinked and yawned, exposing two rows of gleaming needle teeth, before getting leisurely to its feet and stretching its back in a long, lazy arch.

It was huge. In the moonlight its coat was a carpet of silver, with spots like inky fingerprints spread all over its shoulders and back, while its legs and tail were covered by feathery, charcoal stripes. It looked more like a small leopard than a cat.

For a few long moments it just stood there, statue-still, its eyes fixed on me. Even in the moonlight they glowed a deep, fiery amber. It was as if it was waiting for something. A thought slipped into my mind. *As if it was waiting for me.* Another thought quickly followed. *It looked just like the cat I had drawn lying beside the flat-roofed house in the desert.*

Just as the thought formed, the cat turned and stalked away

with its tail held tall and straight behind it. It disappeared into the jungle beside the house.

The garden seemed empty after it had gone. I stood up and went inside.

CHAPTER 15

Ezra soon appeared in our bedroom with two bowls of steaming rice topped by chunks of chicken and a nose-tingling garlic and tomato sauce. 'This is *fatteh*,' he said. 'Mrs Dora thought you might like to try her most favourite Egyptian dish.'

We sat on our beds with the bowls on our laps. The chicken tasted sweet, slightly spicy and delicious.

Ezra closed the shutters and left while we ate, but soon returned. As he collected up our bowls and glasses, he looked at Lily and asked, 'Your bracelet, Miss Lily, it is very beautiful. Was this a gift from Mrs Dora?'

Lily nodded and raised her wrist so he could see the bracelet more clearly.

Ezra turned to me. 'And did you too receive a gift, Miss Rose?' His voice was casual enough but I felt he really wanted an answer. Something made me reluctant give him one. To distract him I asked, 'There was a huge cat in the garden just now. Does it live here?'

'A cat?' Ezra replied raising his eyebrows. 'We have no cats here. Mrs Dora does not like cats. It must be a stray. You must chase it away if you see it.'

I couldn't believe there was anything "stray" about the cat. 'But it looks so at home. I thought you must at least feed it.'

'Certainly not. Beside the Nile, there are many cats. They are everywhere. Most especially they like to be where they are not wanted,' said Ezra. 'Now I will wish you goodnight.' He shut the door firmly behind him.

I stared after him. 'Did Aunt Dora sound like she hated cats when she was talking about them in the library just now?'

Lily was at the dressing table twisting rags into her hair. She pulled a face. 'No. But she might not like them in her garden.'

I turned my back on her and started getting ready for bed. As I dropped my skirt onto the floor there was a small clunk. The stone cat. My heart missed a beat. I'd forgotten it was still in my pocket. I quickly retrieved and inspected it. It was undamaged. I breathed an enormous sigh of relief and stood it carefully on the bedside table. I climbed into bed.

Lily turned down the wick on the lamp. It spluttered and went out. The room was suddenly in total darkness.

I tried to keep my voice steady. 'Please, Lily, could you open the shutters?'

'Honestly, Rose,' grumbled Lily, 'You still hating the dark, it's ridiculous. And you haven't had your nightmare for ages.' But I heard her padding across to the window. As she opened the shutters, the moonlight crept in and the black softened to silver grey.

'That's better. Thank you.' I said, managing to resist making any comment about spiders. I closed my eyes. On the ship I'd almost forgotten about my nightmare. With Mama and Papa just next door, and Lily sleeping below me in that tiny cabin, I'd felt safe; even the appearance of Mr Baxter failed to bring it back. But here in this House of Shadows, nothing felt safe anymore. I remembered when I had my nightmare for the first time.

Mama and Papa had taken us to visit the British Museum on our sixth birthday. Papa said we were now so grown up that we deserved a grown-up birthday treat. We wore our Sunday best dresses with hats and gloves. The museum was quite one of the biggest buildings I'd ever seen. It was all very new and splendid. There was a collection of ancient Egyptian pieces on display that Papa thought we would like to see. There were so many people there. One moment Mama was holding my hand, then a crowd of people pushed past us and swept me away. Mama and Papa vanished. And Lily too.

I searched for them in gallery after gallery, past endless wood and glass cabinets filled with the strangest things. Things I'd never seen before. Then I found the animals with gold and white patchwork coats. They stood tall and silent in the centre of a huge hall. Their necks stretched towards the sky and their legs were so long I was sure a carriage could have driven beneath them. I thought they were alive. I thought they were going to eat me. I turned and ran. Then everything goes blank. Three hours later, I was found. My knees were grazed, and there was a large lump on my head where I must have bumped it.

I had the first nightmare soon afterwards. It was always exactly the same.

I open my eyes. All I see is darkness. Where am I? The air is still and smells of dust. All I can hear is the frantic pumping of my heart.

Slowly my eyes adjust and I see shapes. Shadow-monsters. Black against grey. I feel their eyes on me.

'Lily,' I whisper.

But she doesn't answer. I feel so alone. There is a gaping, aching, emptiness in my head where she should be. The shadow-monsters have shut her out.

The shadow-monsters are changing now. They are bigger than before. My stomach twists as I understand – they are closing in on me.

All around me there's a faint clattering, like twigs in a breeze. Then I realise... they are voices. They grow louder and louder until the words buzz round my head like a swarm of angry bees. Strange words. Words I don't understand.

I have to shut them out. I jam my hands over my ears. I sink to the floor. Something lands on my head. It covers my hair, my eyes... my nose... I can't breathe...

I'd always wake up sobbing and gasping for breath. Mama took me to see a special doctor. He told Mama and Papa not to worry as I would grow out of the nightmares. They did stop worrying about me; they worried about Lily's cough instead. And I did grow out of the nightmares, but not out of my fear of the dark.

The house was so quiet I could hear Lily breathing, slowly and steadily. It soothed me. In the end, I must have fallen asleep. But suddenly I was wide awake. I opened my eyes and stared into blackness. I realised the shutters must have swung closed again. It was dark. Totally and terrifyingly dark.

I had to hold back the fear. If I listened carefully, I would hear Lily breathing. But all I could hear was the frantic pumping of my heart.

I turned onto my side, curled into a ball and pulled the sheet over my head. Gradually I became aware of a strange sound.

Scratch... scratch... scratch...

Was it a rat? I wasn't usually frightened of rats. Not in daylight anyway. At night... it was different. And this did sound like a particularly large rat.

I jammed my hands over my ears.

SCRATCH ... SCRATCH ... SCRATCH.

I couldn't lie there any longer.

Forcing my legs from under the bedclothes, I stood up. The floor was cool under my bare feet. The darkness, thick and heavy, surrounded me.

Slowly I moved forwards, my hands in front of me, feeling the air. Where was the door? At last my fingers touched wood. I fumbled for the handle and turned it until there was a small click. I eased the door open.

The passage was flooded by moonlight, which poured in through the glass-panelled door. I could clearly see the pictures on the far wall.

Something made me look down. And there it was at my feet. I recognised it at once. The cat from the garden. It sat there like a statue and stared up at me with amber eyes. For some strange reason, I wasn't surprised. I leaned down and held out my hand towards it.

'Hello,' I whispered. But as the word left my mouth, I found I was talking to the air. The cat had vanished.

I returned to the bedroom and, leaving the door ajar, got back into bed. My little stone cat still sat on the bedside table, watching me. Maybe that was what had made me think of the cat in the garden? Perhaps it had been some strange sort of waking dream. Grasping it tightly in my fist, I slid the cat under my pillow. Now it couldn't watch me anymore. Cats, I thought, cats. Everywhere in Egypt, there were cats. I wondered about Miut. And Hori. What had his father wanted him to do?

My eyes closed...

CHAPTER 16

'THE BOOK OF MIUT'

II

A sudden jolt woke Miut from her doze. She opened her eyes. Hori had come to a halt in front of a large, square building. The morning air was still cool and the buzz of the kitchens had faded to a distant whisper. He was staring at something.

'Oh no, not them,' he whispered, his arms tightening round Miut.

Her body vibrated with the rapid thudding of his heart. She mewed softly and rubbed her head against his chest.

He stroked between her ears. 'But today, I have you with me and maybe they will leave me alone...' His voice trailed away and his lips tightened.

Miut followed his eyes. A group of boys were sitting on the steps, which led up to the main doorway. She recognised the biggest one. He had the eyes of a snake.

The group stood as they approached, blocking their way.

Snake-Eyes stepped forward. 'Why are you here, Hori? There are no classes today.'

'Let me pass, Neshi. I have business here in the House of Life. I come at the command of the High Priest.'

Snake-Eyes raised an eyebrow. 'How is that? Are you such a fool that you do not know that High Priest Heteb,' he sneered, stressing the name, 'is no longer within.'

'It is my father, High Priest Khay, who asks me to attend him.'

Snake-Eyes glowered. 'Your father is not High Priest yet.'

'But he will be. It is the wish of King Ramesses.'

Snake-Eyes sniffed, then wiped his nose with the back of his hand. 'A king may change his mind, if a priest fails in his duty.'

'My father has not failed.'

'He has been lying in his bed, letting others do his work,' sneered Snake-Eyes. 'It is my father who has prepared the tomb of High Priest Heteb. My father is the one with the power. Your father is as weak as the leg which cripples him.'

'His leg will heal. It will just take time.'

'And what exactly was it that caused such suffering?' Snake-Eyes' mouth twisted into a bitter smile.

'It was a fall. You know that.'

'That is indeed what he has said. But the truth is very different, is it not?'

Hori shook his head. 'What are you trying to say, Neshi?'

'If you truly do not know, then ask him,' spat Snake-Eyes. 'Ask your precious father how his leg was crippled. Ask him if he is still the all-powerful magician he thought he was.'

Hori's grip tightened on Miut. Did he want to break her in two?

'Miaooow,' she protested.

The grip eased slightly.

Snake-Eyes slid a sideways look at his companions. They sat motionless, with closed faces, watching... waiting...

Waiting for what? Nothing good. Miut shivered in the warmth of Hori's arms.

'Maybe all is not yet lost.' Snake-Eye's voice deepened until it oozed like river-mud. 'Maybe a very special offering would make the gods look with kindness on your father.'

Hori stared at Snake-Eyes, 'What do you mean, special?'

Snake-Eyes was so close now that his sour breath surrounded Miut. The boy's thundering heart filled her ears. She moved restlessly in his arms.

'Only,' Snake-Eyes paused, his eyes resting on Miut, 'that you are holding the High Priest's cat.'

Hori scowled defiantly. 'So?'

'Surely he would wish for his cat to walk with him through the afterlife?'

Hori gave a small smile and his fingers stroked Miut's ears. She purred.

'That is the one true thing you have said, Neshi,' said the boy. 'When her time comes she will indeed lie in the tomb of the High Priest.'

'But why should he wait so long? Let her go to him now and surely he will be grateful. He will ask the gods to thank you by returning your father to health.'

Hori's heart roared in Miut's ear. 'Are you saying I should sacrifice her? Before her time? When she is heavy with kittens? This is madness, Neshi. To harm her would be to risk great punishment. You know the law, it forbids – '

'But this cat is different,' interrupted Snake-Eyes. 'It is right that her ka should walk at the feet of Heteb through the afterlife, and her kittens with her. Indeed, she would wish it to be so.'

Hori stepped back, 'Keep away. I will not listen to more of this.'

Snake-Eyes held out his hands, and his eyes burned. 'If you are too weak to do it, Hori, then let me. Just a grasp round the neck and a sharp twist. That is all. And I will have set her free. Or the blade of a sharp knife would speed her on her way. I have one here.' He smiled without warmth and patted his kilt. 'The gods will then surely smile on both of us.'

A shudder passed through the arms that held Miut. 'You are mad, Neshi. There is nothing wrong with my father that time will not heal. The gods will smile on him without the spilling of any blood.'

Snake-Eyes threw back his head and laughed. 'You are wrong. Give her to me.' He dived at Miut with the speed of a cobra. Hori ducked back, but not speedily enough. Snake-Eyes gripped Miut's neck tightly for a heartbeat, but then froze.

'What's this round her neck?' he sneered. 'Some sacred charm?' He grasped the pouch and pulled, but the cord was too strong. It tightened around Miut's throat. Her lungs ached for air.

'Stop it, Neshi. Let go. You are hurting her.' Hori tried to drag Miut free.

The watching boys jeered. 'Give him the cat. Give him the cat.'

'You truly think a pathetic worm such as you can stop me taking her?' laughed Snake-Eyes.

Miut had had enough. She opened her mouth of needle-teeth and bit down on Snake-Eyes's nearest grasping finger just as hard as she could.

He jumped back, clutching his hand, fury flaming in his eyes. Blood dripped onto the ground. 'You will regret this,' he snarled at the boy. 'You and that cursed daughter of Bastet.' He wheeled towards his companions. 'Come with me. The worm has much to think about, and we have more immediate matters to attend to… for now.'

With his words hanging in the air like a threat, the boys set off towards the main courtyard.

Hori stared after them. 'I hate him. I hate them all.' Then he turned away and with Miut still in his arms, he climbed the steps and passed into the House of Life.

~

They were in a small, pillared hallway. Miut knew the way well. With a squirm and a determined wriggle, she freed herself from the cage of the boy's arms and landed with a thud on the stone floor. She set off down the passage.

'More river-cow than cat,' she heard Hori mutter as he followed her. They reached a heavily carved door. The boy eased it open.

'Father,' he called out, 'may we enter?'

Miut pushed past the boy's legs and led the way through the doorway into a large chamber. Light fell through openings in the ceiling, and lay in pools on the floor. Several narrow openings led off the main chamber.

The Lame-Priest sat awkwardly on a low stool, his bandaged leg stretched out in front of him, a palette propped up in his lap. He looked up as the door swung open and replaced his brush in its holder. His eyes fixed on Miut.

'At last, little mother,' he said, holding his hands out to her.

Miut trotted across to him and found herself swept into his arms, his fingers searching her fur with spiky urgency until they closed round the leather pouch.

'Ah,' he breathed as he felt the contents.

'What is the matter, Father? Are you ill again?' Hori came and knelt beside the priest.

He looked at the boy and a smile flickered. 'I am no worse. But Miut has answered a desperate question.'

'What do you mean?'

'This pouch round her neck. Have you not wondered what it contained?'

'I saw it earlier when I found her waiting for food ...'

'Earlier? Today?' The priest looked at Miut and said softly, 'I do not understand. It must have hung from her neck for many days...'

'It might have done,' interrupted Hori. 'I looked for her each morning, but she was never there. I had no time to search for her. In your absence, Dedi has kept me too hard at work.'

'Do you remember when you last saw her?'

There was a pause before Hori replied softly, 'I am not certain, but it could be about the time the High Priest left us for the afterlife.'

The priest's brow furrowed. 'Did you not wonder at her absence? Or fear that some ill might have befallen her?'

Hori shook his head. 'I thought she had gone to the village. In the past, I have seen her near the houses of the fishermen.'

'It is possible she went there. There is a handsome he-cat who lives beside the river, and Miut has certainly found a mate. Somehow, the gods have kept her safe.'

Hori's eyes opened wide. 'Safe? I know Neshi doesn't like her, especially now she is with kittens. But he would not actually harm her? He would not dare...'

'Neshi?' the priest interrupted. 'What has that unpleasant boy got to do with this?' A thought seemed to catch at his mind. 'Unless ...' he shook his head. 'No, it is not possible.'

'What is not possible? Tell me. If Miut is in danger, I need to know. How else can I protect her?'

The priest's lips tightened. He went on as if the boy had not spoken. 'Has Neshi said anything more? Anything about me?'

'About you? Only that his father should be the High Priest, not you.'

'And he said nothing about my leg?'

'He said I should ask you about it, and about your magic not being all-powerful.'

'Did he indeed?' The priest frowned. 'Maybe he knows too much.'

'About what?'

'About the heku. Let me finish this scroll and order my thoughts.' The priest released Miut and picked up his brush. Bending over the papyrus in front of him, he set to work, his brush scuttling over the surface like a river crab.

Miut yawned, stretched and padded over to the nearest shadowed doorway. It led to an alcove where rows of scrolls lay in carved recesses in the walls. She sniffed. She could smell the power. It was all around her. It made her whiskers tingle. But there was something else too. Her tail twitched. Mice. She crouched down. Her body tensed. All she had to do was to wait.

The room was silent as the priest bent over his work and the boy sat cross-legged on the floor staring into the distance.

A large spider with brown-haired legs descended towards Miut on a silver thread. She flexed her claws. But spiders made a poor meal; their many legs tickled her throat. They did make good sport though. However the spider landed out of range and she felt too heavy and too lazy to chase it.

At last the priest straightened up and put down his brush. He blew softly on the wet ink.

'It is dry enough,' he said and rolled up the papyrus, tying it with a strip of white linen. He handed the scroll to Hori.

'Take this and treat it with great care. You will cross the river and enter the temple of Ptah. There you will find Hapu in his chamber in the House of Life. You will hand this scroll to him and to no one else. He will add this to the casket of scrolls he has already completed. On it is written the final spell the High Priest must speak in the Hall of Judgement.' He paused. 'You do know about the Hall of Judgement, Hori?'

Hori nodded. 'Dedi has taught me.'

'He is a good scribe and a respected teacher, but still you must *tell me,' insisted the priest. 'I must be sure you know the importance of this scroll.'*

'After High Priest Heteb is placed in his tomb,' said Hori, 'he must begin his journey through the Underworld. He will have to pass through twelve gates to reach the Hall of Judgement. Each is guarded by a great and terrible monster and he will have to speak the correct spell to defeat each one. All the spells that he needs will be written on the scrolls we place in the tomb.'

'Good. But what happens within the Hall of Judgement itself?'

'The goddess Ma'at waits beside her weighing scales for the High Priest to arrive. Anubis, the Jackal-God of the Underworld, also waits. He will place the High Priest's heart on the Scales of Justice. Every evil thing the High Priest has done in this life will make his heart grow heavier. On the other side of the scales, the goddess Ma'at will place a feather. If his heart weighs more than the feather, then the foul creature Amenti, who is half crocodile and half river-cow, will gobble up him up and he will be no more. If his heart is not heavier than the feather, then the High Priest will pass into the afterlife where Osiris will welcome him, and the High Priest Heteb will live in happiness forever.'

The priest touched Hori's shoulder and said softly, 'Dedi has taught you well. So how will High Priest Heteb make sure that his heart passes the test of Ma'at?'

'By speaking the Final Spell.'

'The scroll I have just given you holds extraordinary power. It calls on the god Osiris himself to help Heteb.' The priest's eyes held the boy's as he added, 'It must be in the High Priest's tomb before it is sealed. Do not fail in this task, Hori. Things are not as they should be here in the Temple of Osiris. High Priest Heteb must pass safely into the afterlife, then he will speak for us, and the gods will smile again on our temple.'

The boy tucked the scroll into his kilt. 'I think Hapu used to visit us when I was younger.'

'He came when he could. He was fond of you, Hori. But now that he works in the Temple of Ptah, he has no time to spend time with

his old friends. However, I would trust him with my life.'

The boy's eyes widened. 'Why do you say, trust?'

'Neshi is right. I did not fall. On the morning after High Priest Heteb began his journey into the next life, I woke with a great pain in my leg. It was as if it were broken, yet there was no break.' The priest rubbed his bandage. 'There is no doubt, heku has been used against me.'

'But now High Priest Heteb has left us, you are the greatest of magicians. How could another have power over you?'

The priest shook his head. 'I have spoken every spell. I have searched the most sacred books and the ancient writings. I have even read the words of Imhotep, the greatest magician of the ancient world.' He gestured towards the alcove where Miut still awaited the appearance of a mouse. 'The pain remains. To destroy the magician who has turned his magic against me, I must know his name.'

Hori's eyes were wide and dark. 'And you have no idea who he is?'

'All I know is that he is clever, powerful and I believe he is a priest in this temple. I fear he lives secretly among us, pretending to serve Osiris, but his heart belongs to a more dangerous god. The god of darkness, storms and chaos.'

'Seth?' whispered Hori.

'What other god would seek the destruction of a Temple of Osiris? It seems the followers of Seth are no longer content with the balance of Ma'at. They want Seth to have a final victory over Horus and to destroy Osiris forever.' The priest's mouth twisted as if he were in pain. 'Most of all, they want the great riches that belong to this Temple of Osiris and power over all our land.'

'Do you know who these followers of Seth are?'

'Some I know. Others I can guess. One may indeed be Paser, father of Neshi. How else would his boy know I had been defeated by another's heku?'

The boy's eyes widened suddenly. 'Maybe,' he spoke almost as a whisper, 'it was Paser who spoke the spell against you?'

'He is just a fool. I do not believe he has the knowledge. But whoever they may be, these priests of Seth do not have the High Priest's Seal.'

'Why would they want that?'

The priest lowered his voice. 'Heteb wrote down each spell he cast, and used the Seal to close each scroll. The Seal holds the magic of all those spells. The followers of Seth have been searching for it.'

'How do you know?'

'The High Priest's rooms had been… disturbed.'

'Anath told me that.'

The priest's brow wrinkled. 'The girl knows too much. But she told the truth.'

'Are you certain they have not found it?'

'I am now that I have seen Miut. It is clear that before the High Priest died he must have known he was in danger and hid the Seal, entrusting it to his most favoured goddess.'

'So the Seal is in Miut's pouch?' whispered Hori.

Miut felt his eyes rest on her. She purred and put out a paw to trap the spider, which had now scuttled within range. She missed, and it skittered into the shadows.

'Yes. He must have thought that amongst her fur it would not be noticed. If it were, then it would be thought she was carrying an amulet of no special worth, such as the Eye of Horus she wears on feast days'

'Neshi noticed the pouch. He tried to open it.'

'But he did not succeed?'

'No. But he was most interested in it.'

There was silence for many heartbeats before the priest said softly, 'I fear the passing of the High Priest can be laid at the feet of the followers of Seth. The scorpion that stung him had no place in his bed.'

'A scorpion? I did not know.'

'No one did. I removed it to examine it properly. I soon realised it was a creature of great venom. It had no place in the Two Kingdoms.'

Hori's face paled. 'Someone put it there?'

'I fear so. But before I could investigate further, I was imprisoned in my bed by my crippled leg. That was no coincidence. So now, not only must you carry the scroll to Hapu, you must also carry the

Seal. Hapu will hide it within the tomb of the High Priest, which lies at the foot of the stepped pyramid of Sakkara and beside the tomb of Imhotep, who was the architect of the pyramid and the greatest magician of all.' The priest looked intently into the boy's eyes and added softly, 'Then Heteb will use its magic in the afterlife, and no priest of Seth will steal its power and so destroy the balance of the Two Kingdoms. Will you do this for me?'

'I will,' said the boy firmly. 'But Miut? What shall I do with her?'

'Her birth-time is close. She should remain here, but Heteb trusted her with the Seal…'

'There's Neshi too. I fear what he may do to her.'

The priest nodded. 'She must go with you.' He rubbed his bandaged leg. 'Tell Hapu that I am determined to come to the tomb later, even if I have to be carried there.' He sighed. 'I must see all is as Heteb wished it to be.'

He held out his hand to the boy, who helped pull him to his feet. The priest laid his arm round the boy's shoulders and looked deep into his eyes. 'Go at once. And may the Eye of Horus watch over you.'

'Trust me, Father,' said Hori gravely. He crossed the room and gently lifted Miut from the floor. She struggled a little, but there was no escape, so she rested her head against the boy's shoulder.

From beyond the door came the whisper of running feet. Far too big for a mouse, she thought, and too heavy. Her eyes shut and she slept.

CHAPTER 17

When I opened my eyes, the room was full of sunlight. I looked across at the other bed. Lily was peering at me. 'When did you open the shutters?' I asked.

Lily yawned. 'Last night, of course. You insisted. Don't you remember?'

My head ached. I was sure that when I'd woken up in the middle of the night the shutters had been closed. It had been so dark. I remembered climbing out of bed and feeling my way into the passage where I had found the cat from the garden, sitting there in the moonlight. And then I'd dreamed about Miut again. It felt so real. Hori and Miut were in danger. Usually dreams fade with daylight, but this one, like the last, was still clear in my head, every detail of it. My thoughts whirled like a merry-go-round. I sat up and realised that the little stone cat was no longer under my pillow, but clutched tight in my hand.

At that moment there was a gentle tap on the door and Aunt Dora's voice called out, 'Breakfast is just about ready. Be quick, please. Remember, we have a guest joining us.'

As I splashed water on my face, pulled on my skirt, blouse and clean pinafore, and dragged a brush though my hair, my thoughts continued to whirl. I tried to picture Miut, but I realised I'd never seen her properly. Just bits of her as she had licked herself clean... stripy tail and legs, and spots like fingerprints along her sides... it was as if I'd been right inside her head.

Lily was still pulling rags out of her hair by the time I was ready. I went to help her. I noticed the bruises under her eyes had gone. 'You look like you slept well.'

She smiled. 'I did.' She studied me in the mirror. 'You don't look like you slept at all. Are you alright?'

I forced a smile. 'Of course. Come on, your hair looks perfect.'

We were just about out of the door when I remembered the little stone cat was still under my pillow. I retrieved it and dropping it into my skirt pocket, I hurried after Lily. She looked so much better today. I wasn't going to worry her by telling her about my dreams. She would think I was fit only for the madhouse. They were just dreams after all.

The dining room had two tall, narrow windows. These had been hooked open and a warm breeze breathed into the room. We could see out into the green jungle at the side of the house. Like the hall, there was little sign that a maid had been there for some time. While the table had been laid for breakfast, the mantelpiece was thick with dust. A small, brass clock stood in its centre, and its short, sharp ticks were the only sound in the room.

We were wondering whether to sit down when Aunt Dora swept in. She seemed brighter than yesterday, even a little flushed. 'Good morning girls, I hope you are both fully refreshed this morning.'

Before we could answer, she half turned and I saw someone was following her into the room. I only saw his silhouette, but it was enough. I heard myself gasp, which I managed to turn into a cough.

'Goodness, Rose, are you quite well?'

'Yes, thank you, Aunt Dora,' I managed.

'So,' she said with a small smile, 'let me introduce Mr John Baxter, your uncle's colleague and friend. He has been in America for many months, so it is a wonderful surprise to have him back in Egypt.' She turned to Mr Baxter. 'May I introduce my nieces, Rose and Lily Evering?'

Mr Baxter gave a small bow. 'The young ladies and I have met before.'

He was smartly dressed in a light tweed suit and waistcoat, and in his buttonhole, he wore a scarlet rose. His mop of grey hair was now oiled and lay smooth to his head, but the same steel-grey eyes peered at us from behind his spectacles.

Aunt Dora looked puzzled, 'Really, how is that?' Then her face cleared. 'Of course, you must have travelled on the same ship from Naples.' She frowned at us. 'Have you both forgotten your manners?'

'Sorry, Aunt Dora,' we chorused and obediently dropped into our curtsies.

I realised that Mr. Baxter's eyes were now fixed on Lily's wrist.

'What a beautiful bracelet you have there, young lady,' he said. 'May I look at it?'

Lily obediently held out her arm. 'It came from Uncle Arthur's Collection of Curiosities.'

'Ah yes,' said Mr. Baxter examining the bracelet closely, 'he had some interesting pieces in there. I remember this. It has cleaned up very well.' He swung round to face me. His eyes held mine. 'And you, child, did you also receive a gift?'

My voice seemed to have frozen in my throat. What if he didn't remember seeing my cat before and there had been a terrible mistake? What if it was taken away from me?

Aunt Dora was watching me with a puzzled look on her face. 'Has the cat got your tongue, child?

My heart missed a beat. The cat had certainly got my tongue, and my heart too. 'Yes,' I managed through wooden lips. 'It's in the bedroom.' I gazed wide-eyed at Mr Baxter as I lied.

'Perhaps if you would fetch it, I could tell you more about it,' he suggested. 'I could show you what to look out for so you can spot genuine pieces yourself.'

His tone was light, but I could hear the iron in it.

Before I could think of a single excuse, Aunt Dora came to my rescue. 'I have to say, Rose, you do not look at all well.' She glanced at Mr Baxter. 'I think the child needs her breakfast. Her gift is a mere trifle. Arthur found it in a market. There's no more to be said about it.'

Mr Baxter's eyes still held mine. Behind the prison of his lenses, they were as grey and as hard as steel. 'Of course, Mrs Sinclair, you may well be right, but sometimes even a copy tells a story.' His quick smile failed to reach his eyes. His cold, insistent eyes.

'Just a quick look,' he continued softly,

I opened my mouth, but still no words came out.

To my huge relief, Ezra arrived just then, carrying a large tray on which stood a steaming pot of coffee, a bowl of fresh fruit, bread, jam and a large plate of ham and eggs.

Aunt Dora smiled at me. 'If you feel better, you can fetch your gift for Mr Baxter to examine after breakfast.'

We sat down and Ezra handed round the plates. I realised I was shaking. I slid my hand under the table and into my pocket. My fingers closed round the silky coolness of the little cat. It steadied me.

'It is so kind of you to offer to help me at such short notice,' said Aunt Dora, her eyes on Mr Baxter. 'I fear poor Arthur's affairs are in a dreadful muddle.'

Mr Baxter leaned forward and touched Aunt Dora's hand. 'My dear, I am very pleased to be able to assist you.'

'That's so kind,' said Aunt Dora. 'I've no idea what I must keep, sell or throw away, but decisions must be made.'

Mr Baxter raised her hand to his lips. 'It will be an honour. After all, it could be some time before your nephew will be well enough to travel to Cairo.'

'Oh,' said Aunt Dora, her cheeks flushed with pink, 'it amazes me how news flies around this city.'

He nodded. 'It was all most unfortunate and I...'

'But what happened?' I interrupted, ignoring Aunt Dora's disapproving look.

Mr Baxter, however, didn't seem to mind my interruption.

'I am told he was being lowered into a newly opened shaft. The rope broke and he fell. He was lucky.'

Lily's eyes were huge and dark as she asked, 'How was he lucky, Mr Baxter?'

Mr Baxter shrugged. 'I meant simply he was lucky not to be more badly injured. The shaft was not deep.'

I stared at my plate. What if the shaft had been deep? The thought of Max falling into a bottomless pit made my stomach twist. Mr Baxter had sounded so casual about it.

There was silence for a few minutes while the others ate and I pushed food round my plate, before Mr Baxter said softly, 'You know, Rose is a perfect Egyptian name.'

I looked up and realised he was studying me intently.

'Yes, indeed,' he continued and glanced down at his buttonhole. 'Roses were the flowers most beloved of the goddess Isis in the time of the Pharaohs. They were grown in many temples dedicated to her.'

A memory flared of Hori and Miut walking together in a garden.

They passed bushes of sweet-scented roses. They were as red as the setting sun-disc and armed with spikes as sharp as cats' teeth.

'I know,' I said slowly, trying to steady my racing thoughts.

Lily stared at me. 'What do you mean, you know? I don't believe Papa ever told us about roses growing in Egyptian temples. I would have remembered. I like roses.'

'It was in that book of Egyptian Gods and Goddesses Papa lent us,' I said quickly, but Lily didn't look convinced.

'Are you alright, Rose?' asked Aunt Dora anxiously. 'You look very pale.'

'I am just tired. I had a strange dream last night and slept badly.'

'Dreams,' said Mr Baxter, 'are powerful things, especially in Egypt.'

'Why especially in Egypt?' asked Lily.

'This is an ancient country built on the stories of the ancient gods and the dreams of the people who believed in them. These stories and these dreams are filled with power and magic beyond your wildest imaginings.' Mr Baxter's voice was low and dark, his eyes held mine.

Magic. Papa had told us he had written a book about it. My heart had begun to race. He seemed to be looking right inside my head. Could he see my dreams? My fingers closed round the little stone cat in my pocket. Once again it calmed me.

'What do you mean,' Lily was saying.

'I mean sometimes these stories are much more than they seem,' continued Mr Baxter turning his gaze on her. 'In Egypt, magic has been practised for thousands of years. They called it *heku*.'

'So,' said Lily with a small laugh, 'we had better be good or we will all be *hekued* into rats – or even spiders.' She gave a dramatic shudder.

Mr Baxter frowned. 'Do not make light of it. For years, I have researched the magicians of ancient times. Just be aware there are things here in Egypt far more powerful and dangerous than they seem.'

I stared at him. His words were a warning. Why?

'Now, now, Mr Baxter,' said Aunt Dora disapprovingly, 'you should not be filling the girls' heads with ideas that will give them nightmares.'

Mr Baxter gave a small, apologetic smile and seemed to relax. 'I am sorry, my dear Mrs Sinclair, it was thoughtless of me.'

Aunt Dora glanced at Lily. 'If you have any questions about the history of this extraordinary country during your stay, I am sure Mr Baxter will be happy to answer them. He only lives a short walk away.'

He nodded. 'Indeed, I do. And two such charming guests will always be welcome.' There was an oddly insistent note in his voice as he added, 'I really mean that.' He pulled a small silver case out of his jacket pocket and slid out a white card. 'My address, should you need it.' He handed the card to Lily, who slipped it into her pocket.

He stood up. 'Now, Mrs Sinclair, if you would like me to make a start on poor Arthur's papers, I am at your disposal for the remainder of the morning. Indeed, if you will excuse me, I shall make a start right now.' He gave us a small bow and headed towards the door.

He had put his hand on the door handle before he paused, directing a stern look in our direction. 'I should warn you that there are many thieves about in Cairo. I would leave anything you value behind.' He gestured towards Lily's snake bracelet. 'That should certainly stay here.' Then he was gone.

Aunt Dora stared wistfully after him. 'Such a kind and thoughtful man,' she murmured.

Kind wasn't how I would describe Mr Baxter. Quite apart from his unnerving curiosity about us, I remembered all too well his treatment of the donkey in Port Said.

Aunt Dora turned to us. 'I am very sorry, girls, I had wanted to show you round Cairo myself, but unfortunately it seems I will now be too busy.' She gazed sadly round the room. 'Now that I am alone, I cannot bear to stay here in this large house one moment longer than I must. Without your Papa here, I must take advantage of Mr Baxter's timely offer of assistance. You have seen the muddle of boxes in the library.'

'Can we help?' asked Lily.

Aunt Dora shook her head. 'I fear not, unless you are experts on ancient Egypt. But thank you for offering.' She sighed. 'I shall not be sad to see Arthur's papers go. They have brought nothing but worry and unhappiness.'

She picked up a small silver bell from the table and rang it. 'I have asked Ezra to arrange for his nephew, Zaccariah, to act as your guide in my place. He's a nice boy. His English is really quite good. You'll be safe with him.' She glanced out of the nearest window and added, 'It will be hot today. Do take your sun bonnets with you.'

CHAPTER 18

'I really truly, dislike him,' I said as we made for our bedroom to collect our sun bonnets. Zaccariah was expected shortly. 'I thought we would never see him again. Now we find him right here, in this house. Don't you think that's strange?'

Lily shrugged. 'Coincidences happen.'

'It's more than a coincidence, it's suspicious.'

'He's a friend of Aunt Dora's. She must like him or she wouldn't have asked for his help.'

'I know,' I said remembering how Mr Baxter had called her "my dear", and that Aunt Dora has spoken of him as "kind and thoughtful". I continued, 'Something's not right. Why did he vanish off the ship? What has he been doing since? He has said nothing about that. And why is he always staring at us? He's a wolf and I'm Red Riding Hood. It's quite horrid.'

Lily frowned. 'But Aunt Dora needs his help now Mama and Papa are with Max.'

A terrible thought that had been hidden in the back of my mind, hit me. 'Do you think that's a bit too convenient?'

A short laugh burst from Lily. 'You actually think Mr Baxter left the ship, went to Alexandria, sabotaged the rope so Max fell down a shaft, then came straight back to charm Aunt Dora, knowing that Mama and Papa would go straight to Max and leave us here?'

She had put it perfectly. 'Yes,' I whispered. 'If he didn't cut the rope himself, he ordered someone else to do it for him.'

She frowned. 'Why?'

'I don't know.'

Lily shook her head, exasperated. 'This is nonsense.'

I said mildly, 'Perhaps. But as we are here, we can keep an eye on things just in case.'

'Anyway,' said Lily, 'if Mr Baxter so desperately wanted Aunt Dora to himself for whatever reason, he would have made sure we went with Mama and Papa.'

I felt my breath freeze. She was right. We were here, and there must be a reason for that. Whatever that reason was, I was sure it wasn't going to be good for us, but there was no point frightening Lily. I took a deep breath, forced a smile and said, 'I expect you're right. Shall we see if Zaccariah is here yet?'

'Yes,' said Lily as she tied the ribbons of her sun bonnet under her chin and checked her reflection in the mirror. 'And I'm sure there's an explanation for everything. There usually is.'

She slipped off her snake bracelet and put it on the bedside table. 'What about your cat?'

'I'll take it with me. It'll be quite safe in my pocket.'

I jammed on my bonnet and tied the laces on my boots. While I hoped she was right about there being a good reason for everything that was happening, I was sure she was wrong.

We had only been waiting a short while in the hall before Ezra appeared. 'Come,' he instructed, and led us out of the House of Shadows into the bright, white heat of the day.

Beyond the iron gate, a boy was waiting for us in the street. My breath caught in my throat. For a moment, in the glare, I'd thought he was Hori. This boy had the same dark brown curls with dark brown eyes to match, and the same tall, slim build. 'Like a palm,' I whispered.

'What's like a palm?' demanded Lily.

I shook my head. 'Sorry, I have no idea what I was thinking about.'

This boy wasn't dressed in a white kilt, but in a sky-blue cotton robe which reached his ankles, however the leather sandals on his feet were similar to those that Hori had worn. Finally, I noticed the boy was glaring furiously at the ground.

'Oh look,' breathed Lily, 'aren't they gorgeous?'

I saw that the boy was holding the reins of three donkeys. One was pale grey with a light brown muzzle, the second was the colour of rain clouds with a cream muzzle and the third was the darkest of all with a muzzle which was almost white. They all had big dark eyes, short tufty manes and huge, fluffy ears. The saddles were unlike any I'd seen before: pads of bright, stripy fabric and a large pommel on the front.

'This,' Ezra said proudly, waving his hand towards the boy, 'is Zaccariah, we call him, Zac.'

'*Salaam alaikum,*' mumbled Zac still staring at the ground.

Ezra ignored his nephew and pointed at the light grey donkey, 'and she is Djinn, which means she is a magical spirit.' He laughed. 'She is indeed most magical as she is always escaping and coming home on her own. Make sure she is always well tied.' He waved at the rain-cloud donkey. 'And this is Bashir. His name means the-one-who-brings-good news. He is a most handsome donkey.'

'And the darkest one?' I asked

'She is Ata,' said Zac quickly, 'her name means gift, and she is mine.'

Lily was gazing thoughtfully at the donkeys. 'I would like to ride Bashir. Will you have Djinn, Rose?'

I nodded. I didn't mind which I rode. I went over to Djinn and gently stroked her velvet muzzle. She twitched her ears and snorted gently.

I realised Zac was looking curiously at me. 'You know donkeys?'

I nodded. 'We have ridden them at the seaside.'

His dark eyes studied me for a moment. 'I think you will like riding these donkeys.' He was suddenly looking rather more cheerful.

'Where are we going?' I asked.

'Oh, please can we go to a market?' said Lily. 'Our Papa has told us so much about all the wonderful things you can see there.'

Zac nodded. 'Today we shall visit the Khan el-Khalili.' He added proudly, 'it is the biggest bazaar in all of Egypt. For many hundreds of years it has been here. Tomorrow maybe, we will travel to the pyramids.'

Lily was smiling as Zac helped her onto her donkey. I swallowed a sigh. I disliked the thought of the heat, the noise, the crowds of a busy market....

We sat astride and hitched our skirts over the pommels. There were no stirrups so our legs hung loose.

We set off, Zac on Ata in the lead, then Lily on Bashir and I following on Djinn. It was surprisingly comfortable. Djinn's stride was short and it was easy to sit down in the saddle even when she trotted.

At first the streets were wide, and then they opened out into a large open area in the middle of which was a garden, but it was like no garden I'd ever seen before. It had a mountainous rockery at its centre, a waterfall and there even appeared to be caves.

All around the garden it was a building site, apart from one rather grand building which Zac told us was the Shepheard's Hotel, where all the wealthy tourists stayed, and another, even grander, which was apparently the new Opera House. The air was full of the sound of hundreds of blue-clothed workmen singing '*La ilaha illallah*' as they climbed up ladders carrying buckets full of bricks, stones and mortar. They climbed down again with empty buckets, which they refilled from panniers slung over the backs of the donkeys and camels waiting patiently below.

'What are they singing?' I asked Zac.

'It means there is no god but Allah. It helps them keep working,' said Zac proudly, 'and soon this *Ezbekiah* Square will be most magnificent. Indeed, Cairo will be as fine a city as Paris or London. When I am a famous archaeologist, I will come here and visit my grand friends in the Shepheard's Hotel.'

I stared at him. 'Is that what you want to be? An archaeologist?

Zac smiled, and a flash of sparkling white teeth lit up his face. 'Yes, and I will search for hidden things like Mr Sinclair.'

The cat in my pocket was a hidden thing. 'What sort of things was he looking for?' I asked.

'For the tomb of a priest. He spent many years searching. But when at last he found the tomb, it had been robbed many years before. There was almost nothing there, except some pictures on the walls. Mrs Sinclair said she thought it stopped his heart.'

'Broke,' corrected Lily. 'That is what we say if someone is very sad or disappointed about something. Stopped would mean he died.'

Zac nodded. 'That is what I do mean. After Mr. Sinclair found the tomb, he became ill and his heart stopped.'

Before I could ask anything more Lily began to cough. I realised the air was full of dust from all the building work, so we trotted on through ever narrower streets, past secretive houses, many with darkened windows hidden behind metal grills.

'Is Cairo so very dangerous?' I asked Zac, pointing up at the barred windows of the nearest house.

Zac shook his head. 'These are windows of a harem. Behind them, the women live. No man but their husband is allowed to see inside.'

Lily and I looked at each other. We were both wondering what it would be like to live forever hidden from the world.

I remembered Mr Baxter's warning to leave anything valuable at home. 'But there must be a great many thieves in the streets?'

Zac looked shocked. 'Most certainly not. A punishment for stealing is to have your hand cut off, or even death. No one wants that.' He smiled. 'But do not trust a seller in the market to give you a fair price. If he can steal from you that way, he will.'

So why had Mr Baxter warned us not to take our valuables with us? Then I realised. If we didn't take them, we would leave them behind. He was working in the library all morning. Easy enough for him to slip upstairs to see what he could find. I slid my hand into my pocket and checked the cat was safely there. If that was his game, then Mr Baxter was going to be very disappointed. I almost laughed out loud at myself. Ridiculous. Lily would be quite right to call me mad if she knew what I was thinking.

CHAPTER 19

As we grew closer to the Khan el-Khalili, the streets became more and more crowded. We were soon making our way past stall after stall. As I trailed along behind, my head was soon spinning with curtains of cascading silks, piles of leather sandals and precarious mountains of clay pots of all shapes and sizes. My fingers ached for my sketchpad. Everywhere I looked there was something different: sweet smelling spices in baskets, dishes of Turkish delight and sugar-drenched fruits, songbirds in cages, sacks of plump, golden dates and mountains of spiky, ssun-coloured pineapples. Eventually the streets grew so narrow we were forced to ride in single file. Some of the passages were covered over and were little more than tunnels.

I leaned forward and hissed at Lily's back, 'Have you had enough? Shall we go back?'

She shook her head. 'Please, Rose, I want to explore up there.' She pointed at the wood planked ceiling above.

Zac twisted round and saw where she was pointing. 'You can go up there on foot,' he said. 'I will remain here with the donkeys.'

We dismounted and handed the reins to Zac. Narrow steps led us up to the floor above, which seemed even more crowded with people and sellers. We were just edging away from the steps when we were picked up and swept along by a sudden flood of people. I grasped Lily's hand and held it tight as we struggled to free ourselves from the hot, seething mass. The heat had made our hands slippery with sweat. Lily's fingers slid from mine. She was gone.

'Lily,' I shouted. There was no reply. Pushing and shoving, I fought my way between the bodies until suddenly I was free. I peered in every direction, but there was no sign of her. I realised with a surge of relief that I hadn't been swept as far as I'd feared, and I could still see the top of the steps that led down to Zac and our donkeys. With luck Lily would already be there waiting for me. I reached the steps, which I half ran and half fell down. At the bottom I peered desperately round for the others. My stomach lurched. There was no sign of Zac or Lily or the donkeys. It was then I realised. They were the wrong stairs.

The passage I found myself in was far less busy than any of the others we had glimpsed before. Indeed, after a group of Arabs had passed by, there was nobody around at all. The silence felt strangely uncomfortable. Looking to my right I could see that the street opened out into a small sunlit square and so I made for it. Maybe there would be someone there who spoke English and could give me directions. Then it hit me. Directions to where? I'd no idea what the square was called where Zac was waiting for me, and hopefully Lily too. Worse, after all the twists and turns we had taken on our donkeys, I'd no idea how to get back to the House of Shadows.

It was at that moment I first noticed the heavily built, fair-haired man wearing a cream linen suit. He was standing in the shadow of a doorway, peering up and down the street. I watched him for a moment. He was obviously looking for someone. It was as if he had felt me watching him because he suddenly swung round to face me. His eyes were the iciest blue I'd ever seen. It was only as his eyes held mine that I realised he'd been looking for me. For a moment, I felt relief that someone had been sent to find me. Then, as he took a step towards me, I noticed the furious line of his mouth. Before I could move he was half way across the street. I tried to turn away, but I was frozen in that ice-blue glare. Then something brushed against my leg. It was enough. I tore my eyes free and glanced down.

Liquid amber eyes replaced the icy blue. Familiar. Impossible. But could two cats really have those same amazing eyes? Those markings? The Garden Cat swished its tail, trotted past me into the shadow of the wall behind me and vanished. Not again, I thought. Then I realised it had actually disappeared into the mouth of a narrow alley. I glanced back. The man in the cream suit reached out towards me. There was no more time. I turned and sped after the cat.

The alley stretched away from me, narrow, gloomy and deserted. I ran down it searching the shadows ahead in vain for any sign of the cat. I'd almost given up when I caught just a glimpse of the tip of a tail disappearing around the corner at the far end of the alley. I flew after it, reached the corner and stopped. The alley opened out into a wide street packed with people who all seemed to know exactly where they were going. They weren't chasing around after stray cats. It was mad. I was mad. Why would that man be the slightest bit interested in me? He had probably just been crossing the square. I'd imagined the rest.

I turned around. That was when I knew I really was in trouble. The man was hurrying down the alley towards me, his arms outstretched.

I plunged out into the street. This time I was grateful that the tide of people swallowed me up and carried me with them. I checked behind me, peering frantically through the crowd. The man had vanished from sight, but I was sure he would be close by. I forced back a sob. Where were Lily and Zac? Where was the House of Shadows?

It was then I noticed that the cat was trotting steadily along just a couple of yards ahead of me. I did the only thing I could. I followed it.

I saw nothing else. It was just me and the cat. I was vaguely aware of weaving between people, of crossing roads, of avoiding carriages, camels and donkeys, of the heat, of the shade.

At last the cat stopped and sat down on a doorstep. It lazily licked a paw. I pushed past a man and I was beside it. The cat looked up at me and I blinked. When my eyes opened, I was staring at an empty step.

'Rose… thank goodness.' Lily's anxious voice cut into my confusion. I looked up. Lily was right behind me.

'I've been so worried.' Lily swallowed a sob. 'Zac spotted you vanishing into an alley, or we might never have found you.'

'Sorry,' I said. There was nothing else I could say.

'We followed you for ages. It was as if you were sleep walking. I remembered Papa telling us how dangerous it was to wake people up. But it was horrible. I thought you were going to get flattened by a carriage or a camel or… anything…' Her voice trailed to silence.

I knew if I told her that I'd been following the cat from the garden, she would really think I was mad. 'Sorry,' I repeated. 'But I was worried about what had happened to you too.'

She shrugged. 'There were lots of sets of steps down. I was lucky and found the right ones. Zac was waiting for me at the bottom. When I told him what had happened, he guessed you might have been swept further along. So we went to look for you and were just in time to see you disappearing down the alley way.'

I had to ask. 'Did you notice a man following me? He was wearing a cream suit.'

She looked puzzled. 'No. It was just us following you. It was certainly not easy. We were leading the donkeys too, which didn't help.'

'Maybe you saw a cat? It was walking just in front of me.'

'No,' said Lily sharply. 'No cat. No man. Nothing.' She gave me a searching look. 'You do seem quite flushed. Are you feeling alright?'

'Yes,' I said and gave her a reassuring smile, although I wanted to tell her she was wrong. That the man had been there. And the cat. But I was too tired to argue. I looked round. Lily was alone. 'Where's Zac?'

'He had to take the donkeys back. I said we'd be fine now.'

My heart sank into my boots. 'But how will we find our way?'

She stared at me. 'Come on, Rose, you must know where we are. I've no idea how you managed it, but you led us home.'

It was only then that I looked about properly. She was right. The House of Shadows was just around the next corner.

CHAPTER 20

Ezra was standing on the top step peering anxiously down the street. He smiled when he saw us. 'I am most glad that you have returned. Your aunt has returned also. She asks that you will go to her in the garden.'

Aunt Dora was sitting in the shade, reading a book. 'Come and sit down. Ezra is bringing us lunch out here. I thought eating in the garden would be nice.' She studied our faces and added, 'You both look as if you could do with a quiet afternoon. Can you occupy yourselves? I am afraid Mr Baxter and I have a meeting at the Egyptian Museum in Boulaq this afternoon regarding some of your uncle's papers and artefacts.' She sighed. 'I'd no idea what a hard job it was going to be. Without dear Mr Baxter stepping into the breach, I don't know what I would have done.'

'Can we help?' I asked, struggling to think of Mr Baxter as "dear".

Aunt Dora shook her head. 'I don't think Mr Baxter would approve. He has little experience of girls of your age. He and neither of his wives ever had children.'

I had to ask. 'Wives?'

'Indeed,' said Aunt Dora, 'his first wife drowned in a boating accident. Such a tragedy. She was so young. Then he remarried but before long his second wife fell ill. The doctors couldn't find out what was wrong with her in time. She died too. He was devastated. Poor man. He is so lonely now.'

We hadn't known Mr Baxter long, but he had never appeared to be suffering from some deep grief. I remembered he had been particularly cheerful at breakfast. A terrible thought struck me. I remembered again how Mr Baxter had called Aunt Dora, "my dear," and she in her turn thought he was lonely, and a "dear" man. Could he possibly be thinking that Aunt Dora might be wife number three?

'Oh, I see,' said Lily, looking suitably sympathetic. 'How sad for him.'

Before we could ask anything else about Mr Baxter, Ezra arrived with the lunch on a tray. It was a mixture of rice, macaroni, lentils and a spicy tomato sauce. It smelt delicious.

'This,' explained Ezra, 'is *Koshari.* It is one of the dishes of Egypt I most like to cook.'

I took a cautious mouthful and realised it tasted as good as it smelled. 'It's delicious, Ezra, thank you.'

He nodded, then turned and made his way rapidly towards the house.

While we ate I couldn't help looking round the garden for the cat. There was no sign of it.

'There was a huge cat in the garden when we arrived. Have you ever seen it, Aunt Dora?' I asked at last, my voice cracking the silence.

Aunt Dora raised her eyebrows. 'A cat in the garden? No. I'm afraid Ezra dislikes cats. If he sees one, he chases it away.'

'But you like cats, Aunt Dora?' I needed to be sure.

She looked surprised. 'Of course. Particularly the genuine Egyptian cats. They are descended from the ancient cats you can see painted on the walls of tombs. There are many special things about them. One is how their eyes change colour.'

I thought of Miut. 'What do you mean, Aunt Dora?'

'Young cats often have amber eyes, they turn green as they get older.' She studied me thoughtfully. 'Why the interest in cats, Rose?'

I realised Lily was gazing at me too. 'I was just wondering,' I said casually and stared into my glass remembering Miut's glowing amber eyes.

Ezra had said Dora didn't like cats, but it was Ezra who hated cats. Why had he lied? Was that the only thing he had lied about? Was anyone here telling the truth about anything? And Mr Baxter's wives? An accident and an unexplained illness. If Aunt Dora did marry Mr Baxter, what might happen to her? I felt suddenly freezing cold even though it was a hot day. Mama and Papa must be with Max by now. I let hope creep in. If by some miracle he was already better, then maybe they might even now be on their way to Cairo.

Lily leant across and squeezed my hand. 'Please stop looking like that,' she whispered, 'I'm sure Mama and Papa will be here soon, and Max too.'

I gave her a small smile. 'I hope so...I really, really do.'

Aunt Dora left for the museum as soon as we finished eating. 'I'm sorry to leave you again,' she frowned. 'I hope you won't be too bored.'

We assured her we would be fine.

'Maybe you would find something to look at in the library?' she added, giving us each a hug. 'You're good girls. I will arrange a special outing for you tomorrow. A surprise.'

Then she was gone and we made our way down to the library.

Aunt Dora had left the shutters closed so the room was shadowy and cool. I pulled them open, while Lily went over to inspect the display cabinet.

I picked my way around the boxes and the piles of books on the floor, while inspecting the ones still on the shelves. They were all about Egypt. There were many dull titles like, '*Three Thousand Years of Ancient Egypt*', and some, which sounded more exciting such as, '*Digging for Treasure in the Valley of the Kings.*'

I'd reached the furthest corner of the library when I came across a shelf with just a couple of books left lying on it. One with a faded red cover caught my eye. Its pages were worn at the corners, as if they had been turned many times. I read the faded title, *Magician-Priests of Ancient Egypt*. It was as if time stood still.

I glanced over at Lily. She was still examining the cabinet. I took the book over to the nearest window, sat on the window seat, and turning to the Index, searched for *H.*

I saw the entry almost at once – *Heteb of the Temple of Osiris – Page 32.* My heart was pounding as I read the short entry.

> *Little is known about Heteb, High Priest of the Temple of Osiris. It is believed he lived during the reign of the Ramesses II and that he was renowned throughout Egypt for his wisdom and his magic, indeed he is sometimes referred to as a Magician-Priest. Papyri, which have been found recently, speak of spells he cast to cure illnesses and to punish wrong doers. The High Priest has also been associated with a magical Seal, which was supposed to have great powers.*
>
> *People have searched for it over the centuries, but as with the Holy Grail, no one knows what it looks like, whether it has already been found and lies hidden in some secret vault, or indeed, if it ever existed at all. If his tomb were to be discovered, then we could learn more of this mysterious priest and his Seal.'*

Just a few words and yet they changed everything. I searched my memory. I was certain Papa had never mentioned Heteb and I was sure no one had mentioned him since we had arrived in Egypt. Aunt Dora had talked about Uncle Arthur's collection, but not Heteb. Mr Baxter had talked about magic or *heku* and the goddess Isis.

I had to face the truth, however impossible it seemed. Heteb had been a real man. The Seal was real. So my dreams must be real too. Then I remembered something Zac had said.

'Lily.'

She didn't look up. 'What?'

'Do you remember Zac telling us about a tomb Uncle Arthur had discovered?'

Maybe it was something in my voice that drew her attention because she did look up then.

'Did he say whose tomb it was?'

She frowned. 'Some priest's, I think. Why?'

I shrugged as casually as I could and turned back to the book.

Not some priest's tomb. It must have been Heteb's tomb. I checked the front of the book. It had been published in 1858, thirteen years ago. Maybe it was reading this book that had started Uncle Arthur searching for Heteb's tomb in the first place.

But how was I dreaming about the High Priest and his Seal? I didn't believe in magic. I closed my eyes, letting a thought form and take shape... cat-shape. The little stone cat must be the connection. I was given it... and then I'd started dreaming. Surely therefore it must be genuine. It must have been found in the tomb. I pulled the cat out of my pocket. It sat on my palm and stared solemnly up at me.

I remembered that first night after Mrs Hodges had handed me the cat. I hadn't dreamt about Hori and Miut then. Instead I had that strange, blurry dream. Why? What had been different about that night to the nights when my dream had been so clear. Then I realised. That first night the cat had been deep under my pillow, the next two it had been in my hand. For the magic – if that was what it was – to work properly, I must actually touch the cat.

Strange things did happen. I knew that. People saw ghosts, mediums with special powers gave messages from the dead to the living... but magic?

I glanced across at Lily who was sitting on the floor examining what appeared to be an old map of Egypt. A memory nagged at the back of my mind.

'Lily.'

'What?'

'Do you remember Papa telling us about a lecture he had attended. He said it was all about how it was possible that the stone walls of buildings could absorb memories of things that had happened in them, and that ghosts and spirits were the way that some people saw those memories.'

She frowned. 'Why ever are you thinking about that?'

'Please Lily. Can you remember anything else?'

She frowned. 'Hmm... I think he said that people who see ghosts have peculiarly sensitive minds.'

'Yes, Lily!' The words exploded out of me. 'You are right.'

She stared at me. 'About what?'

I forced myself to sound calm. 'Nothing important, honestly.'

Lily gave a dramatic sigh, shook her head and returned to studying the map.

The cat still stared inscrutably up at me. Somehow memories had attached themselves to it and my brain was sensitive enough to see them when I was asleep, when my mind was empty of other thoughts.

The stone cat must have been close to Miut. It must have been close enough to absorb her thoughts, to see through her eyes, to hear through her ears and to feel through her whiskers. There was only one place it could have been – in the leather pouch that hung from her neck.

It was all extraordinary, but not actually magic. It was then I remembered what Hori's father, the Lame-Priest, had told him was in the leather pouch. The Seal. There was no doubt. My beautiful stone cat must be the Seal.

I retrieved the cat from my pocket and examined it closely. I knew a bit about seals. Papa wore a signet ring engraved with two roaring lions with a castle in the middle. He had shown us how to drop hot wax onto an envelope and then press the engraved surface of the ring into it while the wax was still warm and soft. When he'd lifted the seal away, the imprint of the two lions and the castle had been left in the cooling wax.

My hands were trembling as I studied the cat's base. This was where any engraving would be if it was the seal. The base was shiny and smooth. There were no symbols or hieroglyphs. I was disappointed and confused.

Hori had been told the pouch contained the Seal, but maybe it was somewhere else? If so, where? Also, why had the Lame-Priest lied to his son?

I remembered how insistent he had been that Hori must tell Hapu that his father would come to the tomb. Maybe Hori was just a decoy and the Lame-Priest had the Seal, and planned to carry it to the tomb himself later. But would any father deliberately put their son into danger like that? Perhaps, but only if he was desperate.

This was all guesswork. To prove anything, I had to discover where Uncle Arthur had found the cat. I tried to remember Zac's exact words as we had sat on our donkeys watching the building work. It took a moment, but then I heard his voice quite clearly telling us how Uncle Arthur had been searching for the priest's tomb. My heart was thudding as I remembered his words.

'He spent many years searching. But when at last he found the tomb, it had been robbed many years before. There was almost nothing there. Mrs Sinclair said she thought it stopped his heart.'

'Almost nothing' meant some things had been found. All around me were half-packed boxes. What if the answers I needed were about to be packed up and sent away?

I'd just knelt down by the nearest box and was peering into it, when the door opened and Ezra peered in.

His eyes narrowed when he saw me. 'Please,' he snapped, 'leave the boxes alone. Mrs Sinclair would not like you to touch these things. You should return to your room.'

As we followed Ezra upstairs, Lily whispered. 'What were you doing, Rose?'

'It was stupid. Sorry, Lily. I was just curious.'

Lily looked puzzled. 'What about?'

I stared at her. 'Can you feel it, Lily? Something's wrong here.'

She looked confused. 'What do you mean?'

I couldn't scare her by telling her about my suspicions regarding Mr Baxter. And as for my dreams, I was certain she would think I should be sent to the lunatic asylum. Mama had told us about those terrible places and I knew you could be sent there for all sorts of things such as Grief for a Lost Child, Laziness, Greediness, even Novel Reading and Mental Excitement. I was sure Having Dreams You Think Are Real must be somewhere on the list too.

I couldn't give anyone the idea that I believed my dreams were real, even Lily. It could be dangerous so I simply said, 'If only Mama and Papa here, and Max too.'

Lily squeezed my hand. 'I am sure they will arrive soon. Then everything will feel all right.'

I forced a smile. 'Of course, it will.' How I longed for that to be true.

CHAPTER 21

We left the library and made our way back up to our bedroom. The last time we'd been in there was when we had got ready to go to the Khan el-Khalili. I knew something was different the moment we opened the door, but it took a few moments to work out what. My bed seemed a little less crumpled than I'd left it that morning. There was a heap of clothes on my chair and I was sure my cream blouse had been on top of the pile, now I could see it had slipped onto the floor. I also realised there was a faint smell of tobacco in the air. My stomach clenched and twisted. I needed some fresh air.

I crossed to the window and opened it. A warm breeze ruffled my hair. I took several deep breaths and stared down into the garden. It was getting dark, but was still light enough to see the cat wasn't there.

I turned around. 'Can you smell it, Lily? Someone has been in here. Someone who smokes.'

She sniffed. 'Probably Ezra tidying up. He might smoke.'

'Things have been moved, not tidied.'

Lily picked up her bracelet off the bedside table and slipped it on her wrist. 'I think you are imagining things. It will be supper any minute. We had better get ready.'

I sat on my bed. A burglar would have taken the silver bracelet. Who then? I was so tired, and not at all hungry.

Lily's worried voice cut through my thoughts. She was staring into one of the drawers.

'You could be right. I think someone may have been through

my things. They were tidy when we left.' She stared at me, her eyes huge. 'What were they looking for?'

I shook my head. 'Not your silver bracelet anyway.'

So it had been no ordinary thief. They were looking for something in particular. It had to be Mr Baxter looking for my cat. But if I suggested that to Lily, I would have to tell her everything, and then she would be as scared as I was.

A memory stirred. 'When we were in the garden, did Aunt Dora say something about a burglary before Uncle Arthur died?'

Lily frowned. 'I think so. But she said nothing was taken.'

My mind was suddenly leaping to all sorts of conclusions, the main one being perhaps the burglars had been looking for that something particular the first time. Had that been Mr Baxter too? Had he even been in Egypt? If it had been him, and he had been searching for the cat, it had been far from the House of Shadows as Lottie must have had it in her pocket. This time it had been in my pocket.

Lily was looking thoughtfully again at her drawer. 'Maybe I am wrong. Perhaps I muddled things up this morning when we were rushing to meet Zac.'

'Maybe,' I agreed, though I was sure she had not muddled anything. 'In any case there's no point worrying Aunt Dora,' I said firmly. 'If they were here, they took nothing.'

We brushed our hair and put on clean pinafores so that when Ezra came to get us for supper, we would be ready. I just needed to change my boots for my indoor shoes. As I knelt down to retrieve them from under my bed, I saw something that set my heart pounding. A scarlet rose petal lay just beside them. The last scarlet rose I'd seen was the one in Mr Baxter's buttonhole.

That night as I lay in bed and tried to fall asleep, all the questions about Hori, Heteb and the stone cat buzzed frantically round and round in my head. I was unsure if I wanted to dream about Miut anymore. I was too afraid that it was all going to end badly. But thinking about Mr Baxter was no better. He must think whatever it was that Aunt Dora had given me might be the thing that he was desperate to find. But even worse was the thought that he might want to marry Aunt Dora. If he did, would she be in danger? And what did he want with Lily and me? I was sure he wanted something. And who was that man in the cream suit in the market? Did he have anything to do with Mr Baxter?

There was only one good thing to think about, though that was strange enough. The cat that had led me safely home from the market. How had it done that? And why?

Lily had fallen asleep almost instantly. For a while I listened to her deep, regular breathing. The shutters were open and moonlight flooded in, so the room was shadowy but not too dark. But what if the shutters closed again? I wrapped my fingers tightly round the stone cat. Maybe it would look after me. Maybe I would be able to "almost see" in the dark. Maybe I would be as brave as a lion... as brave as Miut.

As for the dreams, I realised that however they turned out, I needed to know what happened to Hori... and to Miut.

CHAPTER 22

'THE BOOK OF MIUT'

III

The temple docks were busier than usual. Everywhere Miut looked there were boats tied to the quays and men busy loading them.

Hori paused, staring round at the confusion. 'It is no good, I cannot see him,' he muttered at last. He turned towards a nearby barge.

Miut flexed her claws, kneading the boy's shoulder in her excitement. Somewhere nearby would be the woman who sometimes fed her. Her mouth watered at the memories. Silver, straight from the river, whisker-tingling, fish. Her breakfast was already a distant memory.

'Ouch, Miut. No more of that,' said the boy, unhooking her claws from his shoulder.

The barge's gangplank rested on the quay. Rows of baskets waited on the quayside. Miut inspected them eagerly. Some were piled high with dates, gleaming like burnished gold in the morning light. Others held watermelons as big as a man's head. But none held fish.

A tall man, as thin as a stick, stood at the base of the gangplank, with a writing tablet in his hand. He peered at the load of every worker who passed him, and then marked the tablet. He looked up as Hori and Miut approached and gave a small smile.

'Have you come to assist with the recording, Hori?'

Hori shook his head. 'Not today, Huy.' He looked round. 'Are you nearly done?'

The man frowned. 'No, but we have until noon. Then we must cross the river to the Temple of Ptah. There we have much to do to prepare the High Priest for his journey into the afterlife. His procession will leave the House of the Embalmers as the sun-disc sinks into the Underworld.'

The boy glanced skywards in the direction of the sun-disc. 'You have time.'

'Indeed. Will you be joining us?'

'No,' said Hori scanning the docks with anxious eyes, 'I fear I must be across the river before. Have you seen the ferryman?'

The man's brow wrinkled. 'Some time ago. He was going up river on temple business.'

The river breeze swirled and Miut's whiskers tingled with the oily smell of freshly gutted fish. She turned her head to follow the path of the wind, until her eyes rested on a cluster of little reed boats tethered loosely beside the furthest quay. They bobbed like ducklings on the water. The baskets of silver-scaled fish they had carried were piled high on the quayside. A familiar shape squatted nearby. The fish woman. She would feed Miut. Miut's belly rumbled.

She squirmed free of Hori's arms, and the instant her paws touched the ground she sidestepped to avoid his outstretched hands. She trotted with as much speed as she could manage towards her next meal.

'Forgive me, Huy. I must follow that cat.' Hori was already following her as he spoke.

'May Horus protect you,' Huy called after them.

Miut reached the squatting woman and rubbed herself against her robe. The coarse linen tickled her nose. The woman put down the knife she had been using to split the fish in half and scratched Miut's ears. Her hand was as strong and as wide as a man's and her face, beaten by the winds of the river, was as wrinkled as a sun-dried date.

'I thought you had deserted us, little goddess. But perhaps it is the promise of fresh fish that has brought you back. You and your little ones,' said the woman with warmth in her voice. The Fish-Woman picked a fish from the basket and laid it on the ground. Miut grasped it in her claws and bit deep into the soft, sweet flesh.

Hori arrived, breathing a little fast. 'Thank you, Meryet. She is always hungry'.

The Fish-Woman smiled. 'I see she has been busy since the High Priest's death. From the size of her, it will not be long before those kittens see the light of Ra.'

Hori sighed, 'I know, but not yet. First, we must cross the river, and I am in search of the ferryman. Have you seen him?'

The Fish-Woman shook her head, her eyes fixed on the boy. 'You seem worried. Your journey is important?'

Hori nodded.

The Fish-Woman stood up and wiped her fish-scaled hands on a cloth. 'I have these fish to deliver to the city. I will take you over the river.'

A smile flitted across Hori's tight face. 'Thank you, Meryet. You will be doing my father a great service.'

'Your father is a wise man,' her voice dropped, 'and a good one… which is more than can be said for some others within the temple.' She picked up the nearest basket and handed it to the boy. 'If you load the fish, I will find my husband and tell him that I have finished here. Then we will be off.' She strode away towards a long low building, which stood beside the quay.

Hori looked thoughtfully after her for a few moments. Then he turned and carried the basket down the nearby steps to the small boat waiting there. Other baskets soon followed. When he was done, he returned to sit beside Miut in the shade of a pile of empty baskets.

She had finished her fish and was licking her paws clean, when the boy stiffened beside her. He was peering round the baskets. Miut followed his eyes.

The ferryman had returned. His boat was now tied up alongside the adjacent quay. Three boys were talking to him. She recognised the tallest one at once. Snake-Eyes. She unsheathed her claws.

'Neshi,' breathed the boy. 'Why is he here? He still has duties here in the temple.'

Snake-Eyes was speaking rapidly and gesturing towards the far bank. After a short time, the ferryman nodded his head and the boys climbed down into his boat. As soon as they were on board, the ferryman released the mooring rope, and his men began to row rapidly away from the quay.

'Neshi is in a hurry.' Hori's brow was furrowed. 'I do not like this, Miut. I fear he means trouble.'

All of a sudden, the Fish-Woman was beside them. 'If you wish to cross, you had better get in the boat.'

Once Hori and Miut were seated in the bow, the Fish-Woman took up the oars, calling out as she did so, 'May Hapi, the great god of the river, keep us safe and speed our crossing.'

She rowed smoothly and soon they were passing out of the canal into open water. The breeze was fresh and cool. Miut sat upright beside the boy, watching the wind-dappled water dance under the oars.

The river was full of boats. Some with their sails set high were making their way up the river. Others, with their sails furled, were whisking down on the current, their oars easily breaking the water in perfect time. The boy ignored them and stared only into the distance ahead.

After a while he called back to the Fish-Woman, 'The ferryman's boat ... can you see it? It has ... some friends in it.'

The Fish-Woman ceased rowing and letting the boat drift, she turned round to look at the boy.

'Since when has Neshi, son of Paser, been a friend of yours?'

'How did you know that was who I was looking for?'

'I know many things.' She gave a short laugh. 'But this was not so hard. I saw him talking to the ferryman. I also saw you hiding behind the heap of fish baskets.'

'Please, Meryet, forgive me, but I cannot explain. I must get to the Temple of Ptah. I do not want Neshi to see me.'

The Fish-Woman peered towards the far bank, which was lined with palaces, temples and endless rows of mud-brick houses with palm-tree shaded gardens. But Miut's eyes travelled beyond the great city, to the cliff that towered above it. It blazed white in the heat of the day.

She purred quietly. She knew the cliff well. Its face was honeycombed with tombs. She had lived amongst them as a kitten. One had been her home – until the day a man had come to the tombs. He had caught her, placed her in a basket and carried her down to the great city.

Suddenly the Fish-Woman pointed. 'There.... heading for the temple docks. I see the ferryman.'

Hori ducked low in the boat. 'I must not be seen.'

She picked up the oars again. 'I will set you on the bank this side of the city. You will be there sooner and hidden from view.'

The boat swung round sharply, and water splashed Miut's whiskers. She shook her head and sneezed. Boats were all very well as long as the water stayed in the river.

The Fish-Woman leaned into the oars, forcing the boat across the current, until the water calmed and the boat nosed its way through the clumps of rushes hugging the shallow water. Then, with a grinding shudder, it came to rest on the mud at the water's edge.

'If you climb up the bank, you will see a path running towards the great temple,' said the Fish-Woman.

Hori had stood and was preparing to climb out of the boat when she stopped him with an outstretched hand. 'Take this,' she said handing him a small object threaded through with a leather cord, 'and let the Eye of Horus keep you safe, for I fear your path will be full of danger. This may bring you friends when you most need them.'

'What do you know, Meryet?' The boy had swung back to face her. 'What are you warning me against?'

The Fish-Woman spoke softly, 'I have heard talk. There is unhappiness amongst the priesthood. Some even question the power of the Lord Osiris, and they do not like it that your father will be High Priest.'

Hori's eyes narrowed. 'You are not the first to tell me this. But I must have their names so I may warn my father.'

'I cannot give you more.'

'Cannot or will not?'

The Fish-Woman looked round uneasily before continuing softly.

'All I will say is that you must trust no one until your father is High Priest. Then maybe they will take their ambitions elsewhere.'

Hori slipped the Eye of Horus over his head; it hung above his heart. 'Thank you, Meryet, for this amulet and for the warning.'

He slid off his sandals and held them in one hand, while with the other he carefully lifted Miut up and tucked her under his arm. A few moments later, he splashed up onto the riverbank. At the top, he slipped on his sandals again and checked the scroll was still firmly tucked into his kilt.

Behind them the Fish-Woman heaved on the oars and the boat slid back into deeper water. The wall of rushes soon hid her from Miut's view.

Hori placed her gently on the ground. 'Now walk beside me,' he instructed. Shading his eyes with his hand, he glanced towards the sun-disc. It had been drawn high into the sky, and its rays blazed down at them. The boy frowned. 'It must already be well past noon.'

At the top of the bank, they joined the road. It ran between the river and the fields. The floods had receded, although water still lay in puddles over the lower areas. Everywhere Miut looked, green shoots were springing from the rich, dark mud. Her whiskers tingled with the richness of their growing.

There were few people travelling on the road, and none appeared to take any notice of the boy, although some nodded a greeting to Miut. Ahead stood the wall of sun-bleached, mud-bricks surrounding the temple. As they grew closer, it towered above them. The road led to a large gateway. The gate was closed.

As they approached, a guard stepped forward. His face was like stone.

'What business brings you to the great Temple of Ptah, in the City of White Walls?'

Hori drew himself up to his full height and glared back at the guard. 'I wish to see Hapu, Master of the House of Life.'

'And who might you be?'

The boy glanced round. There was no one nearby. 'My name

is Hori, son of Khay, who is soon to be High Priest of the Temple of Osiris.' His voice rang with pride.

The guard coughed to cover a smile.

'Indeed?' was all he said, before switching his attention to Miut. She gazed unblinkingly back. His expression softened. 'Ah, little Goddess your company vouches for the boy. He must speak the truth with you at his side. You may both enter.' He looked back at Hori. 'But I fear that Hapu is no longer in the House of Life. Not long ago I saw him hurrying towards the Sanctuary. Do you know where that is?'

The boy shook his head. 'Can you tell me the quickest way?'

The guard pointed at a paved path, which ran towards a cluster of low buildings. 'Follow that path and maybe you will find Hapu. May Ptah smile on you.'

'And you,' replied Hori, bending down, and before she could take a breath, Miut found herself back in the boy's arms. 'Come Miut, I am sure Hapu will have some milk for you.'

~

Miut heard a faint buzz of voices coming from the main temple, which lay to the right, but the path ahead was deserted. Hori held her firmly as he made for a cluster of low buildings standing within a low enclosure. The gate was closed.

'Hello,' he called, 'Hapu?'

For a long moment there was silence. But then a voice boomed out behind them. 'This is the right place for questions, but who is asking?'

Hori spun round, almost dropping Miut. Her claws spiked into the boy's arm. But he seemed not to feel it; his eyes were fixed on the man who had spoken.

He was the tallest man Miut had ever seen, and as heavily built as an ox. He wore the kilt of a priest, but strands of hay clung to its folds.

Hori started at the sight of him, then his mouth broke into a grin. 'Anhur. Can it be you?

The Tall-Priest arched his eyebrows. 'It is. Who are you?'

'Hori. Son of Khay, soon to be High Priest of the Temple of Osiris.'

The Tall-Priest studied the boy's face. 'I would not have recognised you for you have grown since I last saw you. But it would be strange if you had not.' He added thoughtfully, 'The last time we met, we went fishing in your father's boat.'

Hori's eyes opened wide. 'No. We went duck hunting in the marshes and I fell in the great river. You rescued me.'

The priest laughed and slapped the boy on his back. 'It is truly you, Hori. Forgive me for the test, but in these times people are not always who they say they are.'

'I must find Hapu. Have you seen him?'

'He came earlier to ask the advice of the Apis, then left in a hurry.'

'Did he say where he was going?'

The Tall-Priest shook his head. 'But as I said before, you have come to the right place for questions. I have returned to let my Lord Apis out into the yard. And as all others appear to have their minds elsewhere this day, he may choose to give you the answers you need.'

Hori frowned. 'I have brought no offerings.'

'But you have brought a goddess with you,' said the Tall-Priest, 'That should be enough.'

He lifted the bar and swung open the gate. He led them inside. In front of Miut lay an open yard, part of which was separated off by a wooden barrier.

'Stay there,' commanded the Tall-Priest, as he started towards the building to their right.

Hori placed Miut carefully on the ground. 'Stay close,' he ordered, and crossed the yard to the barrier.

Miut trotted beside him. Then she slipped through the gap beneath the barrier and sat just inside, her tail tucked neatly around her. Hori stood behind, leaning against the top rail. She could sense the tension in him.

Far above her head, a flock of birds with wings shaped like the heads of arrows swirled and swooped after invisible insects. Miut's nostrils twitched. Straw and dung-dust hung in the air, and something else too... a sweet muskiness. It was a smell, long forgotten, that took her back to her kittenhood. She looked around more carefully and knew that she had been here before.

A loud crash broke the silence. A gate on the far side of the yard flew open and a great beast exploded, snorting furiously, into the light. His coat gleamed like black gold and his great horns shone like the finest ivory. After one mighty roar, he tossed his head and set off round and round the yard, his hooves sounding like thunder and the ground trembling under his weight. As he raced, he leaped and twisted into the air. At last he slowed to a bouncing trot and slithered to a standstill in front of Miut. He faced her with heaving flanks, and nostrils flaring blood-red. His eyes fastened on hers.

She stood up and stretched lazily before padding towards him.

'Miut,' Hori called, his voice sharp with fear, 'What are you doing? Lord Apis will kill you. Come back.'

But Miut padded on until the bull towered above her. She headed for his nearest foreleg, and purring long and loud, she rubbed her head against it. The bull lowered his head to sniff at her. She stood fearlessly between the sweep of his horns. He snorted gently.

She purred. This was an old friend. The man who had carried her down from the tombs on the cliff, had stayed here awhile before taking her across the river. She had spent many nights curled up in the great bull's stall.

The Tall-Priest was talking to Hori. 'He will not harm her. They are both gods. They understand each other. Now ask your questions. Just three. And the answer to each must be yes or no. If the answer is yes, then the great Apis will shake his head. If the answer is no, then he will be still. Do you understand?'

Hori nodded and looked gravely at the bull. 'Great and mighty Apis, my first question is: will my father's leg be fully healed?

The bull tossed his head and snorted.

Hori smiled. 'Thank you, that is most welcome news. My second question is: should I stay here in the Temple of Ptah and search for Hapu?'

The bull looked solemnly back, but did not so much as twitch an ear.

Hori gave a small sigh. 'I will travel on then. My final question is: does danger await us on the path to the tomb of Heteb, High Priest of the Temple of Osiris?'

As the boy's voice died away, the bull reared up into the air. Miut shot back behind the barrier as his head tossed wildly, his horns missing her by the breadth of a man's hair. Then he swung away from them and flew round the yard, faster even than before, his hooves sending thick, clouds of sand spinning into the air.

'Enough,' shouted the great priest. The bull slowed at the sound of his voice, then stopped. He snorted and pawed at the ground.

The priest rested an enormous hand on the boy's shoulder. 'I fear for you, Hori. I do not know what this danger is, but the Apis has warned you, it is great. Why not wait and join the High Priest's procession, which is even now gathering in the temple courtyard? There will be safety with people all around.'

The boy shivered and shook his head. 'I cannot wait, but I will be careful. Thank you, Anhur. Miut and I will be on our way, if you will just show us where our road begins.'

The boy stretched his hand out to Miut. She backed away. She was so tired and hot. Deep within her womb, the kittens moved. She must find a place to rest. Somewhere dark and cool. She remembered the sweet-smelling straw of the bull's stall. But first she had a thirst to quench. She set off across the yard and stopped at a low trough cut from stone and filled with clear, cool water. She drank greedily. As soon as she had had enough, Hori, who had followed her, swept her into his arms again.

'I am sorry, Miut,' he whispered, 'but you must come with me.'

~

Miut rested her head on the boy's shoulder as the Tall-Priest led them through a narrow side gate in the temple wall. The guard opened it without question. Ahead of them lay a raised path. It ran as straight as an arrow, across the narrow band of planted land that lay beside the river, towards the desert cliff.

'This is the shortest way, but it is steep,' said the Tall-Priest. 'The procession will use The Covered Way from the Valley Temple where High Priest Heteb now lies, up to the City of the Dead. You have time. The procession will not leave there until night has fallen.' He wrinkled his forehead and added softly, 'Strange it is to be so late. But the High Priest was a mighty magician… and darkness cloaks many secrets.' He fixed the boy with his eyes and his voice was deep as he said, 'May the Eye of Horus that you wear guide you safely up this path and protect you from danger.'

Without waiting for a reply, the Tall-Priest turned back towards the gate. Hori watched it close behind him. He sighed and gently put Miut down. 'Follow me,' he whispered, 'please.'

There was nowhere else to go so Miut followed. As the path left the fields, it narrowed, and became little more than a track. All around them was the bleak gold of the sand-covered hillside. The stones were hot under Miut's feet and her throat was as dry as a mouse's tail.

Ahead of them the track wound on into the shadows and the rocks rose up on each side, forming a roofless tunnel. Miut stopped suddenly. There was something ahead in the darkness. Something terrible. Her whiskers tingled. The fur on her back rose.

Hori stopped and turned. 'What are you doing, Miut? There is no time for a rest. Not yet.' He lifted her once more into his arms, then strode on towards the shadows.

Miut stared ahead, her body rigid, her claws half-unsheathed. The boy leaned forwards into the hill as the path entered the half-tunnel and the gradient steepened. The boy stumbled on the loose stones that littered the ground. His skin glistened with sweat and his breathing grew ragged. 'It is no good,' he gasped at last, 'you are too heavy, Miut, and the path too steep. You must walk after all.'

Miut found herself deposited abruptly on the ground. Hori leaned against a nearby wall of rock and gathered his breath.

'The hours of writing have taken their toll, have they?' A voice sneered out of the gloom ahead.

Miut looked up to see Snake-Eyes moving down the path towards them.

'Why don't you just give me the cat?' he spoke softly. 'You have no choice. Not really.' He raised his hand and Miut saw the dark gleam of the knife he held.

Hori must have seen it too as he moved forwards and stood in front of her. 'Go away, Neshi. You will not harm her.'

Snake-Eyes laughed. 'Who will stop me? You?' He eased closer, until he loomed just above them.

Hori did not move, his eyes remained fixed on the knife. 'You can't do this.' His voice was like iron, but Miut felt his fear.

Snake-Eyes laughed as he slipped his knife into his kilt. 'You are right. I do not need a knife to do what must be done.'

With the speed of lightening he drew back his fist and drove it at the boy. The boy fell back. There was a thud as his head met the rock wall of the tunnel. He crumpled to the ground and lay still. His eyes were closed. A trickle of blood seeped into the sand beside his head.

Snake-Eyes bent over him. 'Knocked your head, did you, worm?' His voice was little more than a whisper. 'Now it will take little to finish both jobs. But Hori, you shall be first.' He glanced round at the deserted path and jeered, 'And who will stop me now?' He pulled the knife from his kilt and raised it high above his head.

But Miut was already in the air. She landed on Hori's chest. Her raised fur doubled her size, her unsheathed claws gleamed like daggers, her needle teeth glistened in the red cavern of her mouth and her eyes blazed like the hottest fire.

Snake-Eyes froze. For a long moment their eyes locked. Miut tensed, ready to spring at Snake-Eyes's unguarded throat.

At last Snake-Eyes lowered his knife and dropped his gaze to the puncture marks which glowed angrily on his knife hand. Miut remembered his hands tightening the cord round her neck and the bittersweet taste of his blood.

Snake-Eyes backed slowly away, his eyes fixed on Miut. 'I will have you, little goddess,' he spat through twisted lips. 'You will walk with the High Priest... soon... very soon.' He slipped the knife into its holder. There was a swirl of dust and he was gone.

Miut watched the dust settle. Far above her, an eagle hovered lazily in the bleached sky. The air quivered in the heat. She turned to Hori. He was perfectly still, his eyes closed.

Miut stretched to lick his face, her tongue rasping at his cheek. But still he did not move. She curled up in the crook of his arm. For a while, she watched the path and listened for footsteps. There was only silence. At last, her own eyes shut and she slept.

CHAPTER 23

Aunt Dora woke us while it was still dark.

'What's wrong?' I mumbled as she, gently but insistently, shook us awake. I was struggling to clear my mind of the picture of Hori lying so still on the path, Miut standing over him, teeth like daggers, fur spiking upright, green eyes sparking, daring Neshi to come closer. I remembered the blood-stained sand.

'Nothing's wrong,' Aunt Dora reassured us. 'Have you forgotten Zac is taking you to Giza today so you can see the pyramids and the Great Sphinx? You have to get there early, before it gets too hot to enjoy exploring everything.'

She briskly instructed us to cover ourselves with sweet, vinegary smelling eau de cologne to keep the flies away. As we mounted our donkeys, Aunt Dora handed Zac several packets of sandwiches and bottles of ginger beer, which he stowed carefully into a leather bag attached to his saddle. A few moments later, we were trotting through the still sleeping streets of Cairo.

It took us about two hours to reach the foot of the Great Pyramid. Set on a sand-covered plateau overlooking the city, it towered above us, its sides a crumbling mess of great rocky slabs that formed rough steps to the sky. People were already climbing up them; they looked like clusters of brightly coloured spiders. Men in smart, tweed suits, and ladies in high bonnets and long skirts were being hauled up by groups of Arabs. It appeared to take at least three Arabs to hoist each lady up, one pulled on each arm and another pushed from behind.

'Oh goodness me,' whispered Lily, 'how brave they are. I could never do that.'

Zac turned to me. 'And you, Miss Rose, will you climb? I will assist you. Or is it too high for you?' He threw back his head and his dark eyes sparkled. Challenging me.

Suddenly I wanted to be high, above everything, free. However I was not going to be hauled up like a sack of potatoes. 'I'll manage by myself.' I turned to Lily. 'Will you be alright if I go?'

She looked anxiously at me. "Are you sure? It's so terribly high. Do you think Aunt Dora would think it was safe?

'Honestly, I'll be fine,' I reassured her, 'but you look exhausted. Why don't you rest in the shade and I will be back before you know it?'

Lily yawned. 'I am rather tired. I will stay with Akil and the donkeys. So yes, go.' Akil, a slightly built man wearing a black robe and blue turban similar to those worn by Ezra, had been waiting for us when we arrived at Giza. Zac told us he and Akil lived in the same village, and that Akil would look after the donkeys while we explored.

'Watch out for scorpions in the crevices,' Zac instructed as we headed for the pyramids, 'and follow me. Don't look down or up, just do what exactly what I do.'

I tied my skirt into a knot so it was as out of my way as possible, ignoring the disapproving looks thrown at me by a group of nearby tourists, and followed Zac. Slowly and steadily we made our way upwards. I did briefly wonder what Aunt Dora would say if she could see me, but then firmly put that thought out of my mind. Just as I was about to call to Zac that I needed to stop and get my breath, he sat down on a wide flat rock and I joined him. We perched like birds high on the side of the pyramid.

'You climb very well. I have not seen a girl do that before.'

'I love climbing. When we stay with our cousins in the country, there are lots of trees in the park. No one minds if we climb them. I have been to the top of most of them. Some are hundreds of years old and very tall.'

Zac then told me it had taken millions of limestone blocks to build the pyramids, and that most of the blocks had been quarried nearby, then dragged here by thousands of workers, about four and a half thousand years ago. 'Some of them,' he said proudly, 'were my ancestors.'

I remembered Aunt Dora telling us that Copts like Zac were descendants of the pyramid builders. Perhaps it wasn't surprising how like Hori he looked.

Zac was staring at me, waiting for me to say something.

'That's an amazing thought,' I said at last, wanting to say so much more, but knowing he'd never believe me if I told him about my dreams.

He nodded. 'Indeed it is. But you would not have been able to climb any of the pyramids in those times because they were covered by a casing of polished white limestone slabs cut from most special quarries just across the Nile. They were loaded onto river barges and brought across the river when it was in flood, to the very base of the pyramid.'

'But why did they cover them like that?'

Zac shrugged. 'No one is certain. But many believe it was because then the pyramids shone like the rays of the sun itself. The soul of the king could rise through them to join Ra, the sun god.

'His soul is his *ba*.'

'It is.' Zac seemed impressed. 'Did your father teach you this?'

'He did. And that the *ka* is the life force and will stay in the tomb and live in the mummy of the dead person.' I sighed. 'I miss Papa so much.'

'He will return soon,' said Zac, giving me a sympathetic look. 'Now, if you have regained your breath, we must climb or the day will grow too hot.'

Sometime later I half fell and half clambered onto the flat stone platform. My heart hammered in my chest, my lungs ached and my legs felt like paper. I risked a brief glance down. The people on the ground far below were no bigger than ants. I'd made it. I would have laughed if I had any breath to laugh with.

Zac held out his hand to steady me. 'You did well,' he said with a broad smile, 'to climb so quickly. Have you ever seen a view so splendid?'

I swung slowly round. Zac was right. I'd never seen anything like this. I was actually standing on top of the Great Pyramid of Giza, hundreds of feet above the desert below and it felt wonderful. The pale blue early morning air was so clear I could see forever. Near us were the smaller – but still huge – pyramids of Khafre and Menkaure, and far below them I could make out the Sphinx emerging from great mounds of desert sand. I knew it was a great stone lion with a man's face, but it looked no bigger than the ship's cat from up here, though Papa had told me it was as high as eleven tall men.

Cairo lay to the east beneath the brilliant orange of the rising sun. It was a mass of toy minarets, golden domes and pale stone buildings huddled beside the dark ribbon of the Nile. Away from the city, the river was edged with groves of green date palms. In many places, however, the Nile had escaped from its banks and flooded the low-lying land so it looked more like a great lake than a river.

Zac pointed to the north. 'That way is Alexandria.'

It felt like a bolt of lightning hitting me. Max. When had I last thought of him... a day... more... How could I have let him slip out of my mind for even a moment? But there had been so much else to fill my thoughts. Mr Baxter, the man in the cream suit, Hori, Miut... I squinted into the far, far distance. Was Max better? Was he worse...?

Zac gestured in the opposite direction and I realised that I could see yet more pyramids. A broken chain of them stretched into the far distance. 'And that way there are the pyramids of Abusir, Dahshur and, perhaps the most ancient pyramid of them all, at Sakkara.'

Zac's words thundered in my ears and a memory danced

out of the shadows. Hori's father was speaking. *'Hapu will hide it within the tomb of the High Priest, which lies at the foot of the stepped pyramid of Sakkara and beside the tomb of Imhotep, who was the architect of the pyramid and the greatest magician of all.'*

'Very soon you will visit Sakkara,' continued Zac. 'It is near my home.'

Visit Sakkara. Stand in Hori's footsteps. My heart was racing. 'When can we go? Will we see Imhotep's tomb?'

Zac looked curiously at me. 'Who is Imhotep?'

I stared at him. Everything I'd been so sure of was suddenly as shaky as jelly. If Imhotep wasn't a real person, then were Hori and Miut? My thoughts churned like a waterwheel. I clung to the fact that I knew from the book in Aunt Dora's library that Heteb at least had been a living, breathing priest,

'I thought he was an architect and a great magician,' I said at last. 'But maybe he was just a character in a bedtime story.'

Zac nodded. 'Maybe. But there are many tombs out there to be discovered. One day perhaps I will find the tomb of this Imhotep, and he will be real.'

I smiled. 'When you are a famous archaeologist.'

Zac smiled back. 'Indeed.'

I then said something I'd never dared say to anyone ever before. Even Lily. 'Actually, I would like to be an archaeologist too.'

Zac gazed thoughtfully at me. 'Maybe you will be. My father tells me, if you want something enough, and it is a good thing, then it will happen.'

I stared into the far distance. 'I am not certain there are any women archaeologists.'

'Well,' said Zac firmly, 'if that is true, you will just have to be the first.'

'Maybe,' I said realising that the rock-strewn desert beyond the Great Pyramid was all lumps and mysterious bumps. Were there long-forgotten tombs and temples lying hidden beneath the sand waiting to be discovered? I felt a thrill of excitement and the world was suddenly full of exciting possibilities.

Someone brushed past me. The platform was getting quite crowded now and the sun felt hot on my back. I felt a flash of panic. How long had we been up here? 'I hope Lily's alright.'

'Here,' said Zac, 'see for yourself.' He handed me a small leather case, which had hung hidden under his robe. Inside was a neat pair of brass binoculars. 'Mrs Dora gave them to me. They used to belong to Mr Sinclair.'

I put them to my eyes. The ant-sized people became identifiable. I looked for Lily. She was with Akil and patting a donkey. It was getting very crowded down there; people were grouping together in the shade cast by the pyramid. A lone figure caught my attention. I focused on it and felt my heart lurch. I recognised him and his cream suit at once. The man who had chased after me in the market was now staring intently at Lily.

I swung round to Zac. 'I'm sorry,' I said forcing myself to sound calm though my heart was racing, 'but we must go down right now.'

CHAPTER 24

'You took ages,' said Lily when we eventually re-joined her.

'Sorry,' I said, checking round. But there was no sign of the man now. I saw Zac watching me curiously.

'Is everything as it should be?' he asked.

'Everything's fine,' I heard the sharpness in my voice. 'I am just tired from the climb.'

Zac looked up at the sun, which hung high in the sky. 'Shall we go inside the great pyramid now, and then we will rest and picnic in the shade of the Sphinx?'

'That sounds lovely,' said Lily. 'Come on, Rose, you've had your fun. Now it's my turn.'

I looked up at the entrance to the pyramid. At the darkness waiting for me. 'Actually, would you mind if I waited for you here?'

Lily rolled her eyes. 'Akil has told me it'll be lit inside, there'll be lamps and magnesium wire.' She glanced up at Zac. 'Is that right?'

'Of course. There will be everything we need to find our way.' He looked curiously at me. 'You were most brave climbing the pyramid, yet you are afraid of the dark?'

I shrugged. 'I always have been. I have to get over it.' I looked at him and managed a smile. 'But not today.'

Lily stood up. 'We'll be as quick as we can.'

I watched Zac and Lily reach the entrance and vanish. I was pleased that Lily seemed so much stronger now. The Egyptian air was certainly doing her good. I sat down beside the donkeys. Djinn nuzzled my shoulder and I stroked her velvet muzzle. Akil appeared to be asleep on the sand nearby. I'd stayed with Akil, not just because I hated dark places, but because I also wanted to make sure the man in the cream suit didn't follow us into the pyramid. If he did, we would have been trapped.

It can only have been few minutes before I saw him. He was heading for the pyramid, just as I'd been afraid he might.

Lily had no idea he was dangerous. I suddenly wished I'd warned her. But that would have meant telling her everything. I wanted to protect her, not frighten her.

The man was starting the climb up to the entrance. My mind spun hopelessly. I had to stop him. But how? Deep in the crevice by my hand, there was movement. Something scuttled in the shadows.

'Akil,' I screamed as loudly as I could, 'there's a scorpion.'

Akil sat up, blinking. The man in the cream suit swung towards me. I pretended to see nothing but the scorpion. I jumped to my feet and ran still screaming into the sunlight. A wave of heat hit me. I kept running, then pretended to stumble, and risked a glance behind me. The man was striding across the sand towards me. I was running again, weaving past surprised tourists. As I raced past, a white-whiskered gentleman shouted, 'Look where you are going, young lady.'

I had to hide. But where? The Great Pyramid was to my right, the desert rose ahead of me towards a low ridge. I struggled upwards, my feet sinking into the soft sand until I reached the summit. I didn't dare look back; all the time I expected the touch of his hand on my back. I could see the Sphinx below me. Now it was huge. Maybe I could hide in its shadow? I ploughed downwards through the sand, half sliding, half running. There was one last bank of sand, which I threw myself down. I somersaulted, then rolled to a halt between the Sphinx's great front legs. Everywhere was sand: in my clothes, my eyes, up my nose, in my hair. Tears cleared my eyes. I spat out the sand from my mouth. I sat up. There was no sign of the man. Yet. I tucked in tight to the Sphinx's left foreleg so I would be hidden from anyone standing on the desert ridge above. Then I eased myself toward the curve of the lion's chest. I patted my pocket to check the stone cat was still there, then crouched in the shadows and waited.

Then I heard it. A soft meow that sent my heart racing. I peered round. There was no sign of a cat. The Sphinx towered above me as tall as a church tower, the gap between its great legs like a street between rows of houses. There were voices. Men's voices. I couldn't hear the words, but one voice was as sharp as a knife, angry, urgent. It must be him. If he just came over the ridge of the leg above my head he would see me.

My heart hammered in my chest. I crouched even lower, making myself as small as I could. There was another meow. This time it came from somewhere near my feet. I looked down and realised the sand was running away, like sand through an egg timer. I peered deep into the shadows. Then I saw it. A gap between the Sphinx's chest and the sand. I threw myself at it. It was just large enough for me to wriggle through. The next moment I was falling in an avalanche of sand into some sort of cavity. I bit back a scream as I landed heavily on a rock floor, bruising my knees. I rubbed them until the pain subsided.

Light filtered in through the gap above my head. I peered round for the cat, but I was quite alone. There was just a soft scuttling sound as some small creature vanished into the shadows. My head was aching. I knew that however impossible it was, once more the cat had saved me.

I was in a small cave formed by the curve of the Sphinx's chest, while in front of me was a wall of sand blown there by hundreds of years of desert storms. I eased myself carefully back up the slope towards the light trying not to dislodge any more sand as I went. If the man had gone, I could make my way back to Akil and the donkeys.

I reached the gap and peeped cautiously out. For a moment I saw no one, and then I felt the air move. I froze as his shoes passed by just inches from my face. His head twisted to and fro as he searched for me. At one moment he seemed to be staring straight at me. I stopped breathing. Then he turned and walked slowly away between the Sphinx's colossal legs. At last he disappeared round the huge feet, and I slid back down into my sandy cave, my heart thundering as if I'd run a mile.

Lily and Zac would be a while, maybe an hour. I was probably safer here for the moment than heading back to Akil and the donkeys. If the man was still searching for me, it would keep him away from Lily. As the sun moved, so would the shadows, and I should have a good idea when an hour had passed. All I must do was stay awake and keep checking the position of the shadows. I began to relax.

It was quiet in my little cave. After the early start, climbing the pyramid, and escaping the man in the cream suit, I was exhausted. For a while I forced my eyes to stay open, but my lids felt like lead. So heavy. Too heavy. In the end I couldn't help it, my eyes shut.

CHAPTER 25

'THE BOOK OF MIUT'

IV

Miut stirred and opened her eyes. The sky was tinged with pink and gold while the sun-disc now rested on a nearby hilltop. Shadows lay long on the ground.

Deep within her womb, the kittens moved uneasily. There was a strength and urgency to their flutterings, which had not been there before.

Beside her, Hori groaned and Miut began to lick his face. She could taste the salt of his sweat and the sourness of dried blood.

Hori turned his head away from her. 'Ouch! Stop that, Miut!' He sat up and rubbed his head. 'Oh… it aches as if the gods themselves have been dancing on it.'

Miut watched him get shakily to his feet. Hori stood for a while as if he were uncertain as to what he must do next. He fumbled suddenly at his kilt and pulled out the scroll. He stared at it. 'I thought Neshi was going to kill me. I thought he hated me that much. Yet he didn't even search for this.' The boy leant down and scratched Miut under her chin.

She purred softly.

'And he didn't hurt you, little goddess. It doesn't make sense.' He sighed. 'But then nothing has made sense since the death of the High Priest.' Hori looked up at the darkening sky. 'It is late. I must find Hapu.'

He gathered Miut into his arms. Holding her firmly, he turned towards the hillside and set off up the stony track.

The way grew steeper as the shadows ran one into the other and the sun sank into the cavernous depths of the Underworld. Hori's breathing grew laboured and sweat dampened his skin, but he kept on climbing upwards. Miut lay unmoving in his arms, while all the time her need to be alone grew stronger.

~

By the time they reached the lower edge of the plateau, the moon-disc had appeared in the night blue sky. Hori placed Miut gently on the ground before throwing himself down beside her.

'Never,' he said through rasping breath, 'have my arms ached so.'

Miut began licking and smoothing her fur. Her throat was sand-dry and she longed for water. Somewhere in the distance, a night bird was calling. Something small rustled nearby. A mouse perhaps? Her tail twitched.

Gradually, the boy's breathing steadied until at last he sat up and lifted the blue Eye of Horus from his chest in the direction of the moon-disc.

'O most mighty, Horus,' he said, his voice strong and clear, 'who looks down at me in the darkness through your great, all-seeing eye, protect me. And protect too, this daughter of Bastet, who is loved by your father, Osiris, and his priests, but who is hated and feared by the followers of Seth.'

Hori put out his hand and gently pushed at Miut until she was forced to stand, then he got to his feet and stood beside her. 'The City of the Dead cannot be far now. We will soon find Hapu, and then we can both rest.' Together they walked on, the path rising in front of them until at last it levelled out. The boy stopped suddenly. 'I never expected this,' he whispered.

They were on the summit of a low rise. In front of them the ground fell gently away to a chaos of silent temples and empty courtyards, which lay between rock-strewn hills. Each hill was honeycombed with the shadowed entrances to more than a thousand tombs. Dotted around the city were small, flat-sided pyramids. Some were covered in blocks of white stone and gleamed at the touch of the moon-disc, others stood as rough-faced and crumbling as the hillsides themselves.

But Hori's eyes were on the great walled enclosure, which now lay directly ahead of them. The run of its immense wall was broken along its length by small temples. A great stone entrance stood at the corner nearest them. Yet no great doors hung there. Instead the doorway appeared to be no more than a shadowy slit, wide enough for a King's procession of his most honoured guests and priests, but no more. However the boy's eyes did not linger there. Instead they turned to rest on the pyramid, which rose from out of the moon-white sand at the far end of the enclosure. It was a colossal, silvered, stairway to the gods.

'Aah, it is truly magnificent,' whispered Hori. 'King Djoser was truly a mighty king indeed to build this so many lifetimes ago.' Without further words, he set off towards the pyramid.

Miut padded behind him. She ached with tiredness and was filled with unease. Her kittens now lay unmoving within her. She knew they were waiting, and soon, too soon, her womb would begin its tightenings, as it had before. Then just two kittens had slid from her womb into the quiet darkness of the Lame-Priest's bed. Now she eyed each shadowed entrance they passed and wondered if within it lay another such safe and comfortable place.

As they approached the entrance to the enclosure, Miut raised her nose and sniffed. The faint smell of roasting meat hung on the night breeze. It was irresistible. She broke into a trot and overtook the boy.

'Stop Miut, we must not be seen.' He grabbed at her. But it was too late. Miut knew where she wanted to be and nothing, not even the boy, was going to stop her now. She swung right, away from the temple gateway, towards the fire, which she was sure burned nearby.

Just beyond the first rise, she saw it. The fire burned red and gold in a small pit dug into the sand. A large, flat, cooking stone lay like a small bridge across the pit and on it, two large slabs of meat sizzled and spat. One man was adding wood to the fire, a second tended the meat. The rich smell that filled the air made her whiskers tingle and saliva pooled in her mouth.

Beyond the fire, two long-legged dogs lay stretched out on the sand. Miut paused. The dogs raised their pointed muzzles and stared at her, but apart from a wave of their feathered tails and a twitch of their feathered ears, they did not move.

Miut watched them uneasily, until she saw the ropes that tethered them to a nearby rock. She moved closer to the fire. The men looked up as she approached, her tail tall and straight behind her. She sat down beside the pit of fire and stared unblinkingly up at the nearest man. He was taller than the other, and his belly was as large as a river cow.

He looked down, saw her, and spat into the sand. 'See what the desert wind has brought us, Penou.'

The second man was as wiry as a desert fox. He studied Miut intently. 'We have seen her before, Kenna. I would know that tail anywhere. Remember when we crossed the river to the Temple of Osiris. She was the High Priest's cat.'

Swollen-Belly stared at Miut. 'What is she doing here?'

Desert-Fox used the back of his hand to wipe away the sweat prickling his forehead. 'How should I know? I do not have the wisdom of Thoth. But we were told to look out for things that are strange.'

'And I reckon this is strange enough. Cats do not swim rivers. Nor do they climb hills when they are heavy with kittens.' Swollen-Belly peered down at Miut. 'What's this round her neck? Something of value maybe.' He reached his hand down. 'Let me see…'

A voice cut commandingly through the darkness. 'Stop. Leave her. She is with me, Kenna.' Hori stepped forward. He nodded at the two men. 'She is with me,' he repeated, 'and our business is ours alone.' He turned to Desert-Fox, his forehead wrinkled in thought. 'And you are Penou. You are both workers in stone. I have seen you working in the House of Books, in the Temple of Osiris. I am sure you know me.'

The two men had been motionless, like statues, since the boy's arrival. However, at this they both came to life.

'Of course, we know you, Hori,' said Swollen-Belly with a small bow, 'son of Khay.'

Miut's ears twitched uneasily at the oiliness of his voice.

Desert-Fox nodded. 'I remember you too, Hori. We were there after the Flood. There was much to repair. The waters rose high this season.'

'You speak the truth,' agreed the boy. He glanced round the empty desert. 'But why are you here, roasting meat in the night?'

'We have spent many days preparing the High Priest's tomb,' said Swollen-Belly. 'Now we wait to wish him well as he passes by on his final journey.'

'So the procession has not yet arrived?'

'Not yet,' said Swollen-Belly, 'but it should not be long. Though why the ceremonies have to be held after the fall of the sun-disc, I do not know.'

'I am sure the High Priest Heteb had his reasons,' said the boy. 'Now I will leave you to your meal. Come Miut.'

Miut lay down, her eyes fixed on the spitting meat. She was not going anywhere with an empty belly.

'Stop, Hori,' Desert-Fox raised his hand, 'do not hurry away. Let us have the honour of feeding the little goddess... and you too if you have the need for hot meat. It is fresh-killed.' He pointed at the dogs and said proudly, 'They are young. It was their first gazelle. They chased it as the sun-disc sank and killed it cleanly.'

The boy gave a tired smile. 'Thank you. If you are sure you can spare some...? I cannot remember when last I ate. My father will surely reward you for your generosity.'

'I doubt it,' muttered Swollen-Belly, so quietly that only Miut heard him. He picked a knife off a nearby rock and turned it so it gleamed coldly in the light of the moon-disc. 'That should be sharp enough,' he said with a smile, which did not reach his eyes.

'Stop teasing the boy, Penou,' cut in Desert-Fox cheerfully, 'or you'll have him thinking all sorts.' He picked up a bowl and handed it to Swollen-Belly. 'Fill this. And if they wish for more, fill it again.'

The bowl was soon piled high with thick slices of steaming meat. Swollen-Belly handed it to the boy. 'Go on then eat, both of you. And take your time. Whatever your business, it will be better completed on a full stomach.'

'Thank you, Penou,' said the boy as he sat down beside Miut. He placed half the meat on a flat rock in front of Miut.

She sank her teeth into the hot, sweet flesh. When she next looked up the two men had returned to their fire, and they were helping themselves to meat. The murmuring of their voices was a soft hum in her ear, nothing more. Hori saw she had finished and refilled his, now empty, bowl with water from a nearby pitcher and set it in front of her. She drank long and deeply.

Leaning back against a rock, the boy drew her towards him so that she lay on the sand in the crook of his arm. The warmth of his body and the fire soothed her. Surely the kittens would wait a while longer...?

Hori leant down and whispered in her ear, 'We will stay here a while, Miut. When the procession arrives, we will find Hapu. Until then we can do nothing for the tomb will be guarded by others.'

For a while there was silence, and Miut listened to the spitting of the fire and the sounds of the desert night. A fox yelped for its mate in a distant valley, a snake rustled behind a nearby rock, bats squeaked as they hunted insects in the night-sky.

Beside her the boy's breathing changed and became deep and regular. She knew he slept. She lay still and watched the two men sitting beside the fire. She watched as Desert-Fox stood up and stole away into the shadows, and later she watched as he returned as silently as he had left.

It was just a little later that she realised there was something familiar about the shape of the rocks surrounding them. A memory stirred from her kittenhood. A tunnel, dark and quiet, lay not far away. She rose to her feet and slipped from the boy's side.

She had not gone more than a few steps before she stopped, her ears twitching. A sound strange to the desert hung on the breeze. At first it was as quiet as a heartbeat, but it grew steadily louder. She knew what it was. Music. People…

It was at that moment she felt the first small tightening in her womb. It was as gentle as the shiver of a spider's web at the touch of a river breeze. But she knew she could stay no longer.

Swollen-Belly and Desert-Rat murmured to each other beside the fire, and the boy slept as Miut stalked out into the desert night.

She climbed slowly up the nearest slope and sat for a while on the rocky summit in a puddle of moonlight, her tail curled neatly round her. Immediately below her lay the dark, cavernous mouth of the Covered Way. As she watched, the procession began spilling out into the desert night.

First came the musicians dressed in white tunics holding drums and pipes, cymbals and bells. As they walked, they played. Miut's ears twitched as the beat of the drums and the high, wild notes of the pipes floated high on the night-breeze.

Next came two oxen with gleaming, sweat-soaked flanks, and behind them the great funeral sled they had pulled up from the Temple of Ptah. On the platform, under the swaying canopy, lay a painted coffin shaped like a sleeping man.

Then out onto the silver sand strode a figure unlike all who had gone before. He wore a tunic made from the skin of a spotted desert cat, and in his hand he held the staff of power. On his head he wore a mask. Its tall, pointed ears, long snout and rows of dagger teeth were all terrible and familiar to Miut. She shuddered and the fur along her spine rose. It was the head of the Jackal-God himself. Only the figure's mouth and chin were free of it.

Behind the Jackal-Priest came other priests. Each wore a long, white robe, and a god-creature's mask, which part-covered their face. There was the Ram, the Crocodile, the Beetle, the Falcon and the Hawk. Miut knew them all. Their chanting rose into the desert night...

'We follow you, oh most powerful, High Priest
We guard your path.
We keep your body safe so that your soul may return.
Soon you will travel the path into the Underworld.
In the Hall of Judgement
Anubis will weigh your heart on the scales of truth.
It will be as light as the feather of Ma'at.

The power of your spells will please Osiris.
You will become whole. You will pass into the Afterlife.
We will bring you gifts. We will guard your name.'

The breeze died and the voices faded. Miut lay down and rested her head on her paws, her eyes never leaving the procession below. The tightenings had left her for now. She could wait and watch a while and feel the cool night breeze on her fur.

An army of bearers now spilled out of the covered way. Some carried stools, small tables and baskets bulging with unseen treasures. Others carried rugs rolled like scrolls, bundles of spears, arrows and knives. In their footsteps came men carrying chests, some so heavy that two had to share the weight of them.

Following the chests, came yet more bearers. These carried baskets of fruit and trays of bread, and behind them others rolled wooden casks along the ground. And in their footsteps came girls in white, but they did not walk, they danced, twisting and twirling among the rocks. At the end came the family of the High Priest. Miut remembered how they had stroked her whenever they came to visit the High Priest in the Temple. She heard the truth of their love for him in their cries of grief at his leaving.

The Lame-Priest was not there.

By the time the tail of the procession had left the causeway, the head had regrouped and was threading its way up the rock-strewn hillside, towards the great pyramid enclosure. As they passed beneath Miut, the air was a tumult of music, chanting and cries of grief.

A tightening sharper than before ran through her. Distracted by the pain and the noise below, she heard the movement behind her too late.

Hard hands held and lifted her. She spat and struggled, her claws spiking at the fingers that held her. But she could not break free.

'Patience, little goddess. I knew you would not be far from that boy. All I had to do was look. You will not escape this time.' Miut knew that voice. Snake-Eyes.

Miut struggled harder. A claw struck at his chest but it hit only metal. An oval medallion glistened in the moonlight, strange symbols danced before her eyes.

Snake-Eyes laughed. 'Struggle as you may but you will not hurt me, Daughter of Bastet, for in the light of the moon-disc the mark of Seth protects me.'

Then she was being forced through an opening. She knew the sweet, wooden smell. He had placed her in a basket of woven reeds. The top closed down on her. There were no more stars and the light of the moon-disc had vanished.

She scratched at the sides with her claws, and she tore at the reeds with her teeth. But they were too thick and too strong. She was trapped.

The basket lurched as it was lifted, and then swung unevenly as it was carried. For a while there was just laboured breathing to be heard. There was more noise, chanting, music, voices…

'MIAOOOOW,' she called as loudly as she could.

Then the noise faded, and there were only whispered voices and soft footsteps.

'MIAOOOOW,' she called again.

The basket jolted once more and then all was still.

The voice of Snake-Eyes slithered into the basket. 'The waiting will not be long, Daughter of Bastet. Soon you will walk with the High Priest. He will soon join you here in his tomb.'

A laugh as sour as an unripe lemon quivered in the airless darkness. Soft footsteps faded into the distance. Then there was only silence.

Miut lay for a while listening, but all she could hear was her own breathing. The tightenings slowed and faded. At last her eyes shut, and she slept.

CHAPTER 26

When I woke up my head was full of Neshi's gloating face and my cheeks were wet with tears. Miut was trapped in the basket about to give birth. What would happen to her and her kittens?

It took me a few moments to remember where I was. Then panic hit me. How long had I been asleep? I pulled myself back up to the gap and peered cautiously out. The sun was high in the sky. It must be after midday. Lily would be frantic. I had to get back. There was no trace of the man as I left the shelter of the Sphinx and made my way up to the crest of the hill. Nor was there any sign of him as I looked down to where I'd left Akil and the donkeys. Lily and Zac were there. Zac gesticulated furiously at me as I hurried down slope towards them.

'Wherever have you been?' demanded Lily. 'We've been so worried. Akil and Zac have looked for you everywhere, while I looked after the donkeys.'

'I'm truly sorry,' I said overwhelmed by guilt as I recognised the fear in her voice. I decided to tell the truth, some of it at least. 'I went exploring, sat down and fell asleep.'

Lily glared at me, even as she held my hand tight. 'I was frightened I'd lost you.'

I squeezed her fingers. 'You'll never lose me,' I said and meant it. 'How was the pyramid?'

Before she could answer, Zac interrupted and said with a most reproachful look, 'We must go now. You must talk as we ride. Mrs Dora will be most worried where we are.'

Zac needn't have been concerned about Aunt Dora. She was still at her meeting when we got back. Lily and I headed for the garden with the picnic bag. I also had my sketchbook and Lily had a book. There was no sign of the Garden Cat.

We ate our sandwiches in silence. I remembered how once we had been so close that it was like we looked at things through the same pair of eyes. We wore identical clothes, never went anywhere without each other and most of the time we held hands or had our arms twined round each other. We would finish each other's sentences and we even had our own language, which only we understood.

But all that had changed. Lily was so very often ill. Mama and Papa seemed to just forget about me and spent their time worrying about her. I did understand, really I did, and I tried not to mind. But there was a wall between us. Lily had to be protected, looked after, kept safe. Now I wanted, or needed, to talk to her as I would have once, but I dared not break down that wall. While she was much stronger now than she had been for years, was she strong enough for this?

Worst of all though was the feeling that I wasn't part of my own life any more, let alone Lily's. Miut's world felt more real to me.

To take my mind off the past, I opened my tin of crayons and settled down to sketch the urns of blazing flowers. I forced myself to concentrate, but my thoughts kept wandering back to the great step-sided pyramid lit by moonlight. In my mind, it had become just blocks of silver-white, and deepest black. Then I remembered Miut sitting all alone on the hillside in a puddle of moonlight. But she hadn't been alone. Neshi had been lurking in the shadows.

And all the time my brush was moving, adding colours, shapes, shadows. Until suddenly I was crying. Tears splattered onto the picture and they wouldn't stop. I dropped the sketchbook and tried to wipe away my tears with the back of my hand.

I realised Lily was staring at me, white-faced. She put down her book and came and sat beside me on the bench.

'Rose,' she said softly, 'I know something's wrong. Tell me.'

I sniffed. She handed me her best lace handkerchief. Her eyes held mine. 'Tell me.'

'It's nothing,' I lied.

'Stop trying to protect me. I'm stronger than you think. You have to trust me.' She looked down at my sketchbook and her face changed.

'Is it that bad?'

She shook her head. 'Just not what I expected.' I looked at the picture and it wasn't what I expected either. There was no garden, just a pyramid, moonlit desert and a cat.

Lily frowned. 'The pyramid is a strange shape isn't it? Why has it got sides like steps? Though I've seen something like it before...' she paused and frowned as she tried to remember. 'So where is it?'

'The City of the Dead.'

'Where's that?'

'Not far.' *Only thousands of years away.*

She pulled a face. 'But why have you drawn it?'

I shrugged. 'Not sure.'

'And you have drawn another cat? Why are you always drawing cats?'

'I'm not,' I snapped. I just couldn't get Miut out of my head. Did I even really want to, however her story might end?

Lily gave me a searching look. 'Talk to me, Rose. You must. Or I'll tell Aunt Dora you're ill.'

I shook my head furiously. 'No. You can't. Papa told us most particularly not to worry her.'

Lily fixed her eyes on me and said with unfamiliar firmness, 'I need to know what's going on in your head.'

I knew keeping everything hidden was eating me up. The wall between us had to be breached. I needed to put the Lunatic Asylum to the back of my mind. 'If I explain, you must never tell anyone. Promise?'

She nodded. 'Go on.'

I had to trust her. I began with the man in the cream suit following me at the market and then at Giza. I told her how frightened I'd been. I also explained that I thought it must all have something to do with my stone cat, which Mr Baxter seemed far too interested in.

'It must be genuine,' I said, 'and it may be really valuable. Why else would anyone follow me? I think Mr Baxter sent that man after me. How else would he know I had anything worth stealing?'

'But you haven't shown him your cat,' said Lily with a frown. 'Maybe if you had, he would know it was just a copy. Whatever he is searching for might be something entirely different.'

I was certain she was wrong. So I told her about Miut, Hori, their mission, and right at the end I told her about Neshi and the basket. All the time I was talking she never took her eyes off my face.

'You believe every single thing you've told me?' she whispered, shaking her head.

I nodded. I was exhausted. Telling her had been like reliving it all.

'You really think,' said Lily slowly, 'there's a man with strange blue eyes, who has nothing better to do than chase you round Cairo. That there's a well-known Egyptologist who wants to steal your stone cat. There's also the ghost of a cat, which keeps turning up to save you from dangerous situations. And you're dreaming about things, which you believe really happened over three thousand years ago?'

I stared at her, my thoughts spinning. Why hadn't I realised it sooner? Lily was right. My ghost cat was Miut herself. Of course, I'd no idea how, but it had to be her.

Lily sighed. 'How can I?' She looked at me with anxious eyes. 'You mustn't say one word of this to anyone else. They'll think you're mad. You'll be locked away in an asylum.'

'Even you thought someone had been in our bedroom.'

She stared at me, her eyes huge and dark. 'Possibly. But I'm so worried about you. Maybe I should speak to Aunt Dora...' Her voice trailed away.

My heart missed a beat. 'No!' I almost shouted. I tried to calm my voice. 'I expect you're right. It must be the heat or something.'

She gave me a long look but then said, 'So no more ancient cats, blue-eyed men or worrying about Mr Baxter.'

'I'll try,' I said.

'Alright then,' she said, 'I'll say nothing... for the moment.' She gave me a small smile before returning to her book.

CHAPTER 27

Rose could hear the passage clock striking four as Aunt Dora appeared in the garden, bringing with her a large jug of *assir limoon*. She was still dressed in black but the silk had a rich sheen to it, and her necklace of black jet glittered as rays of the sinking sun touched it. Her cheeks were flushed pink. She looked years younger. I should have been pleased for her but instead a deep sense of foreboding filled me.

'Did the meeting at the museum go well, Aunt Dora?' asked Lily.

She smiled. 'It did, thank you. Then Mr Baxter took me for tea at Shepheard's Hotel. It was so kind of him.'

I sipped my drink and wondered desperately if I could say anything to warn Aunt Dora about the dark side of Mr Baxter. She knew his wives had died. She had no idea of the wolf hidden inside him. It couldn't have occurred to her that he had anything to do with their deaths. Why should it? I'd no proof either and no motive, just a feeling deep inside me that Mr Baxter would destroy anyone who stood in his way. But what did he want from my aunt? It couldn't be money. I looked up at the House of Shadows. It was so shabby, and there were no servants apart from Ezra. It was obvious Aunt Dora didn't have a fortune. Maybe it had something to do with Uncle Arthur's papers and collection? Maybe some of them were more valuable than anyone thought? Like my cat?

My thoughts were interrupted when Aunt Dora added, 'Oh dear, I nearly forgot to tell you that Mrs Hodges was at Shepheard's too. She enquired what you were doing to pass the time in Cairo and was kind enough to make several suggestions as to other expeditions you might enjoy.' Dora looked at me and smiled, 'She particularly asked after you, Rose. I said you were well.'

Mrs Hodges was probably hoping I'd achieved my mission and replaced the cat in the Collection of Curiosities. While questions filled my mind, Lily was telling Aunt Dora about our day at Giza.

After a while I realised Aunt Dora was looking at me and frowning. 'You are very quiet, Rose. Are you feeling quite well?' She leant over and felt my forehead. Her hand felt cool. 'You are hot. An early night for you. Rest will cool your blood.'

'I'm fine now, Aunt Dora, honestly.'

She looked down and must have seen my sketchbook. 'May I see what you've been working on?'

I handed her the sketchbook. She flipped it open and stared at the picture for a long time. At last she looked up at me. 'This is wonderful, Rose. You are talented. It is a remarkable picture of the Step Pyramid. Did you know that it is thought to be the oldest stone building in the world?'

And it's where Miut is imprisoned. I realised I was trembling. I took a sip of water to steady myself.

Aunt Dora picked up my picture and studied it again. She frowned. 'It really is extraordinary. It's so detailed... and to paint it in the moonlight, most original. But there's something strange about it... I can't quite put my finger on it.' There was another pause. 'Yes,' she said triumphantly, 'the sides of the pyramid are crumbling, but not as much as they are when you visit it now. The enclosure walls are all standing. Even some of the temples are complete. I've never seen anything like it.' She peered at it again, and then at me. 'However have you done this? It's as if you've stepped back in time. Not to when it was built, but to sometime in between then and now.'

I could feel Lily's startled eyes on me. I gave a her a small reassuring smile and said quietly, 'Maybe not so mad after all?'

She looked at me and whispered, 'Maybe not.'

'Bedtime,' said Aunt Dora when we had finished supper, 'Rose, Lily, you both look exhausted. And I'll have an early night too. Mr Baxter is coming first thing to take some boxes away. Just Arthur's excavation notes and diaries. Apparently of little interest to anyone except Mr Baxter, who was kind enough to say he would sort through them. He will let me know if there's anything I should see.'

I gazed at her, horrified. If the notebooks went, so would any hope of ever finding proof that my cat was discovered in Heteb's tomb, that there was a real connection with the High Priest, that there was a reason for my dreams.

We said goodnight. Lily was exhausted and fell asleep as soon as she got into bed. I lay awake, waiting for the house to go quiet.

I heard Aunt Dora going upstairs to her bedroom, and Ezra padding around for a while, and then all was silent.

The shutters were open and the bedroom was lit by moonlight. Elsewhere in the house the shutters would be closed and it would be dark. I slipped the cat into my nightdress pocket. Maybe it would make me brave? However scared I felt, I had to find Uncle Arthur's notebooks.

I eased myself out of bed, picked up the lamp along with some matches and slipped out of the bedroom door. The only sound was the steady ticking of the clock. The corridor was also lit by moonlight, which streamed in through the glass-topped garden door. But the stairs to the library descended into a well of inky blackness. I lit the lamp then lowered the wick so there was just enough light for me to see my way. Holding the lamp tightly, I tiptoed down the stairs.

The library was thick with oily black shadows as I quietly pushed open the door and stepped inside. I made my way across to the nearest window, avoiding the heaps of boxes, and pulled back the shutters. Moonlight from the garden flooded in. I looked in vain for any sign of Miut.

Turning back to the boxes I realised I didn't need the help of the lamp to read the labels. The nearest box was full of books and had "Ramesses II" written across the top in large black letters. The next box was empty. The third was much smaller than the other two. I peered at the label. 'Oh, yes,' I whispered as I read the words *Sakkara - Tomb of High Priest Heteb*. I knelt down and carefully opened the flap. My hands were shaking as I pulled out the first of several leather-bound notebooks.

The cover was labelled *Excavation Journal – Tomb of Heteb* and its pages were covered with close lines of tiny, cramped handwriting. I held the lamp close but it was impossible to read. I guessed I would need daylight and a magnifying glass to decipher it. There were also plans of what appeared to be rooms, a map and some carefully labelled diagrams.

The next notebook was entirely different. The first pages were covered with detailed drawings of beads, fragments of pots and slivers of painted tiles. Every time I turned a page, I held my breath hoping that I would see my little stone cat looking back at me. Twice I thought I did, but when I examined them carefully, they were drawings of other cats. Near the middle of the notebook there were several pages of human figures, some with animal heads. They looked peculiarly familiar. I picked up the lamp and, carrying the notebook, I crossed to the glass display cabinet. I was right. Some of the little figures in Uncle Arthur's collection had definitely come from Heteb's tomb, including the figure of Anubis I'd particularly noticed that first day. I even recognised the cats that I'd just been studying in the notebook.

Somewhere deep inside the walls of the library, something rustled and scratched. I shivered even though the room was hot and stuffy. A floorboard creaked. I froze, hardly daring to breathe, and listened. There was only silence. It must just have been the old house creaking. I longed to be safely back in my bed, but instead I returned to Heteb's box and pulled out the remaining notebooks. There were more plans and notes, but no more sketches.

I was just about to give up when, at the very bottom of the box,

I found a leather folder. Tucked into it were several loose pages. I took a quick look. The pages formed a series of beautiful coloured drawings of ancient Egyptians hunting, cooking, working in the fields. I remembered Zac telling us that the tomb had some wall paintings, maybe these were copies of those paintings.

My knees throbbed from kneeling on the hard floor, and my back and neck ached from bending over to see what I was doing. I'd found nothing about my cat. For the last time, I carefully examined the notebook containing the drawings. It was only then I noticed a small tatter of torn paper between the two cat sketches, and I realised a page had been torn out. I was certain that on the missing page had been a drawing of my cat.

Questions swirled round my head. Maybe Uncle Arthur had realised the cat was valuable or especially important in some way? If so, maybe he had wanted to protect it and torn out the record of its existence, hiding the cat itself in his Collection of Curiosities. What better place to hide the cat than where it would not be recognised as being anything other than a worthless curiosity? I wondered what Uncle Arthur had done with the torn out page. Had he hidden it or destroyed it?

I gazed round at the half-empty bookshelves and sea of boxes. Where would I begin looking for the missing page? It was hopeless.

I was packing the notebooks and folder back into their box, when the strange but familiar sound of claws scratching on wood stopped me. I swung round, but the room was empty. The scratching must have come from outside. Leaving the lamp on the floor by Heteb's box, I peered out into the moonlit garden. At first, I saw nothing unusual. But then a shadow moved. It was far too big for a cat. My stomach twisted as I saw there was a man standing beside a palm.

How long had he been there, watching me through the open shutters? It was at that moment he stepped out of the shadows and moved towards the house. There was no mistaking his silhouette. I couldn't make out what he was wearing now, but I knew he had fair hair and had been wearing a cream suit earlier.

I turned to run, trying to avoid the boxes, but they were too close together. My right foot hit the nearest one and I fell. I found myself sprawled across Heteb's box. I hauled myself upright, grabbed hold of the lamp, and half stumbled, half ran to the door. I pulled it shut behind me, and made for the stairs. I reached the bedroom and slipped inside. Lily was still soundly asleep. I peered cautiously out of the window into the garden. There was no sign of the man.

My thoughts spun. Should I warn Aunt Dora that there had been a strange man in her garden? But Papa had said not to worry her, and the man had vanished. In the end, I simply crawled into bed. I let my mind wander back in time. Miut was trapped. What was going to happen next? I needed to know, even if her story ended badly.

My eyes closed. Perhaps everything would be clearer in the morning.

CHAPTER 28

I was deep in a smooth, velvet darkness when I heard a voice calling my name. I tried to ignore it, but it wouldn't go away.

'Rose. Rose. Do wake up, my dear.'

I sat up and rubbed my eyes. Lily's bed was empty.

Aunt Dora was looking anxiously at me. 'You were in such a deep sleep, my dear, we thought you would never wake. Are you feeling quite well?'

I smiled at her reassuringly. 'I was just tired, that's all.'

She gave a relieved smile. 'When you are ready, we will be in the dining room. Lily is already there.' She closed the door quietly behind her.

I was suddenly aware of two things. Firstly, I'd slept soundly all night. Secondly, I hadn't dreamed about Miut. I flung back my pillow to look underneath. There was no sign of my cat. I dug my hand deep into my nightdress pocket. It wasn't there either. Frantically I searched under the bed, in the drawers, in the cupboard, under the washstand. I knelt on the floor, blood roaring in my ears, trying to steady my racing thoughts. When had I last had it? It was with me in the library, I was sure of that. I remembered searching the boxes, reading the notebooks, seeing the man in the garden, Miut's scratching, and at last I remembered tripping over Heteb's box. I jumped up. I knew exactly where my cat must be.

Without wasting any time washing, I pulled on my skirt, vest, stockings and yesterday's blouse. I dragged a brush through my hair and headed for the library. Without stopping to worry if anyone was inside, I pushed open the door. I saw instantly that many of the boxes had gone, including the one near the window marked Heteb.

As I made my way slowly up to the dining room, I made a plan.

The dining room windows were open as usual and the room was cool. Aunt Dora and Lily looked up as I entered.

'Gracious, Rose,' exclaimed Aunt Dora, 'that was quick. But I'm sure you are hungry after all that sleep.'

I shook my head; the thought of food made my stomach churn. 'Not yet, Aunt Dora. Maybe I can have something later?' I took a deep breath and added as calmly as I could. 'I was wondering if it would be possible for Lily and me to call on Mr Baxter this morning?'

I could feel Lily's startled eyes on me.

Aunt Dora raised an eyebrow. 'I have to say I didn't get the impression that you liked him very much, but now you want to visit him?'

I looked at her wide-eyed. 'After yesterday, Lily and I have a great many questions that I am sure he can answer about the pyramids and the Sphinx. And he did sound as if he would be happy to see us.'

'Very well,' Aunt Dora smiled. 'I'll send Ezra round to see if Mr Baxter will be at home to you this morning. There's a good chance he will be. He was here early this morning collecting the first load of boxes. He said he would start work on them at once.'

I looked down at my hands. They were trembling. What if he'd already found my cat in Heteb's box?

'Please don't bother Ezra,' I said quickly, 'he's so busy here. If we go right now, I promise if Mr Baxter doesn't want us to stay, we'll come straight home.' I gazed at Aunt Dora with what I hoped were huge, pleading eyes.

She laughed. 'Very well. But don't make a nuisance of yourselves or outstay your welcome.' She paused before adding,

'I've planned a real treat for you later today. This afternoon Zac will take you to Sakkara on your donkeys and you'll spend the night there, camping in a tent.'

I gazed speechlessly at Aunt Dora. That very night I was going to be where Miut and Hori had been all those thousands of years ago. It was more important than ever that I found my little stone cat.

I took a deep breath. 'That is a wonderful idea, Aunt Dora,' I managed, 'we love camping.' I ignored Lily's horrified gaze and the wave of guilt washing through me. I knew the possibility of a tent full of huge Egyptian spiders terrified Lily. I pushed the guilt firmly away. My dreams were taking me to Sakkara because there was something unfinished there. I must go there too, but not without my cat.

Aunt Dora stood up. 'Good. I will be in the library when you are ready to go. I will give you a map so you can find Mr Baxter's address easily.'

'How could you do that?' said Lily as we made our way to the bedroom. I could see tears shimmering at the back of her eyes.

I took her hand. 'Camping will be fun, honestly. I will keep every spider away from you, I promise.'

She frowned. 'You'd better.'

We brushed our hair, cleaned our teeth and put on our sun bonnets in silence.

'Alright,' said Lily at last, 'why are we suddenly going to visit Mr Baxter? Aunt Dora was right. You hate him.'

'He has something I want.'

'What?'

I told her about my night time visit to the library and how I'd tripped over the box. 'So my cat must be in the box. Please, Lily, you must help me get it back.' I didn't tell her about the missing page in the notebook, being watched or being saved yet again by Miut's ghost.

Lily sighed. 'What happens if he refuses to give it back?'

I shook my head. 'If we go right now, perhaps Heteb's box will still be sealed. I just need you to distract him so I have time to search for it.'

'I just have to distract him?' said Lily with a worried frown. 'That's all? You're sure?'

'Yes,' I said hoping desperately I was right.

Aunt Dora was at her desk in the strangely bare library. She stood up as we entered and handed Lily a piece of paper. 'This should help you find your way easily enough.' She frowned. 'I wish I'd time to come with you.' She gestured at the remaining boxes. 'Once these have gone I'll have much more time for you two, although I am sure your parents will arrive soon.'

Guilt washed through me yet again. How could I have become so concerned about the past that yet again I'd forgotten about Max.

'Have you heard anything about Max?' asked Lily.

Aunt Dora shook her head. 'I would have told you if I had. I am sure that we would have had a telegram if the news had been bad. There's no need for you to worry.'

A memory stirred. 'Please may I ask a question, Aunt Dora?'

'Of course.'

'The other day you said our uncle's papers and books had brought only worry and unhappiness? I wondered if you would mind telling us why?'

Lily frowned at me. I ignored her.

Aunt Dora sighed. 'He spent four years of his life searching for clues as to the whereabouts of the tomb of a High Priest called Heteb. He lived in the time of Ramesses II. Your uncle spent days and sometimes nights, pouring over old books and ancient documents. When at last he worked out where the tomb must be, it still took nearly the whole digging season to find the entrance. When he did discover it, he was so excited.' A shadow of a smile crossed our aunt's mouth. 'He was like a young boy who had been given the keys to a sweetshop.' Her voice died away.

'But when they opened it up...?' I prompted.

Her mouth tightened. 'It'd been robbed and badly damaged... it was deeply disappointing.' Her voice drifted to silence.

There were still so many questions. Like, why had our uncle become so interested in Heteb in the first place?

'But what I don't understand,' said Lily thoughtfully, 'is how he knew about Heteb?'

I looked at her, but her eyes were on Aunt Dora.

'Arthur came across his name in some book. He was intrigued.'

I'd seen that book. That book had been the beginning of everything. The tomb might have been robbed, but I knew some things had been left behind.

Lily looked thoughtfully at me, then at our aunt. 'Had everything been taken by the robbers?'

'No, my dear, there were a few small things left behind. But poor Arthur was sure there was more to be found. Then he became ill, believing that he was being watched. He even started hiding things in strange places. After we were burgled, he would hardly leave the house. In the end, he became seriously unwell.'

My thoughts spun and the pieces of the jigsaw dropped into place. My guesses had been right. Uncle Arthur had deliberately hidden my cat in the Collection of Curiosities. He had been right about being watched, and the burglar, Mr Baxter, had been searching for things taken from the tomb.

I could see tears glistening in Aunt Dora's eyes. I had to change the subject. I had other questions anyway. 'Were names important to ancient Egyptians?'

Aunt Dora sniffed, then nodded. 'Indeed, they believed that knowing someone's name gave you power over them.'

'To destroy the magician who has turned his magic against me, I must know his name.' Khay's voice was clear and strong in my head.

'Goodness, Rose.' Aunt Dora was gazing worriedly at me. 'I think you need to lie down. You can visit Mr Baxter another day.'

I shook my head. 'I am quite well, truly. Some air will do me good.'

To my huge relief Aunt Dora nodded. 'Very well. Keep together. Be polite and come straight home when you are done.'

CHAPTER 29

Mr Baxter lived about a ten-minute walk from the House of Shadows. We spoke little on the way. I was thinking about how Uncle Arthur had been worried he was being watched, and how he had been hiding things before his death. Had the cat, and any evidence concerning it, been what he had been so desperate to hide? Who had he thought was looking for it and why? What was so special about my cat, apart from it being the loveliest thing I'd ever owned?

The street where Mr Baxter lived was narrow and the houses far smaller than the House of Shadows, but they were well kept and obviously lived in by people of some wealth. I rang the bell and Mr Baxter answered the door himself, explaining that his maid had gone out on an errand and would be back shortly. He seemed delighted to see us, welcoming us in with a wide, wolf smile.

He ushered us into the parlour, which was a small room with a spectacular view out over the Nile. Waving us towards two chairs and small side table he said, 'Do please sit down. You must be thirsty after your walk. Do you like fresh orange juice? Just give me a minute. Oh, and I believe there are some freshly made chocolate biscuits.' Without waiting for us to answer, he vanished, closing the door firmly behind him.

Lily looked at me. 'No sign of any boxes here or in the hallway.'

'No. They must be in his study. Aunt Dora said he was going to start work on them immediately.'

There was a small oval mirror hanging between two

bookcases. Lily went over to it and peered into it, patting her ringlets into place. 'He could have taken them somewhere else,' she said, her mirror-eyes on me.

'I know.'

'It's a pretty mirror.' She pointed to a small brass plaque fixed to the top of the oval. 'Those are hieroglyphs aren't they?'

I went to stand beside her and peered up. I swallowed. I'd seen those particular hieroglyphs before. If only I could remember where.

'The mirror is of interest?'

We swung round to find Mr Baxter staring at us. He was holding a jug of orange juice.

Lily threw him her warmest smile. 'It is such a pretty mirror. We were just wondering about the hieroglyphs?'

'Ah, yes. They say "Welcome". A pretty enough thing but purely a tourist item, I'm afraid.'

I looked up at the hieroglyphs again. There was something about looking up at them... and the way the brass shone in the sunlight. A memory quivered... not in sunlight... but in moonlight.

My legs suddenly felt like they belonged to someone else. I sat down on the nearest chair and leaned forwards trying to steady my spinning head. I heard Lily and Mr Baxter fussing about me. They sounded miles away. Lily was asking for smelling salts.

'I'm fine, truly,' I whispered, opening my eyes to find Lily staring white-faced at me. 'Just some water and I'll be quite well again.'

Lily turned to Mr Baxter, who was peering anxiously over her shoulder at me.

'Could Rose have a glass of water?

'Of course,' replied Mr Baxter heading for the door.

'What happened, Rose?' whispered Lily. I could hear the fear in her voice.

I sat up. 'Those hieroglyphs,' I pointed at the mirror, 'they don't say WELCOME.'

Lily shook her head. 'How do you know?'

An oval medallion swinging from Neshi's neck glinting in the light of the moon disc, strange symbols dancing before Miut's eyes. And Neshi saying they were the mark of Seth.

I went on. 'They say SETH. Why is he lying?'

Perhaps it was because I sounded so certain that I saw real doubt flicker in Lily's eyes.

Before we could say anything else, Mr Baxter was back, a plate of biscuits in one hand and a glass of water in the other.

'So,' he said, handing me the water, 'when you are recovered, Rose, may I ask to what do I owe the pleasure of your visit?' He sat down and helped Lily and himself to a glass of orange juice.

I took a sip of water. I needed time to think.

Lily gave me the flicker of a smile and then looked intently at Mr Baxter. 'We found what you told us about magic in ancient times so interesting and we'd like to know more.'

I gazed at Lily in admiration, then added, 'Maybe you could tell us about the magician-priest and the tomb our uncle discovered?'

Mr Baxter appeared pleased. 'I will most certainly tell you what I can. But where to begin? Aah yes... Heteb was High Priest at the Temple of Osiris. But being High Priest was not enough for him, he wanted to be the greatest magician in all of Egypt.'

Mr Baxter paused dramatically and took a sip from his glass.

'And...?' prompted Lily.

'Heteb wanted to be remembered forever for the power of his magic. He spent many years studying the ancient writings which filled the House of Life , and he did indeed become a great magician...'

And my head was full of dark alcoves where rows of scrolls lay neatly in recesses in the walls.

'... and the story is that he wrote down many of his spells and used a seal to close each scroll, which absorbed the magic of the words written there. This became known as the Great Seal of Heteb. Unfortunately every powerful man has enemies, and Heteb was no exception.' Mr Baxter paused to take another sip of his juice.

'Who were Heteb's enemies?' I asked, although I already knew.

'His enemies were worshippers of Seth, the god of the desert, darkness and chaos. They believed that if they possessed the Seal they would have magic strong enough to take over the Temple of Osiris for themselves. They would own the riches of the temple, and all the land that belonged to it, which was many thousands of acres. But even more than that, they would use the power of the Seal to banish from Egypt, the god Osiris and his son Horus. Horus was the greatest enemy of Seth and they fought endless battles against each other.

'Seth and Horus,' I heard myself whisper.

Mr Baxter threw me a sharp look but continued in the same voice as before. 'The followers of Seth believed that in the end, with the power of Heteb's Seal on their side, that Seth would vanquish Osiris. The Temple of Osiris would become the Temple of Seth. And from this temple, the Priests of Seth would see their power grow with the help of the magical Seal, and in the end, all Egypt would be theirs.'

My head was beginning to swim. I took a deep breath and my head cleared.

Mr Baxter continued, 'However Heteb learned of these plans and determined to protect the temple and Egypt from the League of Seth, as the priests of Seth came to be known. Heteb was an old man and knew he must die soon. Who would protect the Temple of Osiris after he had passed on? But most importantly of all, who would preserve the balance between Seth and Horus...'

'Ma'at,' I heard myself whisper, 'there must be balance in all things.' I was so confused. How did Mr Baxter know so much about Heteb?

This time Mr Baxter gave me a deep, searching look. 'I am impressed at your knowledge, young lady.'

'Papa is an Egyptologist,' I reminded him, 'we have been brought up on stories of the Egyptian gods.'

'Indeed, so he is.' Mr Baxter gave a small, strangely satisfied smile as he added, 'but he is a long way from here now.'

I was suddenly ice cold. I was more certain than ever that Mr Baxter had something to do with Max's accident.

Mr Baxter's cold grey eyes were on me. 'Heteb believed he would be at his most powerful when he was laid in his tomb, and when the cold, all-seeing Eye of Horus would be high in the night-sky. He had his tomb constructed near a place of ancient magic, and prepared his most powerful spells. The Seal must be with him in the afterlife so it must be with him in the tomb. But so well hidden that it would never fall into the hands of the League.' He paused.

'And what happened?' prompted Lily.

Mr Baxter shook his head. 'No one knows. Maybe the Seal survived. If it does, what will it look like? Seals come in many shapes and sizes.'

Even one so small it could hang from a cat's neck. But my little stone statue wasn't the Seal. I knew that, even if Mr Baxter didn't. What else had Uncle Arthur been hiding? Perhaps my cat had yet again been a decoy to protect the genuine Seal.

'Would any of that matter now?' asked Lily.

'There are still those who believe that if they have the Seal,' continued Mr Baxter, 'Heteb's powers will be theirs. People have searched for it throughout the centuries. Some are still searching.'

I stared at him, more pieces of the jigsaw falling neatly into place. I whispered, 'Do you mean the League of Seth still exists?

He fixed his eyes on mine. 'Yes.'

Why not ask the obvious question? 'Are you one of them?'

The Professor raised an eyebrow and laughed. 'Of course not. But if you really mean, am I searching for the Seal? Well, it is true I would like to find it, but not because it has any power – ' he gave a small laugh, ' – except to bring me a good deal of publicity, which should make my book on Heteb a bestseller.'

His eyes flickered and I knew he was lying. He wanted that Seal more than anything else in the world.

'Do you think that Uncle Arthur's papers will help you find the Seal?' I asked.

'Indeed.' Mr Baxter took a long drink. 'He wrote to me shortly before he died. I was in New York. He was excited. There was something he wanted to show me. Sadly he died before I got to see him. I am hoping that the boxes will give me all the information I need. But I am afraid your uncle was not the tidiest, or most organised, person. There may be things still left in drawers or cupboards... so if you do happen to come across anything in the house, anything at all, to do with Heteb, I would be most grateful if you would show it to me... first.'

He then added the words that must have changed everything for Lily. 'Be assured,' he said, 'I am not a poor man. I will really make it worth your while.' He gave us an encouraging smile.

Lily was staring at him with eyes like saucers. I could feel her thoughts spinning. She turned to me. 'A real treasure hunt? It'll be so exciting. Don't you agree, Rose?'

She swung round towards me, and as she did so her hand knocked her almost full glass of orange juice. It spun onto its side and golden liquid flooded onto the table, spilled over my skirt and deluged onto the rug.

'Honestly Lily,' I protested, 'you must be more careful.'

'Oh no... what a disaster... so sorry, Rose....' Her eyes caught mine. And I understood.

Mr Baxter disappeared muttering darkly about clumsy children, reappearing a few moments later armed with a cloth to begin mopping furiously at the orange flood.

'May I clean up?' I asked, already heading to the door.

'The pantry is near the end of the corridor,' snapped Mr Baxter.

The corridor was narrow and dark. The first door opened into another larger parlour. The second door revealed a wood-panelled dining room. Then came the pantry and I could see the kitchen ahead. Opposite the pantry was the only other door. I pushed it open. It was the study. With my heart hammering like a piston engine I stepped inside and closed the door behind me.

I'd never seen a room like it before. The walls were covered in black leather, but the chairs, the desk and even the rug were all a dark, rusty red – *the colour of dried blood.*

A photograph on the desk caught my eye. In all the usual tones of black, white and grey, Mr Baxter posed in front of the Great Pyramid. Beside him stood a woman. Her face was partly hidden by deep shadow. I peered closely. Then my heart missed a beat. I remembered that elusive smell of peppermint and lavender in Mr Baxter's cabin on the *SS Australia.* There was no question. It was Mrs Hodges in the photograph. She and Mr Baxter knew each other, and well enough for him to have her photograph on his desk.

I remembered how she had received a telegram and then appeared so conveniently in the boat with the offer of escorting us to Cairo. Everything must have been carefully planned. The result of all the planning was that Lily and I were in Cairo while Mama, Papa and Max were in Alexandria. Why?

Was everyone plotting against us? What about Ezra? He had stopped us looking in the boxes in Aunt Dora's study... and something else nagged at me. It was something Hori had said in the moonlight...

'... protect too this daughter of Bastet who is loved by your father Osiris, and his priests, but who is hated and feared by the followers of Seth.'

We knew Ezra had lied about Aunt Dora not liking cats. It was Ezra who didn't like cats because he was a follower of Seth. Another memory flickered into life. Both Ezra and Mr Baxter had said that our hair was *'as red as the sun as it sinks into the desert.'* That couldn't be a coincidence.

Whatever the answer was, I knew that Lily and I were in trouble.

Voices drifted through the door. Lily was chatting away

but with a note of rising desperation. Mr Baxter's replies were increasingly irritated. Time was running out.

The boxes were piled up behind the door, except for one smaller one placed on the floor behind the desk. I recognised it at once. The packing tape had been removed, but the flaps were still closed. Maybe we had arrived just in time.

I pulled open the flaps. The notebooks and the leather folder were still all there. I felt down the sides of the box. My stone cat must be in there. I felt all round. Nothing. My palms were slippery with sweat. My heart hammered frantically in my chest.

I was certain it must have been in that box. He must have already found it. Time was running out. I forced down a wave of panic.

Where had he put it? I checked the desk. It was amazingly neat. Just one pile of unopened post. However underneath the post was an architect's drawing of a building. Something about it caught my eye. It looked both strangely familiar, and unfamiliar. The heading read, "The Temple of Seth".

I was still staring at the plan, trying to make sense of it, when the sound of the parlour door opening refocused me. I looked round desperately. Where was my cat?

'How are you getting on, Rose?' called Mr Baxter.

I could hear his footsteps coming along the passage. I could hardly breathe. My cat must be here somewhere. I stared round. There was a tingling in the back of my neck. I swung to the shelves behind me. And there it was, gazing solemnly down at me from the top shelf. I stretched up and my fingers closed round its silky coolness.

When Mr Baxter pushed open the study door, I was standing in front of the window, gazing out. I turned as he stormed into the room.

'What are you doing in here?' he snapped. All pretence of charm had gone. He was pure wolf.

I gave him my biggest smile.

'I am so sorry,' I gushed, 'but the door was open and I couldn't resist looking out of your window. And you have the most wonderful view of the Nile.' At least that was true.

His eyes slid down to the box and its, now open, flaps. He looked back at me. His eyes were cold.

I ploughed on. 'I was SO interested in what you told us just now about Heteb and seeing the box there with his name on, I just had to take a quick look.'

Before he could say another word, I slipped past him and headed for the front door, signalling desperately for Lily to join me. 'We have to go now,' I called over my shoulder, 'thank you so much for your time.'

We left him gaping after us, as if he had been hit by a hurricane. I pulled open the front door and we were out into the sticky heat of the street.

We ran. But it was too hot and we soon slowed to a fast walk. All I could think about was the cat being safely in my pocket. At last Lily said impatiently, 'I assume you found it then?'

I nodded. 'It was on a shelf.'

'He will know you have taken it?'

'Yes. But it isn't stealing. It was mine in the first place. Aunt Dora gave it to me as a gift just as she gave you the silver bracelet. And why would he want to draw attention to himself by accusing me?' I didn't want to frighten Lily, but there were some things she should know. 'I saw a photograph of Mr Baxter with Mrs Hodges together at Giza.'

Lily stared at me. 'They know each other?'

'Yes.'

There was a pause as Lily turned everything over in her mind.

'If it was the Seal he was after, and he thought it might be your cat, he's seen it now, so he must know he was wrong. Maybe he can try and find from Uncle Arthur's papers what the Seal actually is.' Lily added hopefully, 'This'll be the end of it as far as we're concerned.'

I wished she were right. 'But why are we here, and Mama and

Papa are in Alexandria? Max's accident hasn't been explained, nor what Mr Baxter wants with Aunt Dora. And what about the man in the cream suit? Who is he?' I remembered Mrs Hodges pleading with me to put the cat back without anyone knowing. 'Why did Mrs Hodges pretend not to know Mr Baxter?' Although I was trying, I was failing to see her as evil. 'He has some sort of hold over Mrs Hodges.' I added, 'I just wish we knew what it was.'

I realised Lily had shadows under her eyes and her face was pale and pinched.

I took her arm. 'I'm sorry, Lily. I really didn't want to worry you, but it was dangerous to tell you anything.'

She gave me a wry smile. 'And now on top of everything else I have to go camping.'

I laughed. 'At least spiders are well down the list of things to worry about.'

'What I really didn't like was the way he asked us to look for things, and offering to pay us.'

'Nor did I.'

We walked on together through the midday heat.

'You were fantastic in there,' I said. 'Thank you.'

Her mouth twitched at the corners. 'Actually, I rather enjoyed it.'

We walked on in silence, but I didn't feel so alone, and that was really good. Until I remembered Miut trapped in the basket about to give birth to her kittens.

I had to find out what happened to her. The Seal and the League of Seth were important in Miut's world as well as mine. This afternoon, we were going to Sakkara. I was sure there would be answers there. Maybe, if I knew what had happened to the Seal in Miut's time, it could help us now. I slipped my hand into my pocket and wrapped my fingers round my stone cat. It was the key to everything, at least I was sure of that.

CHAPTER 30

I wasn't sure what to expect but everything looked completely different from my dream. Temples which I remembered glistening in the moonlight, had either completely vanished or were little more than heaps of rubble. In fact, the whole area looked a lot more like a derelict building site than a great City of the Dead. And where was Hori and Miut's hill? Or the smaller pyramids? Or The Way That Is Covered? In the centre of it all stood the Step Pyramid. Aunt Dora was right. My drawing was of a very different building. This one was crumbling at its edges and looked far, far older than the one I'd drawn.

I dropped the reins and Djinn came to a halt. She lowered her head, blowing gently. I patted her neck apologetically. I knew she must be tired after our afternoon ride through the hot Cairo streets. It had taken nearly two hours for us to reach Sakkara.

'We should stay together,' said Zac sharply as he and Lily trotted up to me.

'Sakkara has not always looked like this, has it?' I asked trying to keep the panic out of my voice.

'Of course not. Much has been buried by the sand that blows in from the desert. Also, people took stone from the old buildings to use in their own temples. Ancient Egyptians were most practical people and they were good at using again material left for them by their ancestors.' He glanced up. 'We must hurry or we will not have time to see everything before the sun sets.'

I gasped. For that split second he had again looked so like

Hori, all those thousands of years ago, as he too had measured the time by the height of the sun.

Lily gave me a worried sideways glance but said nothing. Zac nudged his donkey on, ours followed suit, and we rode three abreast across the plateau.

Zac gave a wide sweep of his arm. 'For thousands of years this whole area, as far as you can see, was the burial place for the people who lived in the magnificent city of Memphis.'

'Did they call it The City of White Walls?' I had to ask.

Zac looked at me with surprise. 'Yes. But when the Greeks came many years later, they called it Memphis.'

I took a deep breath. I needed to know how much more of my dream was true. 'And the Temple of Ptah was somewhere near here, and that was the home of the sacred Apis bull?'

'Yes,' he said, and I saw something flicker in his eyes. Surprise at how much I knew perhaps?

'And when the Apis died he was mummified and brought up here. He was buried in a chamber cut out of the rock in a place called the Serapeum. I will show you soon. It is on our way.'

Miut's bull would have been buried there. I liked the thought that all his beauty and strength would have been respected.

The late afternoon sun blazed down at us as we rode on. Zac explained that the necropolis stretched all the way to Giza, that many thousands of tombs must still lie hidden under the sands, but that none were as remarkable as the Step Pyramid before us.

He glanced at me with a small smile. 'Maybe your Imhotep was the magician who created this wonder?'

'Maybe,' I whispered.

I was back in the House of Life, Miut crouched in the shadows watching a spider, while Hori sat listening to his father talking about Imhotep *who was the architect of the pyramid, and the greatest magician of all...*

I forced myself back to the present. Zac was still talking. '... and perhaps he built the pyramid as a staircase to the gods.'

I saw that while most of the vast enclosure wall had vanished, the gateway was still there. It towered above us, some ten metres high, and had been built to look like the entrance to a great palace, though with just the narrow slit of an entrance that I remembered from my dream. It had hardly changed at all.

At last, with the pyramid on my right and the gate in front of me, I knew exactly where I was.

'Was there a covered way somewhere over there?' I asked, pointing off to my left.

'Yes, it is just there. Those fallen slabs are, we think, part of the Causeway of King Unas.'

This time there was no doubt that I could hear the surprise in his voice. I glanced at Lily. A smile hovered at the corner of her mouth.

'It is believed that the Causeway led from the Temple of Unas in the valley where the king was embalmed, to the pyramid where he was buried. There was a covered way so that his treasures could be carried there unseen, and thieves would not be tempted by his wealth. Later kings and other important people may have used it too.'

'Like High Priests,' I murmured.

The procession had reached the top and was spilling out into the desert night.

I closed my eyes for a second and I could see them: the priests with their masks, the sled pulled by oxen, the man-shaped coffin, the dancing girls. They were so real I wanted to call out to them and see if they could hear me.

I had to check. 'Were funeral processions often at night?'

Zac raised his eyebrows. 'Burial by moonlight? I do not think so. Burials happened when the chariot of the sun god was high in the sky. The feasting may have gone late into the night while the tomb was closed.'

I stared at the fallen slabs of rock, all that was left of the ruined causeway. The use of the Covered Way at night must have meant that Heteb really had wanted to keep his secrets safe.

Zac led us on into the great enclosure, past all the small

ruined temples and up to the base of the pyramid. 'We will have time to walk around the pyramid.'

'Can we go inside?' asked Lily.

'No. Most of the tunnels are at the bottom of shafts, far beneath the ground. The main shaft is more than eighty-four feet deep. There are many miles of tunnels, with many chambers and galleries beneath the desert. There is much danger. There are shafts that go nowhere, but there are others that drop deep into the earth.'

I shivered and felt suddenly cold. I looked up and noticed that the sun was lower in the sky and tinged with pink. The heat of the day was fading.

Zac swung his donkey round and set off towards the pyramid. 'Now I will show you something that will truly interest you. Come.'

The path took us along the west side of the pyramid, which now loomed above our heads. We must have been about half way along its side when Zac dismounted and led his donkey to a wooden post, and dropped his reins over it. We did the same.

'Can you guess what that is?' he asked, pointing to a nearby wooden fence. It enclosed an area where the sand had been dug out exposing a stone-slabbed courtyard and a section of stone wall built into the rocky hillside below the pyramid. A mud-brick hut had been constructed alongside part of the wall. The door of the hut was wedged open.

Everything round us seemed to have gone quiet; it was as if the desert was holding its ancient breath. My heart hammered as if I'd run a hundred miles, and my legs were like paper. I knew exactly where we must be.

'This is Heteb's tomb, isn't it?' said Lily, her eyes on my face.

Zac studied the open door. 'People must be inside.' He turned to Lily. 'Do you want to ask if they will show you around?'

'Yes, please,' said Lily, her eyes still on me.

Zac led the way through a narrow wooden gate, down some steps and across to the door. '*Marhaba?*' he called, 'Hello... is anybody there?'

There was no answer.

'Do you know who is working here?' I asked.

Zac shook his head. 'Anyone might have applied for the concession.'

I wondered if *anyone* might be Mr Baxter. Then I remembered he had been in New York for months. So not him.

'We had better leave,' said Zac.

'No!' the word exploded out of me. 'Please,' I pleaded. 'Can we have just a quick look inside? The door is open.'

Zac frowned. 'You would see nothing.'

'But they must have light to work by. Perhaps there's an oil lamp? Or candles?' asked Lily.

I held my breath. To be so close to Miut, and then to just turn around and leave was unthinkable. And with Lily and Zac right beside me, surely the dark wouldn't be too frightening.

'Please, Zac,' I repeated.

At last he rolled his eyes and shrugged. 'I suppose a most quick look would not matter.' He opened the door wide and we followed him inside.

CHAPTER 31

The hut wasn't particularly dark as sunlight spilled in through the door to light it well enough. There was a second door opposite us. It stood slightly open, and through that door we could just see darkness. Several oil lamps stood in a row on a wooden table. Tapers and matches lay beside them. There were a number of large, wooden crates piled neatly in a corner. Otherwise the hut was empty.

Zac hesitated.

'Please,' I pleaded, 'just a quick look.'

Zac sighed, but picked up a match and struck it. He lit the nearest lamp. 'Only for a moment then.'

Lily's fingers twisted round mine and linked together, we followed him through the second door.

The lamp beat back the darkness. The same darkness which had surrounded Miut's basket all those thousands of years ago.

I was suddenly afraid. Not just of the dark but of what I might find. Then I remembered. There would be nothing. Just emptiness.

Zac raised the lamp. We were in a small rectangular room with a high ceiling and stone-slabbed floor. It was empty except for some planks of wood propped up against the back wall. Zac crossed the floor to the far wall letting the lamplight light up the wall. The dark shape of a large seated figure appeared out of the gloom.

'The High Priest himself,' said Zac. 'This chamber is his temple where people came to bring him offerings and to ask for spells to help their sick children or to harm their enemies.'

I stared at Zac. 'This is his temple, not his tomb?'

He nodded. 'Of course. The tomb was close by.'

I looked around. 'Do you know where?'

'Yes. I came with Mr Sinclair when it was uncovered.' He pointed at the floor. 'It is a shaft that lies beneath those stones.'

I went over to where Zac had pointed. When I looked carefully at the ground I could see where some slabs had been replaced as there was no sand in the cracks and they looked cleaner than the surrounding stones.

'It is many feet deep,' he explained, 'and it leads to just a small set of chambers. Heteb's mummy was lowered there, and all his most valuable burial goods. Then the shaft was filled with stones and rubble to stop thieves. It was most unsuccessful. Your cousin found the shaft empty of all things.'

Almost empty, I thought, but said nothing.

I suddenly thought of Max suspended over a similar shaft in Alexandria. I shuddered. Mr Baxter had said he had been lucky the shaft had not been deeper. Then it hit me. Had it been luck? It was only because Max was recovering that Mama and Papa were still away looking after him. If Max had been killed, they would already be with us in Cairo, or we would be on our way home. For some terrible reason, that wouldn't have suited Mr Baxter.

As for Miut, I was more confused than ever. I knew Neshi hadn't thrown or lowered her basket down a shaft. I looked round. There didn't seem to be any alcoves or recesses in the walls, so where had Neshi hidden the basket?

There was a sudden flash and the chamber was alive with white hissing, fizzing light. My nose tingled with the smell of burning metal as a cloud of smoke swirled round the chamber. I turned to see Zac was holding a piece of magnesium wire. As the smoke lifted, the temple walls glowed with brilliant reds, blues and greens. Every inch was covered with ancient Egyptians busy with their lives. Some were working in the fields, others were catching fish in the Nile, hunting in the marshes or baking bread in a bakery.

Zac was talking to Lily. '... see how Heteb's hand is raised. It is as if he is holding something, but the picture is damaged. It is believed that it could be a seal of some sort, a symbol maybe of his magical powers.'

At the mention of a seal, I rejoined Zac and Lily who were closely inspecting the seated Heteb. One hand was indeed raised as if he was holding something up to be seen.

I peered at the High Priest's hand. Zac was right about damage. Someone had chiselled away at the wall, obliterating whatever Heteb had been holding. It looked as if it had happened a long time ago.

The magnesium wire spluttered and went out. The chamber seemed almost dark. The pale blue light of the oil lamp couldn't hold back the shadows. They pressed closer. Anything could be hidden in their depths. I moved nearer to Lily.

To distract myself from the deepening shadows, I examined the seated figure of Heteb. His name filled my dreams, but it felt strange to see his face.

'He looks so young,' I said.

Zac looked at me curiously. 'It is not known how old this priest was at his end. But the dead are always painted as if they are young and strong, because that is how they wish to be in the afterlife.'

He moved the lamp slowly across the painted figures until it came to rest on a strange little creature. 'And here is Heteb's *ba* or spirit.' He glanced at me. 'You remember we talked of this at Giza?'

I nodded. I could make out it was the *ba* bird. It had the body of a bird but Heteb's head.

Zac linked his thumbs together and made a small flapping motion with his hands. 'The ancient people believed that when you die, your *ba* flies from your body. When your mummy is carried to the tomb there is a ceremony when the mouth of your mummy is opened and the *ba* returns. You will be alive in the afterlife.'

'But what happens if your mummy is destroyed?' asked Lily.

Zac shrugged and looked upwards. 'If there was still a statue of you, then it could enter that. But if there was nothing, maybe it kept on flying?'

I thought about the great city of Memphis and how thousands of people must have been buried in the City of the Dead, which had been ransacked for centuries. How many *ba* birds were flying above our heads, like flocks of invisible starlings searching for their stolen or broken bodies.

I found myself listening for the beating of wings in the air around me. I couldn't hear any. But even in the stuffy heat of the temple I shivered. I could feel the sadness all around us.

'It seems so sad somehow,' said Lily. 'All those *ba* birds flying around and nowhere for them to land.'

Zac glanced at the door. 'I think it is late. We should go. I will check the way is clear.' He handed Lily the lamp and vanished through the doorway into the hut.

It was then I heard something. Something so quiet I had to strain my ears to hear it. I knew exactly what it was. I'd heard it before through the bedroom door.

'Can you hear that?' I whispered to Lily.

'Hear what?' she asked.

'Scratching.'

Lily closed her eyes to listen.

The sound came again, but louder this time.

SCRATCH...SCRATCH....

I studied the planks of wood propped up against the back wall. Could Miut be behind all that? Maybe I should pull them aside and see. But fear stopped me. What if there was something terrible hidden there that I didn't want to see? A ghostly basket containing the body of a cat and her kittens perhaps? How could I bear it if that had been the end of Miut's story?

Lily opened her eyes, 'Rats.' she shuddered. 'It's time we went.'

At that moment, Zac reappeared. 'The sun is almost gone. Someone will be back soon to lock up.'

He took the lamp from Lily. 'Come,' he ordered. 'We must go now.' He vanished into the hut with Lily close behind him.

I was suddenly alone in the temple. There was a flash of daylight as Zac and Lily left the hut. It disappeared as the outer door banged shut behind them.

'Wait. Please,' I called, but my voice was choked by fear. The darkness seeped into me, filling my lungs. I struggled to breathe. Blood roared in my ears. My legs no longer belonged to me. Blacker than black shadow shapes swirled past my eyes. I stumbled and reached out to steady myself. As my hand touched the wall my fingers tingled. The air fizzed and crackled all around me. Voices whispered in the shadows. Familiar and terrifying, I recognised them. The voices from my nightmare. Sweat pricked at my skin.

'Help me.' I was gasping like a fish out of water. 'Miut, please help me.'

Something soft tickled my leg. I recognised it at once. A cat's tail. Then she was pushing herself against me, purring a deep, rumbling purr. She was warm and soft and real. I felt the terror draining away. The darkness lightened to grey. My hand was free of the wall. A few steps and I was at the doorway into the hut. I bent down to stroke her. For a heartbeat Miut was still there; a flicker of deep amber eyes at the very edge of my vision. I blinked and looked again, but I knew she would be gone.

'Miut,' I whispered, 'what do you want from me?' But there was only silence.

I entered the hut. My eyes had adjusted and I realised the hut wasn't completely dark after all. A slither of light was creeping in under the outer door. I could make out the packing cases piled up against the wall, and the table. Outside I could hear Zac and Lily talking. Something rustled close by. I spun round expecting to see Miut again. The hut appeared empty. The only places she could hide were in the deeper shadows by the packing cases or under the table. I checked the packing cases. Nothing. I leaned down to examine the floor under the table when something about the table caught my attention. I noticed a small jumble of keys, lying half hidden behind the row of lamps. They had labels attached. One caught my eye: "HETEB - Hut Door". An image of Mr Baxter sparked into my mind. Was he involved in the reopening of the tomb? He'd certainly be most interested in it. Maybe at that very moment he was on his way...

'Come on, Rose,' Lily called from outside, her voice cutting through my thoughts. 'Do hurry up.'

A thought struck me as I left the hut. Lily had heard Miut scratching, even if she had thought it was rats. Miut was not just in my head.

CHAPTER 32

I stepped, blinking, out into the deep crimson glow of the setting sun. Lily and Zac were waiting at the top of the steps.

Lily smiled with relief when she saw me. 'What kept you? We were just coming back to see if you were alright.'

'Sorry. I was just wondering what was in the packing cases.' It wasn't a lie because I did wonder what was in them.

We made our way back to the donkeys.

Zac handed us their reins. 'We will leave the donkeys here. There are many shafts and open pits. It is most dangerous. Many are still full of sand. But some have been dug out and are most deep.'

We walked for a while along the west side of the Step Pyramid. The sun was sinking and turning the desert blood red. Except for a small cluster of tents a few hundred yards away, the area was deserted. 'Is that where we're sleeping?' I asked, pointing at the tents.

Zac shook his head, 'No, they are for other tourists. We will stay near my parents' village. But we must hurry. We must be there before it is dark.' He paused. 'But first let me show you how full of danger is this place.' He took our donkeys' reins from us and indicated we should go forward. 'Be very careful,' he instructed. 'Take three steps and no more.'

After three steps we stopped. A shaft dropped away in front of us. There was no barrier. It fell away into blackness. We couldn't see the bottom. Zac was right. It was terrifyingly dangerous. Lily swayed beside me.

I reached for her just as she grasped my arm.

'I thought I was going fall,' she managed.

I didn't tell her how scared I'd been for her. She knew that anyway.

We led our donkeys down the slope away from the desert plateau with its thousands of tombs, towards the river valley. After a while we reached flat ground and saw that a small tent had been erected beside a cluster of date palms. A fire was burning in a pit nearby and a large round pot stood on a grill over the fire. Three rolls of bedding were neatly piled up beside the tent.

I looked at Zac. 'Who did all this?'

He smiled. 'My father put up the tent and made the fire. My mother, she cooked our meal.'

We unsaddled our donkeys and tied them to a nearby palm. There was a bucket full of water for them to drink and a pile of hay for them to nibble. Each of our saddlebags contained the items that Aunt Dora had considered essential for a successful camping trip in the desert where the nights could be cold. Toothbrush, paste, a neatly rolled mosquito net, a spare flannel vest and an extra pair of stockings, a hairbrush and a small vial of peppermint oil to rub on any insect bites.

Zac's parents had provided everything else we needed. There was a large clay jug filled with water, some freshly made flat bread, a slab of cheese and a basket full of amber gold dates. There was also a box of matches, a brass candle lantern, some spare candles and a small roll of magnesium wire.

'In case we want to explore some more tombs tomorrow,' said Zac.

Lily was gazing at the rolls of bedding. 'Do you think the mosquito nets will keep out spiders?'

'They keep out everything,' I said firmly.

The desert night was as cold as Aunt Dora had thought it might be. We wrapped ourselves in blankets and sat close to the fire as we ate. The Step Pyramid on the hill above us was like a great, black hole cut out of a glittering curtain of stars. Later we watched the full moon come up and hang in the sky like a huge, silver globe.

This was Miut's desert. I felt extraordinarily close to her.

After we had finished eating, Zac helped us unroll our beds in the tent. He placed his bed across the entrance. 'This way I can keep the wild animals of the desert from attacking you.' He smiled as he spoke, and we knew he was teasing.

I closed the tent flap to keep out the cold. It would be dark when we snuffed out the lamp, but with Lily asleep right beside me and Zac just outside, I was determined to be brave. I slipped off my skirt and dropped it along with my boots at the end of my bedroll. I lay down and wrapped the blankets snugly round me. Lily must have been happy that she was safe from eight-legged invaders under her mosquito net as she was already fast asleep.

I clutched the little stone cat tight in my hand as my eyes closed. However terrible Miut's story might be, I had to know how it ended. I tossed and turned. Every time I closed my eyes, I saw Miut clawing at the basket. Eventually I gave up trying to sleep and slipped out of bed, unfastened the ties and, rolling back the flaps, let the moonlight flood in to the tent like quicksilver. Zac, at first glance, seemed to be asleep, but as I watched, he opened his eyes.

'Is there a difficulty?' he asked, sitting up and running his hand through his sleep-tousled hair. He looked so like Hori yet again that it took my breath away.

'It was too dark in the tent for me to sleep,' I managed, whispering so as not to disturb Lily. 'But I have never seen a moon as beautiful as this before.' *Except in my dreams. This was Heteb's moon.*

'It is most magnificent,' agreed Zac softly, 'Do you know the story about Horus and the moon?'

'I don't think so. Papa told us quite a few stories about Horus, but I don't remember one about the moon.'

Zac looked up at the stars. 'But you know that Horus is the god of the skies and the son of Osiris?'

I nodded.

'And that the Seth and Osiris were brothers?'

I nodded again. I did remember Papa telling us at least one story about them. We were in his study and he was sitting in his favourite old red leather chair. The room had smelled comfortingly of polish and cigar smoke.

'Seth was jealous of Osiris,' I said, 'and he tricked Osiris into climbing into a magnificent jewelled chest. Seth slammed the lid shut so Osiris was trapped and threw the chest into the Nile.'

'And after that?' prompted Zac staring at me with huge, brown eyes. Hori's eyes.

I took a deep breath and continued. 'But Osiris wasn't dead, and eventually he returned home to find his wife, Isis, who loved him more than life itself. But Seth found out and came and killed Osiris, this time by cutting him into fourteen pieces, which he hid in different places all over Egypt. But Isis found most of the pieces and, with tears and magic spells, she put him back together. She brought him back to life.'

'Horus has been fighting Seth ever since,' said Zac. 'He wants revenge for what Seth did to Osiris.' I noticed that Zac was talking as if this wasn't an old story, but as if it was still happening.

'It was in one of the many battles against Seth,' continued Zac, 'that Horus lost his right eye. Thoth, the god of wisdom, found the lost eye and returned it to Horus, but it had lost its heat and now it rises cold and silver in the night sky as the moon. While his left eye is the sun that burns each day.'

I glanced up at the night sky as a memory tugged at me. I could see Hori holding his Eye of Horus up to the moon-disc and asking for the protection of Horus. Had he received it? Hori would have searched for Miut until he found her. Had he discovered Neshi waiting for him? I shuddered. Neshi's eyes had been so full of hate.

I pushed the memory to the back of my mind. I was curious. 'You know so many stories about ancient Egypt. Who told them to you?

'My grandfather, Ezra, taught me many of the old ways.'

I'd forgotten about Ezra. My heart thudded as I remembered how he stared at us when we arrived. How he watched us in the House of Shadows. Was he involved with Mr Baxter and the League of Seth? An even worse thought struck me. If Ezra was involved, was Zac involved too? And what about Mrs Hodges? If she was part of the League, why had she wanted me to slip the cat back into Uncle Arthur's box and not just given the cat to Mr Baxter herself? My head ached. So many questions and no answers.

Zac gazed up at the moon and continued softly. 'Seth is the god of darkness and chaos, while Horus is the god of light and order. Neither god can destroy the other, for night must follow day, and day must follow night. But there are nights when Horus has the greatest power, for when he opens wide his pale, cold eye, it pushes back the darkness.'

'So tonight the Eye is wide open and Horus is at his most powerful.' I realised we were now both talking as if the story was real.

At last I understood why Heteb had not wanted the power of Ra to help him pass into the afterlife. It had been a full moon the night he had been buried. Magic was a dark power full of secrets. Heteb had believed in the strength of Horus's cold, silver eye to help him wield his spells.

A thought occurred to me. 'What happens when the moon goes down?

'The Eye of Horus is closed, and Seth is strong again.'

Obvious really. 'But what happens if Seth destroys Horus?' I realised we were still talking as if the ancient gods actually existed.

Zac frowned. 'That cannot happen. There must be balance in all things. The goddess Ma'at sees to that. Otherwise all would be chaos. It would be the end of all things.'

Balance. I wasn't balanced. I was torn between the past and the present, and I had no idea where I even wanted to be.

I suddenly felt very tired, and was sure I could fall asleep now. I said goodnight to Zac, slid under the mosquito net and into bed, leaving the tent flaps open. As I pulled the blankets tightly round me again and picked up the stone cat, I heard Zac whisper...

'And you will wake as my ancestors did, and watch Amun-Ra's chariot carrying the blazing eye of Horus rise out of the eastern desert.'

I lay still and tried to calm my tumbling thoughts, although something was nagging at me. There was something I'd seen in the hut, which had prompted me to think of Mr Baxter. But the more I tried to remember, the more confused I became. I had to think about something else or I would never fall asleep. I listened to dogs barking in the nearby village and thought about Amun-Ra's flaming chariot racing across a hot, blue sky. Eventually my eyelids felt like lead and closed.

CHAPTER 33

'THE BOOK OF MIUT'

It was the tightenings which woke Miut. She opened her eyes, but saw only darkness. She sniffed the hot, still air and sneezed as rock dust filled her nostrils. Miut tried to stand, but the basket was too low; she tried to turn round, but the basket was too narrow. Then came another tightening, followed immediately by yet another. There was no more time. She must free herself.

Miut sniffed at the basket, smelling its woodiness. She pressed her nose against the sides and felt the closeness of the weave. It would take many risings of the sun-disc to bite through that. There must be another way. Then she saw it. A band of dried animal skin held the basket shut.

She bit deep at the band, tearing at it until her teeth ached and the iron taste of blood filled her mouth. Still she bit and chewed. At last the band began to weaken and tear. She half stood, arching her back so that it pressed against the lid, and pushed upwards with all her strength. For a long moment, nothing happened, then, all at once, the band split and the lid loosened. Miut clambered out of her prison, and the lid dropped closed behind her.

She shook herself free of the chewings dusting her fur and looked round. The dark around her was now tinged with grey. She sat for a moment waiting for her eyes to adjust. She was in a tunnel. The walls were bare and unevenly cut. The floor was a mess of sand and broken rock. Behind her lay impenetrable blackness, ahead was a rough-cut opening into a chamber filled with silvered light and shadows. She padded through the opening.

She had not been in such a place since kittenhood. The walls had been carefully smoothed and plastered, and were covered from floor to ceiling with painted gods and strange beasts. Their frozen eyes gazed silently down at her. The chamber was lit by the moon-disc. The cold, white light was creeping in through the entrance opposite her. And beyond the entrance lay the desert. Miut crossed the stone-slabbed floor, carefully avoiding a mountain of diggings and the gaping mouth of a newly dug shaft. She reached the doorway and stood for a while, breathing deeply, tasting the cool clean air of the desert night.

Suddenly a breeze stirred the air, and on its breath hung the faint echoes of music and the distant beat of drums. As she listened, they grew in strength. Music carried the threat of people, noise, confusion… and Snake-Eyes.

A tightening shivered through her. There was no more time, and nowhere else to go. Miut padded back to the mouth of the tunnel. Somewhere deep in the shadows, she smelt power, strange and unfamiliar. For now, it slept lost in its ancient dreams. She hesitated, but fear of Snake-Eyes, and her need for darkness drove her forward.

After a short distance Miut sat down, her tailed curled neatly round her and examined the wall nearest her. Its uneven surface formed a tempting ragged stairway, which ended just beneath a narrow ledge. An ungainly scrabble took her up on to the ledge. Behind it lay a small dark recess. Warm, dark and hidden. This was the place.

From the ledge, Miut could see much of the Painted Chamber and a fragment of silver desert through the outer doorway. The music was louder now, and closer. A tightening shuddered through her, then another, until they came like river waves in a storm. Soon, the first kitten passed out into the world. Miut licked the small, wet bundle, drying and cleaning its fur, feeling the kitten's hold on life strengthen with each rasp of her tongue. And all the while she watched the distant fragment of desert and listened. There were voices and music heavy with an unfamiliar beat and the flicker of fire. Her stomach growled longingly as the smell of roasting meat wafted into the tunnel.

Shortly a second kitten joined the first, then a third and a fourth. Each blind-eyed kitten, from the pale sand of its chest to the tip of its striped golden tail, was just like herself.

Later, Miut glimpsed the end of a table piled high with food and a serving girl holding a jug. A dancer twisted past the entrance and then another and another.

In the tunnel beyond the Painted Chamber, the silence was broken only by the restless stirrings and soft mewlings of the kittens as they searched for her teats and sucked themselves full of life-giving milk.

~

At last, Miut settled towards sleep, her contented kittens tucked close against her side. Just as her eyes closed, the quiet was shattered by a voice just beyond the desert doorway. Miut's body tensed. She knew that voice. It was full of shadows and hate.

'Oh great Osiris, most powerful God of this world, and the next.
Guide the High Priest on his journey through the dark places.
Say with him the words of magic that shall open all the gates.
Welcome him into your kingdom,
Let him walk the paths of the Afterlife.'

As the voice ceased, a group of priests entered the Painted Chamber. Each one held a flaming torch. The Jackal-Priest, in his tunic of spotted desert cat, led the way. But Miut remembered them all. They had stumbled from the mouth of the Covered Way into the light of the moon-disc.

As soon as the last priest was inside the Painted Chamber, the Jackal-Priest turned back towards the entrance and raising his voice, commanded, 'Come near all who carry the possessions of the High Priest.'

The priests gathered at the entrance. Two of them left and soon returned, their arms laden with baskets and other goods. A chain of priests formed to pass these across the temple and pile them at the mouth of Miut's tunnel. Eventually the Jackal-Priest stepped forward into the entrance and held his arms wide.

'Enter, High Priest Heteb,' he called to the desert night, 'through this way of darkness, you shall find the light of the afterlife.'

He stepped aside, then waited motionless as four masked priests left the temple, then returned shortly, bearing the coffin case. They placed it upright in the entrance.

'Assist me,' the Jackal-Priest commanded the two priests who had remained beside the coffin. One wore the mask of a crocodile, while the other wore the mask of a desert beetle. Together they removed the front of the coffin.

The Jackal-Priest lifted the wooden rod he held in his hand. One end was hooked, and from the hook sprouted a flat blade. He touched the bandaged head of the mummy with the blade, and as he did so he chanted,

'Your mouth is opened by Ptah.
Let this adze in my hand split wide your bandages.
Let your ba bird return,
Let your ka drink and eat its fill,
So that you may pass through the Netherworld,
And into the Afterlife.
Return to us and offer us your knowledge.
Your name will live on for all time.'

From beyond the entrance came a collective chant, 'Return to us, High Priest Heteb, return to us.'

The Jackal-Priest turned back to the entrance and again raised his hand and spoke to the people who waited outside.

'You have made your farewells. Go to your homes. As the sun-disc rises, you may bring the High Priest your offerings.'

Miut lay perfectly still on her ledge, her eyes never leaving the Jackal-Priest. His power tingled through her whiskers and she felt the danger that lay deep within him. The rustlings and whisperings of the people beyond the entrance soon faded into the distance. The priests stood unmoving until all was quiet.

A priest entered the Painted Chamber. Miut had not seen him before. He wore the mask of a ram with a pair of horns, each twisting to a dagger's point. In his arms, he held a basket filled with scrolls. He bowed in the direction of the silent coffin before turning to the Jackal-Priest. 'Paser, how...'

The Jackal-Priest raised his hand. 'Be silent, Hapu. I wear the jackal mask of Anubis, god of the Underworld. You wear the ram mask of Khnum, god of the river flood!' he ordered. 'This night we all will use our god names in case unwanted ears are nearby. What delayed you? I sent word for you to leave the Temple of Ptah long ago.'

'I could not come without the Final Spell. I waited for the boy to arrive. When he did not come to my chamber, I went to wait for him at the temple docks. Still he did not come. It was only later when I returned to my chamber in the House of Life that I was told he had arrived through the Southern gate. I had missed him.'

The Jackal-Priest's voice was tight with anger. 'I do not care what you thought. When I send an order I expect it to be obeyed.'

The Ram-Priest bowed his head, then continued, 'So has the boy arrived? Do you have the spell?'

The Crocodile-Priest stepped forward. The light from the flaming torches glinted on the two rows of jagged teeth that decorated his long, crocodile snout. 'Neshi has brought word. Hori is on his way.'

'What has Neshi got to do with this? How did he know of Hori's mission?' asked the Ram-Priest, his voice rough with anxiety.

'Doors are not so thick that sound cannot pass through them if someone happens to be close enough to hear,' replied the Jackal-Priest. 'It was not a great secret anyway. Khay had to give the scroll to the boy, who else would he trust? He could not be sure he could bring it himself, not with his leg so unfortunately injured.'

There was a sigh of laughter from the watching priests.

'I see nothing entertaining in Khay's damaged leg,' reproved the Ram-Priest, 'and I fear for Hori. Why is he so delayed? He is an honest, and reliable boy and ...'

'… a stupid boy more like,' interrupted the Crocodile-Priest with a snort. 'He had just one simple task, to deliver you the scroll before you left the temple. He failed.'

The Jackal-Priest raised his hand. 'Enough.' The word spat from his mouth. 'The boy is nothing but a viper pretending to be a lamb. Once Neshi knew the boy had a mission of such importance, he bravely took it upon himself to protect Hori. He tried to follow the boy to the Temple of Ptah but lost him. Eventually he found the boy on the cliff path. Hori drew his knife and attacked Neshi for no reason. Neshi only just escaped with his life.'

'I don't understand,' said the Ram-Priest, shaking his horned head. 'Hori would never attack Neshi with a knife or anything else…'

'All is not lost, however,' continued the Jackal-Priest as if the Ram-Priest had not spoken. 'Neshi found the High Priest's cat wandering in the desert and brought it here for safe keeping…'

A grunt of laughter erupted from the group.

'… and soon the boy will bring you the scroll, Khnum,' continued the Jackal-Priest turning his head to the Ram-Priest. 'Then we will have all we need.'

Yet another rumble of laughter surged through the watching priests. All except the Ram-Priest. He stood apart from the others, his body as tense as a drawn bow. 'I will not believe this. Hori would never hurt anyone.'

'Enough of the boy. But what of the Seal?' demanded the Beetle-Priest. 'We must have that too.'

The Crocodile-Priest turned his snout towards him. 'Do not ask again. The Seal is already here,' he said softly.

~

The fur along Miut's spine pricked upright. Danger sparked in the air. She turned her amber gaze on the sleeping kittens. However much she longed to slip out into the desert night, she could not move from the ledge. She settled to cleaning the dust from her paws. As she worked, the tip of her tail twitched from side to side, and her eyes never left the Painted Chamber.

~

The Ram-Priest was looking round the Painted Chamber. 'The cat? You said you have her here for safekeeping? What danger threatens her?'

The Jackal-Priest shrugged his shoulders. 'The desert is a dangerous place.'

'That cat was born in the desert. She has nothing to fear from its sands. You must give her to the boy when he comes,' instructed the Ram-Priest.

'Give her to the boy who tried to kill my son? I do not think so,' snarled the Jackal-Priest, 'No, she shall walk with the High Priest. She shall join him in the afterlife.'

The Ram-Priest stood statue-still for five heartbeats before he whispered, 'But she is a Daughter of Bastet and to be protected. She is heavy with kittens. What evil is this, Anubis?' He crossed to the mountain of Heteb's goods and started pulling them aside. 'Where is she? We must release her.' He looked wildly round the Painted Chamber.

Then he was in the mouth of the tunnel with his torch raised. The flames pushed back the shadows, and Miut crouched low on her ledge. 'What is this tunnel? It was not here when I last came to the temple,' the Ram-Priest demanded. 'Where does it lead?'

The Crocodile-Priest sounded amused as he answered. 'The High Priest searched the ancient writings in the House of Life for many years to find the right resting place. He chose to have his temple here, for he knew that beyond this wall lay the way to the Chamber of Imhotep.' He pointed at the shaft. 'That was dug only to confuse any watchers or robbers in the years to come. So when we, his most trusted servants…,' a laugh rustled through the watching priests, 'came to prepare the temple for the High Priest's arrival, all that was needed was a few blows of our picks to open the tunnel.'

The Ram-Priest stepped into the tunnel and raised his flaming torch. The dancing flames pushed back the darkness for a short way. 'But why the Chamber of Imhotep?'

'Surely you know that it lies beneath centre of the great pyramid, and is therefore a place of great power and of magic,' said the Jackal-Priest, his voice vibrating with excitement.

The Ram-Priest swung round and faced the watching priests. 'If the High Priest lies in the Chamber of Imhotep, then his magic will be more powerful.' He glanced back up the tunnel. 'I understand that. Is this where you have the cat?'

He was close beneath Miut. She could see the sweat trickle from under his mask. She lay as still as a statue.

'Come out of there,' commanded the Jackal-Priest, suddenly impatient.

The Ram-Priest stepped back into the Painted Chamber.

'Now forget the cat, forget the tunnel and forget the boy,' continued the Jackal-Priest, 'and tell us, Khnum, what will happen when the Final Spell is spoken by the High Priest?

The Ram-Priest faced the Jackal-Priest. He stood tall and straight, his flaming torch held out in front of him. The shadows of his ram's mask danced on the wall.

'The heart of the High Priest will weigh no more than the feather of Ma'at and Osiris will lead High Priest Heteb safely into the afterlife. There he will be welcomed by the gods as one of them. He will hold his Seal high and say the spells that will forever protect the Temple of Osiris from the Followers of Seth.'

'And,' said the Jackal-Priest, his voice low and hissing like a snake, 'what will happen to these Followers of Seth?'

The Ram-Priest's body was suddenly as tense as the string of a drawn bow. 'Osiris will return the Followers of Seth to the paths of peace or he will destroy them, and it will be as if they had never been born.'

As the two priests had been speaking, the watching priests had quietly surrounded the Ram-Priest and the Jackal-Priest. The silence was so thick with hate it caught at the back of Miut's throat.

The Jackal-Priest flung back his head and his laugh echoed round the chamber. 'But my brothers, we will not let Osiris destroy us.'

The Ram-Priest looked round at the men who encircled him. 'Destroy us?' he repeated, 'I don't understand. Who is "us"'

'We are the Followers of Seth,' chanted the priests in unison.

The Ram-Priest spun round as if searching for a way to escape. But there was none.

'And Heteb will not rise from the dead,' said the Jackal-Priest slowly as if to a child, 'His body will be destroyed and his possessions split between us.'

'And the cat?' whispered the Ram-Priest, 'what has she to do with this madness?'

'She is not just the High Priest's cat, she is a Temple cat, a most favoured servant of Osiris. When her blood spills onto the ground, Osiris will be blind with tears. He will be weak...'

'You have forgotten Horus,' interrupted the Ram-Priest. 'Tonight, his eye is wide and all seeing. He will protect his father, Osiris.'

The Jackal-Priest shook his masked head. 'Horus is not forgotten. Remember that before the sun-disc rises, the cold Eye of Horus will close, and then Seth, god of darkness, will be all-powerful. That will be when the cat's blood is spilled. When Horus is blind, and while Osiris weeps, there will be nothing to stop the magic of the Great Seal banishing them forever from the Two-Kingdoms.

'Without Osiris or Horus, who will stop Seth? He will be the greatest god in the Two-Kingdoms, and his followers will be men of wealth and power.' He threw back his head and gave a wild laugh. 'We will be men of wealth and power, for the Temple of Osiris and all its lands will be ours. In time the Two-Kingdoms may all belong to us.'

'No,' shouted the Ram-Priest, 'you cannot do this. You may soon have the scroll, but I do not believe you have the Seal. It was not with the High Priest's possessions when he passed into the West. I searched them.' The Ram-Priest's voice, thin with fear, faded to silence.

The Jackal-Priest laughed again, but there was no humour in it. 'You did not search them well enough. But while it is not in my hand, I do have the Seal. You must believe that.'

The Ram-Priest did believe it. Miut felt his terror wash through her like a desert storm. She wanted to leap from her rock shelf and run out into the cool, clear night. But the soft breathings of her sleeping kittens imprisoned her.

'And who shall stop us?' continued the Jackal-Priest. 'Certainly not you, Hapu.'

The priests swept forwards in a silent wave. A blade gleamed in the flickering light of the torches. A short cry rang out into the night. The wave smoothly receded. The Ram-Priest lay unmoving, his blood oozing like a lengthening shadow across the sand.

~

A kitten stirred beside Miut. She licked it gently, soothing it back to sleep, but all the while her eyes never left the chamber beyond her tunnel.

~

It was the Jackal-Priest who broke the long silence. 'Deal with Hapu and move the goods with as much speed as you can. I need some desert air. I will keep watch outside.'

As he left the chamber, the Beetle-Priest and the Crocodile-Priest bent over the motionless body. They removed the mask, then each took one arm and together they dragged the body to the edge of the nearby shaft. There was a single grunt as they heaved and pushed him over the edge. There was one thud, then another, then silence.

'That was well done,' said the Beetle-Priest. 'Now two of you get the shaft filled in, and the rest of you move the High Priest's belongings. There is no time to lose.'

Two priests obediently picked up shovels and set about filling the shaft from the heap of stone and sand piled high beside its mouth. The remaining priests formed a chain and passed the High Priest's goods from one to another, the last priest in the line stood almost beneath Miut. It was not long before Heteb's possessions covered the ground beneath her. She recognised a mat on which she used to lie, and a bowl, which had once held water for her to drink. Now it was empty, but for the first time she realised that her throat was burning. She could have lapped a whole river of water.

The chamber was bare when Heteb's coffin joined the heap of goods in the tunnel. The backs of the shovelling priests glistened with sweat as they worked until, at last, the shaft was filled almost level with the floor. The watching priests then lifted four slabs of stone, one after another, and eased them into place. They fitted the space perfectly, and it was as if the shaft had never been there at all.

The priest nearest Miut gave a small chuckle. 'I would give a month's wages to see the look on the face of the thief who digs this shaft. One body of no importance awaits them and no gold to reward their effort.'

A dangerous quiet fell as the priests regained their breath and contemplated their work. The silence was broken by the sound of stones clattering beyond the entrance. Muit's ears twitched. She knew those footsteps. All would soon be well. Her thoughts turned longingly to a belly full of meat and bowls of bread dipped in milk.

'You are late,' accused the Jackal-Priest.

Hori's voice, sharp with urgency, floated in through the entrance. 'I must speak with Hapu. Is he there?'

'He is unwell and is resting within the chamber,' soothed the Jackal-Priest. 'You may give me your message.'

There was a pause then the boy spoke again. 'I must speak with Hapu. I have something for him. No one else.'

'A scroll, you mean,' said the Jackal-Priest. 'The one tucked into your kilt?'

'It is for Hapu's hands alone.' The boy's voice was firm.

There was a pause, then the Jackal-Priest's voice resounded in the Painted Chamber. 'Khnum-Hapu come out here now. The boy, Hori, wishes to speak with you.'

The listening priests stared at each other. Then the Beetle-Priest tore off his mask. 'At least I am the same build as Hapu,' he muttered as he slipped on the Ram-Priest's mask and disappeared through the entrance.

'Hapu, is that you?' Hori's voice was anxious.

A loud bout of coughing exploded into the chamber, followed by a hoarse, 'Of course it is, Hori. You are late. Do you have the scroll?'

'Yes.' There was uncertainty in his voice as he continued, 'But my father said I must be certain to hand it only to you. I have not seen you for a long time. Would you remove your mask?'

'No, he would not,' cut in the Jackal-Priest. 'Our masks must be worn until our business here is done or the gods will turn against us. Now do as your father told you and hand the scroll to Hapu.'

There was a pause. The boy's voice came again. 'I can't. I must be sure who… Owww! You did not need snatch it from me.'

Miut's ears twitched uneasily at the anger and pain in the boy's voice.

There was a long pause, then Hori spoke again. 'Have you seen Miut? It is important I find her.' There was an even longer pause. 'It is important for you too, Hapu.'

'If you have lost her,' interrupted the Jackal-Priest, 'she will be in some dark hole with her kittens. She will appear in her own time. Now, go back to the valley. This is a sacred place and we still have ceremonies to perform.'

'But I must…'

Miut's ears twitched as a short cry vibrated through the air.

The Jackal-Priest's voice was as cold as the desert before dawn, 'Make haste, if you do not want me to raise my hand to you a second time. And I give you a warning, if you ever raise your knife at Neshi again, you will wish you had never taken your first breath.'

'What do you mean?' The boy's voice broke. 'What knife? I haven't hurt Neshi. He…'

'Not one more lying word. Go.'

The boy went. Miut heard his footsteps running from the temple. She closed her eyes, and rested her head on her paws. She could feel the quiet stirrings of her kittens lying close by her side, but she had never felt so alone before.

~

'That was easily done,' said the Jackal-Priest, as he and the Ram-Priest returned to the temple chamber. The Ram-Priest removed his mask and replaced it with the beetle mask he had worn earlier.

'But Anubis, why did you let him go at all? What if he guessed I was not Hapu?' he asked.

'Sometimes you see as little as a beetle yourself. The boy will have been seen coming here. He must be seen to leave or questions will be asked. Soon he will return in secret, searching for his cat. We will be waiting. And he will not escape the second time. There will be no witnesses then.' He gave a dark, bitter laugh. 'It is well known that the desert is a dangerous place after the fall of the sun-disc. Few will question it if he has an accident. And we will all grieve at the disappearance of such a noble boy.'

The laughter that rose from the listening priests was as dark and bitter as the Jackal-Priest's laugh had been.

'Now,' continued the Jackal-Priest, 'bring me the cat.'

The Crocodile-Priest crossed to where Miut's basket lay hidden in the shadows. He bent over it. 'She has gone,' he announced, horrified. 'The strap is broken.'

A gasp ran through the watching priests. Immediately, they raised their torches and began searching the Painted Chamber, the flames sending wild flares of light in every direction so that the shadows appeared to dance.

'Stop,' commanded the Jackal-Priest. 'She has not come this way. We would have seen her. She will be in the tunnel, hiding in the dark.' He carried his torch to the mouth of the tunnel, held it high and waited motionless in the flickering light.

Miut lay rock still as she watched from her ledge. For a long moment, there was a thick, unmoving silence in the tunnel. But then a kitten stirred in its sleep. The Jackal-Priest lifted his head and his black eyes burned as they rested on Miut. He smiled, but it was the smile of a hunting snake. He started up the rock ladder and stretched his hand towards her. At once she was on her feet, her back arched, her fur spiked upright. A hiss exploded from her mouth.

The Jackal-Priest hesitated, withdrew his hand and climbed back down the ladder. She heard the black smile in his voice as he turned to the watching priests.

'As I thought. She and her kittens are there, and there they can stay. The Seal will be safe enough.'

'So, we close the tunnel?' asked the Crocodile-Priest.

The Jackal-Priest nodded. 'Oh yes, and make a good job of it. No one must know what lies behind this wall.'

~

Miut lay down, but her eyes never left the Painted Chamber. She watched as the Jackal-Priest left. She watched as the Crocodile-Priest and the Beetle-Priest began placing stone blocks across the mouth of her tunnel. One row above another was slotted into place. As each stone was added, the opening grew smaller and the light of the torches grew paler. After the last slab was added, there was only darkness.

For a moment, Miut felt fear flutter like a butterfly in the unmoving air. But somewhere in this stillness, a mouse or two would be hiding. She was sure of it. Later she would hunt one out, her whiskers would track its path. She closed her eyes. Until then she would sleep beside the kittens and listen to their dreams.

CHAPTER 34

I woke with a start. The tent was still lit by moonlight. My heart was racing. Miut and her kittens had been sealed into the tunnel. The priests had said they were going back. But when? It might be weeks... months, years even. How would she and her kittens survive without water? And what had happened to Hori? He would come looking for Miut, of course he would. When he did... Paser would be waiting. And there was nothing I could do because I was thousands of years away.

I sat up, trying not to disturb Lily, and looked out of the tent. Zac was lying facing me. He was fast asleep and his likeness to Hori made me wonder if I was still dreaming.

I lay down again and tried to clear my mind so I could drift back to sleep. But I couldn't settle. Something was still nagging at me. I'd been alone in Heteb's tomb, terrified by the voices. Miut had appeared, allowing me to escape into the hut. Something had happened there that had made me think about Mr Baxter... I tried to remember but the harder I tried, the more confused I became.

'Miaooow.'

My eyes shot open and I sat up again.

'MIAOOOW.' The sound was louder, more insistent, closer.

I peered out into the night. I was so used to Miut appearing in unexpected places that I wasn't surprised to see a moon-bleached cat sitting beside a nearby palm tree, its leaves clattering softly in the night breeze.

As soon as she saw me, she stood up and raised her tail high behind her. She'd be gone in just a moment. I had to follow her.

It took me just a moment to struggle with my boot laces, pull on my skirt and slip the little stone cat into my pocket. As I did so, something clinked. I thrust my hand into the pocket, past the cat, past my tin of pastel chalks. Right at the bottom my fingers touched something cool and hard. A key. I didn't have to read the label to know what it said. I'd last seen it lying on the table in the Heteb's hut. I had no memory of picking it up, but I must have done.

I shook my head. A cat, a temple, a locked door, a key. I knew what I had to do. I dropped some matches into my pocket. Lily was sleeping peacefully as I crept out of the tent. Stepping carefully round Zac so I wouldn't disturb him, I paused and looked round for Miut. It took a moment before I saw her sitting beside Djinn, who was still contentedly nibbling her hay.

'You want me to ride, do you?' I whispered to Miut and untied the rope that tethered the donkey to the palm tree, attached the free end to the opposite side of Djinn's halter to form reins and swung my leg over her back. I was riding bareback, just as I had on my cousins' ponies many times before.

Miut stood up, raised her tail and stalked off towards the desert plateau. I squeezed my legs against the donkey's side and she obediently set off after Miut, matching her pace to that of the cat. We climbed steadily up a rocky path. It wasn't the same as the one we'd descended earlier, but it was easy to see the way in the moonlight. The desert was a patchwork of gleaming silver white and inky blackness.

It took a while for me to realise that we were following the line of the Causeway of Unas. Nothing felt real. I found myself wondering if it was all a dream and I was asleep still in the tent. Asleep or awake, I knew just one thing – there was no turning back.

The key from my pocket turned easily with just a small click and the hut door creaked open. I hesitated, listening, but the only sounds were the night skitterings of small desert animals.

I struck a match, and stepped inside. Everything appeared to be just as we had left it. Wooden crates... table... I picked up several lamps until I found one that was heavy enough to be full of oil and lit it.

'Miaoow.'

I turned to see Miut standing in the entrance to Heteb's temple. Trying to ignore the sick feeling in my stomach, I made my way across the hut and into the temple. I recognised it now as Miut's Painted Chamber, and knew that the shaft Zac had pointed out earlier was where Hapu's body had been thrown. I shuddered, longing for my bed, but guessed Miut had not finished with me yet.

I turned my attention to the walls. The lamp lit one small patch of painted wall after another, and for a moment it seemed nothing had changed. Until the light touched the back wall. There, instead of the planks of wood, the open mouth of Miut's tunnel yawned. Someone had recently discovered the secret tunnel and opened it up. Miut might have vanished but I guessed where she would be.

In the streets of Cairo and at Giza, she had been an untouchable ghost. But here in her tunnel, maybe because this was where the stone cat's imprinted memories were strongest, it seemed like she was as alive as she had been all those thousands of years ago. I remembered how her whiskers had tickled me and how she had wrapped herself round my legs that afternoon. So warm, so soft... so real.

I stood for a moment trying to decide what to do next. 'Go back to bed!' shouted the sensible voice in my head. Before I could make a decision, from beyond the hut came the clatter of slipping rocks. Someone was outside.

There was only one place to hide. Extinguishing the lamp, my heart pounding and blood roaring in my ears, I stepped over the pile of rubble, which was all that remained of the wall that had bricked up the entrance to Miut's tunnel thousands of years before.

The darkness in the tunnel wrapped itself round me, so thick with dust and the smells of the past I could taste it. I fought to control the fear that churned through my body. Breathe, I told myself, breathe, in... out... in... out...

It was just a movement of air that told me the hut door had opened. My ears strained in the blackness. For a second there was silence, then something moved in the temple chamber. Footsteps whispered on the stone slabs.

My breathing had stopped, but my heart thundered on. It was so loud... too loud. Whoever was out there must be able to hear it...

I heard a rasping sound and a tiny light flamed for a couple of seconds before vanishing. But it was enough for me to see who was holding the match.

'Lily,' my voice could only croak, 'you scared me to death! What are you *doing* here?'

I struck a match and relit my lamp. The light revealed Lily's pale, frightened face.

'Looking for you, of course.'

'With matches?'

She gave a small smile and raised her hand so I could see what she was holding. 'I slipped a candle into my pocket. I was about to light it.' She glared at me. 'But what were you thinking?' Her voice cracked. 'I woke up and you were gone. And Djinn too.'

'But how did you get here?'

'On Bashir, of course. I followed Djinn's hoof prints. They were pretty clear in the moonlight. But I thought the hut would be locked'

'I had a key.'

'How?'

'I found it,' and before she could ask me any questions added, 'You were very brave coming here on your own.'

She gave a small smile. 'I was terrified. Now can we get out of here?'

I couldn't tell her I was chasing Miut's ghost. 'Not yet. I have to see what's down this tunnel. Heteb's coffin and his treasures weren't in the burial shaft. Zac said so, and so did Aunt Dora. They may have been hidden somewhere else. Somewhere like this secret tunnel. Only now, it's no longer secret. It has been opened by whoever is excavating here. And I want to see what they've found.'

Again I was sure there was something about the hut that I should remember. Apart from the crates, there was just the table, lamps, tapers, matches, a jumble of keys, some with labels... It was then it hit me. The handwriting on the labels. The H in Heteb was the same as on the boxes in the library. Mr Baxter had written both. Of course! Mr Baxter was excavating the tomb.

My thoughts tumbled on. It didn't matter that he had been in New York. He had been given the concession and someone else had started the work. Was that where the man in the cream suit fitted in? Was it because they had found the tunnel and Heteb's treasures that Mr Baxter had returned to Egypt?

While some things made sense, I still had no idea what Mr Baxter wanted with us. But I was sure we shouldn't stay to find out. Whatever Miut wanted from me was suddenly of no importance. The only thing that mattered was that Lily and I were as far away from Heteb's tomb as possible.

'You're right, Lily. We must go now.'

I turned towards the hut, took hold of Lily's arm, then froze. I'd felt another breath of air moving. I killed the lamp. 'Someone's just entered the hut,' I hissed.

'Oh no,' said Lily, 'they'll know someone's here because the door was unlocked.'

We stood like statues in the darkness. A crack of pale light seeped into the temple from under the inner door, which Lily must have closed behind her. I could hear voices. 'There's more than one person,' I breathed at last.

'How can you hear that?' whispered Lily.

'And I can see light coming from the hut.'

'Really?' whispered Lily. 'All I can see is darkness.'

I felt in my pocket for my little stone cat. As always it was there, cool and smooth. Maybe it was infusing me with some of Aunt Dora's cat magic?

'I think you imagined it. Come on. We need to get out of here.' Lily grabbed my arm and guided me towards the mouth of the tunnel.

The inner door opened and light spilled into the temple. Three figures appeared in the doorway, just silhouettes. Then one spoke and I recognised the voice at once.

'Oh,' Lily gasped. Her hand froze on my arm. 'Is that Mr Baxter?'

'Yes.'

The figures held their lamps high, crossed the temple and entered into the mouth of the tunnel.

'We have to go further in,' I whispered. Without waiting for a reply, I grasped Lily's arm and pulled her on down the tunnel.

'But how'll we see where we are going?' hissed Lily. 'What about shafts we could fall down? And you hate the dark.'

I stared into the depths of the tunnel and realised that the lamps held by our pursuers lit the tunnel just enough so I could make out the walls, the uneven floor and best of all, the shape of a cat trotting purposefully in front of us. Secondly, because it wasn't completely dark, I wasn't so afraid. Not of that anyway. The figures behind us were another matter.

'Trust me,' I said. And she did.

CHAPTER 35

I hurried Lily along the tunnel, warning her about stray rocks that might trip her up and when to duck her head. The cat was always in front of us, but I never mentioned that to Lily. At one point the tunnel appeared to end in a landslide. As we got closer, we saw a gap had been scooped out between the roof of the tunnel and the slide of rock. It was high enough for us to scramble through quite easily, but the sharp edges of the rock scratched our hands and knees.

After that the tunnel changed. The floor and the roof levelled out and the walls were plastered and smooth. At intervals we stopped and listened. Always the voices and the light, followed us, pushing us steadily on. Like we were sheep. Lily had been right. They must know we were here.

Lily whispered, her grip on my hand tightening. 'They are herding us like sheep.'

I drew a deep breath. 'I suppose they are. We must be in those tunnels under the Step Pyramid, which Zac told us about.'

We kept on in silence for a while. Now there was something else. Sounds floated out of the gloom ahead. I pulled on Lily's hand. 'Stop. Listen.'

We stopped. 'To what?' hissed Lily.

'Voices.' I pointed into the shadowed darkness in front of us.

Lily dropped my hand and tilted her head slightly as she listened. 'I think you're imagining it.'

By then I was certain that my improved senses had to be cat magic, but I said nothing except, 'I can hear chanting.'

'Oh' she whispered. She glanced back. The lamplight was closer now. 'We have to go on?'

'Yes,' I whispered, as we set off again.

Soon the gloom ahead began to fade and there was the faintest flicker of a light. I felt sick. My throat felt like dry sand, my heart was pounding. Who, or what, was ahead of us?

I glanced down and my stomach lurched. Miut had gone. How could she leave us when we needed her so desperately? Beyond the fear, a great wave of sadness welled up inside me. I'd always assumed she had appeared out of nowhere to help me. That she was on my side. Maybe I was wrong. Maybe, in the end, she had led me into a trap. I swallowed a sob.

Lily's grip on my hand tightened, but she said nothing.

Steadily, and inevitably, the flickering light ahead grew nearer and the chanting grew louder. We could both hear it now.

At last we could see that the source of the light was a doorway cut into the right hand wall of the tunnel. Beyond the open door stood two cloaked and hooded figures. They blocked the tunnel ahead. Any thought of running on past the doorway vanished. As we reached it, a bell chimed twice, and the chanting stopped abruptly. Somehow the sudden silence was more frightening than anything that had happened before.

I am not certain what I'd been expecting as we stumbled through the doorway. Maybe a great hall filled with cloaked priests. Instead we found ourselves alone in a rectangular chamber, not much larger than the table that stood in its centre. The table was covered by a black cloth, embroidered with clusters of hieroglyphs the colour of dried blood. I could read them easily. SETH.

A heavily carved wooden chair stood at each end of the table, and there was a solid looking wooden bench on each side. A tall, tallow candle stood in the centre of the table. The flame spluttered and smoked as it burned, its light flickering crazily over the walls.

On the wall opposite us hung a large mirror. We stared into it, seeing our mirror doubles in the candlelight. Our faces were chalk white against the red of our hair.

Suddenly, our mirror doubles were not alone. A great jackal-headed figure stood behind them in the doorway.

'The Jackal-Priest,' I whispered. My lungs seemed to have frozen solid. I stared at the figure in the glass. My mind swirled with possibilities. Was there really a figure there behind us? Or had I somehow stepped back into my own dream and he was just a reflection of the past? Like Miut?

'Can you see him?' I murmured.

Lily nodded. Her eyes were huge and dark. Slowly we turned around.

The figure towered above us. 'I am Anubis. Welcome, Daughters of Seth to the Chamber of Feasts.'

The voice was startlingly familiar and for a moment that steadied me. I wasn't lost in Miut's world after all. He might wear an identical mask, but this was Mr Baxter. And he was dressed in a long black cloak, not the leopard-skin tunic worn by the Jackal-Priest of my dreams.

'You are Mr John Baxter, not Anubis, and we aren't Daughters of Seth, whoever they are,' Lily said furiously, hooking her arm through mine.

The solid warmth of her arm calmed me. I'd never heard her so angry. If I'd not been so frightened, I would have laughed.

Mr Baxter continued as if she had not spoken. 'We have been awaiting your arrival. You must be hungry and thirsty after your long journey.'

'We've only come from the bottom of the hill,' retorted Lily.

Mr Baxter stood aside from the doorway to allow two cloaked and hooded figures to enter the chamber. One carried a silver jug and two silver goblets on a silver tray, the other a wooden platter piled high with bread and fruit. They placed the platter and the tray on the table.

The figures bowed to Mr Baxter and left.

Lily glared at him. 'We don't want food. Let us go right now. If you don't, you'll regret it.'

I stared at her, astonished. I'd never heard her speak to anyone like that.

'You are going nowhere.' Mr Baxter's voice was as cold and hard as marble. 'Eat, drink, make yourselves at home.' He laughed, but it was a dark, bitter laugh, which didn't make me feel any better. 'You will not have long to wait.'

'Wait for what?' I asked, finding my voice at last.

'For the darkness before dawn.'

'What do you mean?' asked Lily.

Mr Baxter shook his masked head as if we were exasperatingly stupid. 'The Eye of Horus will fade and close. His power will fade also. Then it will be time. So, eat and rest. You will need your strength to face what will come.' Without another word, he swung round and vanished through the door, slamming it shut behind him. We heard the key turn in the lock.

CHAPTER 36

Lily turned to me. 'What does he mean the Eye of Horus will fade and weaken? What is going on, Rose? Why did he say he was waiting for us? How did he know we were coming?'

Remember that before sun-disc rises, the cold Eye of Horus will close, and then Seth, god of darkness, will be all-powerful. That will be when the cat's blood is spilled.

I stared back at Lily, trying to organise my churning thoughts. Miut was long dead, so her blood wasn't going to be spilled. A terrible thought struck me, sucking the breath from my lungs. Was it our blood that Mr Baxter was intending to spill? I'd no idea why, except it had something to do with him calling us Daughters of Seth. But there was no point scaring Lily any more than she was already.

I realised I was still holding the lamp. I stood it on the table and lifting the glass I snuffed out the flame. There was no point in wasting oil; we would need the lamp when the candle went out.

'I took the key to the tomb from the hut,' I said as a terrible thought struck me. The hut had been left open and the key left on the table deliberately. They must have guessed I would be unable to resist taking it. But that raised an even more terrible thought. Had Zac been part of it? Had he pretended to be reluctant to show us the temple, knowing we would insist on going inside? Had he known the key would be there? Was that why he'd left me alone?

'They knew I had the key. They must have guessed I would come back tonight.' I thought for a moment. 'You were sound asleep. What woke you?'

Lily hesitated, then said slowly, 'A sort of scratching on the tent… I think.'

The thought of some shadowy figure watching Lily sleeping, then making sure she woke up, was too horrible. I hurried on. 'They must have thought you would come looking for me.' I paused, not really wanting to ask the question but I had to. 'What about Zac?'

Lily shook her head. 'I tried to wake him, to ask him to come with me. But he was too fast asleep, so I gave up and came on my own.'

Had he really been fast asleep or had he been pretending? I sighed, wishing the last thought didn't make me feel so sad.

'Now we're both here,' said Lily thoughtfully. 'But why?'

There was no point scaring Lily. I might be wrong about any harm coming to us. 'I wish I knew.'

She was silent for a while, thinking. 'And what have these dreams of yours got to do with it all?

'There must be some connection with my stone cat. I wish I knew what. It's not the Seal.'

'Are you sure?'

'A Seal has symbols or writing engraved into it. You know my cat has nothing like that on it.'

'Can I see?'

I pulled the stone cat out of my pocket and took it over to the candle. We examined it closely, as I'd done a hundred times before. I had to hold the cat almost in the flame to see anything. My fingers started to burn, and the cat grew almost too hot to hold. Suddenly something black splattered onto the tablecloth.

'Look, Lily,' I whispered scarcely believing what I was seeing, 'the base is covered in some sort of varnished wax.'

Lily fumbled in her pocket. 'Here, use this,' she said handing me a handkerchief.

I carefully wiped the base. We still couldn't see anything but as we ran our fingers across it, we could feel the indentations. I tilted the candle and tipped a puddle of yellow wax onto the black cloth, then, before it had a chance to cool and harden, I pressed the base of the seal firmly into it. I removed the seal and we stared at the wax with its perfect hieroglyphics imprinted into it. I recognised them immediately. *Heteb, High Priest of Osiris.* There was no doubt. The cat was the Seal after all.

I really wasn't surprised. I'd always thought it should be the Seal. I just hadn't seen how it could be.

... And Khay hadn't sent Hori as a decoy. He had trusted him with the genuine Seal. I stood the cat on the table and gazed at it, while I tried to sort out the tangle of ideas still spinning round my head.

'Oh,' whispered Lily, her eyes as wide as teacups.

'I suppose Uncle Arthur realised that he had found something interesting after all. Somehow Mr Baxter must have found out and wanted to know if it was the Seal.'

'Maybe Ezra told him,' suggested Lily. 'Remember, he started working for our aunt and uncle around the time the tomb was discovered. He must have known Uncle Arthur was excited about something.'

'I think that it was Ezra who searched the house. He made it look like there had been a burglary so no one would suspect him.'

Lily nodded. 'But Uncle Arthur had hidden the cat...'

'... in his Collection of Curiosities,' I interrupted triumphantly, 'so no one would suspect it was genuine, disguising it with wax and varnish. Or, maybe it was disguised like that thousands of years ago by Heteb himself, before he hung it round Miut's neck. Uncle Arthur may have been the first person to examine it properly and realise what it was.'

Lily frowned at me. 'I hate it when you talk about your dreams as if they were real.'

I shrugged. 'They are to me.'

She sighed and changed the subject. 'So maybe Ezra was

against us exploring the house in case we accidentally came across something we shouldn't see.'

Everything seemed to be dropping into place. 'Then when he heard we had been given some things he wanted to be sure what they were. But the cat was always with me. They could never examine it. Not until Mr Baxter found it in the box from the library. He would have guessed it was my cat. But then I took it back, perhaps before he had had a chance to examine it properly.'

Lily gazed round our prison with its strange leaping shadows, and shivered. 'But perhaps he was almost certain what it was. And he knew you never went anywhere without it. To get the cat back, he had to get you here too.' She paused for a long time. 'But that does not explain why he wanted me as well, or why he calls us the Daughters of Seth.'

'No,' I agreed. 'But whatever he says we can't trust him. There were plans on his table for a Temple of Seth...' There had been something about those drawings that had unsettled me, and they unsettled me now. A long narrow room, a door in the left-hand corner, two large windows, evenly spaced along the opposite wall.... and yet another piece of the jigsaw slotted into place. I whispered, 'I'm sure they were of the library in the House of Shadows.'

'Aunt Dora would never allow that.' Lily frowned.

'If he married Aunt Dora and something happened to her, then he could do whatever he liked.' I felt sick.

Lily stared at me, her eyes black holes of horror. 'You mean, murder...?' Her eyes fixed on mine, she added, 'But you think he would? And that he intends to murder us too?'

'Of course not,' I said quickly to reassure her. But hearing her say out loud what I'd been thinking made it sound true.

My head was aching with the stuffy heat of the chamber. I longed to be outside in the cool desert air. Would Mama and Papa ever know what had happened to us? The thought of them made my eyes prick. And Max, how was he?

Lily rubbed her forehead as if it hurt. 'Apart from Mr Baxter,

Mrs Hodges and Ezra we have no idea who else is involved. What about your man with those ice-blue eyes?'

'Or even Zac?' I hated saying his name but I had to. 'He could have been leading us here. Ezra is his grandfather after all…' I let my voice trail away. I hated where that particular line of thought was heading.

Lily shook her head. 'I can't believe that.'

I wished I were as sure. 'Anyway, none of that really matters now. What does matter is getting out of here.'

I went over and rattled the door. It remained shut fast.

'What CAN we do?' asked Lily.

I eyed the platter of food on the table and realised that in spite of everything I was starving. 'Maybe some food will help us think.'

'Honestly, Rose,' said Lily 'how can you eat at a time like this?'

But even she managed some dates and a chunk of bread. There was also a jug of lemon cordial. It tasted quite bitter but we were so hot, we drank our fill of it. Lily had two goblets full to the brim. In spite of ourselves, the food and drink did make us feel somewhat better. However it also made us feel extremely sleepy. We pulled the cloth off the table and laid it on the floor. It was uncomfortable to lie on but better than bare stone slabs. We curled up together and closed our eyes.

I should have wished that Lily was safely back in the tent, not here with me in danger but I was too selfish. I was just too relieved not to be alone.

'Rose,' said Lily softly, 'whatever happens I'm glad I'm here.'

'Really?'

'Yes, really.'

'Whatever?'

'Yes.'

'Me too.'

Then there was silence. After a while, her breathing deepened and steadied, and I knew she was asleep.

I lay for a while, my mind turning things over and over. Somehow

Lily and I had to get away. We had to warn Aunt Dora about Mr Baxter's plans for her and the House of Shadows.

I was exhausted, but sleep wouldn't come. I watched the candle on the table spluttering and tried to control the fear that was seeping into my bones.

I slipped the stone cat from my pocket. It felt reassuringly cool in my hand.

'Miut,' I whispered under my breath, 'we need your help. We'll help you too. Whatever you want. Just tell me how. Please.'

My eyes did begin to feel heavy. I couldn't keep them open one minute longer.

CHAPTER 37

'THE BOOK OF MIUT'

VI

Miut woke with a thirst that burned in her throat and a grumbling ache in her belly. Her eyes searched the blackness. It was darker than night. She was blind but her ears were full of sounds. Beside her, the kittens slept. She could hear every fluttering heartbeat and every breath they took. She nosed the nearest, feeling the softness of its fur, breathing its warm milkiness. They slept now but soon they would wake. The growing need to fill her empty belly and to quench the burning in her throat was impossible to ignore.

Quietly she stood and moved away from the sleeping kittens. Pausing only to stretch, she made her way down the rock ladder. She felt the way carefully, first one paw and then the next. At last she reached the ground, where she sat for a while, letting her whiskers test the air, feeling for those tiny vibrations that would tell her that a mouse, or even better, a rat was close by. Nothing stirred, not an ant, nor a scuttering beetle, and certainly not a rat.

She sniffed the air, seeking the sweet liquid scent of water, but again nothing. The tunnel was drier, and more lifeless, than the desert itself. She got to her feet, and began pacing further into the tunnel, feeling the stagnant air with her whiskers, searching for the smallest wisp of desert breeze to guide her. But the air was still and the only movement was hers. She paused for a moment, her ears straining to catch the faintest echoes of sounds beyond the tunnel. There was only silence. She continued making her way along the tunnel.

Shortly she found she could walk no further as a mountain of rocks had sealed the way. For a while she climbed over the rocks, butting at them with her nose, testing their solidity, looking for a way through. But there was none.

Far behind her, a kitten mewed in the blackness. Miut turned back the way she had come. This time she moved faster, more sure of her way, even the rock ladder was familiar now. It was not long before she lay beside the soft warm bodies of her kittens, letting them fasten greedily to her. But too soon her milk stopped flowing, and for a while the tunnel was filled with discontented mewlings. Eventually exhaustion quietened them, and the kittens fell into an uneasy sleep while Miut stared into the endless blackness, listening.

~

After what seemed like forever, the silence quivered and vanished. From beyond the tumbled barrier far beneath the great stepped pyramid came the sound of clatterings and scrapings. Somewhere rocks were being moved aside. Then came voices. Blurred at first, but gradually they grew clearer. Then Miut felt it on her whiskers; the faintest tremble of clean desert air.

At the same time the blackness lightened to deepest grey, and she was no longer blind. She could see the shadows and the shapes that surrounded her.

The voices were near now. She could hear exultation in them, but there was darkness too. They carried torches in their hands. Orange flames leapt and sent shadows dancing on the walls. In the lead, with his torch held high above his head, strode the Jackal-Priest.

'Hurry,' he snarled, 'We have wasted too much time already. The ropes should have been left ready for our descent. Any fool who lets me down again will pay with their life.'

Miut could feel his fury vibrating through the air. She eased herself into a crouch, each muscle drawn tight. Her eyes glowed amber, her unsheathed claws bit into the rock beneath her. She would defend with her life the kittens sleeping at her side.

The Jackal-Priest came to a halt beneath the ledge. The masked priests that followed drew close, and fell quiet. He turned towards the Crocodile-Priest, and pointed to the ledge where Miut waited. The words spat into the silence. 'Why look who is here waiting for us.' He raised his hand and pointed. 'Fetch me that cat.'

Miut heard the threat. As still as stone, she waited. Below her, the Crocodile-Priest started up the rock ladder. Too soon, he was level with her, his black eyes gleaming through the long-nosed mask, daring her to move. A hand slid towards her. She watched it, waiting for it to come within range of her needle teeth. She did not see the flick of his hidden hand, nor the cloth dropping towards her. Not until it was too late. With a movement swifter than the strike of a snake, she found herself scooped off the ledge and wrapped tight in the cloth. Only her head was left free. She hissed and spat out her hate. The Crocodile-Priest laughed and then, holding her at a safe distance from his body, he dropped her into the outstretched hands of the Jackal-Priest.

The Crocodile-Priest explored the recess with his hand. 'There is a nest of kittens here too? What shall I do with them?'

The Jackal-Priest grasped Miut tightly. 'Now I have you, my little goddess. And I have your kittens. Soon, very soon, it will be your time to re-join your master. And your kittens can make the journey too.' He laughed. But there was no joy in it. Only hate. He turned to the Crocodile-Priest. 'Bring them,' he ordered, 'use the basket.'

The Crocodile-Priest obediently scooped up the kittens and dropped them into the basket the Beetle-Priest held ready. He cleared his throat nervously as he climbed down the stone ladder. 'The treasures of the High Priest? Shall we remove them now?'

The Jackal-Priest threw a short glance at the burial goods. 'There is no need for haste. They will come to no harm here. When the Temple of Osiris is named the Great Temple of Seth, then we will return and collect what is ours.'

The Beetle-Priest cleared his throat again. 'And what about Hori?'

'Oh, I have plans for him,' said the Jackal-Priest. 'He will be here soon. He cannot give up his search for the cat and the Seal.'

'He said nothing of the Seal,' muttered the Beetle-Priest.

'Of course, he would not. He does not think we know of it. Kenna and Pemou are on watch nearby. Neshi also. As soon as they see him, they will bring him to us...'

THUD, THUD, THUD. The sound came from the Painted Chamber, resounding from other side of the newly built wall.

'Ahh!' whispered the Jackal-Priest, his voice throbbing with sudden excitement, 'it is almost time. Kenna warns us that the Eye is closing,' He indicated with his hand for the Crocodile-Priest to lead on. 'Now follow me.'

The procession moved off along the tunnel. The Crocodile-Priest led with his torch held high, the Jackal-Priest followed with Miut grasped tightly in his outstretched hands, and behind came the masked priests in twos, gliding noiselessly on their sandaled feet.

Miut twisted and turned, trying with all her strength to bite at the hands that imprisoned her. The hands that carried her from her kittens. The hands who meant her harm. But their grip was too tight.

The priests slowed as they pressed their way through a narrow gap between the fallen rocks. After that the tunnel became a passage with plastered walls and a stone-slabbed floor. They passed an opening, but the chamber beyond was dark and empty.

Soon they came to a second opening. This one was an arch cut from rock; strange black and red symbols decorated its edge. The priests halted and turned to pass through it into a large chamber. The chamber was longer and wider than the Painted Chamber of Heteb, and it was twice as high. Two rows of five slender columns ran its length. A statue carved from black rock stood at the base of each column. Each statue was the same as every other. Its snout was long and curved, its ears stood tall and square. Behind its back was a tail forked like a snake's tongue. In its right hand it held a tall and slender sceptre, and in its left hand it held the ankh, the key of life.

Once inside, the priests fanned out, placing their glowing torches in brackets, one to each column.

As the light from the flames forced back the shadows, it revealed walls that glowed with brilliant colour. Every scene showed the standing figure of the same god. And each painted god was the same as the carved stone statue that guarded each pillar.

Their hair was the red of rust and blood that had dried, while the skin of their bodies was as pale as milk. Each wore a kilt of gold. The painted gods towered above the many smaller figures, all of whom bowed or knelt, before them. Some carried food or drink, while others held treasures in their arms. The images were as clean and bright as if they were freshly painted.

The Jackal-Priest came to a halt in the centre of the room. He stood statue-still, waiting for the priests to turn to him, and fall silent. Miut remained imprisoned in his hands.

'We are in the Chamber of Seth, the Chamber that once belonged to Imhotep,' he said at last, 'and all that we have worked for lies in our grasp. We have the scroll and we have the Seal. The Eye of Horus has closed and Osiris is without protection. Ra and the Sun-disc have not yet risen. The time of Seth approaches.'

'SETH… SETH…SETH…' chorused the watching priests. They then fell silent.

Miut's ears twitched. Footsteps were approaching along the passage. There were two sets. One set was as familiar to her as her own breath. And the voice too, the sound of it warmed her, even though she could hear the fury in it.

'Ouch! Remove your hands, Neshi. I can walk by myself.'

The priests turned expectantly towards the entrance. Suddenly Hori was there, framed against the darkness behind him. His eyes were wide and black, his lips were clenched shut and his hands were behind his back. Snake-Eyes was at his shoulder.

'Get in there, you worm,' spat Snake-Eyes as he pushed the boy so sharply he was sent sprawling on the floor of the chamber. Miut could see the band of animal skin that bound his hands.

Snake-Eyes turned to the Jackal-Priest. 'He followed you, Father. Kenna and Penou saw him climbing down your ropes. I followed and found him hiding in the tunnel. He did not hear me coming.' He gave a bark of laughter.

The Jackal-Priest nodded. 'This was well done, my son.' He dropped his gaze to the boy on the ground. 'Welcome, Hori. This ceremony would not be complete without you.'

The Beetle-Priest crossed over and pulled the boy to his feet, then he held him tight. Blood oozed from Hori's knees. His face was pale and his eyes were dark with shock.

'What ceremony? What are you talking about?' Then the boy's eyes narrowed and his mouth dropped open as he grasped what the Jackal-Priest held in his hands. 'What are you doing with Miut?' His voice was raw with horror. 'She is so no longer heavy with kittens. Where are they? What is happening here? What is this place?'

'Questions, questions,' sighed the Jackal-Priest gently, 'and there is so little time for answers. For you and this little goddess.' There was a pause, as if he weighed the possibilities. 'But perhaps you should know why you will never leave this place.'

'Never leave? What do you mean?' Hori's face twisted as if he was in pain.

The Jackal-Priest continued as if he had not spoken. His voice was soft now and gentle. It was as if he was soothing a young child. But Miut could hear the iron beneath. 'We are in a chamber beneath the centre of the pyramid. Imhotep, the great architect of King Djoser, knew the magic of this building. He knew the centre of power lay in this chamber.

'But first Imhotep carried out his duties and he prepared the chamber for King Djoser deep within the complex. It lies far beneath us and is magnificent. Many smaller chambers and tunnels surround it. They were once full of all that the King and his family would need in the afterlife.

'However this pyramid hides more than the secrets of King Djoser. Imhotep was not only a great architect, he was also a great magician. He too wished to become a god in the afterlife. After Djoser crossed to the West, unknown to all but his most trusted workmen, Imhotep prepared this chamber for himself. Here in the very centre of power, he would be laid to rest. From here he would rise to be a god.'

The voice of the Jackal-Priest grew darker as he continued. 'A thousand times the great river rose and fell, and the secrets of

Imhotep were lost. That is, until High Priest Heteb began to plan his own resting place.' The Jackal-Priest snarled, 'He dared to believe he was also a great magician, worthy of walking with the gods. He spent years uncovering the secrets of Imhotep.

'Heteb chose the position of his temple carefully. He had learned that behind its back wall lay a tunnel and other chambers. One of these, he knew, must be the Chamber of Imhotep. Your father, Khay, helped him break through into the tunnel, and along with those they thought as their most trusted workers, they found this chamber.' He gave another triumphant laugh. 'Some of those most "trusted" workers watch you now.'

A small grumble of laughter rumbled through the watching priests. Hori's face twisted again.

'They found the chamber empty. There was no sign that Imhotep had ever rested here. Perhaps he was offered a grander tomb somewhere else. We do not know. So the High Priest had the walls painted and the chamber prepared…'

'With paintings of Seth?' interrupted the boy staring around, his eyes disbelieving.

The Jackal-Priest's laugh cut the air. 'Oh, no. Osiris once looked down from these walls, but when Heteb had taken his last breath, after that unfortunate incident with a scorpion…'

'You murdered him, didn't you,' whispered Hori.

The Jackal-Priest shrugged. 'It was just a small thing to introduce a scorpion into his bed. Afterwards we had to do a little …,' he hesitated as if searching for the correct word, 'redecoration. And of course, your father could not be allowed to interfere.'

'It was you who set your magic against him? You crippled his leg.' The boy was no longer in pain. Now his eyes flamed with anger. 'You are a liar and a traitor. Set me free. Set Miut free too.'

'Silence.' The Jackal-Priest's quiet tone was replaced by a darker one, one which cut the air like a knife. He turned to Snake-Eyes. 'Hold this cat, Neshi. Hold her tight.'

Snake-Eyes stepped forward, his lips twisting into a smile, and grasped Miut. His fingers dug into her as he took her from the

Jackal-Priest. She spat and struggled but his grip did not loosen.

'See, worm,' said Snake-Eyes softly, 'enjoy watching her breathe. She will not breathe for long.'

'You can't allow this to happen, Neshi.' Hori struggled to free himself from the Beetle-Priest's grip. 'Please don't let your father hurt her. I will get you anything you want.' But he was held fast and Snake-Eyes shrugged and turned to the Jackal-Priest.

'So, Hori,' the Jackal-Priest crossed to the wall opposite the entrance, 'your time runs out. But first let me show you some of our redecoration.' He raised his hand. 'See the Hall of Judgement. Here is Heteb standing before Anubis while his heart is being weighed. Look carefully and you will see that the heart of Heteb is heavy with sin. How unfortunate he was not able to speak the Final Spell.'

He pulled a scroll from beneath his tunic and held it up. It was the scroll Hori had carried in his kilt.

'Once the scroll is destroyed, see what will happen,' said the Jackal-Priest pointing at the wall again. 'Do you not recognise the Amenti creature, gobbler of wicked souls? Watch how he slobbers and snarls. Heteb will not save Osiris. He will not save Horus. He will not even save himself. Seth will be master of all.'

He threw back his head and laughed so loudly it echoed round the chamber. The priests all threw back their heads and laughed with him. On and on, the sound reverberated around the chamber. It seemed it would never stop. Then, all at once, the Jackal-Priest raised his hand and silence fell.

Miut felt the boy's eyes on her. They were dark and full of grief. But something sparked behind the darkness.

'It must be time,' the Jackal-Priest called out. His eyes turned to Snake-Eyes. 'Bring the cat here.' He raised his hand. He was holding a knife. The long, slender blade gleamed dully in the flickering light.

Hori screamed 'No!' He threw himself forward but the Beetle-Priest held him tight, his arm round the boy's neck.

'You are mad,' shouted the boy, still twisting and turning, 'just take the Seal. You don't have to harm her.' For a heartbeat, his eyes

rested on Miut and the shadow of a smile flickered. His mouth opened slightly, his head bent towards the arm that imprisoned him. Then the Beetle-Priest screamed and his arm dropped from the boy's neck, blood running from a crescent of teeth marks. In that moment the boy jerked free and threw himself at Snake-Eyes.

Miut felt the hands that held her slacken. It was enough. The cloth loosened. She twisted, using her claws and her teeth to thrust herself free. She again tasted the rusty-saltiness of his blood. A cry of agony ripped the air apart, and Snake-Eyes lay moaning on the ground.

But she was already in the air, rotating her body as she fell so that she landed neatly on her feet. For an instant she stood rock-still. Where could she go? A wall of priests stood between her and the entrance to the chamber. She realised not all their eyes were on her. Hori was at her side. His hands were still behind his back but he was forcing them apart, loosening the band that held them. Then his hands were free.

~

Together they stood facing the slowly advancing priests. Miut felt air move across her whiskers. She took a breath. Her nostrils quivered. She could smell the desert in the air. She stepped backwards. And took another breath. There was no mistake. The smell was stronger here. The air was coming from behind her. And beneath her. Then she saw it. In the floor. In the corner of the chamber. A shaft. Not wide. But wider than a cat.

There was no more time. She leapt into the darkness. For a moment she was falling. Then her feet touched the ground. Above her came the sound of something large scrabbling. Dust and small rocks fell. Then Hori was beside her. She rubbed herself against his legs and purred a great rumbling purr. He laughed. His hand stroked her head.

His voice was soft. 'Well, Miut, I know not what sort of trouble we are in now. But at least we are together.'

Above them more stones rattled. And a light flickered

It was Snake-Eyes. She could smell him and his smouldering torch.

Hori's voice was anxious now. 'It is Neshi. No one else would fit. We must move.'

The tunnel stretched in front of them, behind them was solid rock. There was only one way to go. Miut stalked ahead of the boy. It was dark, but not too dark. The light from the torch far behind them lit the tunnel just enough. She could see ahead and the boy could see her. When Snake-Eyes moved faster, Miut moved faster. When he slowed, she slowed. The distance between them did not change. The tunnel ran long and straight. Its sides were uneven. In one place Miut skirted carefully round the mouth of a shaft lying like a puddle of blackness across their path. Her whiskers sensed its depth; it seemed to drop forever.

After a while they came to a junction where the tunnel split in two. Miut paused, her whiskers testing the air. In one tunnel, the air was dead and still. In the other she could smell the desert, more strongly than before. Miut turned towards the desert.

This tunnel was wider than the last. And its walls were broken by the entrances to numerous chambers, each one shadowed and empty. Then came another junction, and another. At each one, Miut stopped and tasted the air. Each time she chose the tunnel that led her towards the desert breeze. Some sections of the tunnels were high roofed and wide, others were low and narrow. In one place the roof dropped so low the boy had to lie on the ground and squirm through the gap like a worm.

As the boy stood up and brushed the sand off his kilt, he muttered, 'It is lucky I have not eaten too much, or I might have been stuck here for a thousand years.'

But Miut was already on the move. She had felt the first strong breath of desert wind on her whiskers and now nothing was going to stop her. Somehow she would find her way back to her kittens. The tunnel ended as another crossed it. Without hesitation she swung towards the breeze. And now she could smell mice, and even better, a juicy, desert rat.

Just then, behind them, the tunnel behind went dark. Snake-Eyes had stopped. Miut paused, letting her whiskers feel the shape of the air, testing the obstacles ahead. They moved more slowly but still they moved. Before her heart could beat eight times the light returned, moving faster and burning, brighter than before.

'If you thought you had lost me, worm,' called out Snake-Eyes, 'you were wrong. And now I am not alone. You will not escape us.'

Hori looked back and frowned. 'The priests have caught up with Neshi. They must have found another path,' he muttered as torches flared in the blackness.

Miut's ears twitched. A crowd of voices now followed them and many feet hurried through the tunnel towards her. She broke into a trot. Hori followed, his breathing becoming ragged as he tired, but his pace never slowed.

The larger tunnel ran into a smaller tunnel, which rose steeply, then levelled out. For a short while it grew darker as the light behind faded. But almost at once, the blackness ahead dissolved to grey. Soon the grey paled to gold.

'It is the sun-disc, Miut. You have led us to freedom,' gasped the boy. 'Well done, little goddess, well done.'

He started to run towards the light. Miut bounded beside him.

A sound cut the air like a dagger. Miut froze and spun round. The sound came again. She recognised it in a heartbeat. The terrified cry of a kitten. She stared into the darkness.

'Come on, Miut,' pleaded Hori, his voice sharp with fear.

But Miut ignored him. The tunnel was suddenly full of masked priests. The Jackal-Priest was in the lead. Miut's eyes were fixed on him.

'I told you she would stop if she heard a kitten,' he said, his voice oozing satisfaction, his eyes watching her every move. 'Move gently. She will not escape from us again.' He lifted his voice and called out, 'Kenna, Penou are you there?'

A voice came from behind Miut. 'Yes, Anubis.'

'The cat is with us. And the boy. Stop them if they run at you.'

Miut glanced behind her to the mouth of the tunnel. The light of the sun-disc glowed enticingly. But between her and the light, two man-shadows now waited. They stood across the tunnel, leaning slightly forwards with legs apart, their hands hanging down and their fingers spread wide. At the same moment she became aware of a movement in front of her.

The Jackal-Priest was moving cautiously nearer, his eyes never leaving her. In one hand he carried a basket. From the other dangled a kitten with closed eyes. It paddled the air helplessly. The Jackal-Priest laughed and shook it. The kitten's frantic mewling filled the tunnel.

Behind him, the remaining priests had formed a moving wall. In their centre was Snake-Eyes. In his hand she could see the dull gleam of a blade.

Miut sank into a crouch. Her mouth opened to reveal her needle teeth. She spat out her hate in a dreadful hiss. Her eyes flamed fire-gold. Her claws were unsheathed. She saw the hesitation in the eyes of the Jackal-Priest. It was enough.

She flew through the air and lunged at his throat, exposed and vulnerable below the mask. She sank her teeth deep into his flesh. He screamed, raised his hands to protect himself and dropped the kitten and the basket. For a moment she tasted the sweet-saltiness of his blood. Then his hands were tearing her free. The air was being crushed from her lungs. There was no more time. Straining every muscle in her neck she turned and bit hard into his hand. Again his scream rang out, echoing through the tunnel. Suddenly she was falling. She was already racing as her paws touched the floor.

She fled towards the light. She must draw him away from her kittens. The flailing hands of the nearest shadow-man touched her fur, nothing more. She recognised his smell as she darted between his legs. Swollen-Belly. There was no one now between her and freedom. She flexed her legs and streaked towards the entrance. She burst from the blackness into the pink and gold of the new day. In the same instant, she saw the danger. In front of her was a ledge no wider than six cats, beyond that nothing but air.

She threw her weight backwards, her legs outstretched. Her claws bit at the rock. For a heartbeat, she teetered on the edge of the void. Every muscle screamed as she scrabbled her way back onto the ledge. She perched there like a fur-covered bird, examining her surroundings. The shaft was vast. Its walls towered above her until they met the sky, and fell away below her into a lake of shadows. Its sheer sides were dotted with black openings. The only movement came from a rope swinging gently to and fro, high above her head. There was no way up, and there was no way down. All this Miut saw, even as the small stones and rocks her scrabblings had disturbed were still spinning down into the depths of the shaft.

Another mewling cry came from the tunnel behind her. Miut twisted so she faced its mouth.

'I will have the Seal,' roared the Jackal-Priest appearing suddenly out of the darkness. His mask had gone. Blood trickled from the puncture marks at his throat and from his hand, which now held a knife. His eyes were wild, his face contorted. From his uninjured hand dangled a kitten.

'And now you will pass into the west. And your kittens too.' His eyes were on Miut. He took a step towards her.

She saw how he gripped the handle of his knife so hard that his knuckles were white. She saw how her kitten paddled the air. She did not move. It was not yet time.

The Jackal-Priest's mouth twisted into a terrible smile. He held up his arm and opened his hand. The kitten fell on to the ledge. It lay there, twitching. Its distressed cries rippled through the air. He raised his knife and took a step towards Miut. 'There is nowhere for you to run, little goddess. I will have the Seal and then you can follow the High Priest. The knife or the fall? The choice will be mine.'

'No, Paser. Stop. You cannot do this.'

Hori burst from the mouth of the tunnel and in one fluid movement he had ducked past the Jackal-Priest and slithered to a halt beside Miut. He spun to face the Jackal-Priest.

The Jackal-Priest threw back his head and laughed, the sound echoing round the shaft. 'Who will stop me, Hori? Not you. Give me the cat.'

Hori stood straight and tall. 'No.'

'You have no choice,' spat the Jackal-Priest. 'Give me the cat. Then I will let you go free.'

The boy shook his head. 'You lie. Why would you let me live to speak against you?'

The Jackal-Priest took another step forwards. 'GIVE ME THE CAT,' he ordered, as if Hori had not spoken.

Miut felt the boy crouch down beside her and slip his hand round her neck. There was a brief coolness against her skin and then the weight of the pouch was gone from her neck. The boy's hand now rested on her head. His touch steadied her, but Miut's eyes never left the Jackal-Priest.

'Let us both go free,' the boy's voice was as hard as the rock beneath her paws. One hand still lay on her head, the other held the pouch out over the void, 'or I will cast the Seal into the shaft. It will surely shatter into a hundred pieces. Is that what you want?'

The Jackal-Priest ducked to the ground. The next instant, the sprawling kitten was back in his hand. 'The choice is yours, Hori,' he snarled, 'give me the Seal or watch the kitten fall. Or perhaps I will crush it in my hand… or cut its mewling throat.'

He held the kitten up high. Its cries grew louder. Its strugglings grew more frantic. Then he raised the knife, his cold eyes fixed on the boy's outstretched hand. 'I mean it. Give me the Seal or the kitten will take its last breath.'

Miut dropped into a crouch. Her eyes blazed. Her muscles tensed. She sprang into the air.

The boy yelled, 'No, Miut.'

Miut was flying towards the Jackal-Priest, away from Hori and away from the Seal in his hand. The air clouded as she passed. It was as if she was jumping through a mist.

Her teeth closed on the Jackal-Priest's knife hand. His fingers opened wide and the knife clattered onto the ledge.

'AAAHHH,' he bellowed, and released the kitten, which tumbled back onto the ground and lay still. Now the Jackal-Priest was pulling desperately at Miut with his kittenless hand. Desperate to

free himself, he lurched forwards. The mist was thicker now. For a moment, the Jackal-Priest and Miut were outlined, shadow-shapes, poised motionless on the brink of the shaft. Then they were falling. Separating as they fell. The Jackal-Priest's scream filled the shaft as he vanished into the darkness below. Miut was spinning after him.

Hori cried out, 'Miut, No. Miut.' His voice was an agony of terror and grief.

And then another so very familiar voice came from far above, from the place where the desert met the sky.

'Miut,' shouted the Lame-Priest, 'save yourself.'

As if the voices had shocked her into action, Miut suddenly twisted in the air, spreading her legs out wide, so the air cushioned her. Her angle of fall was now carrying her nearer the shaft wall. She touched it with her outstretched claws. Shards of rock flew into air at her wild scrabblings, but still she slid on downwards.

The boy held his breath as his eyes followed Miut. 'Please Osiris. Please let her live.' His voice was little more than a whisper. The mist thickened round Miut. She seemed to fade. She was gone.

The mist was denser now. It swirled on upwards towards the light. It was enveloping everything it touched. The boy, the priests, the shaft itself, were all hidden. All was silence. All was darkness.

CHAPTER 38

'Rose, Rose, wake up, PLEASE!'

I kept my eyes closed. Inside my head there was just the darkness and the silence. I knew that shaft. It was the one Zac had shown us. It was so deep. Miut's desperate scrabblings filled my head. Could she possibly have survived the fall? Why did that terrible fog have to hide everything?

I closed my eyes even tighter. If I went back to sleep I might find out. I remember Hori cutting the Seal from Miut's neck. That was when the mist appeared. I tried to work it out. The Seal may only have absorbed Miut's thoughts when it was really close to her? Touching her. It worked when Hori was first holding it though....

It took a few seconds before I remembered Hori resting his hand on Miut's head. There was still a link then. But the link was broken when Miut leapt away from him to attack the Jackal-Priest.

'WAKE UP.' Lily was shaking me. I groaned, and turned away. I wished she would leave me alone.

What about Hori? Neshi had a knife. And the kittens? The one on the ground lay so still. Too still. I couldn't bear to think about what might have happened to them.

'Go away Lily,' I mumbled, 'I just want to sleep.'

'I can hear them. They are coming back. What are we going to DO?'

It was the desperation in her voice that made me sit up. The candle was still burning... just. I wasn't sure if this was all a dream too. I pinched my arm. It hurt.

We heard a key in the lock and the door swung open.

Mr Baxter entered carrying a burning torch. He was still cloaked and wearing the Jackal mask. I could only see his eyes. They told me nothing.

He looked across at the crumpled cloth on the floor. 'I see you have managed to rest. I thought it would be better if you slept a little.' He sounded strangely satisfied.

I remembered how tired we felt after we had eaten...

Lily stared at him, open mouthed. 'You put something in our food?'

'Not the food, the drink. Just a little laudanum,' he said, his voice like silk. 'We did not want you wasting your time trying to escape.'

I remembered the other cloaked and hooded figures. 'Who is w...we?' I couldn't control the tremble in my voice.

Mr Baxter shook his jackal head. 'Enough questions. It is time to go.'

The group of cloaked figures waited for us by the door. But now they wore masks not hoods. I recognised most of them. The Crocodile, the Beetle, the Ram, and the other strange and fantastical gods of my dreams. Each was as motionless as if they had been carved from stone. Each held a blazing torch. The only movement came from the wavering flames and the gleam of the eyes behind the masks. They followed our every move.

Reluctantly we stepped out into the tunnel. The masked figures turned to follow us. Were they people we knew? Was Ezra one of them? Or the man in the cream suit? Or was Zac glaring at us through one of those terrible masks? And what about Mrs Hodges?

My legs felt like straw. I glanced at Lily. Her eyes were huge, her face was ghost white and her mouth trembled. She looked as if she was struggling to breathe too. I realised I was looking at myself. I held out my hand. She took it, and the solid warmth of her grip steadied me.

I take a deep breath. 'It will be alright,' I whispered, 'truly it will. They wouldn't dare hurt us.' I was lying of course. 'They are just trying to frighten us.'

A flicker of a smile twisted Lily's lips. 'They're succeeding,' she murmured.

The figures moved aside and lined the passage. There was only one way we could go. The figures fell in silently at our side. Their feet were hidden by the sweep of their cloaks and they appeared to float rather than walk.

We continued down the tunnel in silence. It was only the warmth of Lily's hand in mine that stopped me screaming. It wasn't long before I saw a doorway ahead.

'Oh!' I breathed. There hadn't been a wooden door when Miut was carried through the opening in my dream but I recognised the arch all the same.

'What?' demanded Lily.

I pointed at the doorway and hissed into her ear, 'I can tell you what we'll see in there. Huge paintings of Seth on every wall. He'll have red hair and white skin. There will be two rows of five columns and there will be a statue of Seth beside each one.' I touched her cheek so she turned to look at me. I held her eyes with mine. 'You must believe me about Miut and my dreams. You really must.'

We were pushed through the doorway. It was just as I remembered. Well, almost...

'No statues,' whispered Lily, 'but the paintings of Seth... the columns... I don't understand how you knew.'

'My dreams, I told you.'

Lily stared at me as she tried to make sense of it all.

The chamber had changed in other ways too. There was just one torch fixed to the central pillar. Stone slabs covered the floor and there was no sign of Miut and Hori's shaft. At the far end stood a table covered by another black cloth decorated with blood red hieroglyphs. Standing on the table were two silver candlesticks, and between them a silver chalice. It reminded me of an altar.

I glanced back at the door. Only Mr Baxter had entered the chamber, the others remained in the tunnel.

'Daughters of Seth, you are most welcome here in the Chamber of Seth.' He fixed us with his glittering eyes. 'We have waited long for this moment.'

'I don't understand,' said Lily staring at him. 'We've only been in Egypt for a few days.'

'Let me show you something.' Mr Baxter crossed to the far wall and indicated for us to join him. He raised his torch lighting up the wall. I saw a group of Egyptians kneeling before a towering Seth.

'Look closely,' he commanded.

At first I didn't understand what he was showing us. I hadn't noticed the painting in my dream but then I realised what we were looking at. The shock drove the air from my lungs. The figures were all young women. Each wore a long, white tunic dress. Each had skin as pale as milk, and each had hair that glowed as red as the hair of the god they knelt before.

'Oh!' whispered Lily, 'I see.' Her voice fell away.

'Seth has been alone far too long.' Mr Baxter's voice was triumphant. 'He has slept for many weary years. Now your presence will wake him. He will walk again amongst the living and the dead, more powerful than ever before. All will tremble before him and his mighty power.' Mr Baxter was ecstatic at the idea. 'You will have the greatest honour of all. You will be his companions in the afterlife.'

'The afterlife? You mean you want us dead?' My mouth felt like it was made of wood.

'You wouldn't dare hurt us,' said Lily.

'People will be looking for us,' I added.

Mr Baxter gave a wide, wolfish smile. 'Everyone knows that the desert at night is a dangerous place. Some ripped clothing will be taken from your tent, smeared with blood and left far out in the desert. That will send those who seek you after the desert jackals and hyenas who must have attacked you when you unwisely went for a ride by moonlight. Your donkeys have been set free and will have wandered far from here. Nothing will link you to this place.'

At the mention of the donkeys being released, I felt the first tremble of hope. If Djinn went straight home, as Zac had warned me she would if ever she found herself free, then that would surely start a search for us. Maybe her hoof prints in the sand would lead the searchers straight here? I glanced at the figures waiting in the shadows beyond the doorway. The tremble of hope faded. If Zac and Ezra were there, watching us now, they wouldn't be raising any search for us.

'But I am not going to kill you.' Mr Baxter crossed to the altar. He pulled a silver spoon and a piece of folded paper from under his robe. He placed the spoon on the table, and carefully opened up the paper so that a stream of powder spilled into the chalice. He picked up the spoon and stirred the liquid. 'You'll have no need to be afraid of a long painful walk into the afterlife,' he said softly. 'One sip of this, and you will arrive there.'

I wanted to laugh. He sounded as if he was reading the script of a really bad play.

'We aren't drinking anything,' declared Lily. 'Let us go NOW.'

I stared at her. I'd never heard her sound so fierce before.

'Oh, there is no question of forcing you, my dear,' said Mr Baxter softly. 'You will take it gladly enough when you understand the alternative... hunger that will twist in your belly like a knife, thirst that will burn your throat. You will long for the afterlife soon enough.' His voice drifted to silence.

I realised then that he was quite mad.

Beyond the doorway, a sigh breathed through the listening priests. They moved uneasily. Mr Baxter glanced at them. 'Quiet,' he snapped before turning back to us.

'This is ridiculous,' said Lily. 'Mama and Papa will find us long before that happens.'

'You are hundreds of feet beneath the Step Pyramid. No one will ever find you.'

He was right. No one would ever find us. Not alive anyway.

He turned to me. 'Now Rose, Daughter of Seth, give me the Seal. Its power and its magic are mine. For thousands of years the League has waited. Now is our time.'

I fought to control my fear and said carefully, 'What seal?'

Mr Baxter tossed his jackal head. 'I mean, give me the stone cat, stupid child.'

'Why? It's just an amulet. And not even an old one.'

Mr Baxter took a step closer. 'Do not treat me like a fool. I know what it is. Why else would your uncle have gone to such length to hide it from me?' He let out a bark of wild laughter and held out his hand. 'But I will have it now.'

I wanted to distract him for just a little longer. Not that it would help much. As he said, no one knew we were here. No one would be rushing to rescue us.

I took a couple of deep breaths and my head cleared. I felt an icy calm spreading through me. 'The burglary before our uncle died, that was your idea?'

'The burglary was unwise. We were not sure what we were looking for. Then we were interrupted. Your uncle felt unwell and returned home sooner than expected.' Mr Baxter held out his hand. 'Stop wasting time. Give me the cat.'

I had to make him see reason. 'Why? You've seen it. It's just an amulet. Let us go and we'll forget all about you keeping us here.'

'Not one word. We promise,' agreed Lily staring at Mr Baxter with desperate eyes. 'No one will even know we are missing yet. You can safely let us go.'

He gave a snort of laughter. 'As if I believe that. And as for your cat, surely you have learned by now that things in Egypt are seldom what they seem. I was almost certain what it was when I found it in the box your aunt so kindly had delivered to me.'

'You're not having it,' I said furiously.

'Give it to me now,' Mr Baxter's words shot out like bullets. 'I must have it.'

'No!' I glared at him. 'Never!'

Mr Baxter took a step towards me. I backed away. He took another step and another, forcing me backwards. And as he moved he chanted...

'The Eye of Horus is closing,

The hour of Seth is coming.'

Suddenly Lily was pulling furiously at his cloak, shouting, 'Leave her alone!'

With one thrust of his arm he sent her stumbling backwards, then turned back to me.

My back was now pressed hard against the wall. There was nowhere to go. Mr Baxter towered over me, his mask a nightmare silhouette in the gloom.

The stone cat was in my hand. I ducked to the right. But he was too quick. His hand clutched my arm. His steel fingers held me fast.

'I will have what is mine,' he hissed.

He forced my fingers open one by one. Then I was tumbling onto the floor, and the stone cat was clasped in his raised fist.

'Give it back. It's not yours.' I screamed the words at him, but I just sounded pathetic, like a child who has lost their favourite toy.

He examined the base with his fingers. Suddenly he threw back his head and let out a strange, high-pitched shriek. 'I knew it. It IS the Seal. And now it is MINE.'

My eyes pricked with unwanted tears. I blinked furiously. I wasn't going to give him the satisfaction of seeing me cry. I sat on floor hugging my knees and stared stonily up at the triumphant Mr Baxter.

Without another word he crossed the room and slammed the door shut behind him. I heard the key turn in the lock and footsteps retreating. Then, there was only silence.

CHAPTER 39

Lily came and sat down beside me on the floor. She was rubbing her elbow.

'Are you alright?' I asked.

She nodded. 'I scraped it on the wall when he pushed me away. I'm quite unhurt otherwise.'

'Thank you for trying to help.'

She sighed. 'I'm sorry I failed. But what now, Rose? Will your cat be appearing to rescue us?'

She sounded as if she wanted to believe Miut would help us.

I shook my head. 'No. He has the stone cat. It only appears when I have it. We're on our own.'

For a while we sat in the dim flickering light of the one smouldering torch. The only sound was the soft sizzling and spitting of the flames.

Earlier I'd been glad that Lily was with me. But now I realised how incredibly selfish that was. My eyes filled. I closed them tight, but burning tears slid down my cheeks. Lily put her arm round my shoulders, and that was worse. I'd let the dreams and Miut take over my life and that was why we were in such danger.

'I'm so sorry, Lily,' I said, 'I'll never think of Miut again. The only thing that matters is that you get out of here safely.'

Lily shook her head. 'No. The only thing that matters is that WE get out of here safely.'

But as we sat in the silent emptiness of the Chamber of Seth, Miut refused to be banished. She was in every shadow, in the dust on floor, in the air we breathed. How could I not think of her?

Believe in her? Worry and wonder about her and her kittens?

I gave up trying to forget and closed my eyes to remember her. The flickering torches, the masked priests, Hori standing beside Miut forbidding them to hurt her, their escape down the... shaft.

I jumped to my feet and pulled the torch out of its holder.

'What are you doing?' asked Lily.

'Looking for any sign of the shaft that was here in my last dream. Miut and Hori escaped down it. They were imprisoned here, just like we are now. It must be under one of these slabs.'

She raised her eyebrows but came over to stand beside me, and we both peered at the floor. 'They all look the same to me. Heavy. How are we going to shift them?'

I studied the stone slabs carefully. 'It looks like they have just been laid on sand. If we clean out the cracks, we should be able to lever one up.' But what could we use as a scraper? I felt in my pockets. There was only my tin of crayons and some charcoal.

'What about the spoon he stirred the poison with?' suggested Lily, handing it to me.

I closed my eyes and tried to remember exactly where Miut had been when she became aware of the fresh desert air. I went and stood in what I thought was the same place. If I was right, then the shaft should have been right behind me. I peered at the nearby slabs.

'I think the shaft was about here.' I said at last, pointing at a large grey slab, identical to all the others.

'Are you sure?' said Lily doubtfully.

'No. But it's worth trying. Unless you have any other ideas?'

She shook her head, knelt down and began using the spoon to remove the sand round the slab. I searched round for something to use as a lever. There was nothing. Feeling useless, I went over to see how Lily was getting on. The sand around the slab was almost completely excavated.

Lily glanced up at me. 'Maybe we can lift one side with our hands if we pull together?'

We hooked our fingers along one edge of the slab. 'One, two, three, LIFT,' I ordered.

We pulled until our fingers went white and the muscles in our arms screamed for us to stop. Just when we thought nothing was ever going to happen, we felt the slab shift slightly. Another heave and the top edge was raised enough for us to get our fingers underneath and we could get a proper grip on it. The slab was heavy but between us we managed to pull it upright. It toppled backwards out of the way and crashed loudly onto the floor.

We froze, listening for the sound of voices coming to see what we were doing.

The silence was unbroken.

I looked down and could hardly believe what I was seeing. The mouth of Miut's shaft yawned darkly at our feet.

'Oh,' whispered Lily, staring first into its depths, and then at me. 'That's impossible. I didn't really think that shaft would be there.'

'Neither did I!' The thought of dropping into that blackness was suddenly even more impossible. Yet Miut did just that, and Hori, and they had escaped to the ledge and that terrible drop.

'Are you sure about this?' asked Lily, with a quiver in her voice.

'Not really,' I admitted, 'but we can't stay here.' I didn't want to scare Lily but how were we going to find our way? If I still had my stone cat, Miut would have helped us. The torch wouldn't burn for much longer. And a candle with a bare flame would drip hot wax on our hands and blow out in the slightest draught.

Lily stood up and crossed to a nearby pillar. From the shadows at its base she retrieved an oil lamp. I recognised it immediately as the one we had brought from the hut.

She handed it to me. 'I thought we might need it. I hid it in the folds of my skirt.'

'That was really clever.' I gave her a hug.

Lily gave me a brief smile. 'Are we really going down that black hole?'

I fought to keep my voice steady, to sound calm. 'We must, but we need to tie the lamp to one of us. If we just drop it down, it will shatter.' I looked at her and I had to laugh. 'Only you, Lily, would have tied ribbons in your hair before coming after me.'

She gave a small laugh too, and we both felt a little better.

I knotted the ribbons together and tied both ends to the lamp's handle. I then slipped the loop of ribbons over my head so that the gas lamp hung neatly level with my waist.

Lily looked thoughtfully at the lamp. 'When we were in the tunnel and being followed by Mr Baxter, it was as if you could see where we were going even though it was so dark.'

'Do you remember Aunt Dora telling us how the ancient Egyptians used to believe that wearing an amulet gave you some of the amulet's powers?'

Lily nodded.

'Maybe because I had the cat amulet, my night sight was like a cat's. But Mr Baxter's got it now.'

I retrieved the palely glowing torch from its bracket and lay flat on the edge of the shaft. I lowered the torch down as far I could reach. The shaft was just darkness below.

'Do we have to do this?' whispered Lily, 'We don't know how deep it is.'

'Trust me. It's not deep.'

'In your dream, maybe. But what if it has been made deeper during the past few thousand years?'

I'd been trying not to think just that. 'We've no choice.'

I peered into the gaping blackness at our feet. There could have been anything down there... snakes, rats, spiders...

Lily broke the silence. 'D.... do you think there are spiders down there?'

'If there are,' I said, as reassuringly as I could, 'I'm sure they will be more scared of you than you are of them.'

Lily shivered. 'I doubt it.'

A new sound entered the chamber. Voices. Somewhere in the tunnel beyond the door.

'Maybe they've come to let us out?' said Lily.

I remembered the wolf in Mr Baxter's smile. 'I don't think so. We must go. Now.'

I sat on the edge of the shaft with my legs dangling down. I whispered under my breath even though I knew it was hopeless, 'Miut, please help us.'

The voices were getting louder. Any minute, we would hear the key scraping in the lock.

I was suddenly beyond fear. I thrust the torch at Lily. 'Drop it down to me.' I lowered myself into the darkness. My feet scrabbled at the side of the shaft, then kicked at air. I was going to have to let go. Would dying hurt very much?

'They are just outside the door,' hissed Lily from above. Her voice cut through my panic. I opened my hands and dropped.

CHAPTER 40

I crumpled onto rock. Sore knees, nothing worse. I checked the lamp. It seemed undamaged. I struggled to my feet and called up to Lily, 'It's not deep. I promise...'

I saw her leaning over the shaft above me, then the torch was flaming towards me. I caught it just before it hit the ground. Lily was suddenly beside me.

We listened for the sound of voices above our heads but heard nothing.

'Maybe they just went past the door?' suggested Lily, 'it might be sometime before they realise we've gone.'

'I hope so. Shall I go first?'

'What about lamp? Shall we light it?' asked Lily.

'Let's save it for later.'

I held the torch out in front of me. It wouldn't be long before it died. It only lit a few feet of the rough-walled tunnel immediately ahead of us.

The air was musty and warm. I wondered how long it was since anyone else last breathed it. Probably thousands of years.

The tunnel appeared to run straight ahead. I held the torch high in front of us. But as its glow faded, the darkness around us deepened. The shadow of a memory nagged at me. I'd forgotten something. Something dangerous. It was then I noticed a patch of solid blackness lying across the floor of the tunnel immediately in front of us, like a giant puddle of spilled ink.

It took me a moment to realise what I was looking at, and when I did, I stopped dead. Lily cannoned into me, pushing me forward. Suddenly I was teetering on the edge of the emptiness of a shaft. A stone fell, loosened by my feet. It clattered on down forever. I threw myself backwards with all my strength. The glowing torch dropped from my hand and spun downwards. There was a horrible thud as I landed in a tumbled heap, my skirt twisted tightly round my legs. I lay frozen, not daring to move. The torch flared brightly for a moment far below and then vanished. I realised I was lying across Lily. Carefully I untangled myself.

'Lily, are you alright?' My voice sounded far too loud in the darkness.

It was so quiet. Too quiet. My hand shook as I fumbled for a match, struck it on the wall and lit the lamp. Lily was lying beside me, unmoving, as pale as a ghost. Her eyes were closed. I gently felt all round her head with the tips of my fingers. There was a lump near her right ear. I found her wrist and felt for a pulse. Thankfully it seemed steady enough.

'I'm so sorry,' I whispered, 'I forgot about the shaft. Are you alright?'

The silence only seemed to thicken. I took hold of her shoulders and shook her.

'Lily, WAKE UP.' A tidal wave of fear swept through me as she lay as still as death. What if she never did wake up?

I swished the lamp gently to and fro. It was only about half full of oil. The wick was turned as low as it could go. I had to get help and there was no time to waste.

I slid my hands under Lily's arms and dragged her away from the edge of the shaft. I looked round for somewhere safe to leave her. Somewhere Mr Baxter wouldn't find her if he came after us. I noticed a small recess in the tunnel wall. It was half hidden behind a pile of rocks, which had fallen from the tunnel roof. I pulled and pushed Lily into the recess, and then managed to pile up the rocks so they made a low wall, which would hide her from view. All the time I listened for sounds of pursuit. There was only silence.

I checked the candle was still in Lily's pocket, and some matches. The flame in the lamp danced in a sudden draft. My heart skipped a beat. Maybe the locked door above had been opened. I had to go.

I whispered in Lily's ear, 'I'll be as quick as I can, I promise.' I picked a yellow crayon out of my tin and scribbled a small rose on a rock near her head. 'Hansel and Gretel,' I whispered into her ear, 'the roses will lead me back to you.'

Leaving Lily there was the hardest thing I'd ever done. My head was spinning with 'What Ifs'. What if I fell down another shaft? What if I didn't escape the tunnels before the oil in the lamp ran dry? What if Mr Baxter found me?

I inspected the shaft. It spread almost across the tunnel floor but on one side there was enough of a rim left to form a narrow path. The shaft itself looked hungry and dangerously dark.

I edged my way carefully round the rim and carried on along the tunnel. I remembered just how scared I used to be of the dark but knew that recently other things scared me more. Miut had shown me that the dark was just a different way of seeing.

I came to a junction and hesitated. I was certain Miut had stopped here, testing the air for traces of the desert breeze. But which way had she chosen? Something had changed.

Suddenly I understood. Long ago the tunnel walls were pierced by openings. Each had been the entrance to a darkened and empty chamber. Now the entrances were blocked up and invisible behind layers of plaster and long-faded scenes of the afterlife. I was sure Miut took the left-hand path. I marked the tunnel wall with a second small yellow rose.

It seemed as if I was walking forever. I kept my eyes on the tunnel floor, watching for the black nothingness of further shafts. I longed for a glimpse of a cat trotting along in front of me but I was quite alone. And so was Lily.

Even as I thought that, I realised I was quite wrong. That part of me somehow linked with Lily was still linked. I knew she was alive... for now. I also knew that could change at any moment.

I kept on walking. Another junction... another. At every one, I paused to try and remember which path Miut took, and drew a rose to mark the way. Just as I became convinced I must have taken a wrong turn, I walked straight into a rock wall.

'Ouch.' My voice exploded into the darkness. My head swam dizzily. A trickle of warm wetness ran down my nose. I tasted it. Blood.

But I did remember this place. It was here Hori had laid down flat and wriggled through the narrow gap between the roof and the floor. I knelt down. There was still a gap. It appeared to go on further than I remembered, and it would be an even tighter squeeze for me than for Hori. I knew if I stuck fast, no one would ever find me.

I pushed away thoughts of the thousands of tons of crumbling pyramid above me and eased myself forwards on my stomach, using my elbows to pull me along. The rock roof scraped my back. It was awkward trying to push the lamp, keeping it upright and the flame alight. Every muscle in my arms was aching. Sweat dripped into my eyes. But I kept on going. I had to. At last the rock roof began to rise again.

I clambered to my feet and looked round. This was where Miut had smelled the desert air and turned right to the ledge and the shaft where I could try and call for help. However I had no notion what the time was. But I did know that if it was still dark, no one would have been around. I could have been trapped there until someone heard me calling, which might have been hours. Lily might not have had hours. And what if it was Mr Baxter who had heard me?

I shuddered at the thought and studied the left-hand tunnel. A memory stirred.

'If you thought you had lost me, worm,' called out Snake-Eyes, 'you were wrong. And now I am not alone. You will not escape us.'

Neshi must have been near where I was standing when the other priests joined him. Many of them were too large to fit through the gap I'd just squeezed through. They had to have come from the left. Therefore, left must lead back to the Chamber of Seth and eventually to Heteb's temple. I could get out through the hut. As long as the door was unlocked. And as long as I could get past the League. So that was the choice, left to the hut and the League... or right to the ledge where the Jackal-Priest fell into that terrible shaft?

I had to clear my head of everything. I had to make a decision. 'Miut,' I whispered, 'where are you? Tell me which way I should go.'

But there was only silence. Help lay in the village, not with me trapped on a ledge. I set off up the left tunnel. The lamp felt alarmingly light, I managed to turn the wick down a little further to save what oil I could. The dim light was enough for me to see that I wasn't about to fall down another shaft, but not much more. The only sounds were the tread of my feet and the rhythm of my breathing. The only thoughts in my head were of Lily. She was all that mattered.

CHAPTER 41

The tunnel sank steeply for a while before levelling out. The rock floor was now covered with a scattering of sand. The desert couldn't be too far away. A tunnel joined from the left. I hesitated. The thin covering of sand continued on the rock floor of the new tunnel, there was none on the floor of the tunnel ahead. I followed the sand and left another rose on the wall.

I took about twenty paces and froze, listening. From out of the darkness ahead came the distant murmur of voices. I wanted to turn and run, it was only the thought of Lily that made me creep forward, keeping close against the wall. The voices grew louder.

I recognised where I was. The door to the Chamber of Seth, from which we had escaped, was on my left. It was still shut. I pressed my ear to the wood, but heard nothing. Carefully I tried the handle. The door was still locked. They must have no idea we were no longer inside. Yet.

The Chamber of Feasts, where Lily and I were first imprisoned, lay ahead. This door stood open, half blocking the tunnel, and the voices were coming from inside the chamber. How could I pass the open door without being seen? I tiptoed up to the door and pressed my cheek hard against the wall and peered through the gap between the hinges.

The black cloth, covered with blood-red hieroglyphs, was back on the table. Between a clutter of silver goblets, empty dishes and dirty plates, stood six silver candlesticks. Each was a great, coiled cobra, its head raised ready to strike. Mouth open. Fangs like daggers. Hood spread wide and a black candle sprouting from its head. The six quivering flames were all that lit the chamber. The cobras were beautiful yet terrifying. But not as terrifying as the ten figures that sat round the table, their masks removed and their faces just visible in the gloom. Some I recognised.

Ezra was there, shifting uneasily on a bench. A woman sat at the head of the table facing me. For a moment I didn't recognise her. Gone was the fluffiness and the dishevelled hair, but it was Mrs Hodges who sat straight-backed in her chair, her grey hair scraped into a tightly coiled bun at the base of her neck. I searched for the blue-eyed man in the cream suit. There was no sign of him, nor of Zac. Hope stirred. Maybe Zac was already searching for us?

Mrs Hodges' gaze swept across the now silent figures. 'Then we are agreed,' she said. 'The girls can never leave. If they speak of what has happened here, then it is prison for life – or death – for us all. There's no other way.'

Ezra shook his head. 'This I do not like. If you had not given Miss Rose the Seal...'

'Do you think if I'd known it was the Seal I would have let it out of my sight?' interrupted Mrs Hodges. 'Or that once our leader said he wished to examine everything that Arthur Sinclair might have excavated from the tomb, that the girl would refuse to let him see it?'

Under the watchful gaze of the other figures, she took a long drink from the goblet in front of her. 'Anyway,' she continued, so softly that I could hardly make out the words, 'from the moment he saw their red-hair and pale skin, their fate was sealed. He ordered me to get the girls here and said that the cat would come with them.' She sighed. 'It was all too simple. I knew Rose would like to camp here in Sakkara. She told me how much she enjoyed camping with some cousins in England.' She glanced at Ezra.

He nodded. 'I spoke just a word to Mrs Sinclair. To her I said that the young Misses might like very much to camp here at Sakkara.'

A grey-haired man cleared his throat. He seemed strangely familiar but why?

He spoke. 'But how did you get them right here, in the tomb of the High Priest?'

Ezra frowned. 'A moment, Mr Fielding, please, and I will tell you all. I heard the girls speaking in the library. They spoke of the High Priest. They sounded most interested in seeing the tomb discovered by Mr Sinclair.' He hesitated. 'They spoke also of other most strange things, like ghosts and visiting the past. These things I did not understand but I sent them at once from the room. I told Mrs Hodges what I knew.'

Ezra had watched us while we were in the library. In fact, he must have been watching us from the moment we arrived in the House of Shadows, and reported back to Mr Baxter everything we did or said. But I wasn't surprised. Ezra had always been just too interested in us.

Mr Fielding broke the silence which followed. 'You could have refused.'

I swallowed a gasp as I suddenly recognised him. He was the elderly man I'd nearly knocked over as I ran screaming in imaginary terror from the scorpion at Giza. Had other people been following us too, not just the man in the cream suit?

Mrs Hodge gave a short bark of laughter. 'Refuse him. How? We all have secrets, things that could ruin us. He knows them all. He can destroy every one of us.'

'If we allow this,' said Mr Fielding shaking his head, 'he will own us forever.'

Mrs Hodges turned to him. 'Indeed he will. But then all Zac had to do was to bring the girls here. He did his job well.'

Suddenly I was fighting for air. I leaned against the tunnel wall, my head spinning. If Zac was involved, then Djinn returning alone wouldn't raise the alarm. All hope of rescue vanished. It was all up to me. I had to get past this door. I had to escape... I looked cautiously round the edge of the door. The tunnel stretched into darkness. If I ran my very fastest maybe I could make it out of the hut before they caught me. Then I remembered the rock fall. That would slow me down.

Mrs Hodges' voice pierced through my panic. '... it was simple enough to leave a clearly labelled key that she must see. Our leader said that the power of Seth would lead her back here tonight, and that her sister would follow. He said it would be simple. As simple as it was to arrange the boy's accident and send their parents to Alexandria.'

'And if they hadn't followed the call of Seth?' demanded Mr Fielding, frowning.

'Then,' sighed Mrs Hodges, 'they would have been fetched from their tent. They couldn't escape their fate. Nothing we can do will stop this. Our lives are in his hands.' She added sharply, 'And I won't risk Lottie's life. I believed sending her to England would keep her safe. But I have learned he has followers there too.'

Even as I realised my wild guesses had been right, I also realised although Mrs Hodges might not want us dead, she wouldn't help us. I could understand why, if the price of helping us was Lottie's life. Probably none of them truly wanted us dead. It was entirely Mr Baxter's fault we were in danger.

Mrs Hodges is still speaking, '... and we all know why you, Ezra, daren't disobey him.'

Ezra swallowed nervously. 'But it was an accident. I did not mean to make her so very ill. I needed her only to keep to her bed while Mrs Sinclair stayed with her friends after the death of Mr Sinclair. Mr Baxter wanted to search the house most thoroughly for all that came from the tomb of the High Priest.'

'Do you think anyone will believe that? The maid nearly died,' snapped Mr Fielding. 'In Egypt, if you're found guilty of attempted murder, the sentence is death.'

Ezra looked anxiously at Mrs Hodges. 'Where is he now?'

'The statues are being collected tonight. He has gone to fetch the men and their camels from the village.' Her mouth lifted into a wistful smile. 'I have to say he is right about that at least. The statues will look magnificent in the new Temple of Seth.'

And suddenly yet another piece of the jigsaw dropped into place and I knew why the plan I saw in Mr Baxter's study was so oddly familiar. Aunt Dora's library would be the new Temple of Seth. I tried not to think about Mr Baxter's plans for Aunt Dora, who would never allow the House of Shadows to be a temple of anything.

Mrs Hodges was still talking. 'I have no doubt that, by the time he has finished with the house, it will be magnificent. After all, Mrs Sinclair is an extremely wealthy widow, just what he likes. Isn't that true, Ezra?'

My thoughts spun. Aunt Dora was wealthy? I couldn't believe it. No maid. All that dust. The general shabbiness of the House of Shadows. Then I understood. Since Uncle Arthur had died, Aunt Dora had been too sad to care.

'It is true indeed,' said Ezra. 'I saw from the accounts that Mr Sinclair was a most wealthy man. His brother made much money from gold he dug in California. He had no wife or children. When he died, he gave all his money to Mr Sinclair. When Mr Sinclair died, he gave all his money to Mrs Sinclair. And the House of Shadows too.'

'Baxter will have to be careful,' muttered Mr Fielding, 'the authorities will doubtless be suspicious if his third wealthy wife also dies in peculiar circumstances.'

Aunt Dora was in real danger. Everything I'd feared was coming true. I had to escape. Somehow. I peered down the tunnel searching for a distant prick of light, which would tell me Mr Baxter was returning. There was just darkness. I had to get past this doorway.

A large bearded man, who had been sitting silently at the far end of the table, slammed his fist onto the table.

'Enough of this madness,' he shouted. 'Murder was never part of the deal Baxter had with me. I paid for the excavation in return for a share of the finds. The statues are coming back to the States with me. The men arriving with the camels are mine, not Baxter's.'

There was a stunned silence, and all eyes were on him.

I saw something metal glint in his hand. A pistol.

A gasp exploded into the silence.

Ten pairs of eyes swivelled towards the door. I realised the gasp had come from me. I was discovered. Chairs and benches crashed as the League leapt to their feet. I darted a glance at the lock. The key was still in it. I flung myself at the door and pushed with all my strength. It was too heavy. It moved so slowly. I would never get it shut in time. Suddenly someone else was beside me and pushing too.

The door clicked shut. I reached for the key and twisted. An instant later, the door shuddered under the weight of people pushing from the other side. An outburst of banging and shouting followed. But the door held.

My knees were like paper, and my head felt like it belonged to someone else. I collapsed onto the floor. Arms were around me, holding me tight.

'Are you alright?' asked Lily.

'Oh, Lily.' I was dizzy with relief that she was alive and there with me. 'I'm so glad to see you.'

'Likewise,' she said.

I heard the smile in her voice. For a moment I was so relieved that I forgot the trouble we were in, but then the fear came flooding back.

'We have to hurry. Mr Baxter could be coming up the tunnel any minute.'

Lily pulled me to my feet and I relit the lamp, still with the wick as low as we could turn it. We made our way down the tunnel towards the hut. The shouts from the prisoners in the Chamber of Feasts faded. The shadows pressed in all around us. I kept my eyes fixed on the blackness ahead, watching for the tiniest pinprick of light from an oncoming lamp.

Lily said quietly, 'Thank you for leaving the extra matches. The candle kept on blowing out. And thank you for the roses you drew on the walls. I followed them.'

'They were really so I could find my way back to you.'

Lily squeezed my arm.

From behind us came a loud crack. It made us both jump.

'Do you think they can shoot their way out?' I tried to keep the fear out of my voice, and failed.

'Probably not,' said Lily. 'The door is really solid.' However she threw a worried look over her shoulder.

Then the thudding started. The prisoners must have been using something, maybe a bench, as a battering ram. However solid the door was, eventually it would give way. We tried to move faster but loose rocks on the ground make us stumble and slowed us down.

Behind us, the thudding stopped. The silence was even more terrifying. I imagined them racing down the tunnel after us. My throat was dry. I risked a glance over my shoulder. The tunnel remained dark and silent.

Reaching the rock fall, we helped each other scramble through the gap. We were approaching Heteb's temple. Miut's ledge was just ahead of us. We'd soon be in the hut. I longed for breaths of cool, fresh desert air. Suddenly we froze.

'Can you see?' Lily breathed into my ear.

'Yes.' I snuffed out the lamp.

We stood statue-still. The darkness ahead turned to grey. Someone was coming. I knew it must be Mr Baxter.

'We'll have to turn back,' I hissed, 'but I'll have to relight the lamp,'

'He'll see us.'

'We will have to get as far ahead of him as we can, then hide in the tunnels beyond the Chamber of Feasts.'

I struck a match and relit the lamp. 'Come on, Lily.'

'Who's there?' called Mr Baxter, his voice echoing up the tunnel.

We turned on our heels, and as we did, I stumbled on a rock. My ankle twisted and stabbing pains shot up my leg. To stop myself falling, I grabbed hold of Lily's arm.

'Ouch,' she exclaimed, too loudly.

"I said, who's there? Answer, damn you.' The voice was urgent, furious.

Lily glanced at me, realised I was hobbling, and put her arm round me. 'Come on. Let me help.'

I could see the light itself now, bobbing up and down. Mr Baxter was approaching fast.

I hobbled beside Lily for a few steps. My ankle screamed at me. It was hopeless. 'You must go on without me. I will slow you down.'

'No. I...'

'You must. Go straight up this tunnel. Ignore any other turnings. At the end is a ledge which hangs out over that deep shaft Zac showed us yesterday.' Yesterday seemed a whole world ago. 'Remember that tent we saw? The campers may be up by now. Scream for help.'

Lily stared at me. 'How do you know the way?'

'Miut. My dream...'

She looked intently at me for a second, sighed and said, 'Alright, I believe you.'

'You, with the lamp. Stop where you are,' shouted Mr Baxter.

I grasped Lily's shoulders, forcing her to turn away from me. 'I will be safe enough on my own. He needs both of us together. But hurry.'

'What about the lamp? Lily's face was drawn tight with fear.

'You take it.'

'I hate leaving you in the dark.'

I glanced round at the light bobbing and dancing ever closer.

'It won't be for long. Now go.' I pushed her away. 'And remember there's hardly any oil left. Keep the flame low.'

Lily gave me one last desperate look, then turned and hurried away up the tunnel. I stumbled after her. I'd never felt so alone.

CHAPTER 42

I watched the light from her lamp disappear through the rock fall. As her light faded, Mr Baxter's lamp was getting brighter all the time. I kept on going. My ankle was already twice its usual size, but I could put some weight on it.

'I see you now, Daughter of Seth,' shouted Mr Baxter. 'Stop. You have nowhere to go.'

He was closing on me. I reached the rock fall and was almost through it before I heard the rasp of his breath. I risked a glance behind. He was so close. His arms were out-stretched, his mouth open, his lips curled back in a snarl of fury, his eyes behind the prison of his lenses, were wild.

With one last effort I threw myself forward, but his hand was on my shoulder. My left foot hit something soft and warm. It unbalanced me. I crumpled to the ground. He stumbled over me. There was a clatter as his lamp also hit the ground. The flame flared for a second and then went out. I lay there in the dark struggling to breathe, the air punched from my lungs. He was sprawled across my legs. I heard him groan as I wriggled free and rolled away from him. I felt something hard under my hand. My fingers closed round the familiar silky smoothness of my stone cat. It must have fallen from his pocket when he fell.

'Miut,' I breathed. Then I scrabbled through the gap and on to my feet. I remembered how the tunnel ran straight and level ahead. Keeping one hand on the wall, I hobbled onwards as fast as I dared in the blackness. I risked a glance behind me. A light danced. Mr Baxter was through the rock fall and, having relit his lamp, was following me again.

'Miut,' I whispered, 'where are you?' Gradually I became aware I could make out the tunnel ahead. I looked down and saw the cat stalking ahead of me with her tail held high.

'Thank you, Miut,' I murmured into the shadows as I followed her, limping faster than before.

The sound of thudding ahead told me I was nearing the Chamber of Feasts. Silence fell as I reached the door. Again, silence was more frightening than noise. Were they resting or plotting their escape? A movement caught my eye. The key twisted and trembled in the lock. I realised they must be pushing it from inside the chamber. Looking down I saw a piece of cloth had been pushed out from under the door. If the key dropped onto the cloth, they would be able to slide it back into the chamber and make their escape. I held out my hand and caught the key as it fell. I dropped it into my pocket along with my stone cat and tin of chalks.

With every step, my twisted ankle sent daggers of pain up my leg, but I forced myself on. A glance over my shoulder showed me the light was getting closer. I arrived at a junction and hesitated. The Chamber of Seth, from which we had escaped, lay to the right, while to the left lay a labyrinth of tunnels, where I could be lost forever. Miut's ledge and Lily were straight ahead.

Miut led me straight ahead. Pain and terror had clouded my thoughts, and too late I realised what a terrible mistake I'd made. If Lily hadn't been able to raise the alarm, then Mr Baxter would have exactly what he wanted trapped on the ledge. Lily, the Seal and me.

I had to give Lily more time. I threw myself to the ground as if I'd tripped. I crouched, rubbing my ankle. I heard the scrunching of footsteps on loose stones and looked up just as he grabbed my arm.

'Where is your sister, Daughter of Seth?' demanded Mr Baxter as he pulled me roughly to my feet.

'I don't know,' I gasped. 'Let go. Please. You're hurting me.'

'Do you think me a fool? I am not about to let you run off again.'

'I've twisted my ankle. I can hardly walk.'

He ignored that. 'Where is she?'

I looked at him with, what I hoped, were wide innocent eyes. 'Lily ran off when I fell. She could be anywhere.'

'Liar,' exploded Mr Baxter. 'You were following her. You were going this way and so will we. Now move.'

We continued along the tunnel, slower now, his grip on my arm vicelike as he half dragged me limping beside him. Miut paced silently in front of us, apparently invisible to Mr Baxter.

Far ahead of us the darkness of the tunnel softened and faded to a misty pink. I guessed we were approaching Miut's ledge, and that the sun was rising.

Mr Baxter pushed me out of the tunnel, then paused to deposit his lamp on a nearby rock shelf. As he did so, his grip loosened and I pulled myself free. I stood for a moment as my eyes adjusted to the dawn light, then looked round for Lily. My breath froze. There was no sign of her on the ledge.

'Where is she?' Mr Baxter hissed, his lips white with fury

I shook my head, genuinely confused. I peered cautiously down into the shaft, dreading what I might see. The bottom was lost in shadows. A stone clattered onto the ledge beside me. I twisted round and stared upwards. High above us, Lily was glued like a starfish flat against the shaft wall, her skirt tucked into her bloomers. However did she get there? Then I saw that she was clinging to an irregular run of stones, which protruded from the shaft wall. They ran from the ledge to the desert plateau far above us. I remembered the Jackal-Priest complaining about some missing ropes. They must have used the ropes to help themselves down this stone ladder to re-enter the tunnels after everyone else had left and the entrance to the tunnel had been sealed. It was the most precarious ladder I'd ever seen. I didn't notice them in my dream, but then my eyes had been on Miut and Hori.

Lily was staring down at me, her eyes huge with terror.

'Lily,' I shouted, 'what are you doing? If you fall...' my voice faded away.

'I shouted and shouted. But no one came.' Her voice was high-pitched with fear. 'I had to try to get help.'

'Get down here at once, you stupid girl,' barked Mr Baxter, glaring upwards.

Lily shook her head. 'So you can lock me up again. I don't think so.'

I'd never seen such a determined look on Lily's face before, nor heard her speak so sternly. If I hadn't been so scared, I'd have cheered.

Fingers bit into my shoulder. 'You get down here right now, or your precious sister will need wings.' As he spoke Mr Baxter swung me round so my feet were scrabbling at the rim of the ledge. I gasped as a cluster of stones clattered downwards into the shadow-lake far below.

Lily screamed. 'Leave her alone.'

Mr Baxter's fingers pressed deeper into my skin. 'Only if you come down, then I will let her go.'

I tried to think. I had to keep calm. Make a plan. Suddenly, I remembered my dream.

'No, Lily, stay there,' I shouted, and digging deep into my skirt pocket, I pulled out the stone cat and held it out over the void, just as Hori had done thousands of years before. 'Let me go, or I'll drop the Seal.' My voice sounded amazingly steady, although my heart was racing.

There was a shocked gasp as he swung me back from the edge and released me. Fear had frozen his face.

He plunged his hand into his pocket and pulled it out empty. He groaned and shook his head. I kept my arm stretched out over the shaft. Lily was all that mattered.

'How do you have the Seal?' His voice was little more than a horrified whisper.

'You dropped it when you tripped over, by the rock fall.'

A movement above his head caught my eye. With one hand, Lily was frantically trying to loosen a chunk of rock from the shaft wall. I had to keep his attention on me, and away from her.

'I'll drop it, unless you let us both go,' I said, and I meant it. 'My sister is more precious to me than anything else in the whole world.' I heard my voice as if it was coming from someone else. It was as hard as the rock, which was now in Lily's hand. I leaned towards the shaft.

'No,' screamed Mr Baxter. 'Come away from that edge, Daughter of Seth.'

Suddenly, miraculously, from far above, a familiar voice bellowed, 'Who is the Daughter of Seth? Have you gone mad, Baxter?'

Everything happened at once. Mr Baxter looked up at Papa, whose horrified face was peering over the mouth of the shaft, just as Lily flung the rock. It landed at Mr Baxter's feet. Startled, he staggered backwards, nearer the edge. Right on the brink of the shaft, he stopped, swaying as he struggled to keep his balance. He stretched out his arms to me. An instinct to save him forced me nearer. I held out my hands. We leaned towards each other. Just an inch more and our fingers would touch. I could save him. I was sure I could. There was a heartbeat of silence.

'No, Rose!' screamed Lily. 'He'll take you with him.'

Miut, soft and warm, pushed against my legs, her tail wrapped round my knees. I froze. Mr Baxter floundered for a moment more, then he was gone, spinning downwards into the void, his scream echoing round the shaft as he fell. Just as the Jackal-Priest screamed all those thousands of years ago. My paper legs collapsed beneath me, and everything went dark.

CHAPTER 43

'Rose, dear. Do wake up.'

Someone was holding me tight in his arms. The wonderfully familiar smell of pipe tobacco filled my nose.

I forced open my eyes and looked up into Papa's anxious face. 'Oh, good, you really are here, Papa,' I said, and shut my eyes again.

'No, Rose,' ordered Papa, giving me a small shake, 'you have to wake up. We have to get you out of here.'

I sat up as memories came racing back, and looked round. The ledge was surprisingly crowded. Apart from Papa, Lily was there, pale, but apparently unhurt. Zac was there too, studying me with wide, worried eyes. He didn't look like someone who had led us into a trap, and then discovered that somehow we'd escaped.

I looked back at Papa. 'How are you here? We thought you were still in Alexandria.'

'With Max recovering well, we arrived in Cairo last night. We wanted to surprise you, but found you had gone camping. We had a most pleasant evening with your Aunt Dora. Then we went to bed only to be woken up by Zac arriving in the middle of the night, most alarmed that you were missing.'

Papa nodded to Zac, who took up the story. 'Djinn woke me with a nudge of her nose,' he explained. 'I saw you were not in the tent and that Lily and Bashir were gone also. I looked for you nearby and, when I could not find any sign of you, I thought you may have returned to the house of Mrs Dora. But you were not there.' He shook his head as if in pain.

It seemed Zac didn't have anything to do with the League of Seth. I managed to smile at him.

Papa frowned. 'You cannot imagine how worried we all were. Your dear Mama....' His voice faded, and he took my hand.

'Sorry,' I murmured. Mr Baxter's scream still filled my head.

There was a sudden commotion as another man suddenly appeared on the ledge. He had been lowered on a rope from the desert above. I couldn't at first see his face but then he turned and looked at me, and I stared into a pair of ice-blue eyes.

'Why are you here?' The words burst out of me, like air out of a balloon. I sprang to my feet, preparing to run for my life.

'Rose,' said Papa sharply, 'remember your manners. This is Mr Roberts. He works for the British Museum. He was staying at the Shepheard's Hotel last night. When we heard you had gone missing, we asked for his help. He is an expert on Sakkara.'

'For the British Museum? I don't understand... You've been following me. Why?'

'I'm sorry if I frightened you. It was not my intention.' His voice was soft, and he sounded truly apologetic. He glanced at Papa. 'Your father will tell you that we have been on the trail of an antiquities smuggling gang for months. I was sent out from London to investigate. I kept hearing John Baxter's name, even though he was in America. He was apparently interested in anything and everything connected with the Tomb of Heteb. This made me curious. It was considered a rather insignificant tomb with little found in it. I asked myself, what was going on? Then Baxter arrived in Egypt, and soon afterwards your brother had his accident. There were rumours that he, Baxter, had something to do with that.'

I looked at Papa. 'Where's Max? Is he really alright now?'

Papa nodded. 'He's waiting with the donkeys. His leg is healing, but it's still too painful for him to walk far. He certainly couldn't climb down here.'

Lily was studying Mr Roberts. 'But I don't understand why you were following Rose.'

Mr Roberts gave me an apologetic smile. 'I heard Baxter wasn't just interested in Heteb's tomb, but in you as well. After your brother's accident, I was concerned for your safety and decided I should keep an eye on you. Now, finding you here, perched on this ledge, with Baxter lying dead far below, I was right to be worried. I can only assume that the smugglers are involved in your predicament.'

I'd no idea what to say. It wasn't about smuggling. At least not for Mr Baxter and the League. Just for the American. Lily was also silent. I knew what she was thinking. A tear ran down her cheek.

I went over and gave her a hug. 'It was his fault he fell, Lily, not yours. It was an accident. Your rock missed him completely.'

Papa stood up. 'Well said, Rose. It most certainly wasn't your fault, Lily. But there are a great many questions that will need answering once we have you out of here.' He smiled at me. 'But you were very brave, Rose, trying to save him even at the risk of your own life.' There was an unfamiliar warmth in his voice, and I felt warm too.

Mr Roberts peered down into the shaft. 'I am afraid there's no hope Baxter can have survived the fall, but we will have to try and retrieve his body.'

'Indeed,' agreed Papa, 'but first, we must get the girls back home. We can knot the rope to make some sort of seat.' He turned to Lily. 'Do you think you can manage it, if we do that? Or maybe we can get out through the tunnels. I assume you came that way? Though it might be too far for Rose's ankle.' He frowned.

Lily looked pale but determined. 'The rope will be just fine, Papa. The tunnels are full of ghosts.' She threw me a look.

I was amazed. Had she seen Miut after all?

Papa was also surprised. 'Ghosts? What ghosts?' But then he smiled at Lily. 'I am impressed with you too, Lily. First, you are able to climb half way up the shaft wall, and now you are happy to dangle from a rope.' He ruffled her hair, and for once, I wasn't jealous.

Papa and Mr Roberts had started tying the rope so it formed an odd sort of cradle in which we could each sit in turn and be pulled skywards.

I watched them for a moment wondering why Lily was suggesting being pulled up the shaft. I was sure she'd really much prefer going through the tunnel. Lily cleared her throat to attract my attention and gave me a long meaningful look. It was only then I remembered the prisoners in the Chamber of Feasts. How could I have forgotten them?

Kidnapping. Attempted murder. They were so much worse than smuggling. I remembered Lottie far away in England, sent there to keep her safe from Mr Baxter, and how unhappy she was. How could we be responsible for Lottie losing her mother? And what about Zac? He could lose his grandfather, and Ezra had not meant to harm the maid.

Everything bad had happened because of Mr Baxter's insane obsession with Seth, and his greed for Aunt Dora's money. But he was dead. As for the American with the pistol, I was certain that given a chance he would be on the next boat back to America, and the crates of statues would shortly be discovered by the Egyptian Authorities. Nothing would have actually been stolen. If the League of Seth escaped unseen then maybe we could forget any of this ever happened.

Mr Roberts and Papa were talking to Lily. I limped quietly over to Zac picking up Mr Baxter's discarded lamp and pulling the last few matches out of my pocket as I went. I whispered fiercely in Zac's ear, 'Your grandfather and his colleagues are locked in a chamber in the tunnels behind us.' I ignored the astonishment in his face. 'You must let them out. This tunnel will lead you to them, just keep going straight. Hurry.' I handed him the lamp and matches. As an afterthought I added, 'And don't tell them I gave you the key. Just say you were exploring the tunnel looking for us and found it on the ground by the door.'

Zac stared at me for a moment. He was probably wondering if I was joking or mad. Whatever he saw in my face must have convinced him for he turned and vanished. I swung round in time to see Lily pale but attempting to smile as she was hauled slowly up on the newly constructed rope cradle. We watched as arms stretched out and pulled her to safety as she reached the top. The cradle dropped back down. It looked extremely precarious. But if Lily could do it, I knew I could too.

Papa said, 'Ready, Rose?'

I nodded and let Papa slip an extra loop of rope round my waist.

'This will keep you doubly safe,' he explained. 'Now hold tight,' he ordered as I carefully eased myself into the cradle.

A wave of weariness washed through me and I closed my eyes.

'Are you alright?' Papa asked anxiously.

'Yes, truly, Papa.' He really did care about me. I managed a reassuring smile.

Papa called up, 'When you are ready, pull.'

At that moment Zac reappeared from the tunnel mouth and gave me a nod. Then I was flying up through the air on my rope seat. Away from the darkness that had tried to swallow me up. Away from the screams of Mr Baxter and the Jackal-Priest. I slipped a hand into my pocket. My little stone cat was still there, although something told me her story wasn't quite finished. But that would have to wait. All I wanted just then was to be in the sunlight where Lily and Max were waiting for me.

CHAPTER 44

It was late. The Cairo night was soft and black. Lily and I were tucked into our beds. It had been a long day of questions. We'd explained that we'd returned to Heteb's tomb after dark because I'd discovered I'd dropped the stone cat Aunt Dora had given me.

I'd been desperate to find it before someone else did. We'd found the hut door open and couldn't resist exploring. Mr Baxter had discovered us and, believing we'd discovered the crates were full of things he was stealing from the tomb, chased us through the tunnels to the ledge, where he'd tripped and fallen into the shaft.

Papa and Mama had seemed happy enough with our story, although Papa had asked several times what Mr Baxter had meant by calling me a Daughter of Seth.

'Honestly Papa, I really don't know,' I'd said firmly. I wasn't sure Papa believed me but he'd just ruffled my hair and then said something about Lily and me both being very brave.

Mr Roberts wasn't at all pleased by the failure to catch a single smuggler. The fact that the boxes containing the statues of Seth were found, however, made him rather more cheerful.

Max too, gave us long, very thoughtful looks as we told our story but had only commented, 'That doesn't explain why Mr Baxter should have had anything to do with my accident.'

We'd just looked blankly back and agreed.

He'd then gave us each a huge hug. 'Do you have any idea how worried we all were about you? Life without the Holy Terrors would be unthinkable.'

'We were worried about you too,' I'd said, thinking how pale Max looked, and tired. 'Are you sure your leg will be alright?'

Max had nodded and smiled reassuringly. 'It'll be fine. Quite good enough to catch up with you if you play any of your childish tricks on me.'

Lily had looked gravely at him. 'After all this, we aren't children anymore.'

Max had gazed back at her, his hazel eyes pensive. 'No indeed, I'm sure you aren't.'

Aunt Dora was shocked on hearing the news of Mr Baxter's fall and that he had been involved with a gang of smugglers, but not grief-stricken.

'It's a dreadful thing,' she said, dabbing her eyes with a lace handkerchief, 'but he was not who I thought he was at all.' She sighed. 'I have to admit that even though he has been immensely helpful sorting through poor Arthur's papers, I have found him far too intense about many things.' She paused, then added thoughtfully, 'His difficulty was that he had absolutely no sense of humour, not like my poor, dear Arthur. He could always make me smile.'

One odd thing was that although there was an extensive search for Mr Baxter's body, it wasn't found. From the remnants of food and drink in the Chamber of Feasts, everyone knew that the smugglers were there during the night. Papa said they must have removed Mr Baxter's body themselves after we had all left and before the authorities arrived to search the tunnels. There were certainly enough of the League there to do that. But I wondered why they would have risked one more moment in the tunnels once they had been released by Zac.

Lily and I were exhausted and went to bed early. Mama swept into the bedroom to say goodnight. She looked tired and pale, but gave us a warm smile as she sat down on the end of my bed. 'You know, my dears, we've been so very concerned about you. Are you truly well? You look a little flushed, Rose.' She leaned forward and touched my forehead. Her hand was cool.

I nodded. 'I think all we need is sleep.' Then I added, 'without dreams, good or bad.'

Mama gave me an anxious look. 'Bad dreams? Has your nightmare returned?'

For a moment that confused me, then I understood she was talking about the nightmare I used to have before Miut and Hori. Suddenly, I was curious.

'Mama, please tell me about when I got lost when I was little.'

She looked thoughtfully at me, then nodded. 'I suppose you are now old enough to understand.'

'What happened?' I pleaded. 'I know it was in the British Museum...'

Mama frowned. 'We just took our eyes off you for a moment ... and you vanished. Someone had left one of the service doors open. It led down to the basement. We guessed you must have gone down there. But it ran under the whole museum and houses thousands of objects. You were one little girl. Even though we had help, it took nearly two hours to find you because for some strange reason you were hiding under a dust sheet.'

Suddenly I was struggling to breathe. 'Where exactly was I, Mama?'

She said softly, 'Sobbing your heart out between two colossal Sekhmets.'

'Cat goddesses,' I murmured. Everything in my life seemed to involve cats.

'Indeed,' Mama stood up and tucked me in, then Lily. 'All the way from the Temple of Mut in Luxor.'

She crossed to the window. 'Now Rose, shall I open the shutters? Or should I leave a candle burning?'

'Neither, Mama. It's fine. I'm not scared of the dark anymore.'

'Really?'

'Yes, really. I believe I've become used to it. I have learned it's just another way of seeing.'

Mama nodded approvingly. 'How sensible. Now go to sleep both of you. And if you must dream, may those dreams be sweet.' The door clicked shut behind her.

I lay with my eyes closed, holding the stone cat tight in my hand. I tried to fall asleep but my thoughts kept spinning wildly. So many things were suddenly clear. Incredible as it seemed, when I was little, I must have 'read' the Sekhmets in the museum, like I had 'read' my little stone cat. It must be something I had always been able to do. My nightmare, and those angry whispered words which had buzzed around in my head like a swarm of angry bees, did at last make some peculiar sort of sense.

Eventually I fell into a deep and dreamless sleep.

CHAPTER 45

It had been several days since our rescue, and the hut looked different, emptier. The crates had been removed and taken to the new Egyptian Museum in Boulaq. I had to plead with Papa to let us come back to Sakkara. Miut had protected and guided me to safety so many times. I knew that she needed me to complete my mission.

Zac lit the lamp and we entered the shadowed temple.

'You know,' whispered Lily, 'I don't really understand about your cat or the dreams. But when Mr Baxter fell,' she hesitated, 'I thought I saw a shadow at your feet... and the shadow was cat-shaped.'

'So I'm not for the madhouse?'

A smile flickered. 'No. Or if you are, then I am too.' She squeezed my hand.

Together, we stared up at the painted Heteb on the wall, wielding his erased Seal. Hori's mission had been to return the Seal to the High Priest. And that is exactly what he must have done as the Seal was found in Heteb's original tomb.

I knew that Miut wouldn't rest until Heteb was reunited with his Seal. It should have been simple enough, except for one thing: I didn't know where the High Priest had been reburied.

I looked round for any sign of Miut. There was no sign of her. I wrapped my fingers round the stone cat in my pocket. Still nothing. Then the fear, which had been lurking at the back of my mind, surfaced. Even though I'd been sleeping with the stone cat in my hand every night since our escape, I hadn't once dreamed of Miut.

I'd guessed that once the Seal was no longer round Miut's neck, then it would no longer be imprinted with her story. However, I'd hoped once we were back at Sakkara and close to where her story unfolded, that she would reappear. She hadn't.

The truth was I might never know what happened to her. My eyes filled with tears, but I brushed them away. I couldn't allow anything to distract me. I must find where the High Priest had been hidden, and if Miut couldn't help me anymore, then I would have to work it out for myself.

Standing there in the gloom with Heteb's painted gaze on me, a memory twisted and shivered into life. All those endless tunnels Miut had led me along in my dreams, and recently when Lily and I had been escaping from Mr Baxter. Something I'd seen nagged at me.

'Rose, are you alright? You're whiter than a sheet.'

'I'm thinking, that's all.'

'What about?'

'Something I noticed when we were in the tunnels, something that has changed since Hori's time. I can't quite remember what…'

Lily gazed expectantly at me.

All those dark openings and empty chambers.

'I've got it,' I said suddenly. 'I think I know where Heteb's buried. We must hurry, though.'

Lily nodded. 'Mama won't be happy if we are late.'

'I know.'

Mama had given us strict instructions to be back at the House of Shadows by noon. Aunt Dora had hired a *dahabiya* for us all to sail up the river Nile to Luxor, and we were leaving that afternoon. Max was coming too, so his leg could recover properly from his accident. Aunt Dora was coming with us because she said the river breezes would blow away the sadness and worries of the last year.

Papa said we would need a reliable donkey boy to make sure we always got the very best donkeys at the very best price when we went exploring ashore, so Zac was coming as well and would sleep with the crew under the stars on the riverbank. Papa said we could all sleep on the riverbank if the weather was kind.

Ezra would look after the House of Shadows in our absence. He had arrived for work the day after our escape, looking rather nervous. Because we behaved towards him as if we had no idea he was one of the League of Seth, he relaxed and got on with his job of looking after us all.

Mama said we might be away all winter, and then we would be on board the first ship sailing back to England. This could be my last chance to complete my part in the ancient quest.

Zac reluctantly agreed to wait for us in the hut. I promised him we'd be back very soon. He handed me the lamp and Lily and I set off through the opening and into the tunnel. I was relieved that my twisted ankle hardly hurt at all. We scrambled over the rock fall.

'This is so exciting,' said Lily after we'd been walking for a while. 'If we find where Heteb has been hidden, and if he has lots of wonderful treasures with him, we will be rich.'

'No, we wouldn't. I expect most of the things, if there are any, would be shared out between the British and the Egyptian museums.'

Lily looked at me with eyes that sparkled in the flickering light of the lamp. 'But not all. And just think of the exciting time Max and Papa will have inspecting everything, and writing books about all their discoveries. They'll be famous.'

I'd never before heard Lily so excited about anything. I understood then just how much Egypt and our adventures had changed her. She had been so brave standing up to Mr Baxter, and was so enthusiastic about finding Heteb's tomb. Lily was certainly no longer my invalid sister. That was going to take some getting used to.

Lily chatted on as we made our way along the tunnel. I only half-listened and added just an occasional comment. All the time

I was worrying about Heteb's hiding place being discovered by other people, and all his things being removed from his tomb. Even worse was the idea of his mummy being on show in some museum, looked at by thousands of strangers. What was the point of bothering to return the cat if everything was going to be removed anyway?

The further into the tunnel we went, the shadows thickened and our voices seemed strangely muffled until eventually we found ourselves walking in silence. We passed the Chamber of Feasts, where the door stood open and the room sat empty.

We came to the junction where straight on led to the Jackal-Priest's ledge. We turned right towards the Chamber of Seth, our prison. We were surprised to see the door was still locked. I guessed that Mr Baxter must have taken the key with him and without it, the heavy wooden door would have taken some breaking down. Apparently, there were still people searching for his body, but no sign of it had yet been found.

'I wonder where Mr Baxter's body went?' said Lily breaking the long silence.

I shivered, cold even in the dusty warmth of the tunnel. 'I think the other members of the League must have taken it away.' Anything else was too frightening to imagine.

'Why would they do that?'

'I don't know.'

We lapsed into silence again. 'I hope you know where we're going,' said Lily after a few minutes.

'Back the way we escaped. We'll just follow my roses.'

The little chalk roses were easy enough to spot, and we soon reached the place where the tunnel roof almost met the ground. We pulled ourselves through that crushing space. I had reached the end and was standing up when the lamp slipped out of my hand, landing on its side. Lamp oil spilled onto the rocky floor and the flame went out. I heard Lily gasp behind me. There wasn't a glimmer of light as blackness enveloped us.

My heart began to race, but then I heard my voice say calmly,

'It's alright. I brought magnesium wire just in case. Give me a moment to find the matches.'

'And I,' said Lily proudly, 'have brought another candle.'

I laughed. 'Well done. We will have plenty of light.'

At that moment, I became aware that the black had thinned to grey. I could make out the faintest shadow of a cat sitting in front of us, her tail wrapped neatly round her. I was so relieved to see her.

'But I don't think we'll need the magnesium wire or the candle,' I whispered taking hold of Lily's hand. 'I can see, can't you?'

'No, of course not. It's pitch black.' I heard the surprise in her voice as she continued, 'Oh yes, I can see now, how strange.'

So Miut's magic was working for her too. We carried on again in silence, this time following Miut's elegantly waving tail. At last, we arrived at the junction, which had so confused me when I was on my own. This was where Miut had seen the entrances to a row of dark and empty chambers, but they had now vanished. I inspected the wall carefully. I could see the entrances had all been blocked up and then plastered over.

'What now?' asked Lily.

'We need more light.' I struck a match and lit a piece of magnesium wire. The brilliant hissing light hurt our eyes for a few seconds before they adjusted. I held up the wire to examine the wall. It must once have been covered with amazing pictures of the ancient Egyptians going about their daily lives. Not anymore. Over thousands of years, they had faded, and bits of plaster had fallen away. I could make out odd disconnected things like a cow's head, a basket of fish, a crocodile swimming in blue water, a man's arm holding a spear, a basket of bread, even a girl's white dress.

I looked round the tunnel for Miut, but yet again she had vanished. I hoped that was because we were in the right place. But how would we find the right sealed chamber?

'I'm sorry, Lily. This is just a waste of time. I'm sure there are burial chambers hidden here. But they could belong to any priests or nobles. How do we find which one belongs to Heteb?'

There was a thought-filled pause, then Lily said, 'Miut has brought you this far. I admit I thought you were crazy for ages. Not anymore. There has to be a reason we were brought here now.'

Out of her pocket she produced a small saucer-shaped piece of rock and the candle. She dropped some spots of hot, liquid wax onto the rock's surface and pushed the base of the upright candle into it. The wax cooled almost instantly, and the candle was stuck fast. She had made a perfectly usable candleholder.

Lily looked at me. 'It's what I did before, when I was looking for you...' Her voice trailed away.

'I hated leaving you.'

'I know.'

Lily moved further down the tunnel taking her candle with her.

I stared at the damaged paintings. It was hopeless. I'd never be able to fulfil Miut's mission. I'd run out of time.

The magnesium wire spat and died. Hope died too. The shadows closed in around me. We would never find Heteb's final resting place.

Lily's voice, sharp with excitement, cut through my thoughts.

'Come here, Rose. Quickly.'

I joined her to find that she was removing chunks of stained, but undecorated, plaster off the wall.

'You can't do that,' I whispered furiously. 'Stop it, Lily.'

'Look here, Rose... I knocked into the wall and a chunk of plaster fell off and I saw something underneath... '

I peered at some dark shapes on the wall where the fragment of plaster had fallen off.

'Light some more wire,' instructed Lily.

As the light flared and the smoke cleared, I understood. Where she had pulled off the top layer of plaster, I could see glimpses of brilliant, glowing colours. Someone, a long time ago, had gone to great lengths to hide whatever was underneath.

Side by side, we carefully pulled the top layer of plaster off an area no bigger than my hand to reveal the painting underneath.

A man in a leopard skin tunic. My heart was beating so fast it felt like it was going to explode. I removed more plaster and saw he was standing proud and upright on a boat. It was Heteb. I had no doubt. As we cautiously pulled off yet more plaster, we saw the boat was sailing towards a pair of gates. They were closed and guarded by a great snake. Heteb was holding his hand out in front of him, palm up, and sitting on his palm was a perfect image of my little stone cat.

'Ohh,' I breathed, 'Heteb is using his Seal to cast the spells he needs to open the first pair of gates.'

'The first?' questioned Lily.

'Don't you remember Papa telling us about the Book of the Dead?'

Lily shrugged. 'Not really.'

'He said that when someone died, their spirit had to cast magical spells to pass through twelve gates, on the way to the afterlife. I think the first gates were guarded by a snake.'

'Oh yes,' said Lily, 'and didn't they have to have their heart weighed somewhere on the way?'

'Yes,' I remembered Khay explaining it to Hori, 'in the Hall of Judgement. If it weighed no more than a feather then the person was allowed to carry on into the afterlife, but if it was heavy with evil, then a monster would leap up and eat the heart, and the person couldn't reach the afterlife.'

'Mr Baxter's heart will be much heavier than a feather,' said Lily softly.

'And will have been eaten by the monster,' I said with some satisfaction. But I felt uneasy too. Why hadn't his body been found?

To distract myself, I studied the image of Heteb's outstretched hand holding the Seal. Without the real Seal in his new resting place, had he reached the afterlife, or was he still waiting for the gates to open?'

Lily had set about carefully easing plaster off lower part of the wall. 'Look, Rose.'

I saw she was pointing at a striped and spotted cat sitting on the bank watching Heteb, her tail neatly curled around her.

'Do you think that could be your Miut?'

I knelt down. The cat certainly had all the right markings. I looked more closely. 'Oh yes,' I murmured as I realised that from her neck hung a small leather pouch. I eased more plaster away to soon reveal a whole line of cats of descending size sitting beside her. My mind was spinning. Miut had given birth to her first litter in my dreams, so to be mother to all these other cats, she must have survived the fall.

'Oh yes, Lily, it's her.' I was crying with relief. I hadn't realised just how worried I'd been about her. Lily handed me a neatly folded, clean handkerchief.

Lily was beside me, peering at the cat. 'But didn't you say that she had amber eyes? This cat's eyes are green,' she said frowning.

'But that's even better,' I said. 'Don't you remember Aunt Dora telling us that when proper Egyptian cats are born with amber eyes which change to green as they grow older? This is just more proof that Miut did manage to save herself.'

I still had questions, but there was so little time. More plaster hit the tunnel floor and more of the scene was revealed. There were other figures watching on the bank. Beside the row of cats stood a young man whom I recognised at once as Hori. The slim girl who stood next to him with her hair tied into a plait at the side of her head, must be Anath. At their feet were four smaller figures, two girls and two boys. They must have been be Hori and Anath's children. Finally, behind all the smaller figures towered a larger figure in a leopard skin tunic, leaning on an intricately carved walking stick. He stared across the water at Heteb, one hand out-stretched towards him. I knew him at once. It was Hori's father, High Priest Khay, the Lame-Priest, who wore the tunic of a High Priest. So the League hadn't succeeded in removing him.

I was just about to look away when something made me

wonder why Khay was holding out his hand out to Heteb, as if he was offering him something very precious. I peered closer, and then I understood. He was giving the magic scroll to Heteb.

The magnesium wire fizzled out. I lit another piece, which I handed to Lily.

My eyes returned to Miut sitting there so proudly beside Hori. I took the stone cat out of my pocket, knelt down and began very carefully to ease away a small chunk of unpainted plaster near the floor of the tunnel. Behind the plaster were mudbricks, old and crumbling. I began scraping out the pieces.

'What are you doing?' asked Lily. 'We can't be much longer or we'll run out of magnesium wire.'

'I just need a couple of minutes. I'm sure Heteb's tomb is behind this wall.'

I kept on working at the hole until I felt nothing but air. There was a strange musty smell coming from the hole.

Lily handed me the blazing magnesium wire, which I eased carefully through the hole I'd made. With my heart still pounding I peered inside.

For a moment I was confused. I was looking at something black and round, surrounded by brown. Then I began making sense of it all. I was looking at an eye. A statue was lying on its side looking back at me. Suddenly I couldn't breathe. Where there was one statue, there would be many more. I was certain Heteb was lying there, on the other side of the wall, with all his treasures.

I remembered how Lily had been so excited at the prospect of Papa working on Heteb's treasures. For the second time in my life, I knew there were secrets that were too important to tell. I must keep Heteb and Miut's secret safe. Even from Lily.

'What can you see?' Lily's voice cut through my thoughts.

I composed myself and said sadly, 'Nothing. Just a very large, very dead ancient spider, and a very ancient spider's web. It's huge.' I looked up at Lily. 'Do you want to see?'

She shuddered. 'Heights are one thing. But spiders, no thank you. And unless Miut is going to help us find our way out of here, we'd better go now or everyone will be hot and cross waiting for us.' However, she gave me a very knowing look and I guessed that she knew just what I was about to do, and why. But as long as she kept the secret, that was all that mattered.

'My little cat will be safe here. Heteb won't be far away,' I said, pushing it carefully through the hole. I picked up a chunk of plaster and eased it back into the wall. It was like adding the last piece of a jigsaw puzzle. A few touches of pastel crayon round the edges, and the wall looked as it did before.

I stood up. 'Goodbye Miut,' I whisper, 'and thank you.'

We stood for a moment lost in our thoughts. The silence was broken at last by the faintest rustling, followed by a mewing so soft I wondered if I'd imagined it.

'Did you hear that?' I asked.

'Yes,' said Lily, and smiled.

We made our way back to where Zac was waiting impatiently for us. I didn't see or hear Miut on the way. Now that the Seal was with the High Priest, I believed that Miut was finally at rest too.

The sun was high in the sky as the donkeys carried us towards the House of Shadows. My pocket felt empty and so did I. I was sure it had been the right thing to do to leave the Seal with Heteb, but I missed Miut already.

'Come on,' said Lily. 'Cheer up. We're going to have a wonderful time on our trip up the Nile. We can forget all about Mr Baxter and your dreams and everything.'

'I suppose so.'

We carried on in silence for a while lost in our thoughts and memories. 'I wonder where Mrs Hodges is now?' I asked at last.

Zac, who had been leading the way through the evermore-crowded streets, swung round in his saddle to look at us. 'My grandfather told me that she has gone away.'

'To India to join her husband?' suggested Lily.

'Her husband?' said Zac with raised eyebrows, 'I do not

think she has a husband. He died two years ago. That is what my grandfather told me.'

The world swam dizzily round me. 'Oh,' I heard myself say. 'But she said she couldn't take Lottie to India, so that was why she took her to England.'

Zac shook his head and shrugged. 'I do not know why she said that.'

My thoughts were a whirlpool. No husband. And she had vanished. As had Mr Baxter's body. I remembered again her warning that nothing in Egypt was as it seemed.

Suddenly I was extremely glad that we would soon be on board our *dahabiya* and a very long way from Cairo.

'Are you alright?' asked Lily with a searching look.

'Yes. And you are too. You haven't coughed for days.'

'I meant without Miut,' said Lily with a toss of her head.

'I know.' I smiled at her. Wherever Mrs Hodges and Mr Baxter might have been, it suddenly didn't matter one bit. We were going to have the most wonderful time travelling up the Nile with Papa, Mama, Max and Aunt Dora. And Zac too. Nothing bad could happen if we were all together.

'Everything is very good indeed,' I said. 'In fact, it is just about perfect.'

A HISTORICAL NOTE

It was 1871 when fourteen-year-old May Tyssen-Amherst and her parents arrived in Port Said on a steamship, just like the *SS Australia*. May was my great grandmother. She didn't have a twin, but she did have six younger sisters left at home in England.

From the moment she stood on the ship's deck and saw Egypt appearing on the horizon, May fell in love with the country. Years later she wrote a memoir called '*A Few Egyptian Memories,*' which was mostly about that first trip to Egypt. She described all sorts of things she did, such as travelling through the Suez Canal, visiting markets, having her hat eaten by a cockatoo, camping beside the pyramids and racing donkeys in the desert.

Some of those events have sneaked into *Nile Cat*. I think May would have enjoyed reading about the adventures of Rose, Lily and the evil Mr Baxter.

If you want to find out more about *Nile Cat,* or about May and her early travels to Egypt, as well as a great deal more about her extraordinary family, you can visit **www.nilecat.co.uk**. If you have enjoyed *Nile Cat* please do write a review on Amazon, Goodreads or Waterstones – reviews are very important to authors as they encourage others to read their books.

ACKNOWLEDGEMENTS

Nile Cat has taken some time to write and I owe a great debt of thanks to the many people who have supported and encouraged me along the way. I particularly want to thank Cilla Lancelyn Green who many years ago encouraged me to write in the first place. She also introduced me to the Oxford Writers Group who have been a huge support over the years, particularly Linora Lawrence who sadly died this year. I must also thank Egyptologist, Pat Remler, who very kindly read through several versions of the *Nile Cat* and made sure that my recreation of the ancient Egyptians' world and belief system, along with Rose's travels through nineteenth century Egypt, were as accurate as possible. I must also acknowledge the importance of my great-grandmother, May Tyssen-Amherst, to this story. It was her passion for all things Egyptian and her memoir describing her childhood travels to Egypt which inspired the Victorian setting of *Nile Cat,* and my own interest in Egypt. Finally, and most importantly, I must thank my long-suffering family.

FURTHER **NILE MYSTERIES** TO FOLLOW SOON:

BOOK TWO
The Eyes of the Nile

Rose and Lily have travelled up the Nile to Luxor where they are looking forward to exploring the Valley of the Kings. When Lily is kidnapped, everything changes. To save her sister, Rose must unravel an ancient mystery and overcome many dangers... but time is running out.

BOOK THREE
Wings over the Nile

Rose and Lily are exploring the banks of the river Nile at Aswan when they find the entrance to a long-lost tomb. With the help of their Egyptologist father and brother, they begin excavating. When strange accidents start occurring and valuable items go missing, Rose realises that they are all in great danger. They know too much. The tomb holds a secret that someone will stop at nothing, even murder, to keep.

CPSIA information can be obtained
at www.ICGtesting.com
Printed in the USA
BVHW042200080623
665676BV00012B/130